Lynnie kept her ——————————— y anything. Most of th——————————— cco or rolling a cigarett——————————— ne not smoking.

Ace ambled up to her, his expression still quizzical. "You ain't smokin' or chawin'?"

Lynnie kept her head low. "I—I forgot my makin's."

"Here." Ace handed her his little sack of tobacco.

"Much obliged." She took it and the little paper he handed her. Her hands trembled as she tried to roll it.

"Lordy, kid, you're wastin' tobacco," Ace grumbled, took the makings from her, and expertly rolled a cigarette.

Lynnie took it, stuck it in her mouth. Maybe he wouldn't have a light.

But Ace struck a match across the seat of his pants and lit it for her. Even as he did so, he stared hard. "I swear I know you from somewhere, kid."

"Uh, don't think so." She fought off a fit of coughing as she inhaled the acrid smoke. To her, it tasted like burning hay.

"What's your name?"

"Ly—Lee. Lee Smith." She didn't look up at him.

"Okay, Lee, we'll take a leak and then we'll mount up and see how far we can get before sundown."

"What?" She looked around in horror, realizing some of the cowboys around her had their pants unbuttoned. She'd never seen a full-grown man with his plumbing on display for everyone to see. "I—I already went." She stumbled toward her horse in confusion and stubbed out her cigarette against her saddle. She made sure it was extinguished before she dropped it in the dirt. A prairie fire would be the devil of a thing to deal with. Red dust choked her and she was having a difficult time seeing without her spectacles, but she was afraid to wear them, certain Ace would recognize her. Oh, this was going to be a long, long trip, and it had barely gotten started. The worst of it was going to be dealing with Ace Durango, who thought he was God's gift to women.

She grinned to herself and began to plan revenge.

Also by Georgina Gentry

Apache Caress

Apache Tears

Bandit's Embrace

Cheyenne Captive

Cheyenne Caress

Cheyenne Princess

Cheyenne Song

Cheyenne Splendor

Comanche Cowboy

Eternal Outlaw

Half-Breed's Bride

Nevada Dawn

Nevada Nights

Quicksilver Passion

Sioux Slave

Song of the Warrior

Timeless Warrior

To Tame a Savage

Warrior's Heart

Warrior's Honor

Warrior's Prize

TO TAME A TEXAN

Georgina Gentry

ZEBRA BOOKS
Kensington Publishing Corp.
http://www.kensingtonbooks.com

ZEBRA BOOKS are published by

Kensington Publishing Corp.
850 Third Avenue
New York, NY 10022

All Kensington titles, imprints and distributed lines are available at special quantity discounts for bulk purchases for sales promotion, premiums, fund-raising, educational or institutional use.

Special book excerpts or customized printings can also be created to fit specific needs. For details, write or phone the office of the Kensington Special Sales Manager: Kensington Publishing Corp., 850 Third Avenue, New York, NY 10022. Attn. Special Sales Department. Phone: 1-800-221-2647.

Zebra and the Z logo Reg. U.S. Pat. & TM Off.

First Printing: May 2003
10 9 8 7 6 5 4 3 2 1

Printed in the United States of America

Sisters. They bring out the best and the worst in you. Sometimes you want to kiss them. Sometimes you want to kill them. My sisters and I have laughed and cried together, suffered triumphs, defeats, and heartbreak, always together. No one knows me as well as my sisters do. So this is for you: Georgie, Carol, Steffie, Angie, and in memory of Cindy, the one we lost too soon.

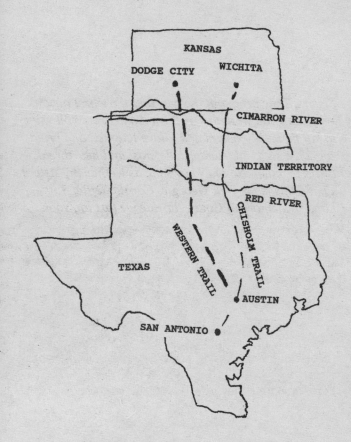

The Chisholm/Western Trail. 1880s

Prologue

You are about to meet Ace Durango, the tough, half-breed heir to the Durango Texas ranching empire and now the trail boss of a big cattle drive up the Chisholm Trail to Dodge City, Kansas. This handsome, charming rascal can handle his cards, his liquor, and his women. Well, most women. With Lynnie McBride, he doesn't even want to try. To put it bluntly, he can't stand the lady!

The feeling is more than mutual. The prim school-teacher and suffragette finds Ace about as appealing as a buzzard. She's appalled by this untamed Texas brute, but she's desperate to get to Dodge City for a Women's Rights meeting. Which means Lynnie's determined to come along on this cattle drive, whether Ace wants her or not.

Trust me, this may be a l-o-n-g, l-o-n-g trip. . . .

One

The Texas hill country
Late January 1885

"Ace is in jail again." Cimarron paused to deliver the news in the doorway of the ranch's library.

"Not again!" Her husband muttered a curse in Spanish and got up from his comfortable leather sofa before the huge fireplace, unceremoniously dumping the small brown Chihuahua dog from his lap onto the floor. "I don't know what I'm going to do about our son."

"Now, darling, don't get riled." Cimarron gestured in a soothing manner as she watched her half-Cheyenne husband. He was almost fifty, but still as handsome as the day she had met him during the Civil War, although now his black hair was streaked with gray. Don Diego de Durango III had a temper like a firecracker, although never with her.

"Riled? Riled?" His voice rose as he paced before the fire. The Chihuahua, Tequila, moved to stay out from under the master's boots. Smoke from Trace's cigarillo billowed like a dragon's breath. "We've spoiled him, that's what. Who brought the news?"

"Comanch."

At the sound of his name, the half-grown boy stuck his head around the library door.

"Comanch!" Trace roared, "I sent you two down to Mexico to buy some blooded horses from my cousins. How in the hell did my son end up in jail?"

The half-breed cowhand twisted his Stetson in his hands. "Well, sir, we got just across the border and Ace wanted to do a little more New Year's celebratin'—"

"New Year's?" Trace Durango threw his hands up in despair. "New Year's? It's late January, for Christ's sake! He's as irresponsible as any saddle tramp. All he does is play cards, drink, and chase women."

"Now, darlin'," Cimarron said, brushing back a wisp of graying blond hair, "Ace is a pretty good cowboy—"

"When we can keep his mind on horses and cattle," Trace snapped and tossed his cigarillo into the fire. "Would I be wrong to presume there was a woman involved in all this?"

Comanch looked at Cimarron helplessly and twisted his hat into a shapeless mass. "Uh, no, sir."

Cimarron saw the expression in her husband's dark eyes and moved to calm things. "Well, now, darlin', you know how the ladies love his easy-going charm—"

"Aha! I knew it! Comanch, what happened?"

"She—she was real purty, sir, and kinda wild—the one that caused the trouble."

"Does my irresponsible son pick any other kind? On the other hand, what nice, respectable girl would risk her reputation with the rascal?" He sighed and sank back down on the leather sofa. The Chihuahua promptly jumped into his lap, and he stroked it absently.

"It wasn't perzactly Ace's fault, sir," Comanche said.

Trace snorted.

"No, really. Some *vaquero* took offense at her sittin' on the arm of Ace's chair in a card game and tried to slap her around. Now, you know no Texan would stand still for that. Ace threw him across the bar, broke the big mirror, and then everybody started throwin' punches."

"You see?" Cimarron came into the library as she defended her son's reputation. "That just shows he's gallant. Ace would always rush to the rescue of a lady."

Trace snorted again. "I doubt she was a lady. Real ladies never attracted our errant son." He reached for another cigarillo. "Comanch, you can go back to the bunkhouse."

"Yes, sir." The half-grown boy fled.

"Double damnation, darlin'," Cimarron sighed, "you scared the poor boy to death. Anyway . . ." She smiled at her husband, remembering. "Your son's not any wilder than you were at that age."

"You're trying to change the subject." Trace seemed to shift uncomfortably at the truth of her words. He looked up at the big portrait of her that had hung over the fireplace for more than twenty years, and for a long moment, neither of them spoke, remembering all the good times and the bad that had brought them together. "But when I was that age, I was already taking charge of the ranch for my father."

She looked out the window at the blustery winter day and felt sadness. The grand old patriarch of the Triple D had only been gone a year. *Tres,* pronounced "trace," meant three in Spanish, and her husband was the third in the line of Durango ranching. Their son was the fourth—if he lived long enough to take over their empire. "Your only son will make you proud yet," Cimarron said.

"Ha! If we could keep him out of jail." He gestured for her to come sit beside him.

"He just needs to find a respectable girl." Cimarron sat down and snuggled up to him. She didn't mention that she already had one in mind.

"His reputation is so bad, no respectable girl would be seen with him. I've got half a mind to let him rot in that Mexican jail."

"Oh, now, darlin', you don't mean that." She kissed his cheek.

"Well, I might. Teach the young scoundrel a lesson." His expression changed, and he looked at her. "You've already done it, haven't you?"

Cimarron bit her lip. "Well, you know how Ace likes his comfort."

"Spoiled, that's what he is. Why, when I was that age, I thought nothing of sleeping out on the prairie or eating by a campfire. He ought to have to live like a real old-time cowboy—toughen him up."

"Yes, dear." She nuzzled his neck, glad to have the subject changed.

He turned his face and kissed her, the kiss deepening. "Wait a minute. You're deliberately distracting me."

"What?" She blinked, keeping her eyes wide with innocence.

"Cimarron Durango, you know what I'm talking about. You've already sent someone with the bail money?"

She laid her head on his chest. "Well, I reckoned the food would be bad in that jail. . . ."

"We both know Ace would seduce the sheriff's daughter into bringing him the best food from her father's house and providing other comforts, too."

She knew it might be all too true. Ace was not only a rascal; he was a devil with the ladies. "Maybe he's learned his lesson."

"Ha! When hell freezes over, maybe," Trace said. "Who'd you send?"

"Pedro. He said the sheriff was his second cousin's brother-in-law."

He put his arm around her and laughed quietly, his anger fading. "Darlin', you are a wonder. Everybody else around here trembles when I raise my voice—everyone but you and Tequila."

The little dog wagged his tail, and his red ribbon of tongue licked his master's hand.

"That's because we both know you better than anyone." She looked up at him and put her arms around his neck.

"I'm just worried that Ace will never grow up to handle the responsibilities that go with his share of this ranch. Now, his sister could handle it. However, I've got my doubts about our wayward son. . . ."

"He just needs to find the right girl," Cimarron said again. Yes, she already had a girl in mind. She started to tell her husband, decided he would roar with laughter at her choice. "In spite of his shady reputation, every young lady in Texas has set her cap for him."

"They all want to be mistress of the biggest, richest spread in the Texas hill country," Trace said.

"Ace would have women chasing after him even if he were poor."

"Isn't that the truth? He's an untamable rogue."

"But a charming one." Cimarron snuggled closer. "All we've got to do is find a girl who can tame our Texan."

"Not possible," Trace said. "One thing for certain: the rascal is beholden to you on this deal. I would have left him in jail."

Cimarron smiled, thinking about her plan. "Ace always pays his debts, and you're right; he owes me now."

His hand went to unbutton her bodice. "You know, it's a cold afternoon, and there's no one around. I can think of better uses for this big couch."

She looked up into his dark, smoldering eyes. "I can, too." She reached to kiss him.

* * *

Two days later, a rumpled, sheepish Ace steeled his courage and ambled into the dining room, Stetson in hand. His head was pounding, but he forced a smile. "Hello, folks. I'm much obliged for you gettin' me out of jail."

"Honey, are you all right?" Ma jumped to her feet to embrace him. He kissed the top of her blond hair. "Oh, you've got a black eye."

"Doesn't hurt." He reached to touch it with one big hand.

His father glared at him. "Don't thank me; thank your ma. Enough's enough. I would have left you there."

"Oh, Trace, you don't mean that." She hugged her tall son again.

Ace favored her with that crooked smile he knew women found so irresistible. "Lordy, Dad, I was tryin' to mind my own business—"

"Your business was to go down to our cousin's *rancho* and bring back some horses." Dad glowered darkly at him over his coffee cup.

Ace grinned good-naturedly. "I only meant to play a hand or two, but there was this girl—"

"Comanch told us," Trace grumbled. "Pretty, was she?"

Ace sighed with remembrance. "Oh, my, was she! Just the kind I like: dark, wild, and hot."

"I don't think I need to hear this," Ma interrupted, and sat back down and gestured him to a chair. "Have some breakfast."

He took a chair with easy grace and looked with disbelief at his father's half-eaten breakfast. The bacon was burned, the eggs half raw. "Old Juanita losin' her touch?"

"She's gone to visit her sister," his mother whispered, "so Cookie is filling in for a few days."

Ace groaned aloud. "That old goat has been poisonin' our cowboys for years; now he's startin' on the family."

"I heerd that!" The bearded old man stuck his head out the kitchen door.

"If you didn't eavesdrop, you wouldn't hear so much," Ace said.

"Listen, you young whippersnapper, I been cookin' on the Triple D ranch as long as you been born—"

"Now, now, Cookie," Ma soothed, "I'm sure Ace is just out of sorts. Bring him some of your delicious cooking."

The grizzled old man wiped the flour off his beard and smiled at Ma. Everyone knew how much he adored her. "All right, Ma'am, I'll feed him, but tell him to shut up about my cookin'." He disappeared back through the door.

"Besides being a lousy cook, he's as cranky as a rattlesnake," Ace said.

"Heerd that!" Cookie yelled.

Ma looked over at Dad, who took a sip of coffee and shrugged. Ace and Cookie had never gotten along in all these years. As a small boy, Ace had delighted in playing tricks on the old cowboy, who was a fixture on the Triple D spread, and Cookie called the young heir "the devil's spawn."

"Don't forget a fresh pot of coffee, Cookie," Ace yelled.

"You'll regret it." His father took another sip and shuddered.

"I heerd that!" Cookie yelled from the kitchen.

Ace put his hand to his head and groaned. "I've still got a headache like a stampede run over me."

"You get no sympathy here," Dad snapped.

"Now, Trace, darling, he's learned his lesson. He's going to do better, aren't you, honey?"

Was he? He liked his lifestyle just fine . . . except ending up in jail or being chased by some girl's irate brother was sometimes a little too exciting. He gave Ma his most charming, lopsided grin, the one that turned all women to jelly.

"I'm sorry, Ma, for causin' so much trouble and bein' a bad boy." He knew all women loved bad boys. Women were reformers deep at heart, and they all saw him as a perfect candidate to civilize. "I'll owe you forever for gettin' me out. . . ."

"In that case, I'm going to call in my marker now," his mother said and smiled sweetly.

"Anything for you, Ma." Ace grinned.

Dad looked up, evidently mystified.

Old Cookie limped into the room, reeking of vanilla, and slammed a plate down in front of Ace. "Here's your breakfast, you young pup, you, and I don't want to hear no complaints."

Ace looked at the burnt eggs and almost-raw steak. He poked at the meat with his fork dubiously. "I seen steers hurt worse than this get well."

"Oh, shut up!" Cookie ran his hand through his flour-dusty beard. "You don't deserve no respect. You're not a real man like your daddy—just a saloon-crawlin' boy."

It was true. He'd never live up to his father's reputation, so he didn't try. "Don't I get some coffee?"

Cookie snorted and returned to the kitchen, leaving the faint scent of vanilla on the air.

"I feel sorry for our cowboys," Ace muttered as he picked up a fork. "They have to eat like this all the time."

"I heerd that!" came from the kitchen.

"Back to the subject about you being obliged to me, son . . ." Ma leaned closer. "It seems the governor is throwing a big Valentine's ball in Austin."

Ace grinned and cut up the eggs. They tasted like some of that rubber he'd heard about. "Lordy, that's great news. All the most beautiful girls in Texas will be there, won't they?"

"I reckon they will." Cimarron nodded. "I've had a note from your aunt Cayenne."

Ace nodded happily, only half listening as he dug into the horrible food. "How are Uncle Maverick and all the family in West Texas?"

"Just fine," Cimarron said.

"That's an understatement." Her husband pushed back his plate and lit a cigarillo. "I never saw so many kids. I don't think that couple ever gets out of bed—"

"Trace!" Ma's face flamed. "That's no way to talk about your adopted brother and his wife."

Cookie limped in with a pot of coffee and a cup and slammed them down before Ace.

"Do you have to make so much noise?" Ace groaned. "I've got a bad headache."

"Cheap tequila and bad women will do that," Cookie snapped.

Ace poured himself some coffee. It was so thick, it looked like black mud. "You know, most ranch-house cooks show a little respect for the boss—"

"You ain't the boss," the old man corrected him. "Your dad's the boss and he's earned respect. We been runnin' this ranch while you were still in diapers, right, Trace?"

Dad smiled and nodded. "Right, Cookie; couldn't run the place without you."

With a satisfied look, the old man limped back into the kitchen. Ace sighed and drank the coffee. The old codger couldn't cook worth a damn, but he knew his father had made a place for Cookie after a horse fell on the veteran cowboy, crippling him. Everyone ignored the fact that the old man drank too much—mostly cheap but potent vanilla from the kitchen.

The little Chihuahua whimpered under the table, and Ace slipped him a bite of the almost-burnt eggs.

Dad whispered, "Be careful, Tequila's old, and Cookie's food . . ."

He didn't need to finish. Ace nodded.

"Double damnation." Ma looked a little exasperated. "Can we get back to the subject at hand if all you men are through snarling at each other?"

"Sure, Ma." Ace nodded, buttered a burned biscuit, and crunched down on it. "Anything you want; I'm much obliged for you bailin' me out."

"Good." She settled back in her chair. "I want you to attend the Valentine ball."

Ace paused with his cup halfway to his lips. "Is that all? Why, Ma, you know that's something I'd go to on my own and—"

"I think it's a trick, young'un!" Cookie yelled from the kitchen.

"Cookie," Ma yelled back, "don't stick your nose in this."

"Women!" came the disgusted snort from the other side of the door.

Ace grinned at his mother, his headache lessening and his mood brightening considerably. She was the only woman he knew that he thought he could trust—she and Aunt Cayenne. "Ma, I'd love to go to the ball."

Dad made a wry smile. "Lots of girls there. It's like sending a coyote to round up lambs."

Ma glared at Dad. "I didn't ask for you and Cookie's comments."

"Got 'em anyway," Cookie yelled from the kitchen.

Ace favored his dear mother with a warm smile. "Sure, I'll be happy to go." He thought of the dozens of winsome, pretty girls he would dance with, and how he might lure one or two outside on the terrace or even into the dark interior of a comfortable carriage.

"I don't think you quite understand, Ace," Ma said. "I want you to escort someone."

Immediately, Ace sensed a trap, and he was as wily as a coyote about self-preservation. "Who?"

"Well, she's bright and has a great personality."

Ace put his coffee cup down and glanced at Dad, but the other man only shrugged and shook his head. Evidently, the senior Durango wasn't in on this. "I said who?"

"Just hear me out," Ma said.

Ace shook his head. "When a mother starts talkin' about what a great personality a girl has, I reckon she's coyote ugly."

Ma gestured. "Beauty is only skin deep."

"But ugly goes all the way to the bone," Ace retorted. "Cookie was right: there's a trap here."

His mother chewed her lip as if she were trying to control her temper. "Double damnation. You gonna take that fractious old cowboy's word against mine?"

"I heerd that!" came from the kitchen.

"Well, you wouldn't," Ma yelled back, "if you'd stop eavesdropping."

"Ace," Ma said, "you owe me. Is a Texan's word no good?"

"You can take a Texan's word to the bank," Ace said, "you know that—especially a Durango's. Dad, what is she up to?"

His father leaned back in his chair and smoked his cigarillo with a smile. "I haven't the faintest idea, but never underestimate your mother."

Ace got up from the table. In his mind, he heard the distinct sound of a trap snapping closed on him. "Tell me who the girl is."

He knew the answer couldn't be good. If it were the kind of girl Ace favored, Ma would have already told him. On second thought, the kind of girls Ace liked wouldn't be allowed into an event as respectable as a governor's ball. "Ma, what's the girl's name?"

"I bailed you out of the lockup when your dad would have left you in there," Ma reminded him.

"Who is the girl?" Ace felt panic like he'd never known before. "Who needs an escort bad enough that a fella's own mother ambushes him?"

"She's a lovely girl," his mother insisted.

"'Lovely' as in 'pretty,' or 'lovely' as in the plain, wholesome kind of girl mothers pick out?"

"Oh, Ace, stop thinking about looks. You're going to have a lovely time."

That word again. "This is someone I reckon I wouldn't escort to a goat-ropin' if my mother didn't blackmail me. Does this 'lovely' girl have a name?"

Ma sighed in defeat. "Very well, it's Lynnie McBride."

"Lynnie McBride?!" He and Dad almost shouted the name aloud. Dad looked as stunned as Ace felt. There was a moment of silence as the name sank in. Maybe Ace had misunderstood. Surely his own mother wouldn't do that to him. "Lynnie McBride? Aunt Cayenne's younger sister?"

There was a cackle of laughter from the kitchen. "I told you, you young whippersnapper. Women is always up to trappin' a man."

"Cookie," Ma yelled, "this is a family matter."

The grizzled old man stuck his head out the kitchen door. "I know. You're the onliest family I got."

"Go back to the kitchen," Ma ordered, and the cook disappeared.

Ace was oblivious to the wordplay between the two. His mouth went as dry as a Texas dust storm. He had to swallow twice, and he felt suddenly sick. He didn't know if it was Cookie's bad cooking or the prospect of taking that redheaded, plain, and opinionated Lynnie McBride anywhere. He couldn't breathe. Now he knew how a condemned man felt when they yanked the trapdoor open and the noose tightened around his neck. "You want me to take Lynnie McBride to the dance?"

"Well, she can hardly attend without an escort," Ma said, "and Cayenne and I decided you would be perfect—"

"Lordy, no!" Ace set off an anguished howl like an injured wolf. "I'll be the laughin'stock of all Texas if I have to escort Aunt Cayenne's old-maid sister."

"Now, Ace, she's not much over twenty," Cimarron said, "and remember, she's smart—"

"Smart? Men don't go with girls because they're smart!" Ace threw up his hands and looked toward his father. "Dad, can you say something?"

Dad scowled. "Cimarron, have you lost your mind? Lynnie is a nice but very naive girl. If Ace ruined her reputation, I'd have to answer to brother Maverick."

Ace was outraged. "Ruin her reputation? You think I'd get close enough to Lynnie to do anything that might . . . ?"

"She's a very nice girl," Ma said stubbornly, "and a schoolteacher."

"Ma, besides bein' plain-lookin', she's opinionated and stubborn. Why, when we were kids at family reunions, she'd want to play school and make all us boys sit up straight and do spellin' and arithmetic."

Dad shook his head. "Send that innocent, sweet girl to the ball with our son? Maverick will kill Ace."

"No, he won't," Ace said, " 'cause I ain't gonna do it."

Ma looked at Dad. "Honey?"

Dad smoked for a long moment. "Ace, a Durango's word is his bond, I reckon. Sounds like to me you gotta do it."

"Well, if men don't want a smart girl, they should," Ma insisted. "You'd end up with smarter children that way."

"Children?" Ace howled again. "I can't even imagine kissin' her, much less gettin' in bed with that straitlaced little schoolteacher. I'll be the laughin'stock of all the cowboys if I have to escort that prim, uptight old maid."

"As many fights and gun duels as you've been in, and you're afraid of being laughed at?" Cimarron said. "You're not only trying to go back on your word, you're a yellow polecat, not fit to be a Texan."

Ace bristled. "No man could call me yellow and live, but I'm rememberin' you're my ma."

"And you owe me." Her eyes brightened in triumph as she reminded him.

"Ask me something else, Ma—*anything* else," Ace implored. "Why, she's skinny as a rail and so flat-chested, you can't tell if you're lookin' at her front or back. And her eyes, behind those glasses, are green as glass. I like a woman with big brown eyes and big . . . well, you know." He gestured out in front of his chest.

"You've just described one of our cows," Cimarron said, "and most of the girls you cotton to are about as smart as cows, too."

Dad leaned back in his chair. "Your mother has a point, Ace. Lynnie may not be a beauty, but she's smart."

"Smarter than me, I reckon." Ace threw down his napkin and stood up. "And she's always talkin' about women gettin' equal rights; I don't know what to think about that."

His mother smiled. "So she's got a brain."

Ace paced around the dining room. "I can't even imagine Lynnie suddenly wantin' to go to a dance. I reckon she'd think a dance was silly."

"It doesn't sound like Lynnie, does it?" Ma admitted. "Your aunt and I were mystified, too. Maybe Lynnie's changed and she's hoping to meet a nice young man at the ball and settle down."

"Lordy, what man would marry plain Lynnie McBride?"

"A woman is always beautiful to the man who loves her," Ma said gently.

"Love? I don't even *like* her."

"Ace, that's not nice," his mother scolded. "Will it hurt you to escort her to one dance?"

"My reputation will be ruined forever," he groaned.

"What about *her* reputation? Being seen with the biggest rake in Texas won't do hers any good."

Ace snorted. "All she does is read books and talk about women votin'. I'll bet you she can't even dance."

There was a long pause. He turned and looked at his mother. "Ma?"

"Double damnation, you do try my soul," Cimarron said. "All right, so she can't dance."

"I knew it! I just knew it!" Ace ran one hand through his blue-black hair. "I'm not only takin' the plainest girl in Texas to a big ball—she can't even dance."

"Well, we're all staying in Austin for this. We'll get to the hotel early that afternoon, and you can teach her a few steps. Then you make sure all the young men fill up her dance card. . . ."

"Lordy, Ma, you ask too much." Ace turned to his

father. "Dad, she wants me to pressure the other fellas to ask her to dance."

His father nodded. "Just think, son; you get her dance card filled, you can dance with the other girls."

Ace's dark eyes lit up. "Hey, that's right, isn't it? Maybe that pretty Emmalou Purdy will come."

"You know what we think of the Purdys." Dad frowned. "All hat and no cattle, that family. Her brother is always tryin' to marry her off into money. Besides, he's a big windbag and a sidekick of the Forresters."

The Forresters were old enemies of the Durangos. Ace would still like to get Emmalou alone in the back of a carriage for a little tickle-and-fun session.

"Young man," Ma threatened, "you'd better not abandon Lynnie and leave her on her own at that dance."

"From what I've seen of that gal," Ace said, "she can take care of herself. Why don't you ask me to take Stevie or Gracious? They're pretty."

Ma shook her head. "You know full well Lynnie's younger sisters are away at school with your own sister."

Ace paced up and down the dining room. The Chihuahua dodged his big boots deftly as it followed him about. "Ma, if I'd known what you expected, I'd have stayed in that Mexican jail. At least the jailer had a pretty daughter who was bringing me barbecued *cabrito* and good tortillas."

"You gave your mother your word," Dad said.

Ace groaned. He walked over and looked out the window at the rolling hills beyond. "I feel like I came into this game with a few good cards and came up against a stacked deck."

Dad smiled. "Don't ever gamble against a woman."

Cookie stuck his head out the kitchen door. "Women ain't to be trusted, you young squirt; even I know that."

"Cookie . . ." Ma turned. "Don't you have dishes piled up in the kitchen?"

With a disgusted snort, the old man disappeared.

Dad nodded. "Let that be a lesson to you, Ace. Women are sneaky creatures and smarter than we are."

"I don't want smart, I want pretty," Ace groaned.

"For the Valentine dance, you'll get Lynnie McBride," Cimarron said firmly, "and after that, you can return to your hot little *señoritas.*"

On the afternoon of February 14th, Ace took a deep breath and hesitated before he knocked on the door of the hotel suite.

"Go on," his mother urged behind him.

He turned in mute appeal to his father, but the senior Durango only mouthed the words: *you owe your mother.*

Lordy, what had he gotten himself into? Could he teach this plain old maid to dance in less than two hours? Of course not. What a miserable evening this was going to be. Well, Ace had learned his lesson; he'd been cold sober and stayed out of the cantinas ever since he'd gotten back from Mexico. The thought of all the fun he'd missed annoyed him, and he rapped harder.

After a moment, the door swung open to reveal a horrible sight. Ace gasped and stepped backward, staring. The creature blinked at him nearsightedly through a mask of white goo and wire-rimmed spectacles. The reddish hair was tied up in hundreds of little rags. Worse yet, the figure wore a faded pink bathrobe tied at the waist and a pair of fluffy, faded house slippers. Ace wanted to turn and run, then realized his retreat was blocked. His mother stood behind him, pushing him forward. He was trapped, and he'd get no mercy. Now he truly understood how his heroes, Travis, Crockett, and

Bowie, had felt in those last desperate minutes at the Alamo. His heart sank. "Lynnie?"

"Of course, you dolt, who else could it be? Hello, Aunt Cimarron and Uncle Trace." The skinny, grease-smeared mess standing in the doorway gestured the trio inside.

Lordy, she was worse than he remembered.

Two

As Lynnie opened the door, she was so taken aback that she could hardly speak. She had forgotten how handsome and broad-shouldered Ace Durango was. She hadn't forgotten he was supposed to be a devil with the ladies. The very kind of man she hated most, she thought, but she needed him tonight. As she gestured the trio inside, she said to Ace, "You're early."

Big drops of sweat gathered on his dark, rugged face. "Reckoned I might as well get it over."

"Excuse me?"

He fumbled with his Stetson, took a step backward. His mother seemed to be nudging him in the ribs. "I—I meant, I was in a hurry to see you again."

"Humph!" She didn't believe it for a minute. "Come into the parlor, where the family is sitting." All three were staring at her in mute astonishment, and she remembered her outlandish appearance. Thunderation. She had meant to have herself presentable by the time Ace arrived. "Aunt Cimarron and Uncle Trace, how good to see you. Don't hug me"—she gestured them off—"I don't want to get lard on your clothes."

"Lard?" Ace looked as if he'd like to turn and run out the door. Lynnie could only imagine what Cimarron had had to do to get her errant son here.

She saw herself in a nearby mirror and winced.

"Sorry I'm not presentable, but they do say lard softens and beautifies the skin."

Ace grinned. "I never saw a beautiful hog."

Oh, the rascal. He was as arrogant and annoying as she remembered from their younger days. If she didn't need him to escort her tonight, she would whack him so hard . . .

"Cimarron! Trace! Long time no see." Maverick and Cayenne came in from the parlor just then, followed by a bevy of their many children. As usual, big sister was expecting again.

The women hugged each other and the men shook hands.

Cimarron smiled. "I'm afraid we're a little early; Ace was so eager to teach Lynnie to dance."

"Uh-huh," Lynnie said, looking up into Ace's stricken face. The only thing he looked eager to do was run like a scalded hound. *Coward.* "Ace, we can all go into the parlor so everyone can sit down."

"And have everyone watch us dancin'?" Ace sounded as if he were choking.

Lynnie frowned at him behind her thick glasses. "I'm sure they will all find it amusing."

One of the twins, Jefferson Davis, peered up at Ace, his freckled face smudged with ice cream. "You gonna marry Aunt Lynnie?"

"Certainly not!" Lynnie felt as horrified as Ace looked, which annoyed her even more. "He's only escorting me to the governor's ball."

As the group walked into the parlor behind her, she heard her pregnant sister saying, "Cimarron, I can't imagine why Lynnie suddenly wants to go to this event; it's not like her at all. But I'm so glad Ace offered to escort her."

"Offered, ha!" Ace muttered under his breath, but Lynnie heard it and gave him her coldest glare.

"Thunderation, you oaf. It's no picnic for me, either," Lynnie whispered through gritted teeth, "but I couldn't go alone."

Behind them, the older couples were catching up on family gossip.

"Ace said he was really looking forward to tonight," Cimarron said a little too brightly.

Liar! Lynnie thought and turned toward Ace. "How do we start?"

"You can't dance at all?" The lanky cowboy tossed his hat onto a table and surveyed her with disbelief.

"Not a step," she admitted. "I always had more important things to do, like improving my mind."

"Lordy!" She thought she heard Ace groan slightly as the whole crowd of family and Ace's parents settled into chairs expectantly. There was ten-year-old Annie Laurie, her sister's oldest daughter; then the twins, young Sam Houston and Jefferson Davis; and the three stair-steps brothers: Bowie, Crockett, and Travis, all named for the heroes of the Alamo. Lynnie's baby sister, Angel, who was now twelve, had stayed at home with the elderly patriarch of the McBride clan, Papa Joe.

Ace licked his lips nervously like a man about to be executed. "Seems like half the county's here to watch," he muttered, "except for your younger sisters."

"Stevie and Gracie are away at school, you dolt, along with your sister, Raven. Angel's at home with Papa. Now, how do we start?"

Ace sighed. "You might start with wiping the goo off your face so you won't get it all over my coat."

"Ace, don't be rude," said his father.

"He's right," Lynnie admitted and went to get a towel. She glanced at herself in a mirror and shrugged. So she looked terrible, so what? The kind of man she'd be attracted to would be interested in her brilliant mind, not her looks.

She returned to the middle of the floor, where Ace stood, sweat shining on his handsome face. The whole crowd had settled down to watch.

"You know," Ace said to the group, "this would be easier if half of Texas wasn't watchin' us."

Maverick, the dark half-Comanche with the knife scar down one cheek, laughed. "Looks to be more fun than a goat-ropin'. What you think, brother?"

"A sip of tequila might add to the fun," Trace said.

"I was just fixin' to suggest that very thing." Maverick grinned and went to get a bottle.

Ace looked at his audience. They were as big-eyed as a bunch of owls, and he felt very ill at ease. "I—I was worried Lynnie might feel self-conscious."

"I'm a liberated woman," Lynnie said grimly, "and I'm not worried about appearing ridiculous—but then, I'm more secure mentally than most men."

"Lynnie," said her big sister, Cayenne, "that was rude."

Lynnie shrugged. "You see what an uncouth rascal I'm dealing with here."

Ace flushed and shot her a look that said he'd like to push Lynnie out the hotel window, and they were on the third floor. "We'll need some music."

"Walk me through the steps first," Lynnie said.

He seemed to be sweating a bucketful, although it was February. "Well, first I put my hand on your waist and take your other hand."

The red-haired children burst into snickers. "He's going to hug Aunt Lynnie. Is he gonna kiss her?"

"That's enough!" warned their mother. "If you don't be quiet, you can't watch."

Lynnie hesitated, suddenly aware of how tall and

masculine Ace Durango was. Very slowly, she put her hand on his wide shoulder and put her small hand in his big, callused one. She had to look up at him, and it gave her a powerless feeling. Lynnie didn't like that; she liked being in control. She took a deep breath to still the nervousness that suddenly overcame her, and smelled the scent of masculine shaving lotion on his dark skin. His big hand went to her waist. She couldn't remember a man ever touching her so intimately. She peered up at him through her spectacles, and he glared down at her.

"Now," he said, "I will lead off on my left foot and you will step backward at the same time with your right one."

"Now, why is that?" she demanded. "Why can't the woman lead?"

Behind her, she heard the resigned sigh of her big sister, who didn't understand Lynnie's obsession with the women's rights issue.

"Lordy, girl . . ." Ace shook his head. "I don't know why men get to lead; that's just the way it is; that's all."

"I think," Lynnie returned primly, "that when women get the vote, we will change all that."

Ace grimaced. "Are you one of those suffragettes?"

Lynnie bristled. "As a matter of fact, I am, and what's wrong with that?"

"Lynnie," said her sister, "we don't have time for all this debate if Ace is to teach you to dance in the next hour."

"And it's gonna be the longest hour I ever spent," Ace muttered as they took their positions again.

"For me, too," she snarled into his ear as he pulled her into the dancing position.

They took a few steps, and one of his big boots trod on her toe.

"Lynnie, don't you know your left foot from your right?" he whispered.

"If I had a better partner, maybe I would do better," she whispered back.

"What? I'll have you know, Miss McBride, that half the girls in Texas would be thrilled to have me as an escort tonight."

"Oh, shut up," Lynnie said. "You big, egotistical brute."

He hesitated, and she was sure the cowboy didn't even know what the big word meant. Behind them, the family chatter continued.

Damn his hide, Lynnie thought. If she didn't need him in her plan, she wouldn't be caught dead with Ace. Why, everyone in Texas knew his reputation. "Well, we might as well get right at it," she snapped. "Houston, wind up the phonograph."

Ace took her hand in his and took a deep breath.

In turn, Lynnie looked down at her fluffy house slippers and wished she did not need to get to the ball so desperately that she would have to attend with Ace Durango. He had a reputation across the whole Lone Star State for being a rascal, a womanizer of the first order, who defied every girl's effort to trap him and tame him. Other women said he was charming, too, but Lynnie was mystified as to why they thought that. She had clashed with him at family gatherings for as long as she could remember, because he wanted to take charge of every game and every situation and Lynnie was not about to be bossed by some male brute.

Young Houston finished winding the big phonograph and put on a wax cylinder. "The Blue Danube" waltz began to play, with a noticeable scratching noise.

"Now, Lynnie, remember, I step forward and you step backward as I lead."

"Remind me again, why is the man allowed to lead?"

Ace started to say something, turned in silent appeal to the watching relatives. They all either shrugged or rolled their eyes, indicating that this was his mess to deal with. "Just do it my way and you can change things when women get the vote, okay?"

"And I suppose you think that will be never?" Her red hair was showing her temperament now.

"Let's just get through this evening"—his voice was grim—"and we'll fight that battle later."

"All right, you big oaf, you can lead this time," she conceded, "but don't think that I'll forget about it."

"I'll just bet you won't." He sounded tired and more than a little annoyed. "Now, remember to let me lead."

She didn't like his being in charge, but he took charge anyway as he deftly guided her around the room to the strains of the music. Besides shaving lotion, he smelled of sun, tobacco, and maybe bourbon, all distilled into a masculine scent that made her a little shaky in the knees. She wasn't used to that feeling, but then, she'd never let a man hold her this closely before. Pure biology, she decided.

Behind them, her sister and Cimarron applauded, but the children giggled and hooted.

"Why, Sis, you're doing just fine. You'll be the belle of the ball tonight," Cayenne said.

Ace snorted, "Not if you keep trying to lead."

"Oh, shut up," Lynnie snapped back.

"Ladies don't tell people to shut up," Ace whispered over the music.

"If you'd behave like a gentleman, I wouldn't have to correct you," Lynnie returned, "but you're a big brute of a Texan who's about as civilized as one of our range bulls."

He grinned down at her wickedly as they danced. "And most women like me that way."

"The kind of saloon whores you favor wouldn't know a gentleman if they met one."

He blinked in shock. "Nice girls don't know about such things."

"No, but I'll bet you do."

"Lordy, Dad would kill me if he heard this discussion. He thinks you're the sweetest, nicest little thing."

She smiled up at him innocently and then deliberately stepped on his toe.

"Lynnie, you're scuffing my new boots," he griped.

"Behave yourself and I won't," she shot back.

Just then, the music ended and the needle sawed noisily on the wax cylinder. Ace let go of her waist and hand as if afraid she might bite him. "I reckon that's enough practice."

"Don't be silly, son," his mother said. "It's not nearly enough."

Houston started the phonograph again.

"It's enough for me," Ace muttered under his breath.

Lynnie steeled herself and closed her mouth primly as Ace's big hand settled on her waist and his other big paw enveloped hers again. "All right, I'm ready."

"Here we go, then."

Unfortunately, both of them stepped forward at the same moment, leading to a tangle of feet that almost caused them both to fall.

"Uh, Lynnie, remember what I told you about allowin' the man to lead?"

"I forgot. It seems so unfair."

Ace sighed. "Just do it."

They took a few more hesitant steps to the music.

"There," he said as he attempted to steer her around the floor, "you're gettin' the hang of it." He pulled her closer so that her face was brushing against his wide shoulder.

"I don't like being held so close," she complained.

"And how do you think I feel about you gettin' hog lard all over my coat?" he countered.

"I imagine the little strumpets you usually hold in your arms have rubbed worse stuff on your body."

"I don't know what a strumpet is, you prissy little prig," Ace said against her rag-bedecked hair, "but I know when I'm bein' insulted."

"Good for you," Lynnie answered. "Now let's make the best of this mess, shall we?"

They made two awkward circles of the small room. The music ended, and the crowd of relatives applauded.

Cimarron Durango smiled encouragement. "Why, you two dance beautifully together. Didn't they, folks?"

Everyone murmured approval, but Lynnie didn't see it in their faces. They all looked dubious at best.

"Well," Lynnie said, "I suppose that's quite enough practice. It's getting late, and I've got a long way to go to get ready."

"A long, long way to go," Ace said, looking her over.

Her big sister looked doubtful. "Are you sure, Lyn-. nie? After all, when all those young men ask you to dance . . ."

"It's quite enough," Lynnie assured her. Lynnie's plans didn't include dancing very much tonight. She had her own agenda—important plans.

"Can I go now?" Ace asked.

His mother shot him a hard look, but Lynnie saw it. "It's all right, Aunt Cimarron. I want to take a bubble bath before I dress."

"Be sure and wash the hog lard off," Ace muttered as he turned away.

She could just kill him. But of course, if she did that, she wouldn't have anyone to escort her tonight.

"I think this calls for another drink," Trace said, "down in the hotel bar."

Uncle Maverick and Ace perked up. "Count us in."

"Why is it?" Cimarron said, "that with men, everything calls for a drink?"

"Oh, let them go," Cayenne said, and waved them out the door. The men scattered like spooked quail.

Cimarron came over to hug Lynnie. "You two danced beautifully together. Why, I can't tell you how thrilled my son is to be escorting you tonight."

You can't tell me because he really isn't, Lynnie thought. "Aunt Cimarron, it's nice of you to say that, but we both know Ace wouldn't be eager to take me to a chicken-plucking. I don't know what you did to get him to agree to take me, but I'm grateful for it."

Cimarron and Cayenne exchanged glances. Lynnie knew that look; she'd seen it before. *Do you suppose there's any chance that at this social event we'll finally find someone to marry this prim old maid and get her off our hands? After all, she's twenty years old and getting a little long in the tooth, with no prospects in sight.*

Oh, why couldn't these two women see that there were so many more things that were important besides marrying some big brute of a cowboy and producing a bevy of children? Well, after tonight, they'd know.

With that, Lynnie retreated to the bathtub to soak and make her plans.

The three men sat in the bar a long time—too long. They talked about things important to Texans—bulls, cows, horses, and guns—while a pretty blond barmaid with big breasts and wearing too much face paint flirted with Ace.

He grinned back, but his Dad nudged him. "Don't think about that, boy. Your evening is taken, remember?"

"How could I forget?" Ace's dark gaze stared at the clock hanging over the big mirror, like a condemned man counting away the last hours of his life. "I'll have another bourbon," he said to the busty girl.

"Ace, you've had three already," his father reminded him. "We'd better go. If I don't get you back upstairs so you can get cleaned up, your Ma will be upset with both of us."

Ace tried to focus his eyes. "Lordy, Dad, you've fought Indians, gunfighters, bad bulls, and unbroke stallions. You ain't afraid of Ma, are you?"

Trace Durango hesitated. "Let's just say a smart Texan picks his battles."

"You can say that again," Uncle Maverick laughed. "Don't know what got into Lynnie about wanting to attend this fancy shindig; it ain't like her at all."

"Looks like somewhere in all of west Texas, you could have found a man willin' to escort her," Ace complained.

Maverick seemed to think a minute. "No," he said, "not one. Sorry about this, Ace. My sister-in-law is a mite stubborn and headstrong."

"A mite?" Ace drained his glass. "I've seen army mules with more give to their personalities."

"Agreed." Maverick rubbed the knife scar on his dark cheek good-naturedly. "Well, I'll see you *hombres* later."

Morosely, Ace watched Maverick leave the bar.

"Come on, son," Trace said, "let's get you ready to go."

"One more drink," Ace begged.

"That ain't gonna make her any more desirable," Trace said.

"Well, it can't hurt."

"That's a fact. I'll have one with you," Trace declared. "Might as well get hung for a sheep as a goat."

"I always wondered what the hell that meant," Ace said somberly.

"Damned if I know. It's just something Texans say."

"Lordy, Dad, she's coyote ugly."

"Coyote ugly" was as big an insult as a Texan could give a person. A girl was coyote ugly if, when a man got too drunk, picked her up, took her to bed, and woke up with her asleep on his arm in the morning, he'd chew his arm off to escape without waking her up.

"Naw." Trace shook his head. "She just looked a little rough with all those rags in her hair and the goo on her face. I'll bet she cleans up pretty good."

Ace tried to picture Lynnie looking better than she had looked this afternoon. Anything would be an improvement. "I hope Ma is satisfied," he grumbled. "I swear I'll never get in trouble again. Ma has no mercy when it comes to callin' in her markers."

"Don't ever try to outsmart a Texas woman," Trace said. "They are as ornery as rattlesnakes and as devious as the devil himself."

"Ma know you think that?"

His father regarded him gravely. "Son, there's some things a smart man keeps to himself, *sí?*"

Ace nodded and glanced at the clock again. He gave the barmaid a final, devilish grin in case he managed to get Lynnie home early.

They were both weaving a little when they left the bar and went upstairs to their rooms. Cimarron met Ace and Trace at the door, her face as stormy as a Texas norther. "Double damnation. Where have you all been?"

"Just chewing the fat in the bar a little," Trace said.

That reminded Ace of hog lard, and he thought for a moment he might lose all that good liquor he'd drunk.

Dad retreated to a comfortable chair, leaving Ace to deal with Ma alone.

"You reek of whiskey," Cimarron complained, grabbing Ace's arm and leading him toward the washbasin. He was still protesting when she poured the pitcher of cold water over his head. "Lynnie might change her mind about being seen with you."

"You think so?" he asked, his soul clinging to that forlorn hope. In answer, he got another pitcher of cold water poured over his head.

Unfortunately, he was almost sober by the time he was dressed and combed like a prize stallion at the county fair.

His mother stepped back and surveyed him proudly. "My, you do look nice. Every girl at the ball will be looking you over."

Ace brightened and smiled at the thought.

Ma frowned. "Hear me, Ace Durango, you are not to flirt with all the girls and leave poor Lynnie standing alone like a wallflower."

"Aw, Ma, give me a little something to look forward to."

Trace called from his easy chair. "You heard your mother. You know no one else will ask that poor little filly to dance, so don't you abandon her."

It was going to be a long, long evening, Ace decided glumly.

"Of course," his mother said, straightening his tie, "if you could get your friends to fill her dance card so she'd look popular, that would be very nice."

"That'd turn my friends to enemies," Ace sighed. "Just remember, Ma, you and I are even after this."

"Until the next time you get yourself in a mess." Ma brushed off the lapel of his expensive black coat.

"I've learned my lesson," Ace declared. "I'm a re-formed man."

Dad snorted from his chair and picked up the newspaper.

"Double damnation, son," his mother scolded, "you might just have a good time tonight."

"Uh-huh," Ace said without enthusiasm.

"Oh, dear . . ." Ma pursed her lips. "I forgot about flowers. Go down to the lobby and get her a corsage. I think I saw a vendor out on the street."

"And don't forget to come back," Dad yelled.

Ma gave him her steely gaze. "Of course he'll come back. Ace is too much of a gentleman to stand up a lady, aren't you, son?"

Frankly, the idea seemed very appealing at the moment. "I said I'd take her, and a Texan's word is good as gold."

"Have a good time, then." His mother pushed him toward the door.

Good time. Hah. "I'd have a better time if I could go alone. Why aren't you and Dad and Maverick and Aunt Cayenne going to this thing?"

"Because your father hates the governor; he thinks he's an idiot. And of course, Aunt Cayenne is in the family way. So go represent our families and be your usual charming self."

"Lynnie doesn't think I'm charming," Ace complained.

Ma laughed. "Now that's a first, isn't it? You're used to every woman in Texas finding you irresistible."

He had to admit it was true. Lynnie McBride didn't seem to find him charming; in fact, she didn't even seem to find him slightly likable. But then, he figured Lynnie felt that way about most men. "I don't know why Lynnie even wants to go to this dance."

"I don't, either." Ma looked puzzled. "Maybe she's finally decided she wants to get married. After all, most of the most prominent, eligible bachelors in Texas will be there tonight."

Ace rolled his eyes. "Like I said, Ma, after tonight, you and me are even. I've learned my lesson."

"Sure you have, dear. Now get along with you." She pushed him out the door and closed it.

Reluctantly Ace went down the stairs to the lobby and found the flower vendor. He hadn't the least idea what to buy, but the bright red roses reminded him of the barmaid's lips, so he chose those. Then he stopped at the bar and had two more drinks to steel himself. He took a deep breath and imagined Lynnie coming out still wearing rags in her hair, goo on her face, and that tacky bathrobe and fluffy slippers. He looked down at the flowers in his hand, wondering idly if Lynnie would insist he pin them on her. Maybe he could stick her with the pin and claim it was an accident.

Holding his corsage, he walked slowly up the stairs, weaving slightly. So this was what it felt like to walk toward the hangman. He was going to be disgraced tonight; he was sure of it—escorting the prim old maid to this ball where everyone in Texas would know about it. There was no telling what she'd be wearing and what she'd look like.

Taking a deep breath, Ace rapped on the hotel door.

Lynnie opened it. "Ace Durango, you're late. I was beginning to wonder if you were coming at all."

He was weaving only slightly as he stared at her. She looked different, very different indeed. Lynnie wore a fluffy pink dress of some soft fabric. Her reddish hair was pulled back in a twist of curls. Of course, being a respectable girl, she wore no makeup, but somehow, the freckles across her clean, shiny face looked appealing, and the lashes around those green eyes were quite long. She was slender, but the front of her ball gown was filled out nicely.

"Stop looking at my bosom," she snapped. "I swear, you men only think about one thing."

With Lynnie? Not on your life.

"Uh, you look nice," he mumbled awkwardly, and thrust out the flowers. "I brought you a corsage."

"You look nice, too." She acted hesitant, which was unusual for Lynnie, and he realized that she was not used to men calling on her. He almost pitied her: twenty years old and probably had never been invited out by any man—the ultimate old maid. "Thanks for the flowers."

She took them, and he realized suddenly that they clashed with her dress. How stupid of him, not remembering to ask the color of her dress. He'd always been so smooth with women. It wasn't like him to make such a blunder. "You don't have to wear them," he mumbled.

Now she became the Lynnie he remembered. "Wear them? Of course I'm going to wear them. Well, don't just stand there; come in." She gestured and stepped backward. The dim light on her delicate features made her almost pretty.

Pretty? Ace, my boy, you really have had too much to drink.

Lynnie took a deep breath and wrinkled her nose. "You smell like a distillery."

"Sorry." He took a deep breath and realized she smelled of some delicate floral scent. "You want me to pin the corsage on?"

"So you can paw my bosom? Not on your life. I'll pin it on myself, thank you."

He felt the flush creep up his rugged face. Okay, so he had touched a few girls in inappropriate places when he pinned flowers to their dresses, while they giggled with delight. The thought crossed his mind that probably Lynnie had never giggled in her life, and if he was reckless enough to touch Lynnie McBride's bosom, she would certainly poke her small fist in his eye. He looked around and realized the whole family was standing in the background watching. "Well, we'd better be goin'."

"I'll get my shawl and bag."

He watched her glide away and thought she was graceful and not too bad-looking—at least not coyote ugly. Maybe he could bribe some of his friends to dance with her so he wouldn't be saddled with her all evening. There were plenty of fellows who owed him a favor or a gambling debt. "Where's your spectacles?"

"In my purse."

"Don't you need them?"

"Only if I want to see," she answered matter-of-factly. "This is going to be an interesting evening; I'm sure of it."

"At least a very long evening." He offered her his arm and imagined a ballroom full of beautiful, desirable women—and he was stuck with prim Lynnie McBride. Ace almost groaned aloud. Well, the dance wouldn't last forever.

Maverick stepped forward. "Remember, Ace, this is a member of my family." His voice held a warning edge. "I'll expect you to be a perfect gentleman."

What was Uncle Maverick hinting at? Oh, surely he didn't mean . . . ? With *Lynnie?*

"I'll bring her home early," he assured his step-uncle.

"Not too early," Aunt Cayenne said.

If he got rid of Lynnie soon enough, he might still have a chance with the blowsy, big-bosomed barmaid with the red, red lips. That thought cheered Ace a little.

"I've got a carriage waiting downstairs," he said, and they went out the door and down the hall, heading for the big Valentine dance at the governor's mansion.

Three

It was a crisp but clear night as the horse and carriage clopped along the street from the hotel.

Ace sighed. This was going to be a long, long evening. Even if some beauty did show up at the ball, Ace was under orders not to abandon Lynnie. Lynnie's delicate fragrance was overpowered by the scent of the roses and liquor.

Lynnie sniffed with disdain. "Just how much bourbon did you consume?"

"Not nearly enough," he snapped back, then instantly regretted his words. A Texan was gallant to the bone, even when he wanted to wring a lady's neck. With any other girl on such a chilly night, Ace would have used the cold as an excuse to cuddle closer, maybe steal a kiss or two. He glanced sideways at Lynnie. She sat ramrod stiff, her mouth firm with disapproval. He didn't figure she'd ever been kissed in her whole life except by her father and maybe her little nephews. Ace didn't intend to be the first.

All that broke the silence was the creaking of the carriage wheels.

"So," she said, evidently attempting conversation, "how are things at the Triple D Ranch?"

He stifled a drunken yawn. "'Bout the same as they are at the Lazy M, I reckon: just cows and more cows."

Another long moment of awkward silence. In the moonlight, he could see Lynnie chewing her lip. She didn't look very happy to be heading for a big ball. Other girls would have been engaging him in silly, giggling conversation. Lynnie was as stern as a hanging judge.

"So remind me again why your father is called Trace."

Even this feeble attempt at conversation was better than strained silence. "Uh, Dad is Diego de Durango the Third. He's half Spanish, and *tres* is Spanish for three."

"Well, then it seems logical that if you're Diego de Durango the Fourth, you should be called Cuatro."

"I like playin' cards," Ace said, and wished he had a little flask to sip on, "so that's the reason for my nickname."

"I hear you spend a lot of time in saloons and gambling halls." She sounded stiff, disapproving.

"Well, that's where men play cards." He grinned at her.

Another long period of silence that was cooler than the temperature inside the creaking carriage.

"I—I appreciate your volunteering to take me to the ball," Lynnie said. "I've never been to one before."

He almost told her that his mother had volunteered him, then decided it would be terribly ungallant. "So why'd you decide on this one?"

Lynnie hesitated. "The governor and most of the legislators and other influential men in town will be there."

"Dad says the governor is an idiot."

"I think so, too." Lynnie smiled and fidgeted nervously with her small handbag.

When she smiled, she didn't look half bad, but then, he knew he'd had too much to drink, so he didn't trust his judgment at the moment. As they used to say at the cantina: *"All the women get purtier at closing time."*

"Thunderation, it's cold," Lynnie said.

He might have taken that as an offer to cuddle from

some other female, but from straitlaced Miss McBride, he was sure she was just filling the silence.

"Lynnie," he said kindly, "ladies don't usually use a word as strong as 'thunderation.' They say 'goodness gracious' or 'mercy me.'"

She fixed him with a green, nearsighted stare. "'Mercy me' sounds sissy and idiotic. It's the kind of thing that addle-brained Emmalou Purdy would say. You know, she's my oldest pupil."

Lordy, Emmalou Purdy. He sighed wistfully as he pictured the pretty, buxom girl. He'd like to be her teacher. On the other hand, there wasn't much he could teach that lusty girl.

The carriage pulled up and halted in the drive of the governor's mansion. From inside, light streamed through all the windows, and as the big front doors opened to accept new arrivals, Ace heard a faint melody drifting on the cold air. Carriages were everywhere, with people all decked out in their finest arriving for the evening. There would be lots of beautiful girls at this dance, and here he was stuck with prim Lynnie McBride. Ma drove a mighty hard bargain.

The driver came around, put down the step, and opened the door. Ace stepped out and reached to help Lynnie down. She stumbled, and he had to catch her by both arms. She was stiff to his touch. "Unhand me, you scoundrel."

He stood her on her feet. "Lynnie, if you'd put on your spectacles, you wouldn't trip over the step."

"And if you were a gentleman, you wouldn't notice my tripping."

Oh, Lordy. He took her arm in case she tripped over the entry steps, and they went inside. Down the ornate stairs floated music, much laughter, and talk. The butler took their wraps. "Ballroom on the second floor, sir."

He wasn't sure just how much Lynnie could see without her spectacles; she looked as blind as a newborn kitten. In fact, for a moment, she seemed almost fearful and very vulnerable. *Lynnie?* She could cut a man to pieces with just her sharp wit, he thought glumly. He took her elbow as he escorted her up the stairs. It wouldn't do to have her trip and fall all the way down in a tangle of pink silk and petticoats.

Many a young lady turned and gave him her best and most inviting smile, and out of force of habit, Ace smiled back. If he could palm his lady off on some luckless *hombre,* maybe Ace would get a dance or two with some of these eager beauties. He paused in the doorway of the big ballroom and watched the dancers sway gracefully to the music. "Lynnie, would you like some punch?"

"I suppose so." She acted a bit bewildered, and he remembered that she hadn't had much in the way of a social life. Well, it was her own damned fault for being so prudish and smart. Ace parked her against a wall and ambled over to the punch bowl. Half a dozen fellows he knew were standing about, ogling the arriving young ladies.

Ace nodded to several of them. "Hey, *hombres,* good night for a dance."

Bob Anderson nodded. He was a bit of a dandy, Ace thought. "I came stag so I could choose among the girls."

"Me, too," Sam and Howard said. "What about you, Ace?"

Before he could answer, Bob laughed. "Didn't you see? He's escorting Lynnie McBride. What'd it take to get you to do that, Ace?"

He almost admitted that his own mother had called in her marker on him; then he looked toward Lynnie looking a bit forlorn, and his heart softened a little. "I've had enough of brainless beauties. Lynnie can talk about politics and all sorts of stuff."

"Since when does a man want to talk to a girl?" Willis Forrester joined them. He was older and had menacing blue-green eyes as hard as turquoise. "I brought Emmalou Purdy; you know, the one with the big . . ." He didn't finish, and the others laughed knowingly. He looked Ace up and down. "I wager Durango's dad forced him to bring the schoolmarm."

The Forresters and the Durangos were old enemies, and Ace frowned at the other man—a little too handsome and dressed in the latest styles from back east. "Forrester, you should be so lucky to get accepted as an escort for a smart girl like Lynnie. Why, she's even graduated from college."

Forrester sneered. "And just how does that help in the bedroom?"

The others laughed, but Ace grabbed Forrester's arm. "Watch your mouth, *hombre.*"

"All right, all right." The other threw up his hands in surrender. "I didn't mean anything by it. It's just that knowing your reputation with the ladies, we're all surprised to see you escorting that prim old maid."

His reputation was on the line. All four of the men looked at him. He almost weakened then and told them how his mother had forced him to bring Uncle Maverick's spinster sister-in-law, but he looked across the floor at Lynnie, standing there by herself among the more beautiful girls, and for the first time in his life he almost pitied her. "I'm tired to death of brainless women who have nothin' to offer but good looks and hot kisses." He waited a moment to see if heaven would strike him down for his brazen lie, then breathed a sigh of relief when it didn't happen.

He waited until Forrester had walked away, then turned on the other three. "Miss McBride's dance card probably isn't full, if you three are wantin' to hurry over and ask her."

Nobody moved.

Ace frowned. "I *said,* she might have room on her dance card for three fellows that still owe me money from our last poker game."

They looked at him. Then they turned and looked toward Lynnie standing forlornly yet defiantly across the ballroom.

"I might even forgive a gambling debt to a man who'd do the gentlemanly thing."

All three looked as if they were surveying a hangman's noose. With a sigh, all three started across the floor toward Lynnie.

Humming to himself with satisfaction, Ace got two cups of punch, tasted his, and grimaced. Well, maybe someone in the crowd had a bottle of bourbon; that would improve the flavor to a Texan's taste. As he stood there watching his friends crowd around Lynnie, Emmalou Purdy minced across the floor and brushed up against him.

"Why, Ace Durango, mercy me," she giggled. "I do hope you're plannin' on askin' little old me to dance."

He bowed gallantly. "I do hope, Miss Purdy, you'll save me a place on your dance card." He relished the idea of rubbing up against those big bosoms, if only for a few minutes.

"That I'll surely do." She giggled again and floated across the floor toward Willis Forrester, who was frowning at Ace.

Ace looked over the beauties on the dance floor with a sigh before sauntering back over to where Lynnie stood. "Enjoying yourself?"

"Your friends came over and asked me to dance," she said almost as if she couldn't believe it.

What he'd done made him feel good inside. He'd feel much better when he got to dance with some of the other girls during those three dances. "Uh, they all want a chance to dance with a smart girl, Lynnie. All these others have is looks." He was looking down into the top of her ball gown and decided she wasn't as flat-chested as he'd first thought.

"Stop staring at my bosom," Lynnie snapped as she accepted the punch.

He was startled that she was so straightforward. He'd never experienced such honesty from a girl. "I wasn't staring."

"Yes, you were. Besides, my corset top is stuffed with hankies. That's what you're licking your chops at."

He felt a mite foolish. "I don't know what to say to a girl who's frank enough to tell me something like that."

"You didn't know?" She snorted. "Why, half the girls in this room have hankies or socks stuffed in the top of their ball gowns to fill them out."

He turned and stared longingly at Emmalou Purdy as she danced by with Willis Forrester. She winked boldly at Ace over Forrester's shoulder.

"Including her," Lynnie said under her breath.

"You mean, that's what I've been looking at?" Ace felt he'd been robbed. "Of all the cheating, deceitful . . ."

"Knowing you," Lynnie said, "you're probably already imagining taking half of these girls out in the back of a carriage, pawing their corsets and drawers."

He felt the flush rise to his face. "Lordy, Miss McBride, that's hardly fittin' conversation for a young lady."

"I reckon not, but I know your reputation." She looked about. "How long before the grand promenade?"

Ace shrugged. "As soon as the governor comes upstairs and the party's in full swing, I reckon."

"Good. I want us to lead it."

He was mystified. That didn't sound like Lynnie.

"Would you like to dance?" Lynnie asked.

"I'm supposed to ask you," he said.

"Well, now, why is it the man gets to do the asking?"

Yes, it was going to be a long, long evening, Ace thought in resignation. "I don't know; that's just the way it is."

"There are lots of things that need to be changed, then."

He didn't want to argue with the little spitfire. The red-haired McBride women had reputations for being feisty. Unfortunately, the other sisters were prettier. He bowed before her. "Miss McBride, would you like to dance?"

"I suppose we might as well."

They set their punch cups down on a nearby table.

She came into his arms, stiff as an ironing board. "Not so close, you rascal, you. Remember, I'm practically related to you."

"No, you aren't, except by marriage." Thank God for that. Her waist was small, as was the dainty hand she put in his big one. He maneuvered her out onto the dance floor. "Now remember, I get to lead. We'll argue over whether it's fair to women later."

They did reasonably well and only tripped over each other's feet a couple of times as they waltzed.

Lynnie glanced around as they danced. "All the girls are watching you. I'll bet they're hoping you'll ask them to dance."

He'd noticed that, too. Ace sighed wistfully and remembered he was under orders not to abandon Lynnie. "Now why would I want to dance with them when I have someone like you in my arms?"

She looked startled, then smiled. "I know you're lying, but it's nice of you to say that."

He must be drunker than he thought; Lynnie looked almost attractive when she smiled. "Lynnie, please stop tryin' to lead."

"Even that Forrester girl is smiling at you."

Willis Forrester's sister. Her pale turquoise eyes were issuing a frank invitation. Ace smiled back.

"You don't have to ogle her," Lynnie snapped.

"I was only being polite," Ace said. "Besides, doesn't the Good Book say 'love your enemies'?"

"That's not to be taken literally, you dolt."

He wasn't sure what a dolt was, but he knew he was being insulted.

Her face was brushing against his shoulder, and he could smell a delicate fragrance in her reddish hair. If she just weren't so stiff, he might close his eyes and pretend she was a ripe, luscious, and eager female. Ace concentrated on dancing. It was difficult, much like steering a ship that was stuck on a sandbar.

"Ace, did you ask your friends to sign my dance card?"

She sounded almost timid, and he felt sorry for the poor little thing. "You've got it wrong, Lynnie; *they* were askin' my permission to sign your dance card."

"Now, why would they do that?"

Ace sighed. "Because I'm your escort."

"I'm perfectly capable of making that decision myself. Why should they have to ask your permission?"

"Lordy, girl, you do carry this women's rights thing too far. You'll never get a husband if you keep this up."

She stopped in the middle of the floor so suddenly that Ace tripped over her feet. "A husband? Do you think that's all girls think about?"

"Obviously, not you." He led her off the floor, thinking he was going to be in the debt of his friends forever more. Well, he'd let them win at poker next time.

"Would you like some more punch?" He pulled out a handkerchief and wiped his face.

"Yes, please."

Lynnie watched him amble over to the punch bowl. Just then, an older student in Lynnie's one-room school, Penelope Dinwiddy, spotted her and hurried through the crowd. Penny was tall, sweet, and blinked a lot. Tonight she wore a cream ball gown that contrasted nicely with her dark hair. "Oh, Miss Lynnie, are you really going to go through with it?"

"Shh! Penny, you'll spoil the whole thing." She put her finger to her lips. "Yes, I'm just waiting for the grand march."

Penny giggled. "My stars, you're so brave. Let me help the cause."

Lynnie shook her head. "You're only seventeen, Penny, and you're my student, so that makes me responsible for you. Besides, there'll probably be some trouble."

Penny blinked and looked at Ace, standing by the refreshment table visiting with friends. "They say Ace Durango is a devil with the ladies."

Lynnie sniffed. "I'm sure I wouldn't know about that."

"All the girls are talking about him being your escort. How'd you manage that?"

Lynnie smirked. "I prevailed on my sister to help me. She was so excited that I actually wanted to attend the ball, she never questioned anything. I think the whole family's afraid of being stuck with a spinster."

Penny sighed as Ace sauntered toward them in an easy, relaxed gait, carrying punch cups. "But the one and only Ace Durango . . ."

Lynnie made a noncommittal noise. "I just needed him to get here; that's all."

"Does he know?"

"Thunderation, no, Penny. You think he'd have come if he'd known? Ace Durango is the last man who'd favor women's rights. What are *you* doing here, anyway? I thought you were spoken for."

Penelope sighed. "My brother-in-law escorted me, hoping to find me a new beau."

Lynnie smiled at a passing acquaintance. "They don't like Hank?"

"No." Penelope shook her head. "I love Hank Dale and he loves me, but my Pa doesn't think Hank has good enough prospects—owns only a few acres, and the land's so poor, it would take three people to raise a fuss on it. That sticky oil is seeping up out of the ground and killing the grass, so it's no good for cattle."

Lynnie nodded sympathetically. "Sooner or later, they've got to find a use for that black stuff besides greasing a few buggy wheels."

Ace joined them just then, and Penelope grinned like an idiot and blinked again. "Good evening, Mr. Durango."

"Ah, Miss Penelope, and how are you?" Ace smiled a little too warmly, Lynnie thought.

"Miss Penelope was just leaving," Lynnie said, and warned the younger girl with her eyes. She didn't want her student caught in the middle of what might happen soon.

Penelope looked up at Ace and giggled. "Nice to have seen you again."

"Perhaps you might save me a dance," Ace said, and his eyes brightened.

"I think not," Lynnie snapped. "Good-bye, Penny, we'll talk later."

The girl walked away, and Ace handed Lynnie her punch cup. "Lordy, that was rude. You practically chased her away."

"Your tongue was almost dragging on the ground, and she's much too young and innocent for a rogue like you."

About that time, the band stopped playing, and the leader held up his hands for silence. "Ladies and gentlemen, the governor and his lady have arrived upstairs now, so take your places for the grand march."

An excited buzz filled the air as the young ladies giggled and primped, getting ready to show off their fancy ball gowns as they gathered at one end of the giant room. Ace noted there were even reporters present with their pads and pencils, scribbling furiously. Tomorrow's newspapers would be filled with descriptions of lovely gowns of rainbow hues and beautiful young debutantes.

"Ace, isn't it exciting? Let's get in front."

"It don't make me no never-mind," he replied, smiling good-naturedly. One of his friends had improved Ace's punch with a little bourbon, so he was now in a much better mood. He took her arm, and they hurried to the end of the room where the couples were lining up. Confusion reigned as couples moved about, vying for a choice spot so they would be noticed.

Ace was more than a little drunk, but he held his liquor well, and with all the ripe beauties winking and smiling at him, the evening was beginning to seem promising and not nearly so grim as he had expected. Still, for the life of him, Ace was mystified about why Lynnie was so enthused about the Grand March.

She had turned away from him, fumbling in her small purse as the couples bustled about. "Hold us a place in line, Ace."

The orchestra leader rapped for silence. "Is everyone ready now?"

Ace moved deftly to the front of the line. With his family's money and power, no one would dispute his right to lead the march. He looked toward all the stiff, gray-haired politicians, seated on the dais to watch the young ladies and dandies parade. Lordy, everyone in Texas would see him with this prim old maid and think he couldn't do any better. Well, it couldn't be helped. "Lynnie?"

"Here I come." She whirled up beside him, and now she was wearing a banner draped across one shoulder of her pink gown and down her bodice. Ace gasped. The satin ribbon was emblazoned: *Votes For Texas Women.*

He blinked. "You gonna wear that?"

"Of course!" Her green eyes were defiant. "That's the only reason I came."

He'd been used. He felt like a cheap slut on the morning after. Lynnie McBride hadn't been yearning to attend a ball or to dance in his arms; she was looking for an audience for her damned women's rights. "You know you're about to cause all hell to break loose?"

"Are you scared? If so, I can make the march alone." She was almost pretty glaring up at him, her green eyes bright with defiance.

"Them's fightin' words, Miss Priss. I'm game if you are."

He felt her take a deep breath as she took his arm and stuck out her chin. In spite of her defiant attitude, he noted that her arm trembled. They were about to start some serious trouble here. Ace didn't even want to think about the results. Then the music started, and Ace and Lynnie led off the march. They took a dozen steps before the important audience of legislators and their ladies seemed to read Lynnie's banner. Scowls replaced the smiles, and the dowagers began to fan themselves very fast and whisper to each other. The reporters paused, pencils in hand, almost as if they could not believe what they were seeing. The music continued to play, but the buzz along the sidelines grew as the line of couples moved toward the dais. The first lady whispered to her husband, who scowled like an old bulldog and gestured to a footman.

"Here it comes," Ace said through clenched teeth.

"Let them come," Lynnie snapped, and kept marching.

"Young lady . . ." The footman approached. "The governor asks that—"

"No!" Lynnie said firmly and kept moving.

The footman moved along beside them awkwardly, looking at Ace almost as if he could not quite believe what he had heard. "She's defying the governor?"

"I reckon that's about the size of it." Ace shrugged and kept walking.

"She can't do that." The footman was aghast.

"You don't know Lynnie McBride," Ace said. He didn't give a damn about women's rights, and the only good part of this evening was that they were probably going to get tossed out and he'd have her back at the hotel in less than an hour, his part of the bargain fulfilled. He grinned, thinking the barmaid with the big tits and the red, red lips was probably getting off duty about now.

The servant hurried back to the governor, who looked like a big, fat walrus with a gray mustache. The walrus blinked in shock and gestured to several guards, who approached the couple, blocking their path. The music kept playing, and the couples behind them stumbled and ran into each other. Whispers spread up and down the line of march. A tall guard grabbed Lynnie's arm. "See here, Miss, the governor insists—"

"Unhand the lady," Ace growled. He was not at all pleased to have been used as part of Lynnie's women's rights protest, but he was too gallant to allow anyone to manhandle a lady.

The music stopped in sudden confusion, and the hubbub increased. Lynnie broke free of the guard and ran up on the dais, pulled off her banner, and threw it in the governor's lap. "Free women!" she shouted. "Votes for women now!"

Young Forrester drew himself up stiffly and stepped out of the line of march. "This is highly irregular," he said in a loud, irate voice, "but what can one expect from a bunch of rowdies like the Durangos and the McBrides?"

Ace strode up to him. "Are you insulting my family?"

"It appears the lady's already done so," Forrester sniffed.

Ace hit him then, sending him stumbling into the punch bowl. The table went over, and the red punch sloshed across the slick floor. Servants rushing to pull Lynnie from the dais went sliding in the sweet, sticky mess.

"Votes for women!" Lynnie screamed, "Governor and senators, you should be ashamed of yourselves! Give women their rights!"

Forrester stumbled to his feet, swinging wildly.

"Hit him again, Ace!" Lynnie yelled.

"Don't mind if I do!" Ace grinned and nodded. "This dull evening might turn into some fun after all." And he put all his power behind his fist.

Pandemonium broke out across the floor as the line of march broke up and people began to push and shove each other. Ace hit Forrester again and pushed through the crowd, trying to reach Lynnie, who was fighting to keep servants from dragging her off the dais. The band began to play loudly, attempting to bring a semblance of order to the melee, but that only added to the noise and confusion as fists flew and women screamed.

Ace made it to the dais and shoved the footman, who

was trying to peel Lynnie away from the drum, which she was kicking to add to the noise. "I told you you were getting us into a mess."

"I don't give a damn if you don't!" she shouted back as she kicked the footman between the legs and he doubled up and went down, moaning.

Women shrieked and blows flew all over the ballroom now, and the waltz music only added to the confusion. Ace waded into the mob, picked up a man, and slid him across the floor and through the punch. The top-heavy Emmalou Purdy turned and tried to run out of the ballroom, slipped in the punch, and landed hard on her bottom.

"Now," Lynnie yelled, "that was worth seeing!"

"We ought to get out of here!" Ace yelled back, and tried to drag her off the dais.

"And miss the excitement? Hell, no!"

About that time, the police arrived, whistles blowing. Ladies shrieked and fainted; gentlemen who had already had too much to drink waded into the fight for want of something better to do.

Next to them, young Howard knocked a portly senator across the floor. "Wow!" he yelled. "Ace, I thought this was going to be a dull evening! I should have known it wouldn't be if you showed up!"

Ace was too busy fighting to answer, but he noticed Miss Forrester, she of the turquoise eyes and fancy ball gown adrip with punch, fighting to take Lynnie's banner. Lynnie had her hands in the blonde's hair, yanking for all she was worth. Two other elegant young ladies joined the fray, and now Lynnie's fists were flying. For such a thin girl, she had plenty of spunk, Ace thought with a trace of admiration. At least the dull ball had become more interesting in a hurry.

Oh, it was a grand brawl that broke up the party. It

took four cops to drag Ace out of the ballroom. Just ahead of him, they were pulling Lynnie, with her dress all torn and her reddish hair down around her shoulders. "Free women!" she shrieked. "Women, arise and take your rights!"

Two reporters hurried up. "And your name is . . . ?"

"Don't tell 'em!" Ace yelled.

"McBride," Lynnie said to the reporters. "*M-C-B-R-I-D-E,* and I'm making this sacrifice for the enslaved women of Texas! Ladies, arise and cast off your shackles! Votes for women!"

She was still shouting as the police hauled them down the stairs and into the paddy wagon.

"Now you've done it!" Ace said to her as the policeman slammed the door. His head was pounding like a war drum, and he was cold sober. He looked at her, disheveled but triumphant, her green eyes gleaming. "Lynnie, somebody's given you a black eye."

"Nobody gave it to me; I earned it!" She looked proud of herself.

"Oh, Lordy," Ace groaned, "what is Dad going to say?"

Four

"Ace is in jail again," Cimarron sighed as she entered the hotel bedroom and turned up the gaslights.

"What?" Trace mumbled.

"I said, Ace is in jail again." She waited for her husband's reaction.

There was a long pause, and for a moment, she thought he had not heard her. She leaned over the bed, and one of his eyes opened, blinked.

"Say that again."

"You heard me right the first time."

Trace began to curse in Spanish as he got out of bed, stubbed his toe, and hopped about the room, cursing. "How in the hell did that happen? I'll wager Lynnie is so embarrassed . . ."

"She's in jail, too." Cimarron crossed her arms. "Maverick's waiting in the lobby for you to go with him to bail them out."

"I'm gonna kill that boy," Trace promised as he grabbed up his pants and boots. "I didn't figure Ace could get into any kind of trouble escorting a nice girl to a fancy dance."

Cimarron tried to say something, but he waved her off as he buttoned his shirt. "Don't defend him. It isn't enough that Ace is wild and irresponsible, oh, no! He has to drag an innocent, respectable girl into it. Maverick will be madder than hell."

Maverick didn't say much as they took a carriage and headed through the darkness. "I'm sorry, Maverick, I don't know what got into the boy."

The other man shrugged. "Don't apologize yet, brother. Ace may not be the only one at fault here."

Before Trace could carry the discussion further, the hansom cab pulled up before the courthouse. Outside, under the gas streetlights, reporters were clustered around and came running to meet the pair as they recognized the prominent ranchers. "Care to make a statement, sir?"

"Hell, no!" Trace roared, pulling his coat collar up against the chill wind, his gray-streaked hair blowing since he'd left his Stetson at the hotel. "Just say there must be some misunderstanding."

"Is it true the Triple D and the Lazy M between them control almost a million acres?"

"It ain't polite in Texas to ask a man the size of his spread!" Trace snapped.

Ignoring the eager reporters, he and Maverick shouldered their way through, but the men trailed after them as they entered the building. "Is it true Ace Durango turned the governor's ball into a brawl?"

"No comment!" Maverick yelled back. He looked as grim and disgusted as Trace felt as they entered and strode to the desk.

In moments, they had posted the bail, and the amused officers brought the pair out. Ace had a cut lip, and blood on his fine coat. Lynnie's pink dress appeared to be in tatters, and she sported a black eye.

Trace glowered at his errant son. "It isn't bad enough

that you've got to get into a fight; you drag this poor, naive girl into it?"

Poor, naive girl. Ace glared at Lynnie, waiting for her to 'fess up, but she only smiled demurely as her brother-in-law took off his coat and put it around her shoulders.

"Are there reporters outside?" Lynnie asked.

"Yes, but don't worry," Trace assured her. "Maybe we can sneak out the back door and your name won't get dragged through the mud." He scowled at his son again.

Ace couldn't take any more. He didn't mind taking the blame when it was his fault, but this female was going to come out of this smelling like a rose. "Lordy, Dad, I was behaving myself, just like you told me—"

"Ha!" snapped Lynnie. "He was drunk as a lord when he picked me up."

"Is that a fact?" Trace gritted his teeth. "Why, Maverick, I wouldn't blame you if you wanted to horsewhip my son."

Maverick didn't say anything. He was looking at Lynnie as if trying to puzzle something out.

"Dad . . ." Ace glared at Lynnie, but she only smiled sweetly at him. "If it hadn't been for Lynnie and her banner—"

"Now you're tryin' to blame this innocent girl?" Trace's voice rose, "I can't believe I sired you. No Texas gentleman would ever blame a lady."

"Let's get out of here," Maverick said.

"She's no lady," Ace grumbled under his breath, and Lynnie gave him an angelic smile as they headed toward the back door. Damn her, she could look so innocent and demure when she had started the whole thing. There wasn't any use in trying to defend himself. Dad would never believe Ace wasn't at the bottom of it.

His dad and uncle were walking fast, Ace falling

behind, looking at the marble floor as he walked, thinking there was no justice.

They stopped at the back door. Trace looked around and asked Ace, "Where's Lynnie?"

Ace looked up from his survey of the courthouse floor, glancing around. No Lynnie. "I don't know."

"What do you mean, you don't know?" Maverick roared. "She was walking with you."

Ace sighed. "She was here and then she wasn't. I reckon we lost her."

"Lost her?" Dad roared at him.

"She can't see a thing without her spectacles," Maverick said. "There's no telling which way she went."

Dad fixed a withering gaze on him. "Damn it, son, she was your responsibility; go find her!"

Looking at Dad's stormy face, Ace decided this wasn't a good time to argue the point. "It was a straight shot to the back door; I can't see how she lost her way."

Dad's face grew even stormier.

"Uh, I'll backtrack and find her." Ace turned and hurried in the direction they had come.

Lynnie had deliberately fallen behind the little group until they were far ahead of her. Reporters were out front. A courageous woman who was crusading for a righteous cause would not sneak away like a chicken thief. This was a perfect time to take her message to the world. Well, at least to the area around Austin. She took out her little purse and put on her glasses so she could see, and hurried out the front door and down the steps. Immediately, she was surrounded by milling reporters.

"Miss McBride?"

"Yes, I'm Lynnie McBride."

Notebooks came out as the reporters crowded closer.

"Tell us what happened at the ball, miss. Is that a black eye you've got?"

Lynnie nodded. "I was attempting to let the governor and the legislators know that Texas women demand equality and the vote."

"What do you think of the governor?"

"Well, my brother-in-law and Trace Durango think the governor is an idiot, and after seeing the man, I quite agree."

"Can we quote you on that?" Pencils began to fly.

"Of course! Texas women deserve equal rights, and I merely turned the ball into a protest rally."

The reporters crowded even closer, shouting questions. Lynnie began to have second thoughts. Maybe her remarks had been too rash. She wasn't quite sure what the consequences could be. Matter-of-fact, she hadn't thought about anything except getting the message out. The men were loud and persistent, and the crush around her was growing. She was a slender, small girl, and she began to panic at the shoving and pushing.

About that time, Ace Durango came through the doors, took the steps two at a time, and shouldered his way through the mob to her. "Lynnie, what the hell are you doin'?"

"Talking to the reporters." She wouldn't for the world admit that she was a little bit relieved to see him.

"Lordy, Dad and Uncle Maverick will have my hide over this," he scolded, and put his arm around her, elbowing his way through the men. "I'm already in enough trouble over you."

She had forgotten how big Ace was until he was plowing a path through the eager reporters, protecting her from the crush. She breathed a sigh of relief. Uncle Trace and Maverick came around the corner and motioned them to follow. Ignoring the eager group following them, the pair ran to get into the carriage and started off into the coming dawn.

"Son," said Trace, "Lynnie was your responsibility. You should have protected her."

Ace looked at her, evidently waiting for her to speak. Lynnie hesitated. If she did so, she could take the heat off him. Should she? Naw, the brute deserved it. The big, handsome cowboy thought he was God's gift to the female sex; the antithesis of the equal woman. Lynnie blinked and smiled innocently.

Ace glared at her and made a twisting motion with his big hands, as if he were wringing her slender neck.

"Ace," said his father, "what the hell are you doing?"

"Nothin'."

Trace leaned back in the carriage. "Young lady, I'm sorry my errant son didn't do a better job of protecting you. I know you didn't realize when you accidentally went out the wrong door that you'd run into reporters."

Lynnie didn't say anything, only smiled innocently.

Ace watched her and amused himself by thinking about grabbing that skinny neck and shaking her until her teeth rattled and that fire-colored hair fell out of its fancy hairpins. She was crafty and smarter than any woman had a right to be. It wasn't fair that a mere girl had out-manuevered a smart *hombre* like himself and caused him all this trouble.

Maverick sighed. "Maybe we can get the newspapers before Cayenne and Cimarron see them."

"Maybe the whole thing'll blow over," Ace said.

"Hmmph! Not likely," Trace snapped. "And you, Diego de Durango the Fourth, you can forget about going to any more parties or doing anything besides maybe cleaning out the stables for a while."

Lynnie grinned at him, and he fought an urge to open the carriage door and push her out into the street in front of a brewery wagon passing by. If he said anything, he was only going to get into more trouble. He couldn't win against Lynnie, Ace realized with a resigned sigh. Even when they were kids, she'd outsmarted him, and she could get away with it because she was a girl. Here he'd thought he was doing a favor, escorting the poor little spinster to the ball, and she'd used him as part of her plan. No wonder the cunning, headstrong old maid couldn't get a husband; no man liked a woman who was smarter than he was. Well, it would be a cold day in hell before Ace got himself into another fix with Lynnie McBride.

That morning, each family returned to its own ranch. Ace was assigned to clean out the horse stalls in the barn, while his indignant father paced up and down before the library fire with the little Chihuahua trailing after him. "Cimarron, your son is a mess."

Cimarron raised her head from her sewing and surveyed her angry husband calmly. "He's just a young stallion, and someday he'll tame down."

"He may not live that long," Trace grumbled, stopping to light a cigarillo. "I just don't know what it's going to take to turn that young dandy into a man. I'm beginning to worry that he'll never be up to the challenge of running this ranch. His sister, on the other hand . . ."

"Now, Raven will do a good job with her share; we know that," Cimarron soothed as she put down her sewing and walked over to put her arms around him. "I'll bet when Ace finally has to take on some responsibility, he'll come through."

"Ha!" Trace paused. "He's never known what it was like to fight Indians, run off rustlers."

"He can shoot and ride well." Cimarron defended

her errant son. "Maybe he's a little wild and devil-may-care—"

"A little?" Trace looked at her. "When I was that age, Maverick and I were leading cattle drives up the Chisholm Trail."

Cimarron sighed and walked over to look out the French doors at the big fountain in the courtyard. "Things are changing, dear—getting civilized. With railroads coming in and stockyards being built here in Texas, those cattle drives are fading fast."

Trace went over to the sideboard and poured himself a tequila. "Now, there was something that would turn a boy into a man. Driving cattle hundreds of miles up to Kansas across Indian Territory. Why, many's the time Maverick and I slept on the ground and stayed in the saddle most of the night, trying to keep spooked cattle from stampeding."

Cimarron rolled her eyes. She had heard these same stories many, many times. "With Kansas complaining about Texas fever infecting their herds, and barbed wire strung everywhere, I'm afraid those days are almost gone forever."

Trace nodded agreement and sipped his drink. "Less than twenty years. When the Chisholm Trail opened right after the War ended, I thought the drives would go on forever. I reckon you're right. Soon there'll be no reason to drive cattle hundreds of miles to load them on freight cars."

"I remember what a handsome young wrangler you were." Cimarron smiled. "Maybe some of the cattlemen should get together and have one last drive for the fun of it."

"Hmm." Trace went to the window and looked out for a long moment. "I don't know. Last time I had to sleep on the ground, I hurt so bad next morning, I could hardly sit a saddle."

Cimarron laughed. "Middle age catching up to you. It's not an adventure for anyone but the young. Ace has missed one of the great experiences of the old West."

"A cattle drive might make a man of him." Trace sipped his drink and smiled, staring out the window as if remembering the old days. "Old Sanchez's younger brother is a good trail boss. Pedro would probably enjoy leading a cattle drive in one final trip up the Chisholm Trail to Dodge City."

"You're not serious. Why, it must be twelve hundred miles." She looked at him.

Trace shrugged. "I don't know. Abilene and Wichita don't want the drives coming through any more. The Kansas legislature has passed laws discouraging it. If we arranged a drive, we'd probably have to swing out as we reached the Kansas border and take the Western Trail to Dodge City."

"There's lots of young cowboys who've never gotten to go on a drive," Cimarron said, "but it doesn't sound like Ace's cup of tea."

"I reckon not," his father grumbled. "Saloons and card games and fast women: that's all that interests Ace. Look at the mess he got poor little Lynnie into. Why, I wouldn't be surprised if the McBrides never spoke to us again."

"Hmm." Cimarron thought about it a long moment. "I wouldn't put all the blame on Ace. You know, she's feisty, stubborn, and as headstrong as he is."

He whirled on her. "You're not excusing his behavior!"

"Double damnation, Trace, I'm just saying that little red-haired rascal may not be as innocent as she looks."

Her husband looked shocked. "Why, that sweet little thing couldn't possibly . . ."

"Maybe not. But I'm a woman and I know Lynnie better than you. Actually, I think they're two of a kind."

Trace smoked his cigarillo and shook his head. "Of course, I can't expect you to understand that Ace should have protected the lady and—"

"Don't use that glib, superior tone with me, *hombre.*" Cimarron tried to keep the annoyance out of her voice. "Frankly, I think votes for women will come; it's just a matter of time."

His dark eyes blinked. "I never thought I'd hear you say that."

"That just goes to show you that you don't always know everything there is to know about women; nor does your son, but he thinks he does." She slipped her arms around her husband's neck and gave him a quick kiss before returning to her sewing. The little brown dog promptly hopped up into her lap and settled down.

Trace returned to staring into the fire, as if reliving a time past. "You know, darlin', I'll bet a lot of old-timers would like to send their sons or grandsons along for one last, big cattle drive."

"Are we back on that subject?"

"It'd be good for Ace, too," her husband argued.

Of course, Ace didn't think so. When he sat down for breakfast the next morning, he was so stiff from the big fight and cleaning stables that he had to suppress a groan. He took a sip of coffee and shuddered. "Juanita not back yet?"

His mother put her finger to her lips for silence and shook her head.

Every bone in his body hurt, and now the coffee was

lousy. He thought of all the fun he was missing at the local cantina and sighed.

It was then that Dad began to tell him his plans for one last, big cattle drive.

Ace looked at his father. "Let me get this straight, Dad: you want me to nursemaid a bunch of stupid cows all the way to Dodge City?"

Trace nodded. "It'll be fun; you'll see."

Ace grimaced and ran his hand through his black hair. "Don't sound like fun to me: sleepin' on the ground, eatin' dust all day. No women, no cards, no saloons, and what do we do for grub?"

"I'll send Cookie along with the chuck wagon," Trace said.

"Cookie?" Ace's voice rose in dismay. "That's addin' insult to injury. Why, that old geezer couldn't cook a egg so a dog could eat it."

"I heerd that!" The old man stuck his grizzled head out the kitchen door. "I'll have you know, you young whippersnapper, I've cooked on many a cattle drive a dozen years before you was ever born."

"And left a trail of poisoned cowboys all along the way," Ace suggested with a grin.

"I can think of one I'd like to poison." With a snort, Cookie disappeared into the kitchen, and thc sound of banging pans increased.

"Now look what you've done," Ma whispered. "You've upset him."

"Will that make his cookin' better or worse?"

Trace stared at the burnt food on his plate and pushed it back. "You'd be surprised how good Cookie's grub will taste after a long day's ride on the trail."

Ace groaned at the thought. "I don't think so."

"Nevertheless," Trace said sternly, "if I can get this drive organized, you'll be going along."

"Ma," he implored his mother.

"Your father's right," she said. "Every real cowboy should go on at least one cattle drive—make you appreciate what an easy life you've got."

Easy? He had blisters on his hands from shoveling manure, and his best boots were ruined from wading around in it.

"I'm serious about the cattle drive, son," Trace said. "It'll do you good to take a little responsibility and do something besides gamble and chase women."

"What happens if something goes wrong? None of us young guys know anything about a long cattle drive."

"Me and Maverick and Pedro will come along. We've all been on dozens of trail drives; we'll know what to do."

Ace looked doubtful. "This is all because of that brawl at the governor's mansion, isn't it? That ornery little Lynnie—"

"Lynnie is a very proper lady, and you've probably ruined her reputation so she'll never get a husband," Dad scolded.

"Me?" Ace moaned. "Lordy, Dad, Lynnie couldn't get a husband if she owned a gold mine and the biggest ranch in Texas. Why, I never met such a stubborn, opinionated—"

"Seems to me," Ma said as she sipped her coffee, "she's no more ornery than you are."

"Well," Ace huffed, "you don't expect a mere girl to get a fella into trouble."

Dad shook his head. "I never knew you to need any help getting into trouble."

"That little schoolteacher can hold her own in a fight better than most girls," Ace grumbled. It startled him that he felt a twinge of admiration for the red-haired vixen. She had more gumption than most of the women he knew, even if she wasn't very pretty.

"I don't want to hear any more about that nice girl," Dad commanded.

Ace looked with mute appeal to Ma. She started to say something but seemed to think better of it. "She's a mite headstrong," she murmured.

"A mite? A *mite?*" Ace's voice rose; then he realized it was no use. He picked up a burnt biscuit and surveyed it gravely. He imagined eating these for three or four months on the trail. The thought horrified him.

"Hurry up, son," Trace said. "You've still got two more barns to clean out."

"I'm goin'." Ace pushed his plate back and reached for his Stetson. The only thing that made his odious task easier was that when he shoveled, he imagined he was burying a certain red-haired schoolteacher up to her neck in manure.

Five

"Mail just came," Cimarron murmured as she entered the dining room three mornings later, reading a note.

Her husband looked up from his plate of eggs and enchiladas. He was grinning because Juanita was back in the kitchen. "Who's the letter from?"

Cimarron sighed as she sat down and signaled one of the Mexican maids to pour her some coffee. "Cayenne says Lynnie's got to go up before the local school board. She may lose her job."

"Poor little thing." Trace paused with his fork halfway to his mouth. "Well, can't say I'm surprised after the trouble our delinquent son got her into at the ball."

"I know Lynnie better than you do." Cimarron sipped her coffee thoughtfully, still reading the letter. "Some of that was bound to be her fault."

"How can you say that?" Trace looked aghast. "Why, that innocent little schoolteacher—"

"I just know Lynnie. She and Ace are pretty well matched when it comes to getting into trouble. Cayenne wants us to attend the school board meeting as a sign of solidarity."

"*Sí,*" Trace nodded and sipped his coffee. "Although we may not be able to do anything to help. Being thrown into jail is a serious charge for a teacher, and hard to justify."

The Mexican maid set a plate of scrambled eggs, bacon, and biscuits in front of Cimarron. She reached for the tart wild-plum jelly. "Hmm, if Lynnie loses her job, I don't know what she'll do. What she needs is a husband."

Trace threw back his head and laughed. *"Dios!* Who would marry Lynnie McBride? She's very sweet, but not a great beauty."

Cimarron said, "She'll be pretty to the man who loves her. But most men will see her as headstrong and stubborn."

"You can say that again," Ace sneered with disgust as he entered the dining room and took a chair. "I wouldn't care if I ever saw that little wench again after all the trouble she got me into."

"You're pretty good at getting into trouble all by yourself," his father said pointedly.

"Which is the very reason I don't need Lynnie around to make more." Ace signaled the maid, and she went into the kitchen and returned with a plate of steak and eggs.

Cimarron sighed and sipped her coffee. "There must be some nice young man who'd marry Lynnie."

"Don't bet on it." Ace grinned and cut up his steak. It was well done and crisp around the edges, just the way he liked it.

His mother ignored him. "Lynnie's smart, and she's not half bad-looking. She'd give a man fine sons . . ."

"I want sons someday, Ma," Ace shuddered, "but not enough to sleep with Lynnie McBride."

"Don't be crude," his mother scolded.

Her husband laughed. "Now, there'd be bloodlines for you: by the stallion, Ace Durango, out of the mare, Lynnie McBride. Reckon the colt would be dark or have a red mane?"

"Be serious!" Cimarron snapped. There was a moment of silence as everyone enjoyed the good food and strong coffee.

"You know what I could do?" she mused, half to herself, as she looked out the window. "I could throw a big barbecue and invite everyone in two counties—and, of course, Lynnie. There's bound to be someone in two big counties who might marry her."

Ace groaned. "Don't bet on it. Besides, it ain't fair to ambush poor, unsuspecting *hombres* like that."

His father shrugged. "Women do things like that all the time, son. They spend their whole lives trying to rope and tie men up."

"I beg your pardon." Cimarron bristled.

"Everyone except you, darlin'," Trace hastened to add. "I was really lucky to get you."

"Then, it's settled," Cimarron said as she laid the letter aside and smiled with satisfaction. "I'll have to talk to Cayenne about it."

Ace paused with his fork halfway to his mouth and looked at his father. Dad raised his eyebrows and shrugged.

"What's settled?" The two men looked at her blankly.

She looked annoyed. "Why, what we just agreed on about having a big barbecue and inviting most of both counties so Lynnie can meet an eligible man."

Somehow, Ace didn't like the look of this. "Did we agree to that?"

His father laughed. "I reckon your mother's made up her mind, so it'll happen whether we agree or not."

If it involved Lynnie McBride, Ace didn't want anything to do with it. "I think I'll plan to be gone," Ace grumbled.

"No, you won't, son," his mother scolded. "Besides, I'll invite a lot of other young girls."

Ace grinned.

"Not that kind," his father said. *"Ladies."*

"Oh." Disappointed, he returned to his steak.

"In the meantime, we'll go to the school board meeting and see if we can save her job."

Ace frowned. "I don't want to do anything to help Lynnie McBride."

Both his parents looked at him.

"We are going to the school board meeting," Dad said, and glared at him. "You got the poor girl in a lot of trouble, and it's your responsibility to help get her out."

"Me?" Ace started to protest, decided he was up against a stacked deck and couldn't win. It would only mean more stables to clean. He imagined piling the manure on top of Lynnie's fiery head. Lordy, she was a pain in the butt.

"March," Cimarron murmured, and smiled as she left the breakfast table to pack a few things for the trip to west Texas. *March.* Yes, that would be a great time to hold a big barbecue and fiesta. Spring would be coming to the Texas hill country by March, splashing the low hills with a riot of bluebonnets and red Indian paintbrush flowers. She knew her sister-in-law, Cayenne, would be pleased. And it would give the men a chance to all get together and discuss this cattle drive Trace had been talking about organizing. Better than that, it might give Lynnie a chance to meet eligible men.

Less than a week later, the special school board meeting had been called in the west Texas town of McBride. Cayenne had just produced her new baby girl, and the elderly patriarch of the clan, Papa Joe, wasn't feeling too well, so Maverick and some of the many children accompanied Lynnie to the meeting, along with the Durango clan from the Triple D ranch.

Lynnie pointedly ignored Ace as they met just outside the little one-room schoolhouse, and he seemed to be pretending he hadn't seen her at all. That suited her just fine. Why, she never would have been caught dead in the company of a rowdy like Ace if she hadn't needed an escort to that ball.

Lynnie's black eye was still a little green around the edges the night she walked into that meeting. Word must have gotten around that Miss McBride's job was on the line, and there was a big crowd that night in late February. An assortment of McBride and Durango children were sitting on the front row next to Lynnie when the president of the school board, young banker Ogle, rapped his gavel and shouted: "Order! Order! Let's get this hearing started!"

Lynnie watched all the pompous locals file in and sit down. Frankly, now she was a little scared, yet still defiant over the stir her trip to the state capital had caused. She hadn't realized the news would travel far enough to end up on the front page of the McBride, Texas, weekly paper, but then, the owner of the paper was still angry that the Lazy M had succeeded in buying some land the paper's owner, Clifford Schwatz, had wanted for himself.

Some of these people, the Billingses, and some of the others felt obliged to Maverick Durango and the McBride clan for saving the town during the attempted bank and stage holdup eleven years ago. Unfortunately, young banker Ogle controlled many of the others because they owed him money.

The schoolhouse was small and crowded. With not much else to do on a cold winter night, many had attended for the entertainment value of the event.

Young Ogle stood up, smiled expansively, and looked up and down the table next to him to make sure all the school board members were there. He thought of himself as somewhat of a dandy, Lynnie knew, but he was balding and pompous. He had tried to court Lynnie, but she would have none of him, and the whole town knew it.

Elmer Ogle cleared his throat importantly. "You all know we have serious business to conduct here tonight, but first, I want to invite you all to the unveiling of the statue of my father in the town square next Saturday. I was honored that a majority of the citizens thought he should be remembered for his heroism in the great stage robbery."

Lynnie's little sister, Angel, piped up. "He wasn't no hero. Everybody in town knows Maverick saved the town that day and your pa got hisself shot accidentally by walking out in the middle of the gunfight."

"Angel, hush!" Maverick whispered while everyone tittered at the truth of the child's words.

Automatically, Lynnie said, "Angel, it's not correct to say 'hisself.' The proper word is *himself.* And don't use double negatives."

The whole audience laughed again while Elmer sputtered and turned red. "Some people can't control their children," he said, "which is why we're here tonight. . . ."

"I beg to differ." Lynnie stood up, although her whole family was shaking their heads at her. "The fracas at the governor's mansion had nothing to do with my family."

She saw Trace nudge Ace, who stood up very grudgingly. "I—I was responsible for the mess Miss McBride got into."

"I beg your pardon!" Lynnie fired back. She was not about to let that big brute take the role of heroic rescuer. "I planned it all by myself."

An excited buzz ran through the crowded room, and

she shot Ace a triumphant glare. He opened his mouth as if to speak, hesitated, and sat back down.

School board member Winifred Leane stood up and peered at her over her spectacles. "Lynnie McBride, is it true someone gave you a black eye?"

"Nobody *gave* me anything," Lynnie fired back. "I earned this shiner."

The room burst into tittering and whispers. Her brother-in-law shook his head at her, but Lynnie didn't care. She figured banker Ogle had enough power in this town to force the other members of the school board to fire her, and she intended to say her piece.

Mr. Schwatz glared at her. "Is it true you created a riot, along with that terrible Durango ruffian, at the governor's mansion?"

She gritted her teeth. "I did no such thing. I merely wore a banner proclaiming women's right to vote."

"That's ungodly!" Mrs. Huffington, a very plump member of the school board, interrupted her. "It says in the Bible women shouldn't vote, and that's good enough for me!"

A series of murmuring and amens followed.

Lynnie was unruffled. "There's a Bible up there on the desk, Mrs. Huffington. Please point out the chapter and verse that says that."

Mrs. Huffington looked about uncertainly. "I—I'm sure it's in there somewhere."

"Enough!" Maverick thundered as he stood up. "Miss McBride is a jim-dandy teacher. I see all her students are here to speak for her."

"That's right!" yelled little Susan Leane.

"She's a good teacher," Billy Huffington said, "no matter what my ma says!"

More noise and confusion while banker Ogle rapped for order.

But Maverick didn't sit down. "May I remind this board that my father-in-law and I own the biggest ranch in this county, the Lazy M, and my wife and I provide a great many of the students?"

The audience tittered.

"We are well aware of the size of your brood," Mrs. Huffington said coldly.

The crowd laughed, and Elmer Ogle rapped again. "Let's get back to the subject at hand: the firing of one Miss Lynnie McBride for questionable behavior and moral decay."

"Moral decay?" Mrs. Leane whispered.

"Getting arrested," the newspaper editor explained.

"No!" yelled a bunch of children from the sidelines. "We love Miss McBride; she's a great teacher!"

Penelope Dinwiddy stood up. "She's done a brave thing, giving voice to getting women the vote."

Mr. Dinwiddy, a serious, balding man rose. "Please ignore my daughter," the rancher said. "She idolizes Miss McBride. Frankly, our family doesn't know what to think about all this. We like the teacher, but, gettin' arrested—that's purty bad."

Squat, fat Nelbert Purdy, a member of the school board, shook his bald head. "Morally wrong, the McBride girl is. She doesn't have the high morals of my sister, Emmalou."

Emmalou, standing to one side, smiled generously at the audience, proud to be the epitome of virtue.

Banker Ogle rapped his gavel again. "Has the board heard enough?"

"Enough?" Lynnie protested, peering over the tops of her spectacles. "Why, I've hardly gotten started."

Mrs. Huffington's jowly face smiled. "You know, I have a nephew in Philadelphia, young Clarence Kleinhoffer, who is of the highest moral caliber and has just graduated from a teacher's college. He might be persuaded to take the job."

Nods and smiles of approval ran through the crowd.

Trace Durango stood up. "Miss McBride was led astray, I'm afraid."

The newspaper editor favored Trace with a steely look. "We know your son's reputation, sir. The women all say he's somewhat of a scoundrel."

Lynnie watched Cimarron stand up, her face red with anger. "Are you smearing the reputation of my son?"

"On the contrary," Mrs. Leane said. "From what I hear, he's been doing a pretty good job of ruining his own reputation. I certainly wouldn't let one of my daughters go anywhere with him."

Titters from the crowd.

"Mrs. Leane . . ." Cimarron seemed to be fighting to control her anger. "I doubt my son would want to call on one of your homely daughters."

"Why, I never!" Mrs. Leane's fat mouth dropped open.

More titters from the crowd, turning into pandemonium again, with banker Ogle rapping in vain for silence. "We shall retire to discuss our verdict."

The vote was a foregone conclusion because so many of the board members owed the banker money and there was old bad blood between the Ogle family and the McBrides.

The room fell silent, and Lynnie was abruptly a little scared. She hadn't really thought about losing her job. However, if she must make that sacrifice for the good of the cause; so be it. She glared at Ace Durango, and he glared back. She had used him, and he was angry about it. Well, it served him right. No doubt he had used many an innocent girl for his own ends.

In less than five minutes, the board filed back in, and

Elmer Ogle rapped for silence. "The board has made its decision. Miss McBride, having behaved in a manner that is unacceptable for a person of her responsibilities, is terminated as of this evening. We are going to offer the job of schoolmaster to Clarence Kleinhoffer; a fine, upstanding pillar of virtue."

"You can't fire me; I quit!" Lynnie stood up and began to wave her arms. "Free women! Votes for Texas women!"

All the children took up her chant, to the dismay of the school board members. Banker Ogle rapped in vain for order. "The Durangos and the McBrides are a bunch of uncivilized—"

"You can't talk about my family that way!" Maverick apparently lost his temper, strode to the front of the room, and hit Elmer Ogle in the nose. The young man was sobbing like a girl as men moved in to pull Maverick back.

"I'm bleeding!" Ogle sobbed. "Look, I'm bleeding!"

Lynnie climbed up on a school desk, waving the Texas flag she had just grabbed off its pole. "Votes for women!" she shouted. "Free Texas women!"

All the children began to shout: "Votes for women! Texans for women's rights!"

"Now, just see," Mrs. Leane shouted in horror, "just see how she has corrupted our children!"

"Oh, shut up!" Lynnie shouted back, "you pompous old windbag!"

Mrs. Leane collapsed in her chair with the other ladies clustered about, offering smelling salts. The whole room was in an uproar and getting worse by the minute.

"Lynnie!" Maverick yelled, "get off that desk!"

"Votes for women!" Lynnie shouted back, "Give women the vote! Remember the Alamo!"

It seemed to Ace that the Alamo had nothing to do with women's right to vote, but as always, it brought a cheer from everyone in the room—even those who didn't favor women voting.

At that point, Lynnie began to sing "The Yellow Rose of Texas" at the top of her lungs while waving her flag. The children took up the song as she stepped off the desk and led a grand march around the room.

"This is outrageous!" Elmer Ogle roared. "This is uncivilized. The woman has no shame!"

"Oh, shut up, you bloodsucking money grabber!" Lynnie yelled as she led her little parade outside to march around the schoolhouse. Then she stepped aside and watched her young disciples continue to march and sing. Frankly, she was a little scared but still defiant. *Now that she'd lost her job, what was she going to do?*

Her favorite student, tall and thin Penelope Dinwiddy, caught up with Lynnie outside in the bright moonlight. She was as serious as Lynnie herself. "Oh, Miss McBride, I'm so sorry," she wailed. "You're disgraced. What are you going to do now?"

Lynnie straightened her shoulders and watched the marching children with satisfaction. Her frustrated brother-in-law was attempting to pull the various members of his own clan out of the parade so they could go home. "Well, I reckon I can forget about asking the board to sponsor my trip to Dodge City."

"Dodge City?" Penelope looked baffled.

"Don't you remember? There's a big Women's Rights gathering up there for the Fourth of July. I had hoped to attend, cheer the ladies on, and maybe get some help for the downtrodden females in Texas."

"Your folks wouldn't let you go," Penelope said as they walked out to the buggy.

"You're right; I've already asked," Lynnie sighed.

"And Cayenne and Papa Joe aren't going to be too happy over what happened here tonight. They don't seem to understand that I feel it's my calling to help get the vote for women."

Penelope shook her head. "I thought, when I heard that the handsome Ace Durango was taking you to the ball, that you were about to settle down and get married. . . ."

"To Ace Durango?" Lynnie threw back her head and laughed. "Why, that pigheaded, woman-chasing, gambling fool—he'd be the last man an independent girl would want."

"Lots of girls would have given their eye teeth to go to the ball with him," Penelope pointed out.

"He is the most egotistical, arrogant, untamed rascal in Texas," Lynnie said. "I couldn't stay in the same room with him for five minutes without an argument. He thinks women are good for only one thing."

The other girl rolled her eyes and giggled. "Lots of girls would like to find out what that one thing is with him."

"Penny," Lynnie said in a stern voice, "I doubt your conviction to our good cause."

Penelope grabbed her arm. "I believe in women's rights; I truly do, Miss McBride. It's just that Ace Durango is so charming and every girl in Texas has set her cap for him."

Lynnie turned away. "Well, that lets me out, anyway, doesn't it? I haven't got the looks to attract the brute, even if I were interested—which I'm not. Believe me, Penelope, I'm looking for a man who will appreciate me for my fine mind."

"Right!" said Penelope, and turned to look at the crowd coming out of the schoolhouse. "As mad as your brother-in-law looks, you'd better forget about the Dodge City Women's Rights meeting."

"I suppose you're right." Lynnie chewed her lip. "I may have gone too far this time."

"And Dodge City is a long way, Miss McBride." Penelope was always the sensible one. "And even if there was a train there, which there ain't—"

"Isn't," Lynnie corrected automatically. "Do you have any money, Penelope?"

"Me?" Penelope touched her chest. "No more than you do."

"Well, I reckon that lets out buying a ticket on the stage, but I'm not giving up yet."

Her friend grinned. "That's what I like about you: you're so stubborn and determined."

"Still, it's a pretty big challenge," Lynnie admitted.

"Young lady," Maverick yelled, "get in the buggy."

She left her friend and walked over to the family group, who were talking. They all looked upset except Ace. That devil was suppressing a grin.

"Oh, shut up!" she snapped at Ace.

"I didn't say anything," he protested.

"But you were thinking it," Lynnie said, and turned toward her out-of-town family by marriage. "I'm really sorry, Uncle Trace, that you and Aunt Cimarron came all this way for nothing." She felt her lip quiver as the enormity of what she'd done swept over her. "I'm sorry; I didn't mean to create so much trouble. . . ."

"Lynnie," Maverick said, "where you are, there is always trouble. I don't know what your papa and sister are going to say."

Lynnie sighed. "I have a pretty good idea."

She saw Trace nudge his errant son sharply in the ribs.

"Uh, I'm sorry you lost your job, Lynnie," Ace said.

She didn't believe he was sorry at all; he was just sorry she had used him and gotten him into trouble.

"It's all right; I'll find something to do."

Maverick lifted one child after another into the buggy. "Lynnie, I just don't know what's going to become of you—twenty years old, no husband, no prospects of one, no job, and now your reputation is ruined."

Trace glanced at his son again, but Ace only glared at Lynnie. Evidently, he didn't know how to deal with women who could start trouble on their own.

"I've already decided my future," she said matter-of-factly as she leaned on the buggy wheel, "Up to now, I've been spending only a little time on the crusade for women's rights, but now I can give it my full attention."

Everyone groaned aloud, but she ignored them.

"Lynnie," said Aunt Cimarron, "I'm sorry we couldn't help." She hugged Lynnie.

"You did your best," Lynnie said.

"I'm going to have a barbecue next month in your honor," Auntie said.

"That's nice." Lynnie was only half listening, already planning her next move in the great crusade. Maybe she could start a newspaper or, better yet, lead the few liberated women she knew to picket the local newspaper.

"Maverick," Uncle Trace said as they shook hands, "give some thought to coming on that cattle drive."

Maverick nodded. "I'm in. Sounds like old times."

While everyone continued to talk, Lynnie lifted her skirts to get into the buggy. After a moment's hesitation, Ace sauntered over reluctantly and offered his hand in assistance.

"I don't need your help," she said, and got in by herself.

"I was tryin' to act like a gentleman," Ace said.

"A gentleman?" Lynnie snorted. "Everyone knows all you can think of is getting a girl's drawers off."

"Not yours." In the moonlight, she could see he was so annoyed, his nostrils flared.

The family crowd was breaking up; Maverick was bringing over more children to pile into the buggy. They all waved good-bye. Maverick slapped the horse with the reins, and the buggy pulled away. When she glanced back, her uncle and aunt had turned toward their buggy, but Ace was grinning at her as if pleased she'd gotten what she deserved. She forgot she was a dignified representative of women's rights. She did what she had done years ago when the brute had annoyed her: she stuck her tongue out at him and crossed her eyes.

"I hope your face freezes that way!" he yelled at her.

Maverick glanced sideways at Lynnie. "What was that about?"

She gave her brother-in-law her most innocent look. "I'm sure I haven't the faintest idea. You know what an uncivilized oaf Ace Durango is. I pity the poor, downtrodden girl who gets stuck with him!"

Cimarron sipped her coffee and nodded to her husband as he came in from the barn and threw his Stetson up on the coatrack. "Hey," he yelled, "I could use some coffee out here!"

"Keep your shirt on." Cookie limped out of the kitchen and slammed the pot down. "You could get it yourself; I got a cake in the oven." He turned and limped back into the kitchen.

"What happened to Juanita?" Trace poured himself a cup and made a wry face as he tasted it.

"Another cousin's having a baby," Cimarron murmured, and returned to the list she was working on.

"I ought to fire that old bastard," Trace grumbled, "for being so uppity, and besides, he's a lousy cook."

"I heerd that!" Cookie yelled from the kitchen.

Cimarron rolled her eyes. "Trace, you know better

than that. The old don would turn over in his grave if you fired Cookie. He's been here since you were a kid, cooking on the cattle drives."

"And he's poisoned hundreds of good cowboys." Trace yelled toward the kitchen, "Did you hear that?"

"Oh, hush up." The grizzled cook stuck his head out the kitchen door, "You'll cause my cake to fall."

"Won't make it taste any worse," Trace said.

"I'll see you don't get none." Cookie disappeared behind the door.

"That's a relief," Trace muttered.

"Shame on you. Now you've hurt his feelings," Cimarron said.

"The old rattlesnake doesn't have any." Trace sipped his coffee and shuddered, looking around. "Where's our lazy son? It's past dawn; day's half gone."

"Nobody should have to get out of bed this early." Ace stumbled into the dining room, yawning and wiping his eyes.

"Just getting up?" his father grumbled, "I've been up two hours."

Ace sighed. "I know, Dad, you're always up with the chickens, but then, you weren't playin' cards last night."

Trace frowned, and Cimarron rushed in to stop the fuss before it started. "Did you win, son?"

Ace took a chair, grinning. "Took Willis Forrester for a couple of thousand." He surveyed his father's cup and frowned. "Not again. Cookie," he yelled, "can I get some coffee out here?"

"I only got two hands!" the old man hollered from the kitchen. "Can't you Durangos do anything for yourselves?"

"You ought to fire that old bastard," Ace grumbled as he got up and retrieved a cup from the sideboard.

"I heerd that!" the old man yelled from the kitchen.

Trace smiled, evidently in a better mood because a Durango had won over a Forrester again. The Forresters headquartered in Austin and weren't too fussy about how they acquired land and money. He leaned back in his chair and said "Son, I want you to help Pedro and me bring in that herd from the south forty today."

"Today? It's colder than a witch's ti—"

"Don't use that word in front of your mother!" Trace snapped. "You think I don't know it's cold? Hell, I've been out in it since before sunrise."

Cimarron moved to diffuse the tension between the two. "Now, Ace, dear, you are, after all, a rancher. It won't kill you to help Dad with a few cattle."

"Rich, spoiled kid," Trace grumbled. "All you think about is cards, women, and whiskey."

"You forgot fast horses," Ace grinned, and turned to yell toward the kitchen. "Hey, Cookie, I'm starvin' out here."

"I'm comin'! I'm comin'!" The old man limped in with a plate of steak and eggs. "Here, you young pup. If the old don was still alive, we'd be servin' up this breakfast out on the range, makin' plans for a big brandin' and a cattle drive."

"And you'd be right there, cookin' for our cowboys." Ace winked at the cook, and the old man winked back. Despite his orneryness, they were all quite fond of the disabled cowboy, despite the fact that he was the worst cook in the hill country. Still, when Juanita was gone, the old man insisted on stepping into her spot, to the dismay of everyone on the place.

Ace dug into the huge platter of burnt eggs and half-raw steak with gusto and smiled as he thought of winning that big pot last night. There was a certain pretty little *señorita* over at Fandango he thought he'd spend some of it on.

"Cookie," Dad said, looking up at the old man, "I think you're right. I'm still thinking about organizing one final cattle drive."

Ace groaned aloud at the thought. "Dad, I hope you're jokin' about that; I got no time for herdin' cattle all the way to Kansas."

"It might keep you out of jail and the cantinas for a while," Dad said, glowering at him.

"Oh, now, boss," Cookie said, coming to his defense, "you got to expect young fellas will sow a few wild oats. As I recall, you sure did afore the lady here haltered and broke you."

Ma ducked her head, attempting to hide a smile, but Ace saw it. Someday, he'd like a girl just like Ma, but not anytime soon. There were too many pretty, wild girls out there tempting him to drink and dance all night. He wasn't ready to be tied down and branded yet.

Ma said, "There's something I'd like to talk about. I'm planning an old-fashioned Texas barbecue."

All three men looked at her with curiosity.

Ace nodded agreeably. "Sounds like a real fiesta: plenty of beef and beer and pretty girls."

Dad cocked his head and looked at Ma. "You still set on that?"

"Well," she said with a nod, "Cayenne contacted me and said the family would like to come for a visit."

Ace paused with his fork halfway to his lips, like a wary coyote smelling a trap. "They can come anytime without throwing a big party."

"Actually . . ." Cimarron put down her cup and beamed at him. "We're trying to do something for Lynnie."

"Uh-oh," Cookie said, and went back through the kitchen door.

Ace groaned aloud. "Don't even mention that woman to me."

"I reckon not," Dad said, "after you got the poor little thing in so much trouble."

"Me? Get *her* in trouble?" Ace looked at him in disbelief. "Lordy, Dad, she was the one who—she used me," Ace groused.

Ma cleared her throat. "Sounds like what I've heard girls say about you."

"I don't reckon anyone would believe this"—Ace attacked his eggs again—"but Lynnie's smart, almost as smart as a man, and as sneaky as a coyote."

"Do tell." Ma smiled sweetly. "Well, we all know the poor little thing's been fired from her teaching job."

"I reckon so!" Ace snorted, "after causin' a riot at the governor's ball. She's got too much pluck for one girl; it ain't natural."

"Okay, so she's feisty," Dad conceded, sipping his coffee. "The Durango men have always liked feisty women. That's how I ended up with your mother."

"Well, I ain't endin' up with Lynnie McBride." Ace shuddered as he reached for another charred biscuit. "Why, she ain't even got any prospects, much less been spoke for, and she's old to be unmarried."

"Twenty is not old. And besides, Lynnie's choosy," Ma said, rushing to the defense.

"You mean, men are choosy," Ace corrected as he buttered the bread. "No Texan wants to go through life with a headstrong, skinny . . ."

"Why don't you just admit you can't handle her?" Dad leaned back in his chair and grinned. "She's a well-bred little filly."

"I like my mounts wild," Ace snapped back, remembering how stubborn Lynnie was, "but she's the most opinionated, annoying—"

"Don't talk with your mouth full, and stop it, you two," Ma interrupted. "If Cayenne is to be believed—

and I think she is—Lynnie wouldn't have our son if he was the last man in Texas."

Ace felt his mouth drop open. "Why, that snippy, prim little—somebody should tell her girls are linin' up for me; I'm charmin'."

"Evidently, Lynnie doesn't think so," Ma said. "So I'm throwing this barbecue, inviting all the young people in two or three counties, and sort of give Lynnie a chance to meet eligible young men and pick one."

"Won't do any good," Ace said, attacking the steak. "They've all heard about the ruckus she caused at the ball."

"Well, there's bound to be one young man in Texas who can appreciate Lynnie's good points."

"Which are . . . ?" Ace looked at her.

"Don't get smart with your mother," Trace snapped. "Besides, once Cimarron sets her mind to something, she's gonna do it, and you're wasting her breath trying to stop her."

"That's a fact!" Cookie called from the kitchen.

"Cookie," Cimarron yelled, "it isn't polite to eavesdrop on family discussions."

Cookie stuck his grizzled, weathered face out of the kitchen door. "Well, now, if I ain't family by now, I don't know who is."

"You're right, Cookie," Cimarron conceded. "Besides, I'll need both your and Juanita's help to put on this shindig."

"I'll have to look at my social schedule and see if I'm available," the old man said loftily. "When you plannin' this barbecue?"

"End of March," Cimarron said. "It'll warm up by then, and the bluebonnets will be in bloom—a very romantic time."

Ace snorted, "It'll take more than bluebonnets to marry off that headstrong old maid."

"Ace, please!" Ma glared at him. "You only have to make sure that all your friends meet her and maybe ask her to dance."

"Lordy, Ma," Ace protested, "I'm still indebted to my friends over the governor's ball."

Cimarron got up from her chair. "Well, if you can't get your friends to dance with her, then you can just entertain her yourself all evening."

Ace sighed at the thought of verbal sparring with the prim Miss McBride for a long, long evening. "All right, you win. You know, it's a good thing you don't play poker, Ma. You're a hell of an opponent."

Dad seemed to stifle a grin. "Better to get in the way of a stampede than in the path of a determined woman, son. I think the barbecue is a great idea; it'll give me a chance to talk to all the local ranchers about the cattle drive. Now, finish up your breakfast, Ace. We've got a lot of work to do before sundown."

He sighed and listened to the wind whip around the *rancho*. "But it's cold enough out there to freeze the balls off a—"

"Ace!" Ma glared at him.

"Well, it is."

"Such a nancy-boy," Cookie yelled from the kitchen, "me and the old don brought in thousands of cows in weather colder than this."

Cimarron smiled as the two men in her life reached for their Stetsons. Maybe her husband was right: Ace was spoiled and soft and did as little around the ranch as possible. She thought marriage to a serious, responsible girl might snap him out of it, but maybe Ace wasn't through sowing his wild oats. Sending him on a long cattle drive would certainly toughen him up.

Six

Late afternoon, one Saturday
March 1885

Ace leaned against the big beer keg next to Dad in the courtyard, where dozens of men drank and tossed horseshoes. He looked toward the drive, where buggies were arriving. Uncle Maverick's buggy had just pulled up, and lots of noisy red-haired children were piling out of it. He sighed, only a little happy from too much beer, and watched Lynnie, wearing a green gingham dress, sitting in the buggy. Her hair was pulled back from her face, and she wore her spectacles.

His dad nudged him. "There they are; mind what your mother said."

"I remember," Ace grumbled, and ambled toward the buggy. He almost felt sorry for the old maid. She looked a little hesitant, as well she might be in facing a big crowd after all the scandal.

Cayenne, with a baby in her arms, passed him. "Wait till you see what she's wearing. I just couldn't talk her out of it."

Ace nodded and ambled out to the buggy. Maverick had just unloaded many red-haired children and now picked up a picnic basket, nodded to Ace, and headed for the house.

Ace stood looking up at Lynnie, swaying a little on his feet. "You need help gettin' down?"

"You look like you're about to fall down yourself," Lynnie sniffed, "and you smell like a brewery."

He started to say something but thought better of it. He realized he wasn't as quick-witted as the strait-laced schoolteacher, and the thought annoyed him. Nevertheless, he reached up and put his hands on her slim waist, helping her down. She smelled good. Without thinking, he leaned closer and sniffed again.

"Will you stop that?" Lynnie snapped, backing away, "you're fogging my spectacles, snuffling me like a hungry hound looking for a biscuit."

If he weren't a gentleman, it would be so satisfying to pick her up and toss her into the big fountain in the courtyard. That would get him in *mucho* trouble with his parents, to say nothing of Uncle Maverick. Now he looked askance at her costume. "Lordy, what an outfit. Lynnie, your dress is too short; your underpants are showin'."

Lynnie drew herself up primly. "These are bloomers, Mr. Durango, created by Amelia Bloomer as a protest garment for women's rights many years ago."

He leaned on the buggy and grinned. "So Miss Amelia protested by showin' her drawers?"

"Thunderation, I don't know why I bother." She turned to unload some of the food in the buggy. Even when he was drunk, Ace was handsome and so strong, Lynnie thought with annoyance, certain his parents had sent him out to meet her. She looked around with some trepidation into the warm afternoon of the Durango *rancho.* The barbecue was going to be a huge event, all right. Buggies and wagons were tied up at every hitching post, and crowds gathered around the great fountain in the courtyard and the big keg of beer over by the adobe wall. It seemed to her that everyone had paused to stare at her. No doubt it was common gossip about the scandal she had created. Well, she didn't give a fig. The cause was all that was important.

Her older sister, Cayenne, holding the baby, Joey, yelled from the courtyard. "Lynnie, can you get those pies?"

"Certainly." Lynnie nodded as her nieces, nephews, and younger sisters scattered across the courtyard, yelling to friends. She looked at the food in the back of the buggy. She wasn't about to ask this drunken brute for his help. Defiantly, she took a coconut cake in one hand and a rhubarb pie in the other, stuck her nose in the air, and started across the courtyard.

"Can I help you with that?" Ace blocked her path. He was taller and more broad-shouldered than she remembered, but one thing she hadn't forgotten was the arrogant cockiness of the man, as if he were God's gift to women.

"May," she corrected automatically, *"May* I help you with that?"

"I'm offerin' to tote that stuff to the kitchen." He grinned, obviously unaware he was being corrected, or maybe not caring.

"You'd probably drop things," Lynnie said primly, "and besides, you're so drunk, you couldn't hit the ground with your hat in three tries."

He winked at her. "Not as drunk as I'm gonna be later tonight."

Lynnie paused, tempted. It occurred to her that to hit him with the coconut cake might be soul-satisfying, but it would be the waste of a delicious cake that she had worked hours baking. "I'm perfectly capable of carrying this, thank you."

His rugged face lit up. "Is that rhubarb? My favorite."

Had she remembered that? Of course not! "If I'd known, I'd have brought apple instead."

"Like that, too." He grinned down at her.

"Leave me alone," she commanded, and resumed her march toward the kitchen, green skirts swishing.

He trailed along beside her, his long legs easily keeping up with her shorter steps. "Dad said I was to help you; you wouldn't want to get me in trouble, would you?"

"How tempting, although I suspect that with you, Ace Durango, you're usually in trouble anyway."

He looked too drunk to be insulted as he took the pie away from her. "Didn't know you could cook—especially rhubarb pie."

They continued their walk toward the kitchen through the curious crowd. "There's a lot of things you don't know about me, Ace."

"Lordy, girl, you're the derndest thing I ever met. All the other girls here are gigglin' and being agreeable."

"The silly dolts are trying to attract your attention," Lynnie said as they entered the big *rancho.* "All they want out of life is a husband."

"And you don't want one?"

"I have bigger plans in mind," Lynnie said loftily, "and it doesn't include continual cooking and cleaning up after some big, dirty ox like you."

"Lynnie, you sure know how to hurt a fellow." He followed her into the kitchen.

Lynnie ignored him while nodding to the women bustling about the kitchen. "Hello, all."

Aunt Cimarron raised her gaze from a huge platter of deviled eggs she was finishing up. "Well, hello, Lynnie. I see Ace couldn't wait to give you a hand. Remember to save him a dance later this evening."

Lynnie put the cake down, feeling hesitant. "I doubt very many men are going to ask me to dance tonight."

"Oh," Aunt Cimarron nodded, "I'm sure all Ace's friends will want to dance with you, so he can't hog all your evening, right, son?"

"Uh, right." Acc put the rhubarb pie on the table next to the dozens of other pies and fled the kitchen. *Lordy,* he thought as he stumbled away, *if I don't get some of the* hombres *to dance with her, I'll be stuck with her all evening*—and there were dozens of local beauties here to choose from. Now just who owed him a favor?

Inside the kitchen, Lynnie made herself useful. There were mounds of barbecue sandwiches, plates piled high with homemade pickles and hot Texas relishes, mountains of potato salad, and pans of spicy baked beans and platters of steaming Mexican food.

"Really, Lynnie," Aunt Cimarron protested, "you go out and mix with the other young people and leave all this to us old married ladies. I hope you don't mind if I invited members of your school board. I thought, in a better mood, they might reconsider."

"I doubt that."

Aunt Cimarron was looking at her dress with raised eyebrows.

"They're bloomers," Lynnie said without being asked. She didn't really want to leave the safety of the kitchen, knowing people outside were gossiping about her; in spite of her careless demeanor, it really hurt. If it hadn't been for the cause, she would have been quite shy. "I'll go find my friend Penelope."

She started out the back door, past the big tubs of iced lemonade. Children ran and chased each other, laughing and calling. Ladies sat on spread-out quilts, playing with babies and visiting. Lynnie rounded a corner and plowed right into Ace's chest. He reeked of beer and he embraced her without really looking down. "Oh, honey, you smell good," he murmured, and tried to pull her closer, kissing her neck.

"Ace Durango, have you lost your mind?" And she slapped him hard.

He stumbled backward, rubbing his cheek. "I reckon I did for a moment." The frown that crossed his handsome face gave her a funny feeling that she couldn't quite put a name to. Was it anger or just disappointment?

"Who'd you think it was, one of your saloon tarts?"

He drew himself up, weaving slightly. "I'll have you know that respectable women like me, too."

"So I've heard, but damned if I can see why."

"I never heard a lady cuss before."

"That's because you don't spend much time around ladies, Ace. Now, if you'll excuse me—"

He caught her arm. "You're the only girl I know who don't think I'm charmin'."

"Doesn't." She corrected automatically. "Drunken cowboys are not my type. I'd prefer a smart and responsible gentleman. Let go of my arm."

"You don't think I'm smart?" He was looking down at her with annoyance.

"Not judging from the company you usually keep."

"Worse than the Austin jail?" he pointed out, swaying on his feet.

"Don't act so wounded and indignant; you've seen the inside of half the jails from here to Mexico City. Goodbye, Mr. Durango." She pulled away from him and hurried off, leaving him standing there, still weaving slightly. She wasn't about to end up as one of Ace Durango's many conquests. When she finally married, she wanted a very civilized gentleman, the type who would quote Shakespeare and be a true believer in the cause. She sought out Penelope, and the two of them watched couples sashaying around the bubbling fountain.

Penelope sighed. "There's going to be a Mexican band and dancing tonight. I hope Hank Dale shows up and asks me to dance. Who do you want to dance with?"

"With *whom* do I wish to dance?" Lynnie corrected automatically. "Nobody. Men will only distract us from working for women's rights, Penny. They only want one thing from us, and it doesn't have anything to do with voting."

Penelope's dark eyes blinked as she considered that one thing. "Miss McBride, you ever been kissed?"

"Call me Lynnie, since I'm no longer your teacher. I presume by 'kiss' you mean by someone other than uncles and little brothers? No, but I don't think we're missing anything," Lynnie answered, and frowned as she watched Ace Durango laughing with a bunch of silly girls, who were twittering about him like a bunch of birds.

"Well, if you haven't tried it, how would you know?" Penelope, too, watched the girls flocking about the big cowboy.

"I imagine it's like being licked in the face by a hound dog," Lynnie snapped.

"Emmalou Purdy looks like she can hardly wait to find out," Penelope observed. "Look at how she's leaning close to Ace and laughing at everything he says."

"Emmalou Purdy is an idiot." For some reason she didn't understand, it annoyed Lynnie greatly that the girl was leaning so close to Ace, her big bosom almost brushing his arm. For a moment, she remembered the sensation of being in his embrace at the ball, the power and the size of the man. "And Ace Durango is a bigger idiot to fall for all her giggling. She doesn't have a brain in her head."

Penelope sighed. "I'm not sure brains are what a man's looking for."

"Which shows you just how smart the average man is," Lynnie declared, and meant it. "While ninnies like Emmalou are getting kissed and flirting, we'll be leading the charge for women's right to vote."

"I don't know," Penelope said wistfully. "Getting kissed seems awfully nice."

"Penelope, you mustn't desert the cause," Lynnie admonished. "We've got to push for women's rights in every way we can, and that means not succumbing to some brute's wiles and ending up hanging over a hot stove, baking rhubarb pies by the dozen."

"Rhubarb pies?"

"They're his favorite," Lynnie said without thinking. "Next thing you know, you've got a houseful of babies."

"From baking rhubarb pies?" Penelope looked puzzled.

The girl was one sandwich short of a picnic, Lynnie decided, or incredibly naive. "Well, that's what it leads to; kisses and babies."

"Babies are nice; I'd like some, wouldn't you?"

For a split second, Lynnie imagined a baby in her arms that had a cockeyed grin and very black hair. She must be losing her mind. "I can't think of a man I'd want to do . . . well, you know . . . with to get one."

"I don't even know what it is you do to get a baby," Penelope admitted.

Lynnie felt herself flush at the image that came to her mind of that big galoot and how he would look naked. In her mind, his lips brushed across her face and down her throat to her . . .

"Miss Lynnie, are you getting sunburned? Your face is turning beet red."

"No, Penelope." She watched Emmalou Purdy take Ace's arm, and the two of them laughed together like a pair of crazed hyenas. "He has to be stupid not to see through that."

Penelope watched the two for a long moment. "He gets much closer to her, he'll have to answer to her brother."

"Nelbert Purdy?" Lynnie sniffed disdainfully. "Why, Ace Durango would wipe up the courtyard with him."

"Just think how exciting it would be to have men fighting over your honor." Her friend sighed.

"Oh, Penny, you'll never be a modern woman if you keep thinking like that," Lynnie said. Abruptly, she was sick of watching the handsome cowboy fawning all over the giggling simpleton. She used her hand to shield her eyes as she looked up toward the late-afternoon sun. "I wish they'd serve the food. It's too boring to keep watching that pair make idiots of themselves."

Penelope turned and gestured. "Well, there's a croquet game going on the south lawn."

"Croquet?" Lynnie shook her head. "A ladies' game for prissy females. What are all the men doing?"

"What are they always doing? Most of them are over by the beer keg, a few are tossing horseshoes, and the rest are out back by the tables, waiting for the food to be served."

As if on cue, a big gong clanged on the edge of the courtyard, and the grizzled old cook yelled, "Come and get it, folks; we got a beef and a pig roasting!"

"Come on, Penelope; we'll be expected to help."

Lynnie forgot about the annoying Ace Durango, women's rights, and everything else for the next hour as she helped serve the food. A number of people looked at her with questions in their eyes, but Lynnie ignored them. So she'd caused a riot and ended up in jail. Certainly it was not something girls of good family did every day in Texas, but it was all for a good cause. Although she was attempting to put up a good front, it was difficult to be brave with people staring with such curiosity at her bloomers. Perhaps she had gone too far.

She served up barbecue and gallons of iced tea and lemonade. Ace Durango pointedly ignored her while a dozen pretty girls from neighboring ranches gathered around him, giggling at everything he said. They all seemed to be arguing over who was going to bring him a plate of food. Well, she'd never be a giggling slave like that.

Emmalou Purdy appeared to have won the argument and sashayed over to Lynnie, grinning like a possum. "Fill me a plate, Lynnie; Ace is waiting for it."

Lynnie smiled. "Certainly." When Emmalou turned to look back at the drunken cowboy, Lynnie poured chili pepper sauce over everything on the plate—especially the rhubarb pie.

Emmalou took the plate and returned to Ace, her hips swaying outrageously.

"It's a wonder she doesn't throw her back out," Lynnie muttered.

Penelope watched the buxom beauty handing the plate to the grinning Ace. "I don't think he's interested in her back."

"Oh, hush up, Penny, and get yourself a plate of food before these male pigs eat it all."

Ace gobbled the food down without even tasting it, Lynnie thought. She hoped it gave him a bellyache.

As the sun sank toward the horizon, Lynnie watched him and his harem with a growing annoyance. Why couldn't he be smart enough to see through those stupid girls' antics?

When he ambled to the serving table to get another helping of her rhubarb pie, she told him so. "Those girls don't really think you're that clever."

"They don't?" He grinned at her and seemed to be having a difficult time focusing his eyes.

"Of course not, you big oaf; they're just trying to charm you. All of them would like to be Mrs. Ace Durango, although, for the life of me, I can't see why." She cut a big hunk of pie and slapped it on his plate, but with him watching, she couldn't put chili peppers on it.

"You know, Lynnie, you're as annoyin' as a burr under a saddle, but at least you're always honest with me." He grinned at her and took a bite. "Lordy, you can cook. But the piece I had while ago was a little better."

She started to tell him about the chili peppers but decided she'd better not. "You're so drunk, how would you know the difference?"

Ace cocked his head, pie smeared on his mouth. "Do you have to turn everything into a fight?"

"This isn't a fight; it's a discussion," she countered loftily.

"Uh-huh."

She didn't mean to say it, but she couldn't help herself. "I see Emmalou was almost crawling all over you out by the fountain."

He grinned. "She was, wasn't she? She can't cook, but she's got other things to interest a man."

Lynnie felt herself blush to the roots of her hair. "Ace Durango, you are no gentleman."

"I never claimed to be, Miss Priss. I'm a man, a hairy-chested, uncivilized man—the kind most women like."

"A brute," she snapped. "Helping to keep women downtrodden and powerless."

"You, powerless and downtrodden?" He threw back his head and laughed. "Lady, you are the most stubborn, headstrong . . ."

"I beg your pardon! If your mother knew—"

"You gonna tell her and get me in trouble again?"

"You seem to be perfectly capable of getting in trouble all by yourself. Now, you'd better hurry; your harem is waiting."

He winked, turned, and sauntered back to the bevy of eager girls gathered under the giant oleander bushes.

Damn him. Damn, damn, damn him. Oleanders were poisonous. It was too bad she hadn't sprinkled some leaves or blossoms on his pie instead of just chili peppers.

Now that most of the crowd had been served, Lynnie got herself a plate and retreated to the kitchen to enjoy the delicious picnic. The barbecue was juicy and smoky, the fresh bread crusty and thickly spread with home-churned butter. She went back for some of her rhubarb pie, but Cookie informed her that Ace had taken the very last piece. She hoped he choked on it.

Darkness had fallen over the Texas hill country as Lynnie went back outside. The little Mexican band was setting up on the edge of the courtyard, preparing for the dance. Lynnie tried to look busy, bravely walking about the courtyard and nodding first to one and then another, but some avoided her gaze and others paused as she passed, and then the conversation picked up again after she left—she suspected the people were gossiping about her exploits. For the one-hundredth time, Lynnie wished she had stayed home, but her big sister had insisted she attend.

Penelope joined her by the fountain. "I wonder if Hank is comin'?" She said for the umpteenth time.

"We can have a perfectly lovely time without men," Lynnie assured her.

"I so wanted to dance with him," Penelope moaned.

"Speaking of men, where are they all?"

Penelope gestured. "Some of them are over by the band, some are still hanging around the beer keg, and I think some of the others have gone to the library to smoke cigars and talk business and politics. I think I saw Ace drifting that way."

"Politics?" Lynnie's ears perked up. "That sounds more interesting than standing here hoping to get asked to dance."

"Oh, Hank Dale just rode up!" Penelope went running to meet the young rancher. Hank Dale was lanky with brown curly hair. His face lit up when he spotted Penelope, and they laughed together.

Lynnie felt completely alone. She wasn't going to be asked to dance—she knew that—and she really didn't know how, anyway. That short lesson from Ace had only made her aware of her shortcomings in that department. Besides, she didn't want to argue with some dolt over whether it was his right to lead.

Politics. She headed toward the library. The door was open, the air heavy with tobacco smoke, which made her choke, but she suppressed a cough.

". . . and the price of beef will of course depend on if we get enough rain for a good stand of grass," the older Durango said.

Some of the other men standing around him nodded and murmured agreement.

Her brother-in-law, Maverick, said, "Trace, are you really planning an old-fashioned cattle drive?"

"Thinking about it," Trace said. "It'll be like old times."

She watched Ace sip his whiskey and groan aloud. "Lordy, Dad, it sounds miserable."

A couple of the older ranchers made noises of disagreement. "Them was the days," one of them said wistfully.

She reminded herself that she must not correct the older man's grammar as she slipped closer to the sideboard and grabbed a whiskey off a tray. She'd never drunk anything except a little sherry before, but she was feeling brave and reckless.

One of the other men said, "I hear Willis Forrester has heard what you plan and is going to do a cattle drive himself."

Trace Durango snorted. "Sounds like the Forresters. I hear he's been cozyin' up to the governor."

"The governor has some pretty good ideas," one rancher said.

Lynnie couldn't stand any more. "The governor is an idiot," she said loudly.

The men all turned as if noticing her for the first time, and the room grew quiet.

"Ah, ma'am," the older Durango said, "ladies don't usually—"

"Don't usually what, Uncle Trace? Join the men for interesting conversation? I'll have another whiskey, please." She gulped her drink and handed the glass to the Mexican boy behind the bar, who paused, then filled it for her. She saw Trace look toward his son, and Ace pushed through the silent crowd to her.

"That's pretty strong drink for a lady."

"Everyone else is drinking it." With all the men staring, there was nothing to do but grab the glass and gulp it. "Now, as you were saying about the governor, what I'd really like to talk about is his stand on women's rights."

However, no one talked. In the silence, the men all looked at each other helplessly, which annoyed her. She knew more about politics in this state than most men, but they were waiting for her to go join the women and talk about babies and crocheting doilies. "I—I'll have another whiskey, please."

Her stomach was already roiling over the liquor she'd just put in it. How in the name of God did men drink that stuff? Maybe the bartender wouldn't give her another. She could only hope.

The Mexican boy looked toward Ace, who nodded. "If Miss McBride wants to behave like a man, by all means, pour her another." He grinned at her. "Would you like a cigar, too?"

"A cigar?" All the men were staring at her. Her brother-in-law, Maverick, looked annoyed. "I—I—of course. I smoke them all the time."

"Is that a fact?" Ace took one from his pocket and handed it to her. She wasn't quite sure what to do next. Every pair of eyes in the room was on her. There was no backing out now. Ace's father looked as if he was about to object.

"It's all right," she said with as much dignity as she could muster. "I just remembered I don't have a match."

"Allow me." Ace made an exaggerated, courtly bow and pulled out a little silver match safe from his vest.

She sniffed it as she had seen men do, and remembered then that she was supposed to bite the tip off, but she had trouble with it. All that time, Ace was standing there in the silence with his damned match safe.

In the silence, he struck the match. What else could she do? With a shaking hand, she put the cigar in her mouth. Ace lit it, looking much amused. She took a deep puff, trying not to cough.

"Miss McBride, would you like another whiskey?"

"N-no thank you," she managed to gasp as the black smoke fogged around her. Why on earth did men like these things? It tasted like burning hay. No, worse.

Maybe burning manure. She felt all gazes upon her, most of them dark with disapproval, but she wasn't sure how to exit gracefully now, so she took another puff and tried to look nonchalant. "Gentlemen, you may continue with your conversation. I—I think I hear someone calling me."

She was feeling sick—very sick. Almost tottering, she headed out the French doors, past the dancers, and around to the back of the house, where she tossed away the cigar and leaned against the wall.

Ace came around the house, looking a little more sober in the moonlight. "Lynnie, are you all right? Your face looks greener than your dress."

"Thunderation, why wouldn't I be all right? I can do anything a man can do."

"All right, then." He started to walk away, and at that point, Lynnie's stomach couldn't stand any more. She began to throw up all over his boots.

"Oh, hell," Ace said, "my best boots. Little gals shouldn't try hard liquor and cigars." He came to her side and put his arm around her to keep her from falling.

"Go away!" she wailed. "Go away and just let me die! Haven't you humiliated me enough?"

Ace disappeared and was back in a moment with a bucket of cold well water. He began to splash her face. "Here, you little priss, you'll feel better."

"I don't need your help," she gasped, and leaned against the wall.

"Yes, you do." He sounded almost gentle as he caught her arm, handing her a dipper of water. "Here, wash your mouth out while I tend to my boots."

She gulped the cold water, and it seemed to calm her belly.

Then he dipped his handkerchief in the water and gently washed her face. "I'm sorry, Lynnie; I shouldn't

have put you on the spot. Here, let me carry you inside."
Before she could object, he had swung her up in his arms.

She had forgotten how strong and powerful he was. "I hate you!" she sobbed, laying her face against his chest. "You are the most despicable brute of a man. . . ."

"Why don't you try behavin' like a lady and you wouldn't get yourself into these scrapes?"

"Go away!" she yelled at him, fighting the urge to sob.

"Oh, hush, Lynnie." Ignoring her pleas and threats, he strode with big, easy strides toward the house. "I was trying to help. . . ."

"I don't need your help," she wailed.

"Reckon you do," he said as he carried her into the house, with everyone turning to stare.

"You're embarrassing me." She laid her face against his wide chest.

"Gal, you embarrassed yourself, but I'll probably get in trouble for givin' you the cigar."

"I just wanted to talk politics," she murmured, still queasy as he carried her.

"I know, but men ain't used to women with opinions." He carried her upstairs and kicked a bedroom door open.

"Aren't," she corrected.

"What?" He paused, looking down at her.

"Aren't used to women with opinions."

"Damn," he sighed, "I never met a girl who was so opinionated and so much trouble!"

And with that, he dumped her unceremoniously on the bed and strode away, leaving her to her misery.

Seven

Lynnie watched the big cowboy turn and stagger out of the room. Then his big feet echoed down the stairs. Could she have humiliated herself any worse? She managed to get off the bed, went to the bowl and pitcher in a corner, and splashed water on her face. Outside, the merriment drifted up to her window.

Suppose people had seen Ace carrying her upstairs and hadn't seen him come back? Would they think the two of them were . . . ? *Oh, hell, of course not!* She and that uncouth rascal? Besides, what did she care what people thought? Her big sister would care, and Lynnie felt obliged to be a good example for Penelope and the younger women. She lay down on the bed until her head stopped whirling, then tidied herself up as much as possible and went down the stairs and out into the courtyard.

The fiesta was still going strong; laughter and guitar music drifted across the night air. There, under the faint glow of the Chinese lanterns, Emmalou Purdy was draped around Ace Durango's neck, laughing like a hyena.

About that time, Nelbert Purdy rounded the corner. Uh-oh. Lynnie started to yell a warning, then decided the big lunkhead deserved whatever he got. Nelbert crossed the courtyard like a train engine under full steam, grabbed Ace by the arm, and spun him around. "How dare you take advantage of my innocent little sister?"

"Innocent?" Ace said, "she was kissing me and—"

"He was taking advantage of me," Emmalou declared with a pout. "I do think, though, brother, that his intentions are honorable."

"They are?" Ace blinked; obviously, he'd been back at the beer keg.

Nelbert Purdy bristled. "I reckon you are plannin' on marriage with sweet Emmalou, or I may have to ask for satisfaction."

Nelbert must be drunker than Ace, Lynnie thought, because he was older and shorter, and Ace had a reputation as a saloon brawler.

Ace turned pale as a catfish's belly. "Marriage? No, not me."

Emmalou began to cry, although Lynnie thought it sounded fake.

The crowd noise lessened, and some drunk in the back yelled "Fight! Fight!"

Now, besides liquor, fast women, and horses, there wasn't anything more fun to a bunch of Texas cowboys than a good fistfight. A crowd began to form a circle.

Ace grinned good-naturedly. "Now, Nelbert, I wasn't doin' anything—"

"But you was thinkin' it."

Ace grinned and tried to focus his eyes. "I'd be a damned liar if I said I wasn't."

Of course, at that point, Nelbert was honor-bound to hit Ace in the mouth, knocking him back against the wall of the fountain. The crowd set up a yell for a fight. Always obliging, Ace wiped his bloody mouth and charged at the shorter man. They meshed and slugged it out around the fountain, with the men in the crowd cheering them on.

Oh, dear. Where were Trace and Cimarron? Somebody had to break this up. Even as Lynnie looked around, trying to decide what to do next, Emmalou attacked Ace, hitting him in the back and screaming, "How dare you hit my brother! Give it to him, Nelbert!"

Ace was outnumbered—anyone could see that—trading blows with Nelbert Purdy and trying to fend off Emmalou, who was slapping and hitting him. It wasn't fair, especially as drunk as Ace was. Always one to come to the aid of the underdog, Lynnie charged in, grabbing the buxom girl by that long blond hair, which was certainly dyed. Now there were four of them struggling and shouting near the bubbling fountain.

"Let go of me, you old maid, you!" Emmalou scratched and slapped, but Lynnie was used to dealing with overgrown students. She pushed the younger girl, and they both stumbled backward and fell into the fountain with a splash. They both came up wet and gasping. Thunderation, the water was cold. It molded her green gingham dress to her slender form, and the incredulous looks on the crowd's faces as they ringed the fountain was something to see.

Just then, Ace punched Nelbert again and they meshed, both going into the fountain with a shower of water. About that time, she heard running feet, and Ace's dad pushed through the crowd, his face marked by both disbelief and anger.

"Ace, what the hell's going on out here?"

In answer, Ace knocked Nelbert down again, and water sprayed everyone near the fountain. Emmalou stood up, the water molding her dress to her big bosoms, and wailed, "Your son won't marry me, and he's ruined my honor."

"Oh, Emmalou," Lynnie said, "we all know your family's hoping to marry money."

She smacked Emmalou again, and the buxom girl began to wail. "My dress. You've ruined my dress."

"Oh, shut up," Lynnie snapped. "You aren't hurt."

She could see Cimarron and her big sister coming from the house even as Ace's father and Uncle Maverick climbed into the fountain, separating everyone.

"Show's over!" Trace yelled, and then he said the magic words to scatter the crowd. "I think the cook just put out more food and another keg of beer!"

The crowd cheered, and most started drifting away. A drunken cowboy grinned as he left. "More beer and a good fight! Life don't get no better than this."

Any better, Lynnie thought, but she only gathered her sodden skirts around her and stood looking at Cimarron's and her big sister Cayenne's horrified faces. Someone helped Emmalou and Nelbert climb out of the fountain, and little Tequila promptly ran over barking and sank his sharp little teeth into Purdy's leg.

"Dagnab it, even the Durango mutt is dangerous!" Nelbert howled. "I wasn't doing nothin' but protectin' my sister's honor."

"That's right," Emmalou wailed. "I thought Ace had honorable intentions."

"Emmalou," Lynnie snorted, "anyone who knows Ace knows he hasn't an honorable bone in his body. Besides, he couldn't have done anything with you; he was upstairs in the bedroom with me!"

Everyone turned and stared at her, then at the buxom Emmalou. Given the choice, it didn't seem too likely.

Ace looked at her with disbelief, then slowly smiled, realizing her sacrifice. "Can I help you out of the fountain, Lynnie?"

Oh, God, what had she done? It horrified her that anyone might think she would actually . . . and with an uncivilized brute like Ace Durango.

"No, thank you," she replied primly, already regretting her words.

Emmalou began to howl like a cat whose tail had gotten caught under a rocking chair.

"Emmalou," Lynnie said, "he isn't going to marry you. Now stop your caterwauling."

"You Durangos!" Nelbert hissed at Ace, water dripping from his stocky form, "you think you're so high and mighty—too good to marry into regular workin' folk . . ."

"Now Nelbert," Trace soothed, "you're drunk and there's no harm done. Go have another drink and some more barbecue."

"You think your rascal of a son is too good for my poor, innocent sister."

Lynnie started to point out that everyone in the county knew Emmalou hadn't been innocent since she was twelve or so, but decided that it would only add fuel to the fire.

Nelbert's weathered face was dark with anger. "From now on, Trace Durango, you and I is quits. I'm gonna join up with Willis Forrester's cattle drive, and we'll beat you to Dodge City."

The Purdys marched away with as much dignity as they could muster, which wasn't much, considering they were leaving a trail of water, and their wet shoes squished with each step.

Trace turned back to the fountain and cursed in Spanish. "Well, son, now see what you've done."

Ace grinned. He was still drunk, Lynnie thought. "Thanks, Lynnie, now can I help you out of the fountain?"

"*May* I help you?" she corrected, very conscious that her wet clothes were clinging to her.

Ace grinned, evidently enjoying the sight. "No, I don't need no help, Lynnie, but let's get out of here."

Before she could protest, he caught her arm and assisted her as they climbed out and stood there, dripping water. The crowd had headed back for more food and beer, but Trace was glaring at them both. Lynnie remembered he had a famous temper when riled.

"Uncle Trace, let me explain . . ."

"Never mind, Miss Lynnie. I'm sure this wasn't your fault. The two of you get in the house and dry out. We'll be the talk of the whole county tomorrow."

Ace grinned good-naturedly. "That was larrupin' fun, Lynnie. I didn't know you could fight like that."

"Young lady . . ." Her sister took her arm. "This is the last social event you'll be attending for a while."

There was no point in explaining she had only been helping Ace. When gossip got around, she wouldn't have any reputation left.

"I suppose this means I can't go to Dodge City for the women's meeting?" Lynnie asked in a soft, subdued voice.

Cayenne glared at her. "Do you even need to ask? You're not going anywhere, young lady. Now march."

Ace grinned at Lynnie. "Reckon we're even now, Miss Priss. I owed you one for the trouble in Austin."

She tried to kick his shins, but he dodged her as they both walked, dripping water, toward the house.

True to her word, big sister Cayenne put Lynnie under strict supervision, and in the next couple of weeks, she wasn't allowed to go anywhere. However, when word came from the Dinwiddy ranch that Penelope's new sewing machine had arrived and she wanted Lynnie to come help her sew clothes for the Christian Aid Society charity, Cayenne decided it was a worthy cause and let Lynnie take a horse and go. It was a long ride, but even the daintiest Texas girl could handle a horse.

"Hallo the house!" Lynnie dismounted from her gray horse as a dozen mongrel dogs boiled out from under the front porch, barking a greeting. Penelope came out on the porch, shielding her eyes with her hand. "Hey, Lynnie, what have you been doing the last week or so?"

"Not much," Lynnie answered grimly. "Still trying to figure out how to get to Kansas for the Independence Day meeting." She tied her horse to the hitching rail.

Penny shook her head. "Don't you ever give up? You know your sister is not going to let you go."

"If women give up, we'll never get the vote," Lynnie answered as they went inside. "I'm allowed to stay till next Saturday because it's such a long ride over, and the whole ranch is preoccupied with that stupid cattle drive Ace's dad thought up."

"That begins next week, doesn't it?"

Lynnie nodded. "Let's see that fancy sewing machine of yours."

Penelope led her into the parlor, where the new machine sat in state. "Had it shipped all the way from St. Louis. You operate it with your foot."

Lynnie peered at the wonder through her spectacles. "Isn't technology something? I could use a new dress or two. I ruined my green one in the fountain."

Penelope smiled, her eyes bright with curiosity. "How is Ace Durango? Everyone's talking about it."

Lynnie drew herself up proudly. "I'm sure I wouldn't know, and I certainly don't care."

"When you two get together, there always seems to be trouble," Penelope said.

"That's because he's a typical, stupid man. The kind I'd like to meet is a civilized, well-educated man with whom I could discuss poetry and philosophy."

Penelope looked doubtful. "Sounds like the new

schoolmaster, the one who's just been hired to replace you; Clarence Kleinhoffer."

"Oh, did they hire him?" Lynnie's ears pricked up.

"Yes, he's coming to call on my parents since me and my little brother are still in school."

Lynnie decided not to correct Penelope's grammar, because she wanted to know more about the new schoolmaster. "Now, there's the kind of civilized man who would help lead women's emancipation."

Penelope raised one eyebrow. "I don't know about that. I've met him briefly, and he's a Yankee."

They frowned at each other. "Yankee" was not a good thing in post-Civil War Texas.

"Besides," Penny said, playing with her hair, "Mr. Kleinhoffer seems awfully straitlaced and priggish—not like our local cowboys."

Lynnie snorted. "Our local cowboys wouldn't know what the word 'priggish' meant—especially that lout Ace Durango. If there was ever a more savage, uncivilized . . ."

"Some of the girls said he'd be fun to tame." Penelope smiled.

"Tame? That brute? Impossible." Lynnie shook her head.

About that time, the dogs started raising a ruckus out front.

Penelope got up and went to peer out the front window. "I think the schoolmaster has arrived for supper."

Lynnie hurried to join her. "At last, an educated, civilized man."

She peered out, too, and was disappointed. Young Clarence Kleinhoffer was still in his buggy, looking down at the dogs as if terrified and waiting for someone to rescue him. He wasn't much to look at, Lynnie thought—not big and broad-shouldered like that ruffian

Ace, but of course, he would have redeeming qualities like sophistication and education. At least the new schoolmaster wore a very stylish suit with a flowered vest. His hair was parted down the middle and greased so much, it reflected the sunlight.

"My," said Penelope, "I never saw any man around these parts dress that fine."

"He's a gentleman from a big city," Lynnie recalled, "but he's obviously not used to dealing with hound dogs. Yell at your little brother to go rescue him."

Thus rescued, the schoolmaster entered the house. Introductions were made, and Clarence was evidently quite entranced by both young women, although no one bothered to tell him about Lynnie's past history.

In the parlor, Clarence entertained the two and younger brother Billy by playing the old pump organ and reciting verse until supper was ready. Lynnie was impressed, and he was openly flirting with both girls.

He leaned closer, and Lynnie could smell the strong rose-water hair tonic he wore. "Now, which of your two families has the bigger ranch?"

The girls looked at each other in shock. In Texas, it was not considered polite to ask about the size of a man's spread or how many cattle he owned. But after all, Mr. Kleinhoffer was a big-city Yankee, and in these parts, that pretty much said it all.

Penelope cleared her throat. "Uh, the Lazy M and the Triple D are the two biggest ranches in Texas besides the King Ranch. Lynnie is from the Lazy M."

About that time, Mrs. Dinwiddy called from the kitchen that supper was ready.

"Well, well, well!" Clarence's teeth fairly gleamed. "Miss McBride, allow me to escort you in to dinner."

They all stood up, and Lynnie took his arm. The four of them trooped into the big dining room and sat down as Penny's father joined them. He was as dried up and leathery as most cowboys. Plump Mrs. Dinwiddy bustled about serving food. Mr. Dinwiddy seemed less than pleased to meet the new schoolmaster, but after all, Lynnie thought, the older man had been a member of one of the Texas cavalry units in the Civil War and had no use for Yankees.

Lynnie watched in astonishment at the amount of fried chicken, hot rolls, and chocolate pie Mr. Kleinhoffer consumed. Even half-grown Billy, who could eat a lot, seemed amazed at how much the man ate.

The schoolmaster finally sighed and leaned back in his chair, wiping his mouth daintily with a napkin. "Excellent cuisine. Well, Mr. Dinwiddy, I was just asking the girls how much land you owned."

The older man frowned. "Not enough. I'm hoping my girl will marry well and bring a little into the family."

"Now, Pa," Penelope said, "you know I'm promised to Hank Dale."

"Not yet, you ain't." Her pa made a gesture of dismissal. "He has worthless land and not much of it."

The schoolmaster was now smiling at Lynnie. "But you, Miss McBride, your family has a big ranch?"

Old Mr. Dinwiddy frowned at him. "Did the girls explain that Miss Lynnie is the one whose job you took?"

The Yankee looked taken aback. "I'm sorry; I had no idea—"

"Let me assure you, sir," Lynnie said with a smile, "I'm not upset you are taking my position. I'm delighted to have an educated man around who can discuss poetry and who might lead some symposia to teach ladies about their rights."

"Their rights? Surely, my dear lady, you are not one of those suffragettes?"

"I certainly am."

"Me, too," Penelope chimed in.

"When I marry," the schoolmaster said coolly, "I shall be looking for a young lady who is not only pure as the driven snow but also knows her place."

"Which is . . . ?" Lynnie asked, struggling to hold her temper. It was not polite to start a fuss in someone else's home.

"Home and church," Mr. Kleinhoffer said decisively. "These fool women who want to meddle in politics should be turned over some man's knee."

"Any man who tries to turn *me* over his knee," Lynnie snapped, "has a fight on his hands."

"Oh, dear, I think we need some more coffee," Mrs. Dinwiddy said, and got up and went into the kitchen.

Mr. Dinwiddy cleared his throat as the atmosphere at the table turned awkward and silent. "I think we'd best adjourn to the front porch swing."

The schoolmaster's thin face turned pale. "Where the hound dogs are?"

The atmosphere turned even cooler. Next to his horse, his wife, and his guns, a Texan loved his dogs. Well, maybe the wife might fit a little lower on that list.

Mrs. Dinwiddy came in from the kitchen, wiping her hands on her apron. "More coffee, anyone?"

"I'd better be leaving." Mr. Kleinhoffer stood up, and everyone else got up, too. "Mrs. Dinwiddy, it was a lovely dinner."

Yes, he was a Yankee, all right, Lynnie thought. Texans had dinner at high noon and supper at night.

Good-byes were said, and with Billy holding off the hound dogs, the prissy Mr. Kleinhoffer got in his buggy and left.

"What a disappointment," Lynnie fumed once she and Penelope were back inside. "I think he's hoping to marry some girl with a rich father, and he doesn't even believe in women's rights."

"Forget him," Penny said with a smile. "There's bound to be someone else for you: sophisticated, elegant, educated—the man of your dreams."

Lynnie laughed. "Penny, you've been reading too many romantic novels. There's no man like that in Texas."

"Well, if you could get to Dodge City, maybe you'd find him there. Anyway, let's work on some sewing and think about the trip."

"Yes, I'll make another bloomer outfit to wear in Dodge City," Lynnie said. "That is, if I can figure out a way to go."

Spring was definitely coming to central Texas, with new calves and colts, and flowers in bloom. The next week passed pleasantly for the two girls, until the day before Lynnie was to leave and a Lazy M cowboy came riding into the yard. "Hallo the house."

The dogs all ran barking to meet him, and Penelope and Lynnie went out on the porch. "Good morning, Bob."

"Miss Lynnie, don't come any closer," he shouted, holding up his hand in warning.

"What's the matter?"

"There's an outbreak of chicken pox at the ranch, and your sister sent me to tell you to stay at least a week longer."

Lynnie blinked. "What about Maverick? Aren't he and some of our cowboys supposed to leave on the Durangos' cattle drive soon?"

The cowboy shook his head. "Can't help that. Quarantined, all of us. Won't be able to go—and oh, I reckon you ain't heard: Trace Durango got throwed by a bronco yesterday and broke some ribs. He won't be goin' neither."

The two girls looked at each other.

"So they've called the drive off?" Penelope asked.

"Nope. It's goin', all right, but it'll be young Ace, old Cookie and Pedro, and a bunch of young cowboys that ain't never been on a drive before."

Lynnie winced at the grammar. "When are they leaving?"

"Day after tomorrow; gatherin' at the big spring."

She knew where that was. "All right, Bob, thanks for bringing the word. Tell Sis I'll be just fine here."

The cowboy touched his fingertips to his hat and rode away.

"Well," said Penelope, "what about that?"

"Anybody in your bunch going on the drive?" Lynnie asked.

Penelope shook her head. "My dad's rheumatism is too bad to sleep on the ground, Billy's too young, and our cowboys are already scheduled to fix fence for the next few weeks in our west pastures."

An idea began to grow in Lynnie's mind. "You know, Penelope, I could ride out of here and your folks would think I'd gone home, and at my ranch, they think I'll be here at least another week."

Penelope looked puzzled. "So what?"

"So if I borrowed some of your brother's clothes, dressed like a boy, and went along on that cattle drive, nobody would know the difference."

"Oh, Lynnie, you wouldn't!" Her eyes went wide with excitement. "Besides, why would you want to? Don't we see enough of dirty, unshaven cowboys?"

"Silly," Lynnie reminded her, "the women's rights meeting in Dodge, remember?"

The other shook her head. "You'd be in big trouble when they finally figured out who you were."

"Well, in the first days of the drive, there's always a lot of confusion and some new hands, so maybe no one would pay any attention to me."

"You couldn't get away with that," Penelope said, "not riding your horse with the Lazy M brand. Everyone would wonder where you got it."

"You're right." Lynnie furrowed her brow, deep in thought. "Maybe we could hide my horse and take one of your dad's."

Penelope shook her head. "That won't work. Everyone would notice the Rocking D brand and realize you weren't one of our cowboys."

Lynnie paced up and down the porch. "There has to be a way to do this."

"Lynnie, it's a loco idea; forget about it."

"No, this is my only chance to make that meeting."

"You ever been on a cattle drive?"

Lynnie paused and looked at her. "You know I haven't; even most of the young cowboys who'll be going haven't been on one before."

"It'll take weeks," Penelope argued, "and everyone says it's pretty miserable. Besides, after a few days, the secret would be bound to come out."

"So what?" Lynnie challenged. "If we're far enough up the trail, they won't be able to spare the men to escort me back. And they can't let a lady travel alone, so they'll be stuck with me."

"And you'll be stuck with them," Penelope reminded her. "Weeks and weeks on the trail with a bunch of rough, dirty cowboys—and Ace Durango among them."

Weeks on the trail with that uncivilized brute. The thought almost caused Lynnie to give up her idea. No, getting to the women's meeting was important enough to make any sacrifice, even if it meant she had to ride alongside that dreadful Ace Durango. "The biggest problem is, I don't have a horse that won't be recognized."

Penelope's face brightened; then she shook her head. "No, maybe it's not a good idea."

Lynnie grabbed her arm. "What?"

"It's a loco idea, Lynnie; I can't do it."

"Tell me!" Lynnie demanded.

"Well . . ." Penny chewed her lip. "Dad just bought a new mare—paid plenty. This gray is supposed to be able to run like the wind, even though she doesn't look like much."

"But the brand . . ."

"The horse hasn't been branded yet with our brand; it's still carrying a brand from some ranch in New Mexico."

"Where is this horse? I want to see her."

"She's out in the east pasture; Dad's trying to fatten her up, but she looks as bad as she ever did."

"So maybe I could trade out the gray I rode over here, and for a few days, unless your dad rides out to check, no one might notice?"

Penelope shook her head. "I told you it was a loco idea."

"I'm desperate enough to try anything. Let's go see this horse."

They got a buggy and drove out to the east pasture to see the gray mare.

Lynnie sat in the buggy and stared wide-eyed at the bony beast through the fence. "Tell me you don't mean that refugee from the glue factory."

Penelope frowned. "I told you she didn't look like much, but she can run. Dad intends to win a bunch of money off unsuspecting ranchers at the fall races."

Lynnie took a closer look. The gray was not only

ugly, she was slightly swaybacked. "Penelope, this horse couldn't run fast enough to outrace your grandmother."

"I've seen her run. Believe me, Boneyard's better than she looks."

At the sound of her name, the big-jointed, flea-bitten gray horse came to the fence and nickered.

Lynnie shook her head. "That's the ugliest horse I've ever seen. She's got hooves as big as buckets, and her hipbones stick out."

"Be quiet; you'll hurt her feelings. Get down and have a look."

The two of them got out of the buggy and walked over to the fence to scratch the horse's ugly head.

Penelope took a piece of cornbread out of her pocket and handed it the horse. "Boneyard's crazy about cornbread and biscuits."

"Boneyard?" Lynnie said doubtfully. "Well, at least the name fits. Why, a self-respecting pack of coyotes would turn up their noses at this rack of ribs."

The ugly horse nickered again.

"Hush, you'll hurt her feelings. She likes ladies better than men, too."

Lynnie patted the velvet muzzle. Boneyard had big, yellow teeth. "How are you, girl?" she crooned. "You have pretty, long eyelashes even if you don't look like much."

The horse nuzzled her, and Lynnie liked the mare instantly, even if she wasn't pretty. "Penelope, this poor thing doesn't look like she could walk all the way to Dodge City, much less win a race."

"Trust me," Penelope said, "I've seen her run."

Lynnie sized up the horse as she scratched her, and Boneyard fluttered her long eyelashes. Sure enough, she was carrying a brand no one would recognize. "Apaches must have stolen her."

"Who knows?" Penelope shrugged. "Anyway, Boneyard's my dad's pride and joy."

"So I could swap out my gray, and from a distance, your dad wouldn't notice?"

Penelope stroked the horse. "Maybe we should forget the idea. I'll be in big trouble when she disappears."

Lynnie looked at her sternly. "Penelope, are you in favor of women's right to vote or not?"

"Well, yes, but . . ."

"We all have to make sacrifices," Lynnie declared solemnly. "After all, I'm just borrowing Boneyard. Think about what I'll have to endure, riding the trail for weeks with a bunch of uncivilized, loutish brutes."

The other smiled. "You reckon Hank Dale will be going along? If so, I might have the guts to go—"

"Guts?" Lynnie shuddered. "Ladies don't say 'guts,' not even liberated ones."

"You're right." Penelope turned toward the buggy. "Besides, Lynnie, you're the only one I know who would dare go on a cattle drive with a bunch of men. It'll be just miserable out there on the trail."

"I'm willing to make the sacrifice so that Texas is represented at the meeting," Lynnie said loftily as she walked toward the buggy. "Now let's get back to the house and see if your brother has clothes that will fit me."

"Oh, Lynnie, are you sure you want to chance this? When Ace Durango realizes you're along, he'll be madder than—"

"Won't he, though?" Lynnie grinned and peered at the younger girl through her gold-rimmed spectacles. The thought of annoying that big rascal cheered her as the two got in the buggy and returned to the ranch house to make their plans.

Eight

Lynnie was certainly having misgivings as she dressed in Penelope's younger brother's clothes that early April dawn. They'd told Penelope's mother that Lynnie was going home in the morning. Because of the chicken pox scare, it would be a few days before her big sister, Cayenne, came looking for her.

Now, as she pulled her Stetson over her eyes and swung up on Boneyard, she hesitated at the temerity of her undertaking. "Oh, Penelope, I'm not sure I'm brave enough to go through with this."

"You sound terrible, Lynnie. Are you sick?" The other girl peered up at her anxiously.

Lynnie coughed and admitted, "I must be coming down with a cold or the grippe. My throat feels sore."

"Your voice is as deep as a man's," Penelope said, "but maybe that's a good thing."

Lynnie nodded. "I might be able to pass myself off as a boy after all." She peered down at the other girl, who looked a little out of focus.

"Are you able to see without your spectacles?"

Lynnie patted her shirt pocket to make sure the gold-rimmed glasses were there. "Not very well, but if I put them on, I'm sure to be recognized."

The other chewed her lip. "Oh, Lynnie, don't you

want to reconsider? I can't believe you'll make it all the way to Dodge City without being found out."

"It's for the cause." Lynnie squared her small shoulders and hoped her hair would stay secured up under her hat. "You're sure no cowboys from your outfit are going?"

Penelope shook her head. "I told you, the whole bunch headed for the main pastures last night to fix fence."

"Wish me luck. Maybe in all the confusion of getting the herd road-branded and started on the trail, nobody will pay any attention to me."

"Oh, I almost forgot." Penelope pulled a bunch of multicolored ribbons from her pockets. "If you make it to Dodge City, would you try to match some fabrics to these colors?"

Lynnie sighed. "Honestly, Penelope, you think I'll have time to shop for dress goods?"

Penelope's serious face fell. "It's just that there's never much to choose from here at the general store and if I'm ever to catch Hank—"

"All right." She weakened at the wistfulness on the other's face. "Put the ribbons in my saddle bags, and if I get there, I'll see what I can do."

Penelope complied happily. "Good luck."

"Try to keep anyone from finding out as long as possible," Lynnie ordered, and saluted. "For the cause," she said grandly, and rode out, knowing she must make a sight in the faded boy's clothes, with a Stetson pulled low over her eyes and riding a horse that looked as if it were ready to lie down and die. The other cowboys would hurrah her over her mount, she knew, but maybe that would take attention away from Boneyard's rider.

In the early-morning dew, she loped to join up with the herd gathering in the grove a few miles to the east. She didn't gallop Boneyard, because she wasn't certain the horse wouldn't collapse under her if she did.

Frankly, she didn't believe that preposterous story about her speed, but if the old bag of bones could really run, she might want to keep that little secret to herself until needed.

Just as she had expected, the meeting place that early April dawn in the grove near the spring north of town was sheer pandemonium: cattle bawling and milling about, nervous horses neighing and churning among the cowboys, and the crowds that had gathered to watch the send-off. The weather had been dry, and the animals were kicking up so much dust that even the most weathered cowboys were pulling their red bandannas up to cover their lower faces. They all looked like bandits, she thought, but Lynnie did the same, grateful that the kerchief hid most of her face. There was a branding fire going as the cowboys put a road brand on the left shoulder of every steer and cow. In case they got scattered along the way, they'd be able to recognize and recapture the stock this group was driving north.

Her vision was blurred without her spectacles, but she dare not put them on, for fear of being recognized. However, she breathed a sigh of relief as she looked about and was pleased that she didn't see anyone from her immediate family there. Under a tree, Ace looked almost green, with one eye slightly blackened, as his mother scolded him. Good—he was in trouble, Lynnie thought, straining to hear. From Cimarron's expression, she was giving him a dressing-down.

"Double damnation, son," Cimarron snapped, "you'd think with the drive leaving this morning, you'd have known better than gettin' yourself in a drunken brawl last night."

"Sorry, Ma."

Lynnie wondered if the *señorita* had been pretty and worth the fight. Ace looked as if he were ready to lie down and die and kept rubbing his head as if he had a bad hangover. The randy rascal.

"Ace," his mother scolded, "your father will be so disappointed if you don't behave like a Durango."

"I told you I didn't want to go on this silly cow chase," Ace groaned.

"Your father would love to go along if he hadn't fallen from that horse and broken some ribs."

"Lucky Dad," Ace said.

Cimarron looked disappointed in her son. "Why don't you get over there and help Comanch and Pedro?"

Ace nodded, but he didn't seem enthused as he took out his canteen and poured cold water over his head. Then reluctantly, it seemed, he tied up his horse and stumbled over to the branding fire while his mother got in her buggy and drove away.

"Hey," Comanch, the half-breed kid, laughed, "Ace, you look like you've been rode hard and put away wet."

Ace groaned. "I feel that way, too."

The experienced Durango trail boss was a tough, swarthy Mexican. Pedro and some of the other cowboys were already at work by the branding fire. Even in this cool dawn, Ace's shirt was soon wet with perspiration and sticking to his big, muscular body. He looked positively male and uncivilized as he tried to follow the Mexican's orders. Lynnie also recognized a few very young and green cowboys from various ranches, but they were all too busy working to notice her. There must have been three or four thousand longhorns milling about the small valley, bawling and churning up dust, as well as a big remuda of extra horses. Off to one side sat the Durangos' old chuck wagon, hitched to two lop-eared mules, with the cantankerous old Cookie seated on the driver's seat, grumbling and scratching.

Dogs barked; whips cracked; cattle lowed and bawled

as they were branded, while horses neighed and stirred up even more dust. She seemed to be the only one not intent on doing something. Lynnie felt very conspicuous. She dismounted, holding on to her reins and looking about, trying to decide how best to blend in. She needn't have bothered hanging on to her reins; Boneyard appeared to be asleep standing up, completely ignoring the confusion around her.

"Hey, kid," Ace yelled and motioned, "get the hell out of the way!" He made an ill-tempered gesture, and his voice rose. "Hey, you with the nag, get outta the way."

Abruptly, she realized he was addressing her, as a pair of cowboys bumped into her, dragging a bawling steer to the fire.

How dare he speak so to a lady. With a flush of indignation, she almost said something, but then remembered she was a cowboy now, and stepped to one side.

Ace appeared to be glaring at her. She couldn't be sure without putting on her spectacles. Sweat dripped down his dark, handsome face as he pushed his hat back. His hangover must be making him short-tempered. "Kid, ain't you got any work to do? You look as useless as udders on a bull."

The other cowboys chuckled, and she bridled at the insult, then realized she was the only one standing around doing nothing. What to do? She'd watched the cowboys at the Lazy M, but of course she'd never taken part. She strode over to the fire in her best masculine manner. "How can I help?"

Her low voice must be convincing, because Ace never looked up. "Hold on to this damned steer while I cut him."

She felt her face go brick red as she realized what the cowboys were doing to the young male animal. Under Pedro's directions, Ace turned the young bull into a steer and tossed his male parts into a kettle. "Good supper tonight," Ace said, and the cowboys around the fire agreed with guffaws.

She thought she was going to be sick, even though she'd grown up on a ranch. Ace nodded to her. "Hey, kid, take this kettle to Cookie and see if he needs a hand."

Calf fries—a very popular dish in the West. For the moment, Lynnie was grateful that her bad vision didn't give her a very good view of what was in the pot. She swallowed hard and picked up the kettle, almost staggering under its weight. For a long moment, she waited for some cowboy to come gallantly forward and offer to carry her burden.

Ace glared up at her. "You got lead in your butt, kid?"

Damn him, she hoped he choked on his calf fries tonight. She struggled carrying the heavy load over to the sour-looking old cook.

Cookie only nodded to her, and she sniffed a strong smell of vanilla as he wiped his mouth and hastily put a small bottle in his shirt pocket. He climbed down off the wagon and took the kettle of male bovine parts, smacking his lips. "Good eatin' tonight."

"Yep," she agreed, and almost ran to get back to her horse. There was no getting around it: tonight she would have to eat something she had always turned up her nose at around the ranch as an uncivilized, barbaric feast.

Boneyard was definitely asleep on her feet, her ugly head drooping. The only sign of life from the bedraggled gray was the occasional flick of her tail at a fly buzzing about, and the flutter of long eyelashes. Lynnie mounted up and rode about, trying to look busy. Everyone else seemed to have a job to do and paid no attention to her.

As the sun moved toward noon, the people who had come to see the herd off gathered in the shade of the trees, the ladies protecting their delicate complexions under lace parasols. The Durangos' main wrangler, Pedro, was definitely in charge, shouting orders, half in border Spanish. Ace looked as miserable as she felt, and his face still had a greenish hue. His dark eyes squinted in the sun, and occasionally he wiped his perspiring brow. He'd gotten hot enough to pull off his wet shirt, and from her perch on her tall horse, Lynnie could watch his muscles ripple as he worked. She had never noticed how much muscle there was to the man. Were those scratch marks on the broad back?

Lynnie squinted and looked closer, imagining Ace's last evening in a cantina with some spicy *señorita* enjoying that virile male body. The images that came to her mind shocked her. A lady certainly shouldn't be imagining such things. Still, it was hard to look at that big brute and not think about those rippling muscles and those scratches on his back. Lynnie wrinkled her nose in disgust. If and when she finally picked a mate, it would be a well-mannered, civilized gentleman who would do nothing that would cause a woman to behave in such a wild, primitive manner.

Finally, all the road branding was done, and the sun's angle made it nearly noon. The cowboys were now all mounted up, Ace having put on a fresh denim shirt. Pedro and Ace had ridden to the front of the herd, trying to get it moving, but the noise and barking dogs, whips cracking, and all the lowing and neighing and shouting were adding to the confusion. Men yelled "good luck," and ladies waved lace handkerchiefs as the herd began to move. It seemed to Lynnie that an unusually large number of women were waving at Ace, who bowed low on his mount and grinned and winked, doubtless loving all the sighs and coos directed toward him. There was not the slightest doubt that every one of the maidens—and some

of the married ladies—would love to be the next to put
scratches on that muscular back.

The brute. Lynnie gritted her teeth at the thought of
such silly women and nudged her sleepy horse awake.
At least with all this excitement, no one had paid the
slightest attention to her. She fell in alongside the herd,
and it began to move out slowly.

"Head 'em up and move 'em out!" Ace shouted.
"Old Twister is ready one last time to lead this herd to
Dodge City!"

The cowboys took off their hats and cheered, waving
their Stetsons in the air to hurry the beeves along. Lynnie almost took hers off, too, so caught up in the moment
was she, then remembered that her hairpins might come
loose. If a red length of hair cascaded down her back,
she'd be noticed for sure. "Hurray!" she shouted in her
strained, deep voice, "Hurray for Dodge City!"

A cheer went up all around as the brown sea of cattle began to move. Everyone down to the smallest child
seemed to sense that this was a historic moment. Some
of the elderly cowboys on the edges of the crowd took
out big bandannas and wiped their eyes. Lynnie herself
was awed by the thought. She was a woman and she was
going on one of the last of the big cattle drives that were
so much a part of Texas legend.

Now most of the cattle were in motion. Slowly at
first, and then one by one, they fell in behind old
Twister, the Durango lead steer with the twisted long
horns, that was famous throughout the county because
he had led so many of the Durango drives north. With
thousands of cattle stirring up the dust, and the remuda
of extra horses rearing and stamping, it took a while to
get the whole herd moving.

Lynnie rode along one side as they began their slow,
dusty walk north. Behind her, from the chuck wagon,

she could hear the crusty old cook grumbling about the rutted trail.

The dust seemed so thick, she was choking as she looked back at the crowd of well-wishers waving goodbye. Up ahead of her, she could see Ace Durango's broad back. Even if he hadn't been riding one of the famed black quarter horses the Durango ranch was famous for, she would have known him from his muscular frame and shoulders so much wider than the average man's.

Abruptly, Ace turned his horse and galloped back along the herd, looking things over, motioning to a cowboy to stop a stray from bolting away. He didn't look quite so green as he had earlier in the day. Then he fell in next to her. Oh, thunderation. Had she been discovered already? She'd hoped to make it at least a few miles before she was caught in this masquerade.

"Hey, kid," Ace yelled, "you look familiar. What spread you from?"

"Uh . . ." She took a deep breath, then remembered the brand on the horse she rode. "Double X."

Ace pushed his Stetson back and scratched his head. "Never heard of it."

"From the Panhandle," Lynnie kept her voice gruff.

His dusty, handsome face turned incredulous. "You come that far on that old nag?"

She almost corrected his grammar but caught herself. "I—I wanted to be in on this drive."

"*I* sure as hell didn't." Ace groaned and rubbed his forehead as if in pain, cursing in Spanish as he did so. "It was my dad's idea. They say the Forrester outfit is a day ahead of us; looks like we'll be eatin' their dust the whole way."

Lynnie nodded and ducked her head. He galloped on, and she couldn't help but turn in her saddle and watch him ride. He might be a woman-chasing hooligan, but

the Cheyenne blood in him was apparent from the way
he sat a horse. Maybe that was the reason silly girls kept
sighing over the big brute, even though he had the manners of a caveman.

Halfway through the afternoon, Pedro sent word down
the line of riders to stop the big herd to graze a little. That
gave the cowboys a few minutes to get a drink of water
from the big barrel on the side of the chuck wagon and
eat a cold biscuit and beef that Cookie handed out. Lynnie kept her hat low over her eyes and didn't say anything,
leaning against a big rock. Now most of the men were
taking a chaw of tobacco or rolling a cigarette. Lynnie
seemed to be the only one not smoking.

Ace ambled up to her, his expression still quizzical.
"You ain't smokin' or chawin'?"

Lynnie kept her head low. "I—I forgot my makin's."

"Here." Ace handed her his little sack of tobacco.

"Much obliged." She took it and the little paper he
handed her. Her hands trembled as she tried to roll it.

"Lordy, kid, you're wastin' tobacco," Ace grumbled,
and he took the makings from her and expertly rolled a
cigarette.

Lynnie took it and stuck it in her mouth. Maybe he
wouldn't have a light.

But Ace struck a match across the seat of his pants
and lit it for her. Even as he did so, he stared hard. "I
swear I know you from somewhere, kid."

"Uh, don't think so." She fought off a fit of coughing
as she inhaled the acrid smoke. To her, it tasted like
burning hay.

"What's your name?"

"Ly—Lee. Lee Smith." She didn't look up at him.

"Okay, Lee, we'll take a leak and then we'll mount up
and see how far we can get before sundown."

"What?" She looked around in horror, realizing some

of the cowboys around her had their pants unbuttoned. She'd never seen a full-grown man with his plumbing on display for everyone to see. "I—I already went." She took her cigarette and stumbled toward her horse in confusion.

Ace Durango didn't have any modesty about him at all. As she glanced back in embarrassed horror, he unbuttoned his pants and pulled out his . . . My goodness, that was a big one! Ace Durango had a manhood on him like a stallion. She knew she shouldn't look, but it was difficult not to, with him making a pattern in the dust with the stream. He appeared to be spelling out his first name. She'd seen Cayenne's little boys do that. Well, some things about males never changed, she thought with disgust as he buttoned his pants, swung up on his black stallion, and galloped to the front of the herd.

"Head 'em up and move 'em out!" Pedro shouted, and the herd began to move north again.

With no one looking, Lynnie stubbed out her cigarette against her saddle. She made sure it was extinguished before she dropped it in the dirt. A prairie fire would be the devil of a thing to deal with. Red dust choked her, and she was having a difficult time seeing without her spectacles, but she was afraid to wear them, certain Ace would recognize her. As it was, the dust was so thick, she could hardly see the chuck wagon moving along ahead of her. Old Cookie seemed to be singing, or maybe he was in pain; it was difficult to tell. When she ran her tongue over her lips, it was so gritty, her teeth seemed to grind. She thought about a warm bath in clean water, soft towels, and clothes that didn't smell like horse sweat. Oh, this was going to be a long, long trip, and it had barely gotten started. The worst of it was going to be dealing with Ace Durango, who thought he was God's gift to women. She grinned to herself and began to plan revenge.

Nine

As the day progressed, her saddle seemed to get harder and harder, to the point she wasn't sure she would be able to get off her horse, when they finally camped for the night. Ace didn't look any better. His face grimaced as if he were suffering from a hangover—which he probably was, Lynnie thought in disgust. At least with all the confusion of the first day, no one paid much attention to her, which was good.

Would the day never end? She glanced up at the sun, trying to hurry it along and thinking that in a few more weeks, it would turn blistering hot and the band she wore now to tie down her small breasts would become unbearable. About the time dusk finally spread across the plains, and Lynnie had reached the point she thought she'd fall from her saddle, Comanch rode along the trail shouting, "Creek up ahead! Pedro says we'll camp there tonight."

Thank God! Gratefully Lynnie reined in her horse and followed the chuck wagon as it pulled off the trail. Up ahead, she heard whistles and shouts as the cowboys got the tired cattle headed toward the creek to drink and settle down to graze for the night.

Some of the cowboys were already dismounting, unbuttoning their pants and making patterns in the dust again. Didn't men ever get too old to find that amusing?

"Hey, boy," the cranky old cook yelled at her, "gather me up some cow chips to cook with."

She nodded. Oh, how her bottom hurt. It was all she could do to dismount from her horse and lead it over to drink from the creek. Boneyard seemed as tired as she was.

"Hey, kid," Ace yelled at her, "hurry it up. We got calf fries tonight!"

Oh yes, calf fries. So-called mountain oysters. The cowboys' delight. Yum, yum. She'd forgotten about the bloody things in the kettle. Although she felt as if she could barely walk, she tied her horse to graze on a particularly rich stretch of grass and walked out across the prairie, looking for old, dried-up cattle manure to fuel the fire. In the olden days, she knew the pioneers had used buffalo chips. Prairie coal, they had called the manure on the treeless plains, but the buffalo had been slaughtered long ago. A buffalo was now a rare curiosity. She stumbled across a big pile of old manure and stared at it with distaste.

Ace rode by. "Hey, kid, get a move on," he snapped. "Or we won't save you any calf fries."

Oh, if only she could count on that. She started to suggest he could be a gentleman and get down off that big black horse and help her, but remembered in time. She gritted her teeth and nodded as he rode on, resisting the temptation to throw a clod of manure and knock his jaunty Stetson off. Instead, she bent to pick up the cow pie, then another and another. Even though it was dry, it still smelled terrible. *Parfum de cow.* She wrinkled her nose and kept picking up dung. Finally, her arms were so full, she couldn't carry any more. With her load, she staggered through the dusk toward camp.

Ace sat his horse, watching her, but he didn't offer to

help. Instead, he yelled at her, "Hey, kid, while you're workin', watch out for rattlers."

Snakes. Yes, this was prime country for rattlesnakes. The thought startled her, and she dropped some of what she'd gathered, then started walking again, very cautious in the tall grass. She could only hope that the next time that arrogant Ace Durango whipped out his, uh, maleness to pee, a big coiled rattler would sink its fangs in his . . . well, at least his boot.

Back at the fire, Cookie soon had a good blaze going and opened some canned beans and brought out the big skillet to fry the cowboy delicacy. The smell of the food and strong coffee made her mouth water, and then she remembered what they were about to eat. Up north, they wouldn't believe this.

A young half-breed cowboy ambled up to her. "Hey, we've howdied, but we ain't shook. I'm Comanche Jones." He stuck out his hand.

It dawned on Lynnie that she was expected to shake it, which she did awkwardly. Women didn't generally shake hands with men. "Lee," she growled. "Lee, uh, Smith from the Panhandle."

Comanche turned a critical eye toward her horse. "That the best they got up there?"

She resisted the urge to kick his shins. "Better than she looks."

Ace came up just then and dismounted. "Couldn't be any worse, could she?"

Both cowboys laughed like idiots.

Ace said, "Pedro says somebody's got to ride herd. Lee and you can start." He was staring at her in the growing dusk. "Kid, are you sure we ain't met some place before?"

She gritted her teeth over his grammar, but with a mighty effort, she didn't correct him. "Maybe in some whorehouse somewheres."

Young Comanche flushed to his dark hair, but Ace guffawed. "You don't look old enough to be toppin' no fillies, Lee."

Leave it to this uncivilized stud to put it that way. He was insufferable. She now had her doubts that she could stand arrogant Ace Durango long enough to ride hundreds of miles with him.

Just then, Cookie began to beat on a pan. "Grub's ready! Come and get it 'afore I toss it to the coyotes."

"Why poison a bunch of helpless coyotes?" Ace muttered under his breath.

"I heerd that!" the old man yelled in their direction.

Ace shrugged. "He only hears what he wants to hear, the old bastard. Believe me, this drive is headin' for disaster—a bunch of green hands, and only old Cookie and Pedro know a damn thing about what to do."

She grunted an answer and moved away from him, grabbing up a tin plate and cup. She tried to turn down the calf fries, but the old man wouldn't hear of it. The way the dozen Texas cowboys were wolfing them down and licking their lips was disgusting. Hank Dale, the curly-headed young rancher, was there, but he didn't seem to recognize her, either.

"Hey, Lee," Ace yelled, "eat up! Calf balls will make a man of you."

It'll take more than that, she thought, but with everyone watching, there was nothing to do but close her eyes and take a bite. The thought of what she was eating made her gag, but with the cowboys looking, she'd have to finish her plate. She pretended these were Ace's she was grinding her teeth on, and that made it easier somehow. In fact, she began to eat with relish, wiping up the gravy with a biscuit as hard and heavy as a cannonball. Ace was right: Cookie's grub might kill a coyote. She tucked one biscuit in her pocket for her horse. Maybe they wouldn't give Boneyard a bellyache. Lynnie looked around for a napkin and noticed the other men, hunkered down gobbling their food and wiping their greasy faces on their sleeves. She managed to do the same, but she shuddered as she did so.

As they finished, the Durangos' old Mexican ranch boss stood up. *"Señores,* I know most of you are young and have never done this before, but I will teach you, and after a few weeks it will get easier, *sí?"*

They all looked doubtful but nodded.

Ace licked his spoon. "How do we make sure we're headed in the right direction?"

Cookie snorted. "'Cause I always point the chuck wagon tongue toward the north star as I unhitch my team, and we start off in the morning the way the wagon tongue points."

"Now what do we do?" A young, green hand asked.

Everyone looked toward Pedro, who was rolling himself a cigarillo. "We ride the herd all night, circling it to keep it calm. Two men at a time, two hours at a stretch."

Comanch stepped forward. "I'll take the first watch."

"Good," Ace said with a yawn, "then I won't have to. I'm still recoverin' from last night. Lee, you help Comanch so the rest of us can get some shut-eye."

Of all the irresponsible, gold-bricking . . .

Everyone was looking at her.

"All right," she grunted.

Ace pulled out his bedroll, spread his blankets, and, using his saddle for a pillow, lay down and tipped his hat over his eyes. Even as she walked toward her horse, he was snoring.

She gave Boneyard the biscuit, and the big yellow teeth chomped it up and nuzzled Lynnie's pockets for more. The half-breed kid called Comanche caught up with her, and together they swung up on their horses.

"Hey, Lee," Comanche said as he reined his bay gelding out toward the herd, "maybe tomorrow night we'll reach a pretty good-sized creek so we can all skinny-dip and wash the dust off."

"Good." She turned her horse and started off, wondering how on earth she'd deal with that—swimming with a bunch of naked cowboys. Well, that wasn't tonight's problem. She wondered suddenly how Ace Durango would look naked, and was then properly shocked at herself for the image that came to her mind.

She took her position, riding in a slow circle around the grazing herd. Comanche rode the other direction, and some time within the hour, they passed each other and nodded. Comanch was singing softly, *"As I walked out in the streets of Laredo; as I walked out in Laredo one day; I spied a young cowboy all dressed in white linen . . ."*

She was so tired, her bottom ached, but if she protested or disobeyed orders, her ruse might be discovered and she'd be sent back. Too bad she wasn't more of a tomboy. She kept hearing about these girls who could rope and ride and shoot as well as any man, but she thought they must all be in the dime novels, because she didn't know any girls like that.

It had grown dark and the cattle were settling down, contentedly chewing their cuds, except for old Twister, who was over by the chuck wagon, begging for biscuits. The steer must be a glutton for punishment. A cool breeze dried her damp face, and in the distance a lonely coyote howled. Around her, katydids chirped away, and the smell of Indian paintbrush and bluebonnets drifted to her nose. Despite the fact that she was tired and dirty, she felt a sense of satisfaction that today she had held her own among a bunch of rowdy cowboys, worked just as hard, and was the equal of any of them. Maybe she could make it all the way to Dodge City after all.

When she was so tired she didn't think she'd be able to get off her horse because her bottom was stiff, Ace came riding toward her, yawning and rubbing his eyes. "Pedro says I take the next shift, Lee—interrupted a great sleep. I was dreamin' about the girls at Miss Fancy's place in San Antone; you ever been there?"

"Nope," Lynnie muttered. The leering idiot. Did he think of nothing but women?

"You missed something," Ace sighed wistfully as if he wished he were there now. "They got real cold beer, too, and the card games go on all night."

Lynnie didn't say anything. The boys at the Lazy M bunkhouse had taught her to play poker, and she was pretty good at it, although probably not as good as this rake.

She nodded to him and headed back toward the welcome beacon of the campfire. It was all she could do to dismount, but she still had to unsaddle her horse and rub her down. No good cowboy rode a horse hard and put it away wet with sweat. Then she hobbled the mare and turned her out to graze with the other horses. Comanche was already crawling into his blankets by the fire.

Where to spread her bed? She hesitated, looking around at the snoring men around the fire. She didn't really want to bed down among them. Maybe she could spread her blankets quite a distance away. A lone wolf howled unexpectedly somewhere close by, and she quickly rethought her plans.

Carrying her saddle and bedroll, she tiptoed over dirty, snoring bodies and made her bed as best she could, using her saddle for a pillow. She felt rocks and cockleburrs under the blanket, but she was too tired to move it or search them out. She lay there, tired and dirty, her muscles hurting. She had chigger bites itching in some places she couldn't scratch without taking off some of her clothes, and she wasn't about to do that. Oh, the romance of the Old West. She wished she could get her hands on some of those dudes who wrote dime novels about the thrill of the cattle trail and its lusty cowboys.

She took a deep breath. It was more than obvious that all these cowboys had been eating beans. Here and there, somebody let out a big, noisy sound.

Lynnie wrinkled her nose. *Phew!* Again she was tempted to pick up and move away from the fire. Then the wolf howled again, and she decided to stay where she was—smells and all. Well, she started this and she had to see it through. Lynnie McBride might be a lot of things, but she was no quitter.

About the time she was dozing off, she heard two cowboys get up and head out to saddle their horses for the next shift. Nighthawks, they called the riders, keeping the spooky cattle calmed by singing to them and watching for coyotes or anything that might start a stampede.

As she watched, Ace and Hank rode in from their shifts, dismounted, and unsaddled and hobbled their horses. Then the two came to join the sleeping circle. There was an empty spot next to her, and Ace threw down his saddle and spread his blanket. Without thinking, she scooted in the other direction.

"What's the matter, Lee, you see a tarantula?"

The image of the black, hairy giant spider crossed her mind, so now she had something new to worry about. She muttered something unintelligible, but it didn't seem to matter to Ace. He was already asleep and snoring. He looked as big as a mountain lying there.

The wolf howled again, and it seemed close—too close. She scooted a little nearer to Ace without even thinking about it. Somehow, she felt safer when she lay closer to his big body. The April night had turned chill, and her one blanket wasn't enough. The fire was dying down, but if she tried to build it up, she'd wake people. Very cautiously, she scooted right up against Ace. He not only generated as much heat as a coal stove, he felt hard as iron—and she knew he had a rifle in his bedroll. He was a good shot, too; everyone knew that. She closed her eyes and listened to Ace's steady breathing. Somehow, it was a comforting sound to know he was right there if she needed the big brute.

When she awakened, it was not quite dawn, the sky splashing the first pale pink across the prairie. What a beautiful sight, Lynnie thought; maybe there was something romantic about cowboys after all. And then she turned her head and saw half a dozen cowboys over on the grass with their pants unbuttoned, peeing in the dirt. She needed to go, too. Frantically, she looked around for some bushes so the men couldn't see her, and dashed there as fast as she could. Ace rose up on one elbow and looked at her quizzically in the gray light as she returned. "Kid, you get cold last night?"

She kept her head low and shrugged. "Why?"

"When I woke up, you was curled up against me like a kitten next to a warm brick."

Were, she thought, mentally correcting his grammar. "Maybe *you* were curled up against *me.*"

Ace looked horrified and jumped to his feet, grabbing up his boots.

About that time, Cookie hit his frying pan a couple of times. "Come and get it or I'll throw it out."

"That'd be a blessing," a skinny cowboy near her muttered.

"I heered that!" Cookie limped over to stoke his fire. "Just for that, you don't get much."

The cowboys laughed, grabbed their tin plates and cups, and lined up. She must have been hungry, because the fried bacon and hard biscuits made in the iron Dutch oven tasted pretty good to Lynnie, although the coffee was the way most Texans liked it—strong enough to float a horseshoe.

Ace looked at Pedro. "Okay, *compadre,* now what? Any chance we can forget this whole deal and go home?"

The Mexican stroked his black mustache and frowned at him. "I promise your papa to make a real cowboy of you. Maybe we make more than ten miles today."

Ace groaned aloud. "All those pretty women and cardsharps in Austin and Laredo are going to miss me while I nursemaid these stupid cows."

Pedro shrugged and grinned. "As *Señor* Durango would say, 'saddle up anyway, *hombre.'*"

Ace picked up his saddle, his shoulders slumped with resignation.

Lynnie's muscles hurt so badly that she almost groaned aloud as she slipped on her boots. Ten miles on a horse today. Ten long, long miles on her sore, aching bottom, and hundreds of miles more to the north. Around her, the cowboys were saddling up. She was tempted to take down her hair, give up the masquerade, and get sent back home. In fact, Ace might even welcome the incident. It would give that malingering loafer an excuse to end this ill-fated cattle drive and get back to his saloon whores and gambling. Even as she thought that, she knew she couldn't do it. Her quest was for the cause and for all Texas women who were under the heel of all these male brutes who wouldn't let them vote. She must continue.

"Hey, Lee," Ace yelled at her, "why don't you leave that old crowbait behind to die, and pick another horse?"

She shook her head and grabbed her saddle. The old-time stock saddle was so heavy, she almost staggered under the weight, but she couldn't ask one of the men to saddle for her, as she could have done if they'd known she was a lady. Besides that, they'd all be horrified that she was riding astride like a boy instead of using a sidesaddle.

She staggered over to saddle Boneyard. The gray's mournful expression told her she didn't think much of today's ten-mile ride, either.

Lynnie's locks felt tangled and dirty, but she dared not take down her hair and attempt to comb it. Pulling her Stetson low, she saddled her horse and mounted up. The chuck wagon was already on the trail, and the cowboys were putting the herd on the move. Lynnie looked up at the sun. It was going to be a long day, and it was just getting started. Ace galloped back toward her.

"Hey, kid, pick up the pace; we ain't out on a picnic here."

She managed to bite her lip and not give out with a smart retort. Oh, how she hated him as she glared after his broad back, disappearing toward the front of the herd. Maybe that big black stallion would step in a hole and throw him and break his thick neck, or better yet, toss him into a fresh cow pie or some scorpions. Lynnie urged her horse out onto the trail and gritted her teeth. Only the thought of her noble cause kept her headed north. She watched Ace's arrogant back as she rode and amused herself by imagining his horse throwing him in the dirt. If that happened, it would be her pleasure to ride right across the uncouth brute's big body.

Ten

One miscrable day blended into the next for Lynnie, driving the slow-moving herd north. So far, no cowboy seemed to realize she was a girl, although every once in a while, she saw Ace look at her and scratch his head in puzzlement. Sooner or later, he might just figure out where he had seen her before, but maybe by then, they'd be too far up the trail to send her back.

As May approached and the days grew warmer, she thought all the unwashed bodies seemed to get smellier. Lynnie felt so filthy she could hardly stand it, but there was really no place to wash much, and even if there were, she wouldn't dare risk taking off her clothes. She never took off her hat, either, and she could only imagine what a rat's nest her hair must be.

The cowboys were not only unwashed, they were all growing straggly beards, although most of them didn't seem old enough to be growing whiskers at all. Ace and Comanch, because of their Indian blood, seemed to have few whiskers at all. *Oh, the romantic cowboys of song,* Lynnie thought with a snort of disgust, and tried to stay upwind of the sweaty bodies. *Parfum de dirty cowboy* now blended with *parfum de cow.*

One dull, dusty day seemed to fade into the next, and sometimes Lynnie almost wished her masquerade would be discovered so she could go back to a clean bed and plenty of water. The fact that they were a day or so behind the Forrester herd did not help. The other herd left grass destroyed, cow manure everywhere, and water either used up or so filthy it couldn't be used. Her cold had cleared, but she kept her head low and spoke as little as possible so she could fit in with the others. Whoever said cowboys were men of few words knew what they were talking about.

One afternoon, Hank galloped back along the line, shouting and waving his hat. "There's a pretty good-size pond ahead! I could see it from a distance!"

All the cowboys set up a yell. "Skinny-dippin' tonight! Boy howdy, that sure sounds good!"

Oh, hell and thunderation, now what would she do? Lynnie let out a yell of excitement just like the others, but she was already worrying about how she would handle dealing with a bunch of buck-naked men. Worse than that, how would she explain when she didn't go in the water herself?

However, to her relief, when they finally pulled up to the shallow lake and watched the thirsty cattle wade in to drink, a disappointed moan went up from the crew.

Ace cursed under his breath as he looked at the muddy, fouled water. "Looks like Forresters' bunch deliberately drove their herd through it several times to mess it up so we couldn't use it. It'd be like swimmin' in a cow outhouse."

Lynnie breathed a sigh of relief but didn't raise her head.

Comanche said, "That means no bath?"

Ace shrugged. "Look at that water. It's so thick, you'll be dirtier comin' out than when you went in."

Cookie took a swig off his bottle of vanilla. "We better find a good stream some time soon, or my water barrel will be empty and I'll have to make coffee out of ponds like that."

"Wouldn't taste no worse," a cowhand muttered.

"I heered that! Just for that, young man, no food for you tonight."

The young man grinned and started to say something else, but seemed to think better of it.

"I heerd that!"

"But I didn't say nothin'," the cowboy protested.

"No," Cookie said, "but you was thinkin' it."

Ace looked toward Pedro. "So now what do we do?"

Pedro scratched his mustache. "We camp and move on tomorrow . . . *sí.*"

"We ought to try to pass that Forrester herd." Ace leaned on his saddle horn.

Pedro shook his head. "No, *hombre,* we'd end up in a stampede. We can only pass if they agree to hold their herd and let us."

"Not likely!" Ace said, and let loose a string of oaths questioning Willis Forrester's parentage.

Lynnie winced, not used to hearing men curse in front of her, and tried to keep her face expressionless.

Ace seemed to be in a foul temper as he dismounted. "Hey, you, kid, help Cookie gather up fuel and get the camp goin'."

"That ain't really fair, Ace," one of the cowboys protested. "Lee's been doin' more than his share of the work."

"Then let him do some more," Ace snapped, and while some of the young cowboys exchanged glances, no one argued with him.

It wasn't fair, Lynnie fumed as she dismounted and allowed her horse to drink. It wasn't fair at all that she was the one Ace seemed to be taking all his spite out on. Of course, if she argued or did anything to draw attention to herself, she was apt to be discovered, so she unsaddled and hobbled Boneyard. As the mare began to graze, Lynnie walked out across the prairie, picking up dried cow chips. She carried a stack over to where the old man was laying out his fire.

"Thanks, boy, you'll get extra helpin's tonight."

Yum, yum. "Thanks, Cookie," she muttered. He reeked of vanilla, and she realized that the flavoring was full of alcohol. She hoped he didn't get too close to that fire; his breath might catch fire. As she worked, the other cowboys were settling down the herd for the night, and Pedro was explaining tomorrow's tasks to Ace. As green as everyone in this drive was, if anything happened to Pedro, they'd be in serious trouble, Lynnie thought. Old Cookie stayed half-drunk on vanilla, and Ace Durango was too spoiled and inexperienced to take charge of a cattle drive. The other cowboys were younger and less experienced than he was, so they wouldn't be much help.

It was dusk, one cowboy playing a guitar as they choked down old Cookie's food. Only old Twister, the lead steer, seemed to have any taste for the heavy biscuits—with the exception of Boneyard. Boneyard shouldered the steer out of the way for the delicacies. The cowboys laughed about it. Lynnie was a pretty good cook, and she itched to take over the chuck wagon, but she knew she couldn't do that without raising the cook's ire and everyone else's suspicions.

Pedro had gone off to check on a lame horse when Ace said, "It's time to set the first watch. Joe, you and Lee do it."

Lynnie sighed. She was dog tired.

"Ace," said one of the other boys, "you're picking' on the kid and he ain't done nothin' to deserve it."

"Hell, I'm not, either!" Ace seemed to be in a particularly foul mood. "He knew it would be rough when he signed on."

Comanch said, "But he's doin' more than his share."

Ace glared in her direction. "You hear him complainin'?"

"I'll do it," Lynnie muttered, and picked out a fresh horse and saddled it up. How she wished for just an hour's worth of sleep, but she wasn't about to protest Ace's bullying. She surely didn't want to give him any excuse to fire her. When she mounted up and glanced back, Ace was glaring at her as if she'd done something wrong.

She hadn't gone more than a few hundred yards when her horse stumbled, and half-asleep as she was, she fell from the saddle and lay there, the wind knocked out of her. She wasn't sure whether to get up or not; maybe there was something broken.

Even as she tried to decide, Ace ran over. "Kid, are you hurt?"

"Maybe my ankle," she muttered. "Not sure."

"Oh, hell, you're determined to make me look bad in front of the crew, aren't you?" Ace snapped as he swung her up in his arms and headed back to camp. "Okay, I'll ride your shift for you."

"You're wonderful!" Lynnie said, and without thinking, she threw her arms around his neck and kissed his cheek.

He froze in midstride, his eyes wide and full of horror. "I ain't one of them nancy-boys, if that's what you're thinkin'." And with that, he dropped her in the dirt and strode away to catch her horse.

Damn him, anyway; what was the matter with Ace? Lynnie stared after him, her bottom aching from being dropped so unceremoniously. Thank God they were just over a little rise, and the others hadn't seen what had happened. Had he figured out who she was because of her stupid, spontaneous kiss? No, she shook her head in puzzlement as she stumbled to her feet and walked back to camp. If he had, he surely would have let the whole world know immediately. As it was, he caught up her horse and mounted and rode away toward the herd, seeming to avoid her curious stare.

Lynnie limped back into camp, got her bedroll, and spread it near Ace's by the fire. Rocks under her blanket or no, she was too tired to care. The camp settled down fast on the warm spring night; only the nighthawks' singing to the cattle drifted on the wind. Lynnie kept her hat on, laid her head on her saddle, and drifted off to sleep.

Ace rode his circuit, singing softly to the cattle: "*As I walked out in the streets of Laredo; as I walked out in Laredo one day; I spied a young cowboy . . .*"

His mind was in turmoil over that Lee Smith. He'd never admit it to a living soul, but the young cowboy was beginning to stir Ace's blood, and it horrified him. When the kid had kissed him, he'd liked it. The boy must be one of those nancy-boys who liked men. Well, Ace Durango sure wasn't. Ever since he'd been attracted to the kid, Ace had been punishing him, loading him down with extra work, hoping to make him quit and drop out. Ace didn't like the thoughts he was beginning to have about the boy.

When his shift was up, he rode back to camp, unsaddled his black, and awakened Comanch to take his place. Then he noted with horror that Lee had spread his blankets next to Ace's. Did the kid realize Ace was attracted to him? He must or he wouldn't want to lie next to him. No telling what might happen. Ace had been without a woman for several weeks now—longer than he'd ever been in all these years. He looked at the kid's small form under the blankets and stifled an urge to snuggle down next to him.

Damn, what was happening to him? Ace grabbed up his bedroll and moved as far away from Lee Smith as he could get. As he drifted off to sleep, he imagined the eager saloon girls who would be waiting to pleasure him in Dodge City with their lusty bodies and full breasts. In his dreams, he kissed one, and as he kissed her, she suddenly became the boy called Lee. Ace bolted upright, breathing hard and wiping sweat from his face. No one must ever know about his secret attraction to the boy. Ace just needed a woman; that was all. Once he got an eager whore under him, he'd be all right. However, he hardly slept that night, and when they put the herd on the move next morning, his mood was black. He made sure he kept as much distance as possible between him and young Lee Smith. Lordy, it was going to be a long, frustrating, confusing day.

That evening just before sundown, they finally came to a creek, deep and clean with newly fallen rain. The excited cowboys rode their dusty horses into the water among the cattle. "Oh, boy! After grub tonight, we all get a swim!"

Thunderation, how would she deal with this?

"I—I'll take first watch tonight," she said. Pedro was busy gathering in stragglers from the herd, so Ace and a few cowboys were the only ones to hear her. The young hands looked at Ace accusingly, but he only snapped, "Fine! You can take my shift."

What was ailing the man? Ace Durango had been avoiding her like she'd been bitten by a mad dog, and when he did speak to her, he was surly and ill-tempered. Ever since she had kissed his cheek so impulsively when he'd picked her up off the ground, Lynnie had been holding her breath and waiting for him to expose her disguise. Instead, he had held his tongue and treated her as if she were a Yankee carpetbagger, snarled at her at every opportunity, and never passed up a chance to load her down with extra work. Why he hadn't exposed her masquerade to the rest of the crew mystified her, but she could only breathe a sigh of relief that, so far, he hadn't.

That running stream looked awfully good to her, but of course, she couldn't skinny-dip with the men. Instead, she went to help Cookie get the camp organized. Many of the cowboys, including Ace, were now stripping off their dusty clothes and diving into the water.

Cookie paused to watch the swimmers. "Looks good, don't it?"

"Sure does." She turned and looked. Ace Durango stood on the bank, wearing nothing but a smile as he dove in. She got a quick look at wide shoulders, narrow waist, and—oh, my, what a big . . . She felt the blood rush to her face as she turned and began to help stir up the biscuits.

"Hey, young fella," Cookie said, grinning, "you go ahead and take a dip with the others. I can manage here."

"Thanks, Cookie," she muttered, "but I don't feel like it right now."

"You sure? They seem to be having more fun than pigs in a mud pit."

She turned and looked again. She had never seen so many bare bottoms before. The young cowboys were having a great time splashing and popping each other with wet clothes. She rolled her eyes, thinking men were just overgrown boys after all. Lynnie tried not to stare at Ace, that magnificent brute. Once he glanced up and caught her looking. Immediately, his face grew dark as a thunder cloud, and he turned his back to her. That gave her a great view of his lean hips and the rippling muscles of his back.

"Hey, Lee," Cookie asked, "you gonna help me or not?"

"Sure." She avoided his gaze as she began to peel potatoes.

The old man was mixing biscuits and sipping vanilla.

"You know," Lynnie ventured, "that idea you had about adding a little baking powder sounded good."

He paused and scratched his head. "I say that?"

"Didn't you?"

He thought a minute, nodded, and added a pinch to his mix. While he was putting his bread in the Dutch oven, Lynnie took the big butcher knife and began to cut thick slices of bacon. As she worked, Ace, halfway up to his waist in water, turned and yelled at her, "Stop watchin' me like a buzzard watchin' a dead calf!"

"I'm not." She looked at the big knife in her hand and smiled at the tempting thought that crossed her mind of the cowboys turning young bulls into steers. She'd like to take this big knife to Ace's . . .

"Liar! I saw you watchin' me swim." He was glaring at her, and she wasn't sure why.

She couldn't deny it, and she had a feeling she looked very guilty. "I was watchin' everyone."

"Humph." He returned to his splashing, and she helped Cookie get the food cooking. By the time Cookie banged a pan, they had crisp slices of bacon, fried potatoes, biscuits and gravy, and strong coffee ready.

Half the cowboys headed for the fire without putting any clothes on, but Ace looked at her, turned his back, and put on his pants and boots. Water still dripped from his rugged body as he came to the fire.

Lynnie blinked and took a deep breath. She just couldn't sit down by a fire with a bunch of naked cowboys and keep her mind on her food. Ace must have seen her expression, because he snapped at the wranglers, "You *hombres* at least put your pants on."

A cry of protest went up from the boys.

Ace was still glaring at her, which puzzled her greatly. "Put 'em on, I tell you. How would you like to spill hot grease on your best parts and disappoint all those gals in Dodge City?"

That was enough to get the boys laughing and hurrahing each other as they went for their clothes.

Lynnie hurriedly gobbled her food, keeping her gaze on her plate.

"Hey," one of the cowhands said, "these biscuits ain't half bad—light and tasty."

Cookie beamed. "My new recipe."

Lynnie kept silent and ate.

As the evening shadows lengthened, the boys were all setting their tin plates aside, leaning back against their saddles and belching. There seemed to be a contest between them about who could belch the loudest. Well, at least they weren't doing the other thing. Men were such rude, barbaric creatures when women weren't around to civilize and tame them.

Now the boys had a card game going, with Ace winning most of the chips. It was evident he was a better than average poker player, and Lynnie knew more than a little about poker, having been taught by her own ranch's bunkhouse crew over the years.

Ace glared at her. "Ain't you got the first watch, Lee?"

It took all her control not to correct his grammar. She

nodded and left the fire. She gave Boneyard a biscuit, and as she saddled up, she noted Cookie was soaking leftover biscuits in vanilla and feeding them to old Twister. A drunken steer—just what they needed. No wonder the old bovine hung around the chuck wagon— he had a taste for alcohol.

As she mounted up in the darkness, she heard Ace's triumphant yell as he won yet another hand. Arrogant, cocky bastard. She'd like to take him down a notch by beating his socks off at poker, but that would only make him more difficult to deal with. Ace Durango was a true Texan; he couldn't stand to be bested by a mere girl. As she rode her lonely post and watched the steers chew their cuds, she looked with longing toward the distant creek.

She was sweaty and itchy, and her face felt as if it had a dozen coats of grime. Maybe when she got off her shift, all the crew would be asleep. It was a cloudy night, and maybe, just maybe she could sneak into that water and take a little bath without anyone being the wiser. Lynnie brightened at the thought; yes, that's what she would do. The risk of getting caught seemed small compared to staying dirty and sweaty for even an hour longer.

She glanced up at the stars and thought she had never seen such a beautiful night. A soft breeze carried the scent of wildflowers and crushed sage. For a moment, she almost enjoyed her trip, and then reminded herself that she was not here to enjoy being a cowboy; she had a bigger job to do. She would attend the Suffragette Conference and help bring Texas into the coming century even if she had to do it with untamed brutes like Ace Durango, kicking and screaming in protest. Women were smart enough to vote, and it was time they got equal rights with men.

A relief rider came out, a young man from Bandera named Joe. "I'll spell you now, Lee."

"Much obliged." Lynnie nodded and headed back to the campfire. The other rider had already spread his blanket and was drifting off to sleep as she rode up. Old Twister was asleep next to the chuck wagon, probably waiting for morning's vanilla-soaked biscuits. With all the snoring going on, she couldn't decide if it was Twister, Cookie, or that bunch of cowhands.

Lynnie unsaddled Boneyard, rubbed her down, and turned her out to graze. The fire had died down until the night was as black as the inside of a cow. The moon was hidden by scudding clouds. The discordant symphony of snores told her the crew was sound asleep. Maybe if she got some soap and clean clothes, she might manage a bath without anyone being the wiser. It was worth the risk.

Ace opened one eye cautiously and watched the kid gathering up some things from his saddlebags. *What was that Lee up to?* Curiously, he watched the boy tiptoeing away from camp. He lay there a few minutes, listening. The kid hadn't returned. Maybe he had decided to quit this outfit because Ace had been riding him so hard. No, that ugly gray horse was still here grazing on the prairie. Most cowboys couldn't swim. Could Lee have gone to swim, fallen in the water, and drowned? Ace began to worry about the kid's safety, and that annoyed him. He'd never looked out for anyone but himself before.

Silent as his Cheyenne ancestors, Ace crawled out of his blankets, slipped on his boots, and crept down to the creek. Lee Smith stood in knee-deep water with his back to Ace, sudsing himself. Ace knew he shouldn't watch the boy wash; it was giving him a guilty pleasure, which troubled him no end. Not that he could see much in the darkness, except how pale the kid's body was. Then the moon came out from behind a cloud, bathing the scene with moonlight. The boy's pale form was silhouetted against the dark night. Ace felt his groin tighten at the sight, and he cursed at himself and then at Lee Smith for the torment Ace had been through these past few days.

Now the boy was messing with his hair. Long hair? Long *red* hair? Why would a man have long hair? Ace watched in disbelief as the boy shook his hair loose and began to wash it. Then he leaned over and rinsed it. At that moment, the boy turned and was silhouetted against the moon as he stepped up on the creek bank. Ace gasped, staring hard. His mind or his eyes must be playing tricks on him.

Without even thinking, he charged toward the figure, anger and relief mixing in his soul. At the sound of his footsteps, the boy looked up, startled and grabbing for clothes, but it was too late. Cursing, Ace collided with the naked figure, and they went down, rolling and struggling in the dirt of the creek bank. Ace snarled, "What the hell is goin' on?"

The slight figure fought back, and they were a tangle of arms and legs. They went down, Ace on top. He was only too aware of how soft and curved the naked body was. "A girl! You're a girl!"

"Get your dirty paws off me!" Lynnie shrieked.

The camp was shaken awake at the sounds of struggle, cowboys coming up out of their blankets. She was wet and slippery, she knew, but no match for Ace Durango's strength. His hands were all over her slender body as he tried to hang on to her. Cowboys tumbled out of their beds, coming toward the creek, and she was naked as a jaybird.

"Get your dirty paws off me, Ace Durango, or I'll tell your daddy and Maverick."

He stopped dead and she saw the shock, the disbelief, then the anger in his dark eyes. "Why, I'll be God-damned! It's Lynnie McBride. You conniving little bitch!"

Eleven

"Don't you dare call me a bitch! I'll tell your daddy on you!" Lynnie struggled to get away from him, desperate at the way his angry gaze was devouring her. All the men hurrying toward the creek were big-eyed as well. Not knowing what else to do, she sank her white teeth into his hand.

"Ow, you're worse than a coyote!" He turned loose, waving the injured hand. She grabbed for her clothes as the young cowboys came running.

Ace was so stunned, he could only blink and stare in disbelief as she began to dress. He was both angry and dumfounded that the prim old maid was a naked temptress with a cascade of wet fiery hair. True, she might not be as generously endowcd as the women he usually preferred, but when he'd held her softness against him, he'd had a split-second image of making wild, passionate love to her right there on the creek bank. *Make love to Lynnie McBride?* Lordy, had he lost his mind? He'd been too long without a woman. Now his disappointment turned to anger. "Lynnie, I ought to whip your bottom for this!"

"Don't you dare, you brute of a Texan!" She was almost a temptress in her outraged manner as she struggled to get into her pants, hopping about on one foot.

The cowboys gathered on the creek, and abruptly,

Ace didn't want them staring with such eye-popping interest. "You *hombres* go back to camp. There's not much to see; it's just Lynnie McBride."

"Well, I never!" She had her pants on now, looking about nearsightedly for a shirt.

Her breasts might be small, but they were perfect, Ace thought, and was annoyed all over again because his groin had tightened. He handed her a shirt, and she slipped it on as the crew gathered around them. Old Cookie blinked. "What's going on down here?"

Ace reached out and began to button her shirt, even though she was slapping at his hands.

"Stop pawing me, Ace Durango."

"Damn it, I'm not pawing you; I'm just tryin' to protect your dignity." Yes, she was almost attractive when she was mad, he decided.

"Is that what you call wallowing me all over the dirt, and me buck naked?"

The men circled them, eyes bright with curiosity.

"Nekkid?" Joe said, "Did I hear the word 'girl' and 'nekkid'?"

"It's just Lynnie McBride," Ace said, but he couldn't stop staring at her small, angry face. She looked like she might cry. He didn't know if he was feeling relief that he wasn't a nancy-boy after all, or anger with the sneaky female for her deception.

Comanche looked tousled and incredulous. "Lee Smith is a girl?"

Some of the others grinned. "We got a girl travelin' with us?"

"Not *that* kind of girl," Ace let them know quickly. He didn't want anyone getting ideas about crawling into her blankets. Of course, he told himself, it was only because his dad and Uncle Maverick would be furious if any man laid a hand on her. Which was why Ace resisted the urge to grab her and shake her until her teeth rattled. Tears pooled in her eyes, but she squared her small shoulders as she brushed back the wet mop of fiery hair.

Pedro strode up, looking grim. "Ace, you responsible for bringing the *señorita* along?"

Ace was outraged. "If I was gonna sneak a woman on this trip, you think I'd pick *her?"*

Comanche scratched his head and yawned. "She looks purty good to me."

"Comanch," Ace said, "you've been on the trail too long."

At that point, Lynnie kicked Ace in the shins for this insult.

While Ace hopped around on one foot, howling, Lynnie faced the others. "All right; I'll admit it. I sneaked on this cattle drive because I'm trying to get to Dodge City for a women's rights meeting. No man helped me; I was clever enough to dress like a boy, and none of you are too smart if you thought I was for the last couple of weeks."

Pedro sat down on a big rock and stroked his mustache. *"Señorita,* does your brother-in-law know?"

"Of course not. You think Maverick or my big sister would have let me come? I'm independent; I thought this scheme up all by myself." Now she could finally take her cameo pin from her pocket and pin her shirt closed.

"I ought to paddle your butt," Ace said, and quit limping.

Lynnie drew herself up primly. "That's not a nice thing to say to a lady. Anyway, you just try it, you big lummox."

Pedro sighed. "This trouble I did not need. The question remains, *señorita:* what do we do with you?"

Lynnie took a deep breath and looked around at all the curious male faces. "Thunderation, why do you need to do anything? I was carrying my share of the load as Lee Smith; you've got to admit that."

The boys looked at each other and nodded.

"Lordy, girl," Ace said, "that was before. It ain't right and proper for a girl to be travelin' with a dozen men."

Lynnie snorted. "Ace Durango, a rogue and libertine, is lecturing me on what's right and proper?"

His expression told her he was not certain whether he was being insulted. "Lynnie, you and your big words. None of us even know what a 'libertine' is."

"Well, you're a prime example, you irresponsible brute." She bent and began to put on her boots. "I don't see why I can't continue just the way I was doing before."

The young cowboys all looked at each other.

"Look, Lynnie," Ace said patiently, as if he were talking to an idiot, "you can't, because it would ruin your reputation."

"Ha!" She faced him. "After you caused me to go to jail and lose my teaching position, do you think I've got any reputation left?"

The cowboys all looked at Ace with the kind of scornful contempt they might have reserved for some villain who had said, "Forget the Alamo."

"Listen, Miss Priss," Ace fired back, "as I recall, *you* got *me* thrown in jail."

A gasp went up from the cowboys.

Hank said, "Ace, no true Texan would talk to a lady the way you're doin'."

"This *lady,*" Ace said coldly, "keeps gettin' me in trouble, and then I have to take the blame."

"Why, Miss Lynnie," Comanch said, rushing to her defense, "is a sweet, nice girl."

"Ha!" Ace snarled.

Pedro held up his hand for silence. *"Hombres,* none of this matters. What matters is that we are a long way from home. I don't know what to do next."

Ace said, "Why don't we turn this herd around and go home? I've had my fill of Cookie's food and sleepin' on the hard ground when there's eager girls at Miss Fancy's—"

"Ace!" snapped another cowboy, "you shouldn't talk about Miss Fancy's in front of a nice girl like Miss McBride here."

"Hush, *hombres,"* Pedro ordered, and gestured for silence. "I've got to think."

Lynnie glared at Ace. "You're an irresponsible quitter; that's what you are. Here we've promised to take this herd to Dodge City, and you'd let Forrester and Purdy take their herd in while we quit, turn tail, and go home beaten? You're more spoiled than I thought you were."

"Don't talk to me like that, you old maid. You're the one puttin' this drive in trouble."

Cookie said, "Don't you two ever stop yammerin' at each other?"

"Pedro," Lynnie appealed to him, "I've come this far and I've been a good hand. It isn't fair to turn the herd around and disappoint everyone who's counting on us to get these steers to Dodge City."

The old Mexican nodded agreement. *"Sí.* That's true, *señorita."*

The boys were all weakening, Lynnie thought with satisfaction—that is, everyone but Ace. He looked like he'd like to shake her until her teeth fell out.

"Please," she whimpered in her best helpless-female tone. The others looked undecided and sympathetic.

"No!" Ace shouted. "Can't you see how she's playin' all you *hombres?"*

She batted her lashes at all the men. "Now, could a weak, helpless little lady do anything to outsmart a bunch of big, strong cowboys?"

Hank nodded. "I say we let the little lady go on with us."

There was a murmur of agreement from some of the others.

"Lordy, your fellas are dumber than a rock if you can't see what's happenin' here."

Lynnie managed to squeeze out a tear, which trickled down one cheek while she pretended to stifle a sob. "Oh, Ace, you are so mean. Isn't there any way I could change your mind?"

Ace looked around the circle. Even Lynnie could see that he might lose in a vote. "Tell you what, Lynnie, suppose we have a contest, and if you lose, you go back without causin' a lot of fuss."

Lynnie considered. "What kind of contest?"

His eyes brightened, and he actually rubbed his hands in glee. "What about a game of cards? Pedro, you think that'd be fair?"

The cowboys set up a moan of protest. "Hey, Ace, that ain't fair. No woman can best a man at cards, especially you."

Pedro scratched his head. *"Hombres,* I don't know what to do. I never had a problem like this before."

Ace sneered. "Lynnie McBride, you're a yellow-bellied chicken if you don't pick up that dare."

Lynnie ran her tongue over her lips nervously. "What—what kind of cards?"

Comanch objected. "Don't you do it, Miss Lynnie. Ace is the best in all Texas."

Lynnie sniffed. "I imagine he's had plenty of practice, the kind of places he hangs out in. All right, Ace Durango, I accept your challenge."

Ace's eyes gleamed like a crafty fox. "I get to choose the game?"

Cookie shook his head. "Don't let him, Miss Lynnie."

All the cowboys were glaring at Ace for taking advantage of a nice, innocent girl.

Lynnie stuck out her hand. "Done. You pick the game."

Ace stepped back involuntarily. It was obvious that he didn't want to shake hands with a mere girl. In the meantime, the cowboys were grumbling among themselves at his lack of chivalry. He grinned. "I say poker. None of those sissy lady games like whist."

The men all groaned aloud. One of them whispered, "It ain't right for a cardsharp like Ace to take advantage of an innocent little lady like that."

Poker. He was walking right into her trap. Lynnie controlled her smile while looking about innocently. "Poker? Maybe some of the boys will tell me the rules."

Ace made a sweeping gesture. "All right, back to the fire. We'll get this game goin' pronto. I've got a deck."

Cookie started out in the lead. "I'll make a pot of coffee if we're all going to stay up."

"Aw, not that," one of the younger men whispered.

"I heerd that."

Back at the fire, Ace got out a deck of cards, and they all gathered around a big, flat rock. He shuffled the deck and handed it to Lynnie.

She looked at it as if mystified and slipped on her gold-rimmed spectacles. "What am I supposed to do?"

The cowboys gave her pitying looks, but Ace grinned even bigger. "You cut the deck."

"I'm not sure I know how—"

"Here," Comanche reached and took it from her.

"You do it this way, miss, so they'll be mixed up good." He handed the deck back to her.

While smiling innocently, Lynnie ran her thumb down the edge of the cards. Just as she had suspected, this was a marked deck. She could feel the indentations that had been made with a thumbnail on certain cards. "I think I'd like a fresh deck, please." She smiled demurely.

"What?" Ace said. "What's wrong with these?"

Lynnie gave him her widest-eyed look through her spectacles. "Well, these have been played with quite a bit and they're filthy. I think I'd have to wash these off before I'd want to handle them."

The cowboys laughed, and Ace sighed loudly. "Somebody got a nice, clean new deck so the little lady won't get her hands dirty?"

"I do," said Comanch, and ran to get them. He handed them to Lynnie.

"Now, this is more like it," she said, took the joker out of the deck, then began to shuffle the cards expertly. She glanced up and enjoyed the look on Ace's rugged face as she handled the cards. His dark eyes showed first disbelief, then amazement. He had that shocked, deer-in-the-lantern-light expression. Still, she was certain that with his smug masculine superiority, he didn't believe a woman might be a pretty good poker player. "Now, Ace," she said as she handed him the deck to cut, "what's your pleasure? I hear you prefer five-card stud."

A cowboy laughed softly, and some of the others began to grin. Ace, for once, seemed speechless. "What—whatever you choose."

"Deuces wild, okay?"

Ace only blinked and nodded as he handed the deck back.

Lynnie smiled. "Cut for first deal?"

Again he only nodded, still blinking. He reached and took a card: three of diamonds. Lynnie smiled and took a card: queen of hearts.

"Well, now," she said and shuffled the cards again. She began to deal the hand expertly, one card facedown for him, one card facedown for her. Then she flipped him a card faceup: jack of diamonds. Her next card was a ten of spades. She kept dealing, and as she dealt, his smile grew bigger. He had two jacks and two queens showing. She picked up her cards, wondering what his bottom card might be.

"All right, Miss Priss, now I'll show you how to play poker." He looked at his bottom card and grinned, then began to chew his lip.

Lynnie said nothing. She had two tens and two eights showing. Not so good. She looked at her bottom card and almost yelled for joy. Then she remembered she must not let him know what a great hand she held. "Okay, Ace, what's the bet?"

"You—you played this game before?" His expression told her he refused to believe that he might be about to be taken by a woman.

"A time or two with the boys in the bunkhouse." She grinned at him, and around them the cowboys chuckled.

It was easy to see that Ace was off his game, unable to concentrate. Lynnie kept her face grim. He must not guess how good her hand was. "What's your bet?" she asked again.

"My gold watch." He took it out of his pocket and laid it on the rock.

"All right, I'll take that bet—your gold watch against my best cameo pin." She reached up, unpinned it from the neck of her shirt, and laid it on the rock.

Ace snorted. "Now what would I do with a lady's jewelry?"

"I don't know—maybe give it to your favorite whore at Miss Fancy's."

Ace choked audibly. "Ladies don't know about things like that."

"Oh, don't be so stiff-necked," Lynnie scolded. "I've spent too much time around cowboys."

He snorted. "Obviously, the *wrong* cowboys if they taught a lady about poker and Miss Fancy's. You know, with my bottom card, I might have a full house. A full house is—"

"Don't explain," she said, "I know what a full house is. Are you calling me?" The cameo had held her shirt closed. Now she leaned so that he got a good look down the front of her shirt.

It was evident he was so rattled, he couldn't keep his mind on his cards. He looked at his hole card again and began to chew his lip. That told her he was bluffing; the bottom card was worthless. "Yes, I'm callin.'"

She turned over her bottom card, and the cowboys took an audible breath. "Full house," she said triumphantly, "Read 'em and weep. You got anything better?"

Ace blinked, looking at his hand, and shook his head dumbly as he stared at her cards. "Two pair," he admitted, and tossed in his hand.

"Thought so." She raked the watch and cameo to her and tossed her cards in. "Your deal, and let me caution you, I know about dealing from the bottom of the deck."

"You ain't accusin' me of cheatin'?"

She looked at him in wide-eyed innocence. "Now, did I say that?"

Ace shuffled the deck, but his hands were trembling uncertainly. It had to be evident to all concerned that he was off his game. "Cut it."

Lynnie cut the deck and handed it back to him. It was

so quiet, she could hear the crackle of the fire, and some of the cowboys breathing.

Ace dealt the hand. She had an ace, king, queen, and jack, all of the same suit: hearts. She sneaked a look at her hole card and frowned as if it were a bad card.

Ace looked down at his face cards. He had three aces and one king showing, different suits. He turned up the corner of his hole card and began to chew his lip again.

Lynnie picked up her cards and watched Ace. If he had a king as a hole card, he'd have a full house; but watching him, she knew he was bluffing, because he was so tense he was chewing his lip. "Let's make this worth while and get this over with." She looked into his eyes, taunting him by running her tongue over her lips.

"Stop that," he muttered, "you make it hard to keep my mind on the game."

"What?" She fluttered her eyelashes innocently.

"Damn it, you know what I mean."

She ran her tongue over her lips again, this time even more tantalizingly. "I say let's make the bet a big one. Let's bet our bedrolls."

The cowboys set up a chorus of moans. "No, Miss Lynnie, he's mean enough to take it and make you sleep on the ground."

"What about it, Ace?" she taunted him.

"My bedroll?" He sounded a little desperate, and sweat broke out on his handsome face. She studied him, reading him like a book. He was bluffing, all right. He didn't have that king he needed.

"Maybe I'll raise the stakes a bit," Lynnie said, and leaned forward a little. Without the cameo holding it, the top of her shirt gaped open, and she knew it. "What about letting me come along on the trip, our bedrolls, and shutting up about how dumb women are?"

He looked at his hand again and grinned. "And if I win, I get your bedroll and send you home?"

She nodded.

A murmur of dismay went up from the cowboys. "Oh, Miss Lynnie, watch out. Ace is the best poker player in the county."

"So he thinks," she said, and didn't smile.

Ace leaned back against a rock. "I think you're bluffin', missy. I call you."

She smiled. "You gotta know when to hold them and know when to fold them." There was a sharp intake of breath as Lynnie laid her cards slowly on the flat rock. "All I've got are this ace, this king, a lady, and what do you call this one?"

Ace's eyes were wide with shock. "A jack."

"Oh, and a number card." She laid down the ten of hearts. "Is it important that they all are hearts?"

"A royal flush," Cookie whispered in disbelief.

Ace began to curse under his breath, and the cowboys chuckled and nudged each other.

Lynnie batted her eyes at Ace again. "Does that mean I win?"

Ace tossed his cards down, swearing mightily. "Yes, damn it, you win. I can't believe I've just been beaten by a girl. You must be the luckiest player in the world."

She smiled. "Or maybe one of the smartest, even though I'm just a woman?" She stood up, putting the gold watch in her pocket and pinning the cameo at the neck of her shirt to protect her modesty.

She got no answer, because Ace got up, so obviously angry that he kicked their rock table and then hopped about on one foot, howling and swearing.

"It just goes to show," Lynnie said, brushing off her pants, "that a woman is equal to a man and ought to have equal rights, including the right to vote."

Take A Trip Into A Timeless World of Passion and Adventure with Kensington Choice Historical Romances!
—Absolutely FREE!

Enjoy the passion and adventure of another time with Kensington Choice Historical Romances. They are the finest novels of their kind, written by today's best-selling romance authors. Each Kensington Choice Historical Romance transports you to distant lands in a bygone age. Experience the adventure and share the delight as proud men and spirited women discover the wonder and passion of true love.

4 BOOKS WORTH UP TO $24.96— Absolutely FREE!

Get 4 FREE Books!

We created our convenient Home Subscription Service so you'll be sure to have the hottest new romances delivered each month right to your doorstep—usually before they are available in book stores. Just to show you how convenient the Zebra Home Subscription Service is, we would like to send you 4 FREE Kensington Choice Historical Romances. The books are worth up to $24.96, but you only pay $1.99 for shipping and handling. There's no obligation to buy additional books—ever!

Save Up To 30% With Home Delivery!

Accept your FREE books and each month we'll deliver 4 brand new titles as soon as they are published. They'll be yours to examine FREE for 10 days. Then if you decide to keep the books, you'll pay the preferred subscriber's price (up to 30% off the cover price!), plus shipping and handling. Remember, you are under no obligation to buy any of these books at any time! If you are not delighted with them, simply return them and owe nothing. But if you enjoy Kensington Choice Historical Romances as much as we think you will, pay the special preferred subscriber rate and save over $8.00 off the cover price!

4 FREE

Kensington
Choice
Historical
Romances
(worth up to
$24.96)
are waiting
for you to
claim them!

See details
inside....

KENSINGTON CHOICE
Zebra Home Subscription Service, Inc.
P.O. Box 5214
Clifton NJ 07015-5214

"You stacked that deck!" Ace snarled. "You cheated."

The cowboys' mouths dropped open. "Ace, a true Texan would never accuse a lady—"

"With you doing the dealing? No, you low-lifed varmint," Lynnie said, "you tried to give me a deck of marked cards. Now admit it." Lynnie, confronting Ace, looked up at him towering over her. "I was clever enough to beat you fair and square."

Ace closed his eyes and groaned aloud. "You *hombres* see what you're lettin' us in for? Forget the cards; I vote we send this sneaky little old maid home if we have to cancel the drive."

"Why, you cheat!" Lynnie snapped, angry at the injustice of it all. "You're a rotten sport, Ace Durango, besides being a spoiled woman-chaser. I'm not only a better poker player, I've been doing my share of the work, and you just don't want to admit that a woman might be your equal."

He towered over her. "Ain't no bit of skirt my equal, and if we had to have a woman along on this drive, Lynnie, you wouldn't be my choice."

"Ha, the kind of woman you'd chose never gets off her back!"

The cowboys chortled with laughter at her spirit. "She's a sassy piece, ain't she?"

"'Isn't she?'" Lynnie corrected primly. "What about it, Pedro?"

The old Mexican sighed, then nodded. "She won fair and square, and Ace, you made the deal yourself. Besides, she's been pullin' her share of the load without complaint."

Ace howled in protest. "I say no; *N-O*. We ain't turnin' this cattle drive into a petticoat outfit. Why, the Forrester bunch will laugh themselves silly when we pull into Dodge with a girl along."

"Coward!" she shot back. "You afraid of being laughed at?"

"Lady," he said coldly, "in Texas, when you call a man a coward, you better be able to fight."

She doubled up her fists. "Oh, you'd hit a lady, would you? Very well, put up your dukes!"

Ace looked around at the other men helplessly. "You see what we're dealin' with?" Then to her, "Lynnie, you know I can't fight no girl; I'd be the laughingstock of the Lone Star State."

"Put up or shut up," Lynnie commanded. "You're the one who made the bet when you thought I didn't know the game. By the way, when you've got a bad hand, you chew your lip, even though you're smiling. Any good poker player should spot that. You've been outplayed and, better yet, outsmarted."

"Of all the sassy women in the world, how was I unlucky enough to end up with you on this drive? I ought to whip your butt and teach you proper respect," Ace growled.

"Just try it, mister."

The other cowboys looked at each other.

Hank said, "The little lady's got spunk. You know, Texans like that in their women. She beat Ace; we all saw that. Pedro, I think we should let her finish the drive."

Ace slapped his forehead in frustration. "No!" he protested. "This woman has been the bane of my life ever since my folks made me take her to that dance. She'll make my life a livin' hell all the way to Dodge City."

Lynnie grinned at the thought. She'd be delighted to fulfill that dire prediction.

The other cowboys mumbled among themselves and began to nod. Cookie said, "She won fair and square."

"Sí," Pedro said, "and Ace made the bet."

"Can't you see what she's doin'?" Ace looked around the circle in frustration. "Lordy, are you *hombres* loco? We can't treat her like an equal; she's a petticoat."

Lynnie let her eyes fill with tears that ran down her cheeks. "You're just plain mean, and me a defenseless woman. Worse than that, you welsh on a bet."

He was speechless on that one. "Well," he stammered, "the bet didn't count, 'cause you're a girl."

"I'm a *Texas* girl." She turned in mute appeal to the men. Texans believed in fair play.

Now all the men turned and glared at Ace—even Pedro. *"Hombre,* stop picking on the poor little *señorita."*

"She started it," Ace said. "How come she keeps gettin' me in trouble but I get the blame?"

Lynnie cried some more.

"Enough!" Pedro thundered. *"Hombres,* we let the *señorita* go along to Dodge City."

The boys cheered, but Ace groaned aloud. "We'll regret it. You fellas just don't know Lynnie McBride like I do."

Cookie yawned. "I think it's time we all get some shut-eye. Mornin's comin' purty soon."

The others got up and started for their bedrolls.

Lynnie wiped her eyes and grinned at Ace.

"I knew it," he growled. "Like any woman, you'll use tears to get what you want while whinin' about equal rights."

She sniffed primly and turned to go.

"You are sneaky." He walked along behind her.

"And smart?"

"Well, I reckon you're that, too," he admitted grudgingly.

"Hah! I never thought I'd hear you say that. You yelling 'calf-roped'?"

In Texas, "calf-roped" was admitting defeat.

"Not on your tintype, Lynnie." He grabbed her arm and whirled her around. "I want to be there to say, 'I told you so' to this crew when they get sick of havin' a girl along."

She tried to pull out of his grasp, but his big hand was too strong. They were standing close together—too close. She could smell the hot male scent of him and see the full, sensual lips. It stirred something inside her that startled her. "Oh, by the way, you bet your bedroll, remember?"

He gasped and let go of her, his eyes full of horrified disbelief. "You'd take a man's bedroll and make him sleep on the hard ground?"

"You were planning to do it to me. You welshing on this bet?"

"It's not that; it's just the ground's pretty hard—"

"You welshing on the bet?" She was standing too close to him, but to step backward would be to admit defeat. She kept looking into his eyes, knowing that if a man had said that, Ace probably would have killed him. There were some advantages to being a girl.

"Don't push me too hard, Lynnie. I've had about as much as I can take of you."

He was towering over her, standing so close, his muscular chest was almost brushing against her breasts. She crossed her arms across her chest. "Admit I'm smart."

"Okay," he conceded, "for a woman, you're smart."

"No qualifiers," she insisted.

"What?"

"That means"—she said it slowly and patiently as if talking to an small child—"admit I'm smart as you are."

He shook his head.

"Then give me your bedroll." She held out her hand.

"All right; you're almost as smart as a man."

She raised one eyebrow.

"Okay, maybe you're as smart as some men."

"Maybe?" she laughed. "All right. I'll consider you've yelled 'calf-roped' and let you keep your blankets."

"I didn't yell calf-roped."

"Yes, you did, in so many words. Oh, by the way, I don't have any use for a gold watch, so I'm generous enough to return it." She tossed it to him and started walking back to the fire, humming in satisfaction.

"I did not yell 'calf-roped'!" he yelled after her.

Lynnie grinned to herself and kept walking. She knew she could only push him so far, but this evening had been a triumph for all women against all arrogant male brutes. She'd hold up her end of the work, all right, but if she could make Ace Durango's life miserable the next few weeks, she vowed she would surely do it.

Twelve

The next morning, Lynnie felt a decided difference in the air. Although she was still dressed in boy's pants and denim shirt, the rough, uncivilized cowboys now seemed self-conscious around her. Why, they were acting halfway civilized, Lynnie thought with surprise as she rolled up her bedroll. As she struggled to lift her heavy stock saddle and carry it over to her horse, half a dozen cowhands rushed up.

"Here, ma'am, let me get that for you."

"Miss McBride, I'd be glad to saddle your horse."

"Miss Lynnie, a little thing like you oughtn't to be carryin' that heavy saddle."

"Let her carry it," Ace ordered, his voice as grim as his face. "She wants to be a man's equal; let her prove it."

"I can and I will," Lynnie snapped, and lugged her own saddle across the circle.

Behind her, she heard grumbling among the men. "What's eatin' Ace? It ain't right to let a little lady carry a big saddle while a bunch of men watch her."

She glanced back over her shoulder at Ace. She could see the disgusted looks among the cowboys. Even old Cookie was giving her a look of sympathy. Oh, she was going to make that big brute of a Texan pay for his stubborn superiority.

They saddled up and got the herd moving. The May weather was hot and dusty, and water scarce as they trailed a day or so behind the Forrester herd. She made sure she did more than her share of the work, and she caught the cowboys giving her admiring looks. That is, all except Ace. If looks could kill, she'd surely be dead by now.

That night when they camped, the cowboys were all on their best behavior: no belching or breaking wind in her presence, and there were no ribald jokes. In fact, they all seemed to be watching her with embarrassment, as if remembering some of the ungentlemanly behavior the past several weeks before they had realized there was a girl among them. That is, all but Ace. If anything, he was even more rude and uncivilized to her. She'd heard how charming he could be to women, but danged if she saw any of it. He seemed determined to make her life as miserable as possible. Well, she could give him tit for tat, she promised herself.

Cookie even seemed to have sobered up some, although old Twister was as drunk as ever on vanilla-soaked biscuits. "I suppose you think you'd like to take over my chuck wagon?"

She gave him her most charming smile. "Why, me? No, Cookie, I could never cook the way you do."

That was the god-awful truth, she thought, remembering last night's meal. "Of course, if you'd want me to do the lowly stuff like slice bacon and clean pans—"

"Couldn't ask a lady to do that." The old man ducked his head, smiling shyly. "Now that I think of it, Miss Lynnie, I'd admire to have you give me a hand. I hear as how you're the best pie baker in south Texas."

Ace glowered at her. "I'll admit she's that. In fact, that's where she belongs—in a kitchen, rustlin' up grub for the unlucky man who'd get hitched to her."

Comanch sighed wistfully. "Miss Lynnie, any man who got you would be lucky."

"Comanch," said Ace sternly, "you been on the trail too long."

Lynnie smiled sweetly around the circle at the cowboys, and in turn, they all glared at Ace. He retreated to a rock, sat down and began to roll himself a smoke.

"Now," Lynnie said, rolling up her sleeves, "I believe we passed some sand plum bushes about a half mile back. I might ride there and get enough for a pie."

Most of the boys jumped to their feet, taking off their Stetsons with a sweeping gesture. "Miss Lynnie, I'd be proud to accompany you."

"No, I'll ride back with her—"

"Dagnab it, I spoke first—"

"Hey, I'm the best plum picker there is," another protested.

"You can all go with me," Lynnie said grandly.

Ace didn't smile. "Don't look at me to help. It appears to me ten or twelve skirt-addled *hombres* is plenty to pick a few sand plums."

She gave him her coldest, haughtiest stare. "We can do this without you, thank you."

Immediately, all the cowboys pushed and shoved to see who would be the fortunate one to help her up on her horse. Then they all mounted up and rode out.

Behind her, she heard Ace griping to Pedro. "Damn it, she's disruptin' everything, that gol-darned female."

She turned in her saddle and yelled back, "I heered that!"

The cowboys guffawed, and she knew she had won another round. Of course, she really shouldn't rile Ace Durango. He'd already lost the first round, and she shouldn't be rubbing all this in—he was already almost impossible to deal with. One thing was certain:

he'd never follow her around like a puppy dog like these other cowboys were doing. Maybe this was one Texan who couldn't be tamed, nor did she want to try. He wasn't at all like the genteel gentleman spouting poetry and playing croquet that she read about in romantic novels. The kind of man she dreamed of would be named Percival or Felix, would accompany her to violin concerts and encourage her in her women's rights work.

They returned to camp with more sand plums than they could possibly use. Old Cookie's eyes lit up when he saw the hats full. "If we had time, we'd make some wine."

Pedro shook his head. "No, *hombre,* no wine."

Ace glared at her. "We ain't gonna be on the trail that long."

She fed a handful to Boneyard and petted her. The lead steer, Twister, ambled over, stuck his muzzle in a hat, and began eating plums.

"Shoo! Shoo!" Lynnie chased the old steer away. "Now, you gentlemen wash up for supper, and Cookie and I will get a meal together."

"Wash?" Ace said. "We just washed yesterday."

Lynnie sighed. "I know this might surprise you, Mr. Durango, but gentlemen wash every day, even when they're not going to Miss Fancy's."

The others laughed and headed over to the little stream to wash up.

Ace seemed to dig in his heels. "I ain't gonna wash up."

"Then kindly stay downwind from me," Lynnie said, and reached into the back of the chuck wagon for a can of flour.

"You've turned the whole crew against me," Ace muttered.

"I have done nothing of the sort." Lynnie began to mix her pie dough. "They see it as a matter of fairness."

"No, they don't. They have been on the trail without any women around for several weeks, and now you're beginnin' to look like Lillian Russell to them instead of a skinny little schoolmarm."

Cookie paused in peeling potatoes. "That ain't no way to talk to a lady. I ought to tell your daddy on you."

Ace glared at Lynnie. "You see what I mean?"

With an oath, he got up and went out to sit on a rock and smoke. Lynnie sneaked a glance at him as she rolled pie dough. Did he really hate her so much? Why, when all the others were so nice and so eager to please her, did that ornery cowboy act so contrary? One thing was certain: a respectable woman would find it difficult to put a bridle on that mustang. Pity the poor girl who got stuck with him.

Between them, she and Cookie turned out a meal that was mouthwatering, even if she did say so herself.

She noted, as she dished up the tin plates, that every cowboy except Ace had curried and groomed himself. Their hands were clean, their hair combed, and they had even shaved. Some of them reeked of cheap hair tonic. Ace looked like a dirty barbarian by contrast. "You look like a saddle tramp," she complained as she ladled out the stew.

"You may turn all these others into fawnin' little nancy-boys, Lynnie McBride, but you ain't makin' me act like some lady-broke nag."

"That," she announced coldly, "is the furthest thing from my mind."

"Fine." He took the plate and began to eat. "Hey, this ain't half bad."

"Even modern women who want equal rights can

learn to cook," she answered loftily. "Let's see the girls at Miss Fancy's match that."

"The girls at Miss Fancy's don't have to cook to interest men," Ace shot back.

"And they don't care how many men they interest as long as you plunk down your money," Lynnie pointed out.

The other cowboys were all glaring at Ace again.

Pedro said, *"Hombre,* leave the little lady alone."

"She started it."

Cookie said, "She only asked you to wash up. We got a lady among us; we ought to be a little more gallant."

"I'm gonna hate the rest of this trip," Ace said, and got up.

"Sit back down," Lynnie said, "or you'll miss out on the hot plum pie."

"I don't want any of your damned pie." He stalked away from the campfire, went out a ways from camp, and rolled and lit a cigarette.

Lynnie watched him. He looked as puffed up as a riled horny toad, blowing smoke in short, angry spurts. To hell with him. "Who's for pie, boys?"

Immediately, she drew a crowd of cowboys. "My, that do smell good, Miss Lynnie."

"Miss Lynnie, I'll bet you bake the best pie in all Texas."

"Well, I've won a few ribbons at the county fair," she admitted modestly.

She served up pie, waiting for Ace to come back to the circle, but he continued to sit out on the rock and smoke. He was not only arrogant, he had enough pride to choke a horse. She thought about it a minute and hid the last slice of pie in the back of the chuck wagon.

Cookie saw her do it. "You savin' that for him?"

She felt her face flush. "Of course not. It's just that

there's a slice left and you might offer it to him when he gets off his mad."

Cookie nodded somberly. "He's an awful proud man, Miss Lynnie."

She snorted. "Don't I know it! And undoubtedly the most uncivilized, annoying cuss I ever met."

"You know," the old man said, "it's them wild mustangs that make the best stock when someone finally manages to break them."

"Humph! I wouldn't wish that stallion on anyone." She turned on her heel and went over to the fire, where all the cowboys promptly stood up awkwardly.

"Miss Lynnie, can we get you anything?"

"Miss Lynnie, that was a mighty fine supper."

"Miss Lynnie, here, take my seat, it's closer to the fire."

"Thank you, fellows; you may continue your conversation."

Several faces turned brick red.

Hank stammered, "Miss Lynnie, we was jokin' around—nothin' fittin' for a lady's ears."

"You didn't hold back when you thought I was Lee Smith," she reminded them.

"We're powerful sorry about that, Miss Lynnie," Comanche gulped, "but we can't be tellin' rowdy jokes that ain't fittin' for a lady to hear."

"Well, then, sing some cowboy songs."

Hank broke out a guitar and they sang about the streets of Laredo and dogies and hard trails.

Out of the corner of her eye, she watched Ace. He finally returned from his perch on the rock. Cookie signaled him from the chuck wagon. At first, Ace shook his head, but Cookie insisted. When Ace strode over, Cookie handed him the pie tin with the last piece of plum pie and a cup of coffee. Ace looked her way as if to check and see if she was watching. Lynnie made no sign that she was.

He took a bite. He looked surprised and smiled. Now he was licking the fork. Lynnie winced at his manners but gave no sign that she saw him. Ace dug into the pie again, gobbling like a starving wolf. He did everything but lick the pie pan. It only surprised her that the uncivilized brute didn't do that, too. It occurred to Lynnie that pie or no pie, Ace intended to make the rest of this trip a living hell for her, and it was still a long, long way to Dodge City.

Well, she could go toe to toe with him on that. Once she got to her suffragette meeting, she didn't care if she ever saw that half-breed varmint again, but she was going to have to deal with him day in and day out for hundreds of miles. He knew it, too, and would be as ornery and contrary as a billy goat. What could she do to break that rascal's resistance so he'd treat her halfway decently for the remainder of the trip? She was smart; she'd find a way.

The next morning as the camp was stirring, one of the nighthawks rode in from the herd. "Hey, Pedro, we got three or four new baby calves last night."

Pedro groaned. "You know what to do; it can't be helped, *hombre.*"

Lynnie caught the reluctance in both men's faces. "Wait a minute; what do we do?"

Ace shook his head at her. "Lynnie, we can't be burdened with calves; they don't walk fast enough to keep up with the herd."

She had an uneasy feeling as she looked around the circle. All the cowboys were avoiding her eyes. "So what do we do with them?"

Pedro started to speak, hesitated, then looked at Ace in mute appeal.

Ace chewed his lip. "They can't keep up, and the cows will stay with them unless . . ."

"Unless what?"

"Lynnie," Ace said, looking annoyed at having to be the one to tell her, "we can't leave the cows behind, and they won't leave a live calf. Hasn't your brother-in-law ever told you what they do with calves that happen to be unlucky enough to be born on a drive?"

She shook her head, but she had an uneasy feeling deep inside. "You don't mean kill them?"

Pedro shrugged and sighed. "It can't be helped, *señorita.* I'm sorry."

"No," she said firmly, "we'll take them along, even if we have to load them up in the chuck wagon."

Ace snorted. "I reckon old grumpy Cookie would have a hissy fit about that."

"I heered that! If Miss Lynnie wants to haul calves in the back of my chuck wagon, it's all right with me."

All the cowboys looked at each other, eyes wide with disbelief.

Ace shook his head. "It still wouldn't do any good, Lynnie. Any cowboy knows it's almost impossible to get a cow to suckle any calf but her own, and after you've mixed them up in the chuck wagon, how can they identify their own calf?"

Pedro nodded toward Comanche, who turned toward the herd with reluctance.

"Wait!" Lynnie threw up her hands to stop him. "There has to be a way."

"Look, Lynnie." Ace's voice was almost gentle. "None of us cotton to killin' baby calves, but—"

"I know what to do!" She laughed with relief. "I've got a bunch of ribbons in my saddle bags. Penelope

Dinwiddy sent them along for me to match dress goods."

Pedro blinked. "Ribbons? *Senorita,* I don't *comprendo. . . ."*

"It's simple." She hurried to rummage in her saddle bags. "I tie a ribbon to a cow's horn, then a matching one around her calf's neck. At night, we just match them all back up; that's all."

Ace groaned and pushed his hat back. "Lordy, I can't believe I'm hearin' this. You want tough cowboys to decorate up a bunch of cows and calves like play-pretties?"

Lynnie gave the cowboy a beseeching look. "Please, Ace."

He looked surprised at her begging. Then he looked at Pedro. "I reckon it might work; what do you think?"

Pedro shrugged. "We can try, if it would make the lady happy."

Ace sighed in defeat. "Okay, Miss Priss, get your ribbons and come on. We'll tie up them cows like they was ladies goin' to a dance."

"Those cows," she corrected, and went running for her horse. The nighthawk led them out to where he had found the new calves. The tiny brown beasts trembled on unsteady legs as they nursed.

"Oh, aren't they precious!" Lynnie exclaimed before she thought.

"Just precious," Ace agreed, and seemed to be stifling a grin. "Now, Lynnie, you stay on your horse. These old longhorns don't cotton to anyone messin' with their babies." He dismounted and turned toward her. "Give me your damned ribbon."

"I think pink would be nice for the first pair." she handed him two strands of pink ribbon. Their fingers brushed, and he glanced up, as startled as she was.

For a long moment, they stared at each other, and as

she looked down at him, she realized again how full and sensual his mouth was. As the moment lengthened, it grew awkward, and she laughed. "The calf," she reminded him.

"Oh, yeah." Very gingerly he turned and approached the calf. The mother lowered her head and gave out a warning bellow.

"I must be loco," Ace muttered under his breath. "I'm gonna get myself kilt over a damned calf that wouldn't bring a dollar in Dodge City."

"I think you're very brave to do this," she encouraged behind him.

"Humph! Tell that to my dad when you take my body home."

He slipped the ribbon around the calf's neck and tied it in a knot. "That suit you?"

"You could tie it in a bow," she suggested.

"Damn, Lynnie"—he looked back at her in exasperation—"you're gonna get me killed yet." But he tied the ribbon in a bow. "Give me the other pink ribbon."

She leaned from her saddle and handed it over. When she leaned, she knew he was getting a good view of the soft rise of her breasts, but she pretended she didn't. She had to soften him up somehow, she reasoned. He blinked, took a deep breath, grabbed the ribbon, and turned toward the suspicious longhorn.

"Hey, old cow," Ace crooned softly, "let me hang this on your horn without you guttin' me, okay?"

The cow didn't look like she planned to cooperate.

"Ace," Lynnie suggested, "why don't you make a big bow and drop it over her horn?"

Ace turned and looked at her. "Who's doin' this?"

"I merely thought . . ."

"Let me do the thinkin'. You've gotten me in enough

trouble with this dad-blamed idea." Very slowly he reached out and tied the ribbon on the cow's sharp horn. "Now, distract her and I'll grab the calf."

Lynnie took off her hat and waved it in the cow's face. Immediately, the half-wild cow charged at her, and Lynnie turned the flea-bitten gray horse and galloped away. The cow followed her . . . until she heard her calf bawl behind her. Ace grabbed up the baby and mounted up, laying the calf across the front of his saddle before him. With the calf bellowing and the cow lowing, they all headed back to the chuck wagon.

The cowboys began to laugh as they rode up. "Hey, Ace, you look right purty with that beribboned calf. Wouldn't they give a play-pretty to see this sight back home?"

"They better not hear about it back home," Ace said, and his glare seemed to send fear through the cowboys. "Here, Cookie." He handed the calf over, and the old man placed it in the back of the chuck wagon. The cow hung around, bellowing.

Lynnie smiled. "See? She'll follow along. Don't worry, mama cow, you can have him back later."

Ace looked up to heaven as if beseeching the Almighty's help. "Okay, boys, where's the others?"

They got the second one without incident. Lynnie, after much thought, used matching lavender ribbons on this cow and calf. Then they went out for the third one, which they decorated in blue. Finally, they found a fourth one.

Ace leaned on his saddle horn and shook his head. "Lordy! That's the ugliest calf I ever did see."

Lynnie stared. The calf was runty, knock-kneed, and so weak it could barely stand. Worse than that, it was cross-eyed, which gave it a comical expression. "This is my calf," she announced. "I'm going to keep her."

"This ugly calf?" Ace snorted, and got down from his horse. "Well, it don't make me no never-mind."

"She may not be beautiful, but she's got personality," Lynnie said. "I'm going to named her Daisy Buttercup."

The ugly calf looked toward Lynnie—at least she thought it was looking toward her—with its crossed eyes and bawled loudly.

"See?" Lynnie said. "She likes the name."

"Uh-huh. Give me the ribbon."

She sorted through the ribbons while the old cow lowered her horns. "I think yellow would be a good color for a calf named Daisy Buttercup."

Ace looked back over his shoulder at the threatening cow. "Lynnie, if you don't give me the damned ribbon—"

"You don't need to lose your temper with me." She handed over the ribbon.

"You've delayed the drive for over two hours for four calves that ain't worth a dollar apiece," Ace griped. "I told everyone you'd be a pain to have along, but would they believe me? No, they're all suckers for a woman's tears."

"Oh, hush and give Daisy her ribbon."

Ace sighed and shook his head, and approached the cow slowly. "Here, you walkin' beefsteak, I'm gonna pretty you up."

Lynnie watched him tie the ribbon on the cow and calf. Then, very gently he lifted Daisy Buttercup and carried her over to his horse, the mama cow bawling in protest behind them.

Ace said, "Cookie won't like having four old mama cows trailing along behind the chuck wagon all day."

"He won't mind," she answered. "He likes me."

"Humph." Ace mounted up and they headed back to camp.

"Ace," she said softly as they rode.

"What?" He sounded more than a little annoyed, the cross-eyed, ribbon bedecked Daisy Buttercup bawling across his saddle.

"I just wanted to tell you I'm much obliged for your doing this for me. I couldn't bear to have them kill the calves."

"Don't mention it." He looked over at her, and for a moment he almost smiled. "I didn't want to kill 'em, either, but they'll be a lot of trouble—much more than they're worth."

"We'll put them all in the chuck wagon," she said.

He laughed. "They'll never believe this back home."

Soon they had all four calves in the chuck wagon with four bawling, complaining cows trotting along behind as the big herd got back on the trail. It was a long, hot day, but they made good time.

That night when they camped, Ace got the calves out of the chuck wagon for her, and she matched them up to their respective mamas. He watched her fussing over each one, and her tenderness stirred something in him. In spite of her crusade for women's rights, there was something very feminine and gentle about Lynnie. He softened a little toward her, thinking she was a lot like his ma. Then he was annoyed with himself for being sentimental, because he didn't intend to give an inch to this confounded petticoat.

Cookie grinned. "Now ain't that sweet?" he asked as he watched the beribboned calves nurse.

"Just precious," Ace said sarcastically, and went off into the bush to relieve himself. It was such a nuisance having a girl along. Everyone had to watch his language and his manners, and no longer could a man just unbutton his pants and do what came naturally—not with a girl along.

What really annoyed him was that he'd found himself watching Lynnie McBride all day whenever he didn't think she was looking. Had he never noticed before that her hair reflected light like flames? When she rode past him, he was aware of the roundness of her bottom and how soft her skin looked. He'd never thought freckles appealing before. "Careful, *hombre*," he cautioned himself, "don't let her soften you up and make a lapdog out of you like she's doin' these other loco fools. Keep remembering how hot those busty tarts in the saloons in Dodge City will be—and they'll know how to please a man. Lynnie McBride's never even be kissed."

It would be exciting to the man to show her how, he thought, and then was both surprised and annoyed with himself for that idea. "Lynnie McBride is a stubborn, prim old maid, and no man would want to spend his whole life havin' his grammar corrected and his neck checked for dirt."

Lynnie enjoyed her day chasing stray cattle and adding them back to the herd. Once in a while, she returned to the chuck wagon to check on the calves. Cookie grinned at her and waved. "They're fine, Miss Lynnie; I'm seein' to that."

She gave him her warmest smile. "I knew I could count on you, Cookie." She rode on next to Pedro. "Things going well?"

The Mexican trail boss nodded. "*Sí*. In two or three days, we should make the Red River and be in Indian Territory."

She noted his concerned look. "What's the matter?"

Pedro shook his head. "Worst river on this whole trail. The Red's drowned many a good cowboy tryin' to get a herd across."

She had a sudden picture in her mind of cattle churning up the water, horses caught in the confusion or the current. "We've got you, Pedro, and you'll get us through."

"*Sí,* I've crossed the Red before. I know the shallow spots."

"That's good, since everyone else is so green." She rode on, assured, and reined in next to Ace. He was so sweaty, his shirt was plastered against every inch of his muscular, virile body. She remembered what he looked like stripped down naked.

"Lordy, girl, what's the matter? Your face is as red as a deacon who got caught with his hand in the collection plate."

"Nothing," she stammered. "I—I just wanted to thank you for saving the calves."

He shrugged and grunted.

She studied his body. His pants were tight and his body muscular. The way he gripped that big horse with his thighs betrayed the strength of the man. She glanced toward his crotch, and her eyes widened at the way he filled out those denims. An image crossed her mind of this big, sweaty man naked, and the thought shocked her. Why should she care what he looked like naked and sweating? "Uh, Pedro says we'll be at the Red River in a couple of days."

Ace nodded. "Glad we got him with us. They say the Red's a killer if you don't know what you're doin'."

She saw a drop of sweat run down his sinewy neck and into the open neck of his denim shirt. She'd like to see him without that shirt. *Lynnie, what are you thinking?* she scolded herself. *Why, you're not much better than the girls at Miss Fancy's.* She wondered what it was Ace did to please them. She had a sudden image of his sensual, dark body spread out on white sheets, with those hard hands reaching for her soft, virginal body.

Ace stared at her. "What's the matter, Lynnie? You look as nervous as a long-tailed cat in a room full of rockin' chairs."

"Nothing." His naked image unnerved her so, that she put spurs to her horse and galloped on down the herd of lowing cattle.

That afternoon, a wind came up, blowing swirling dust devils across the rolling prairie.

Pedro frowned and shook his head. "This is not good. Blowing tumbleweeds spook cattle."

"Maybe we should camp early?" Ace asked.

"Sí. Pass the word," Pedro said. "I think there's a creek up ahead."

Lynnie heard the news with a tired sigh. She wouldn't want to admit how weary she was, but she'd like a chance to rinse off and maybe wash out some of her un-mentionables. Maybe she could find some bushes to hang them on where the men wouldn't see them. It wasn't fitting for men to see freshly laundered personal items like a lady's underpants.

The cattle were restless in the wind, stamping their hooves and bellowing.

Pedro yelled, "We'll need double guards tonight, *hombres.* It won't take much to set them off and start a stampede."

The boys hurried to set up camp, and she helped Cookie with a quick meal that had more than a little grit in it. The western sun had turned red on the distant prairie horizon.

Ace looked worried. "Pedro says to keep your horses saddled, boys, in case anything spooks the cattle tonight."

"If nobody minds," Lynnie said, "I'd like to do a little personal laundry."

Pedro nodded. "You go right ahead, Miss Lynnie. Let

the men do the ridin' tonight, you've been doin' more than your share."

She smiled and went to get a bar of homemade laundry soap from Cookie. The old man and Twister were sharing some vanilla, and her calves were nursing on their contented mamas, the pretty ribbons making the scene look homey.

She looked around. All the cowboys seemed to be busy with chores. She got herself some clean clothes and a towel from her saddlebags, and some of her dirty clothes and bloomers. It was not yet dusk as she pulled off her sweaty clothes and swam about in the cold creek. It was indeed a delicious feeling.

Lynnie waded up onto the bank, dried herself off, and dressed. Then she took her soap and began to wash her laundry. These white bloomers with the lace trim were part of her new protest outfit, she thought with satisfaction as she rinsed and wrung the green fabric out.

Lynnie gathered up her wet laundry and looked toward the restless cattle. The wind seemed to be dying down a little. Good, she wouldn't get her wet laundry all dusty. She found some sand plum bushes and began to spread her wash out to dry. She had just hung the last pair of bloomers over a bush near the herd when the breeze picked up unexpectedly. The wind caught her lacy white bloomers, filling them with air like a hot-air balloon. Even as she watched in disbelief, the wind took her drawers and blew them through the air and toward the herd of nervous cattle. Immediately, the cattle began to low and bellow.

"What the . . . ?" Ace, riding past the herd, tried to control his rearing black horse.

The bloomers blew through the churning cattle, creating curses and shouts from surprised cowboys. The cattle milled and bellowed in confusion, their panic building in the blowing wind.

Lynnie cried out a warning, but the surprised men were already fighting to keep the spooked cattle milling.

"Stampede!" Hank yelled, "Stampede!"

And even as Lynnie watched in horror, the herd broke and began to run.

Thirteen

For a split second, Lynnie could only watch helplessly as the big herd of longhorns milled and bawled
like a great, churning brown sea. Then they broke and
began to run.

"Stampede!" Ace yelled, "Goddamn it! Let's stop
'em!"

The spell was broken, and everyone ran for their
horses. Lynnie ran, too, but Ace shouted at her, his face
distorted with anger. "Damn it, you've caused enough
trouble! Stay out of the way!"

"I caused it; I'll help stop it!" She still had a pair of
bloomers in her hand as she swung up on her horse and
spurred Boneyard into a gallop, running along beside
the thundering herd. The chuck wagon was in the way
of the rampaging cattle. She yelled a warning to Cookie,
who grabbed up the last baby calf and clambered inside.
As she passed, the chuck wagon trembled against the
onslaught of the running brown wall and flipped over on
its side. Her mare was caught in the forward momentum, and Lynnie couldn't stop to see if Cookie was all
right. The most important task at this instant was stopping the panicked, headlong plunge of longhorns.

All the cowboys were in the saddle, running along the
sides of cattle, trying to contain them so the herd
wouldn't split and scatter over the prairie, where the

wranglers might never find all the stragglers. Up ahead of her through the churning dust, she saw Pedro galloping. Then his horse stumbled and went down. The momentum flung him to one side so that he didn't fall under the pounding hooves, but the way he cried out, barely heard over the roar, told her he was hurt.

It seemed unreal, she thought. Her ears rang with noise that sounded like a tornado or a thunderstorm as thousands of hooves drummed the ground and the cattle ran on. Her mouth tasted of grit, and she felt perspiration running down her back in the evening twilight. Around her, red dust boiled up from the charging cattle so that her vision blurred and her spectacles became coated with a film of dust. There seemed to be no stopping the spooked cattle, she thought as she topped a rise and galloped down the other side. Here and there, she saw a blurred vision of hard-riding cowboys, but the longhorns charged on like a great brown wave crashing across the prairie. Far ahead of her, she saw Ace riding expertly, attempting to reach the herd leaders. Her heart almost stopped, knowing the men who reached the front of the stampede were putting themselves in grave danger, because their job was to turn the leaders, get the herd milling in confusion so that they stopped running. Sometimes, she knew, the riders trying to stop the lead steers were caught in the whirlwind and fell beneath the steers as they began to mill.

She wasn't going to let that happen to Ace. This stampede was her fault, and she had a fast horse. She urged Boneyard forward, and now they were running neck and neck with Ace and his great black stallion.

Ace looked first surprised and then angry as he glanced to one side and saw her. "Get the hell back!" He waved her away.

She hesitated, then decided to ignore him. She had a good horse and she was an expert rider. In answer, she passed Ace, shouting and waving her bloomers at the cattle. For a heart-stopping moment, she was ahead of the longhorns, seeing the whites of their eyes rolling in terror, their great horns flashing in the last rays of sunlight, dust churning up in a great red cloud. "Ha!" she shouted, and waved her drawers at the cattle. "Ha! Get back there!"

"You little idiot!" Ace was beside her, shooting his pistol to turn the herd. Around the other side came Hank and Comanch, their guns echoing above the thunder of the herd. The cattle hesitated, bawling, then began to mill in confusion, those behind the leaders stumbling as the leaders stopped.

Cattle almost always mill to the right. Lynnie remembered the tales she had heard from old-timers. Knowing that, she reined her horse to follow the leaders and prevent them from starting off again. The cattle appeared as startled as the cowboys when Lynnie waved her underwear.

If they broke the mill and started running again, she and her tired horse would be swept under the longhorns as they charged toward her. Her horse reared, neighing, and Lynnie had never been so scared in her life. If she went down under the great brown mass, they wouldn't find enough of her to bury.

Ace fired his pistol again, charging into the mill. "Hah! Get back there! Hah, cows!"

The cattle hesitated, dusty and lathered with sweat as were the horses, but they began to mill in confusion as the other wranglers caught up with the leaders, cracking their whips, forcing the cattle to stop. Now the herd was a churning, bawling mass, but the stampede was over. Within minutes, the tired cattle were barely moving, lathered and blowing as the cowboys began to sing, soothing the frightened beasts.

Lynnie sighed with relief as she rode off to one side and reined in her horse. There she dismounted and leaned against her saddle, trembling violently as she suddenly realized how close she'd come to death.

Ace galloped up. "Damn you, you nearly got us all killed!" He swung down off his horse, whirled her around, and looked into her face, suddenly concerned. "Are you all right?"

She tried to hold back the tears but couldn't stop herself. "I didn't go to do it," she sobbed. "It just ha—ha—happened."

"Oh hell, I know you didn't go to do it, silly female." He pulled her to him awkwardly and stroked her hair. "It'll be all right."

"The chuck wagon," she sobbed against his big chest. "I saw the chuck wagon go over and Pedro go down."

He swore and stepped away, then swung up on his horse. "Nothin' but trouble on this drive," he muttered, and put spurs to his lathered horse and galloped back down the line.

Yes, she had been nothing but trouble. She couldn't blame him for being furious. She felt so alone and vulnerable now, remembering the comfort of his arms. With a sigh, she wiped her eyes and mounted up, following him to see how bad the damage was. Here she'd been trying to prove that women could do things as well as men, and she'd messed it all up. With eyes downcast, she rode past the cowboys who were now rounding up the strays from the stampede. How they must hate her.

Pedro's horse stood ground-tied where the Mexican had fallen. Ace had propped him up against a stump. She dismounted and ran to join them. "Oh, Pedro, I'm so sorry. I didn't mean—"

"It's all right, *señorita*." He nodded. "I was just tellin' the boy here, I'm not hurt bad, I think."

Ace was examining him. "He's got a broken leg. He's not going to be able to ride. I'll get him some whiskey."

They all looked toward the chuck wagon.

"Thunderation." Lynnie stood up. "We forgot about Cookie."

Ace's dark eyes betrayed his fear. "That old bastard is too pickled to be hurt."

"I heered that!" came from the overturned wagon.

Lynnie laughed with relief, and Ace grinned. "He must not be hurt too bad."

They both ran over and peered inside. Cookie lay sprawled among overturned flour and sugar canisters, with four beribboned calves bawling in protest.

"You hurt?" Lynnie asked.

"Dagnab it, nothin' but my dignity," the old man complained.

Hank and some of the others rode up.

Ace said, "Help me get this chuck wagon back on its wheels, and then we'll see what we can do about Pedro."

Tired, dusty men dismounted. "Pedro hurt bad?"

She felt shame and chewed her lip as Ace said, "We'll have to send him back. Pedro can't ride with a broke leg."

"I'm sorry," Lynnie said. "I'm really sorry."

Ace shrugged. "It's our fault for lettin' a female come along. Women don't belong on a cattle drive."

"Aw, Ace," Hank said, "go easy on the lady. She didn't go to do it."

"That don't make me no never-mind," Ace snapped. "She's still caused a big mess. Hold on, Cookie," he shouted, "we're fixin' to get the wagon up on its wheels."

As she watched, Ace put his strong back into his lift as the other cowboys rushed to help. In seconds, they had righted the wagon, and it didn't seem badly damaged.

Ace peered inside. "Cookie, you hurt?"

"No, but these danged calves peed on me."

"Lynnie," Ace ordered, "get some bandages and the whiskey out of the chuck wagon."

She peered in as Cookie moved a bawling calf off his lap. They were all covered with sugar and flour.

Cookie's eyes lit up. "There's whiskey?"

Ace grinned in spite of himself. "Knowing you, I hid it in the liniment bottle."

"Well, that's a damned dirty trick—excuse my language, Miss Lynnie. At least my bottle of vanilla ain't broke." He began to dust the spilled flour off the bawling calves while the anxious cows clustered around the wagon.

Daisy Buttercup looked like a ghost, but she complained mightily as Cookie dusted off the flour and Lynnie picked her up and put her on the ground for her anxious mother. Then she searched out the bandages and the liniment bottle, then followed Ace back to where Comanch squatted by the injured trail boss. Lynnie held out the bottle, and Pedro took a big swig.

Ace asked, "How bad is it, *compadre?*"

Pedro wiped sweat from his swarthy face. "It hurts, but if I get it bandaged, I think I can go on."

Lynnie exchanged glances with Ace. Ace looked beaten. For the first time, his wide shoulders seemed to slump. If Pedro had a broken leg, they both knew he wouldn't be able to sit a horse.

"Lynnie, go find me some sticks we can use as a splint. I thought we passed a cottonwood tree back there somewheres. Joe, you tell the boys to meet at the chuck wagon in about an hour so we can assess the damage and decide what we're gonna do next."

Lynnie glanced around. All the boys looked depressed. *This is the end of the drive,* she thought, *and it's all my fault.* Without an experienced trail boss like Pedro, they would have to cut short the trip and go home like defeated hound dogs with their tails between their legs. True, Cookie had made the trip before, but with his taste for anything alcoholic, they couldn't count on him to lead them. In the meantime, Willis Forrester and Purdy would get top dollar for their beef in Dodge City and return to Texas in triumph.

She rode back and found some fallen branches that could be cut up for a splint. Following Pedro's instructions, the novice hands helped straighten the leg and bandage it. Then some of the cowboys put the injured man on a blanket and carried him back to camp. In the meantime, Cookie had gotten a fire started and a big pot of coffee boiling.

The old geezer was coated with flour until he looked like a spook, but he seemed cheerful. "Boys tell me one steer got kilt in the stampede, so we got steak if anyone's hungry."

The cowboys grinned.

Hank said, "You ever see a cowboy not hungry?"

After a hearty meal and some broth for Pedro, the wranglers gathered around the fire to talk as darkness fell. Lynnie was so ashamed, she couldn't look at any of the men.

"I think I could sit a saddle," Pedro said, and nobody else said anything, knowing the pain would be unbearable.

Ace shook his head. *"Gracias, compadre,* but you'd never make it. Is there a railroad anywheres near?"

Pedro thought a minute and nodded. "A few miles to the east. It connects with a stage line farther south. Why?"

Ace chewed his lip, thinking. "I reckon we'll have to put you on the train."

"But there's no experienced trail driver but me," the Mexican protested. "If you send me home, you'll have to end the drive."

A moan of protests went up from the boys. "No! We ain't gonna yell 'calf-roped' and let that uppity Forrester and Purdy win this thing!"

"I don't know that we got much choice," Ace said.

There was a long silence. It was so quiet that Lynnie thought the sound of the fire crackling seemed very loud.

Ace rolled a smoke and lit it with a burning twig from that fire. "Lordy," he said softly, "I wish now that when my dad was tryin' to teach me about bein' a rancher, I'd paid more attention. I don't know beans."

Pedro gave him a fond, gentle smile. "It's in your blood. The Durangos have been ranchers for generations. You got what it takes, amigo. Someday yet, you will be a good cattleman."

Ace shook his head. "Now is when I'm needed, and I ain't got the goods." He stood up abruptly and went out on the prairie, staring up at the stars.

Lynnie had never felt so sorry for anyone as she did for Ace Durango at this moment.

Pedro shook his head. "He feels bad about himself."

"He shouldn't," Lynnie said stubbornly. "I'm the one who caused the stampede. I owe you all an apology."

"Gosh, Miss Lynnie," Comanche said, "none of the boys hold it against you. You didn't go to do it, and you risked your life to help stop it."

"That doesn't make me feel any better." She took off her spectacles, put them in her pocket, and wiped the tears that threatened to overflow her eyes.

"Well, Pedro . . ." Hank looked around at the other cowboys. "What are we gonna do?"

The old man shook his head. "Much as I hate to admit it, Ace is right. I can't ride, so I'll be a burden to you, and you can't go on without a trail boss. Maybe we could turn over our cows to the Forrester drive, all of us catch that train if the railroad can work out credit with the Triple D."

Lynnie protested. "Willis Forrester would send Daisy Buttercup to the butcher."

The calf, as if recognizing its name, bawled loudly, and the men laughed.

Joe said, "Pedro, do you reckon Ace could take this drive through?"

Pedro hesitated. "I don't know. It takes a special *hombre* to be a trail boss; it's a tough job. It's in his blood, but whether Ace has the guts and the heart for it, I don't know. He'll have to make that decision."

Lynnie looked out toward Ace, standing under the stars, his outline one of dejection as he smoked. "I think he could do it," she said with conviction. "Ace has just never been forced into a situation where he had to take charge of something this serious with everyone depending on him."

The others looked at each other uncertainly. She knew what they were thinking. Ace Durango was a spoiled rich boy who chased women, gambled, drank, and had never taken responsibility. They weren't sure he was up to the task.

One of the men shook his head. "Even if we thought he could do it, Miss Lynnie, I'm not sure he would. He's been wantin' to quit and go home ever since this drive started."

There was a murmur of agreement from the others.

She turned to Pedro. "What do you think, *señor?*"

"I don't know." The older man sighed. "He doesn't have much confidence in himself as a leader."

"Let me go talk to him." Lynnie hopped up and walked out across the prairie. "Ace . . . ?"

He didn't turn around. "What the hell do you want?" He sounded depressed, sad. She could see the glowing tip of his cigarette in the darkness.

"There's a train to the east you could put Pedro on."

"Yeah, I know." He didn't turn around.

She didn't hate him now; she felt something else. Maybe it was compassion; she wasn't quite sure. "The boys are wondering if we could go on without him."

He didn't answer for a long moment. "Men have to have confidence in their trail boss," he said finally. "You think they'd have any confidence in me? All I'm known for is chasin' women, cards, drinkin', and fightin'. I'm a joke to all the serious cattlemen, and I know it."

"I think you could prove your worth to them." She put her hand on his arm.

"I never felt I was really worth a damn." Ace's voice was barely a whisper. "You know what it's like to try to live up to a father like mine? Trace Durango is a livin' legend in the Texas hill country—respected by everyone who knows him; bigger than life. I never thought I could be the man he is."

"But you can," she protested.

He whirled around to look down at her. "You, of all people, ought to know what a wisecrackin', worthless SOB I am."

He looked so woebegone, she reached up impulsively and kissed his lips.

His dark eyes widened in surprise; then he grabbed her, pulled her close, and kissed her—a deep, serious kiss. She was astounded at his action and at her own reaction. His mouth felt warm and firm on hers, his arms a circle of safety. His body was lithe and strong, and for a moment as they clung together, it was the sweetest, most exciting sensation she had ever felt.

Quick as it began, it ended. He jerked away and stepped back. "What the hell am I doin'?"

She was both insulted and humiliated at the shock in his voice. "I started it, Ace. Reckon you aren't use to girls taking the initiative and kissing you."

"I'm damned sure not. Lordy, you can get yourself in big trouble that way, missy, with the wrong man."

She remembered the sensation of the kiss and almost yearned to find out what kind of trouble he was talking about. "The—the boys want you to come back to the fire. They want to talk about you taking over as trail boss."

"Hell"—he shook his head—"I haven't got the guts or the brains for it."

"Ace, you do. I believe in you." She said it with a certainty that made his eyebrows go up.

"Lady, you do amaze me." Without another word, he turned and strode back to the fire. She walked back slowly, trying to sort out her confused feelings. No man had ever kissed her before, and it had awakened passion deep in her soul—the kind of passion she had never dreamed of. She stopped short. *Ace Durango?* She shook her head. She must have been hit on the head during the stampede—hit hard enough to be loco. When she returned to the fire, the discussion was continuing.

Ace paced up and down before the fire. "All right, maybe we could make this work. We could rig a travois for Pedro so a couple of cowboys could take him on east and get him on the train. The train could telegraph on ahead and Dad could have a wagon waitin' when he got there."

The others nodded in agreement, their rugged faces alight with hope.

Ace paused and looked around the circle. "The big

question is, do we go on? Are you *hombres* loco enough
to take on a trail boss who's green as fresh-cut grass?"

Hank stood up and ran his hand through his brown
curly hair. "I vote yes. I think you can do it, Ace. I ain't
one to go home beaten with my head down like a
whipped hound."

The others set up a murmur of agreement. "Yes, we
think we can do it. We're with you, Ace."

"Yes!" Lynnie jumped to her feet. "I say we go on. I
vote yes!"

"Missy," Ace said, turning on her, "no matter what
the boys decide, you ain't goin'."

She felt her spirit sag. "What—what do you mean?"

"I mean," Ace said, "it's gonna get rough for a bunch
of green hands with the worst part of the trail ahead of
us. I can't take that responsibility. Uncle Maverick
would never forgive me if something happened to you."

"I can take care of myself. Besides, when I beat you at
poker, I thought the bargain was that I could continue."

There was a long silence, and she realized it hadn't
been too clever to remind Ace she had beaten him at
cards.

Ace cleared his throat. "Reckon you startin' this
stampede sort of makes us even, Lynnie."

"No fair changing the deal," Lynnie protested.
"You're just looking for an excuse to get shut of me."

Ace didn't deny it.

"Hey," Cookie said, "she's a real plucky gal. I kinda
hate to lose her."

Lynnie glared at Ace. "Somebody isn't. Talk about a
sore loser . . ."

"Think whatever you want," Ace snapped, "but tomorrow morning we'll get Pedro started for the train,
and you're goin' home, too."

"That's not fair!" Lynnie yelled.

There was a murmur as the crew seemed to agree with her.

"Listen, little lady," Ace said, "I'm gonna have a couple of bad rivers, Indians, and no tellin' what else to deal with, without dealin' with a sassy petticoat, too."

"I told you I was sorry about the stampede."

"That don't cut it." Ace shook his head. "You keep talkin' about equal rights, but all the men will be caterin' to you, lookin' out for you. We don't need the female distractions."

She turned to Pedro in mute appeal.

"Sorry, *señorita*," the old man said, "if he's trail boss, from now on, what he says goes."

"I hate you, Ace Durango." She got up and flounced away, got her bedroll, and lay down near her horse. "You hear that, Boneyard? We'll be getting on a train tomorrow. I can forget about Dodge City."

The horse nickered and reached down to brush her soft velvet muzzle against Lynnie's hair. Absently, she reached up to pat Boneyard. Worse yet, she'd be going home in defeat, with all those eager suffragettes disappointed that she didn't get to the meeting to discuss strategy. Damn Ace Durango. And after he kissed her like he meant it. Or had she kissed him? Now that she thought about it, she wasn't quite sure. One thing was for certain, she wouldn't have cooperated in that kiss if she'd realized the rogue intended to rid himself of her now that the chance had arisen.

She cried herself to sleep, and in her dreams, Ace Durango, that stubborn, smug mule of a man, took her in his arms and kissed her like she'd never been kissed before. "I believe in equal rights for women," he murmured against her hair. That woke her up, knowing that he would never say such a thing. *Oh, Percival or Felix, you civilized paragon of virtue, where are you?*

* * *

In the morning, Pedro was placed on a homemade travois the boys had fashioned from some willow poles and blankets. Ace had assigned Hank and Joe to escort the injured man and Lynnie to the train. "You put Pedro on that train, along with Miss McBride and her horse," he ordered. "Then catch up with us. We'll let the cattle graze a couple of hours, then start ridin' on ahead."

Lynnie tried one more time as she stood next to her horse. "I wish you'd give me another chance, Ace."

He shook his head without looking at her. "You add to my problems, Lynnie, and I got plenty already. Tell Dad I'll wire him from Dodge City . . . if we make it."

She was too angry to look at him. "You're not worried about my welfare; you're worried that I'll make it all the way and show you up."

"Are you gonna get on your horse, or am I gonna put you on it?"

"Try it!"

He grabbed her and, with his great strength, swung her up into her saddle, with her biting, kicking and screaming, "I hate you!"

He nodded to the two cowboys. "Hang on to her bridle and get her on that train with Pedro like I told you." He leaned over the old man. "You gonna be fine?"

The other nodded and held up his hand to take Ace's. "I just regret not finishing the drive with you, amigo."

"I regret it, too." For a split second, Ace's handsome face mirrored his uncertainty as he shook the other's callused brown hand. "Wish us luck; we'll need it."

Lynnie looked down at him, thinking she could be of some help to him if he'd only let her stay, but of course, this big galoot would never admit he might need a woman's assistance.

The cowboys waved their hats as the little party started out. "Good-bye, Pedro; good-bye, Miss Lynnie."

Lynnie waved back at Cookie. "Take care of Daisy Buttercup for me."

The old man nodded and took a swig from his big bottle of vanilla.

They started off at a nice pace. Behind them, they heard the camp coming to life, the cattle lowing as they grazed.

Pedro looked up at her from his travois. "It's just as well, *señorita.* They still have the Red River ahead of them and it's a bad one. Then there's Indian Territory and sometimes braves get off their reservations. Farther north is the Cimarron and it's as wild as its name; full of quicksand."

Cimarron. It meant "wild one" in Spanish and the dangerous river was legendary. She sighed and turned in her saddle to look behind her. "You think he'll be all right?"

Joe said, "He'll get the cattle through, Miss."

"I wasn't worried about the cattle." She said it before she thought and all three men looked at her curiously. "I—I was worried about the men," she blurted. *One man,* she thought with surprise. Damn his ornery hide, he was growing on her.

By late afternoon, they had reached the train station at the tiny hamlet that was nothing more than a freight stop. They had to wait only an hour before the train pulled in, chugging and blowing smoke, its whistle shrieking.

In minutes they had Boneyard and Pedro's horse loaded into the freight car behind the passenger car and Hank went to get the tickets.

"Well," Joe said awkwardly, "I reckon this is it. You gonna be all right, Pedro?"

The old man nodded. "Get in one of those soft seats, I'll be all right."

"Sorry, Miss Lynnie," Joe said. "You know, the boys liked havin' you along. You're a right good sport for a woman."

"It's all right," she said, her head high. "I know it isn't your fault. It's that stubborn jackass of a man back at camp."

Hank returned with the tickets. "They're wirin' on ahead, so they'll be lookin' for you and waitin' with a wagon. I told them Miss Lynnie was comin', too."

The conductor helped them get Pedro to a comfortable seat so he could put his leg up. Lynnie settled in next to him with a sigh. There were a few curious passengers, and they stared at her, attired as she was like a boy, but Lynnie ignored them.

Hank pulled out his watch and looked at it. "Train'll be pullin' out in a few minutes. Tell Miss Penelope I send my regards."

Lynnie smiled up at him. "You boys go ahead and leave. You'll have to hurry some to catch up with the drive."

Joe hesitated. "You sure you two will be all right if we go on?"

Pedro yawned. "Go on, amigos. We'll just sit here and enjoy these soft seats until the train pulls out."

Hank said "Well, if you think it's okay . . ."

Lynnie batted her eyelashes at him. "Now, why wouldn't it be? He's hurt, and I'm just a helpless female, remember? That herd is putting more miles between you even as we talk."

"I reckon we should go, then."

Both cowboys gave a final nod, left the train, and stood out on the platform for a long moment and waved.

Lynnie and Pedro waved back, and the two cowboys strode over to their horses, mounted up, and turned back west.

"Well, I reckon we're bound for home," she said as they watched the pair ride away. She felt defeated and wondered if Ace Durango could possibly get that herd to Dodge City without her assistance.

"I'm *muy* sorry, *señorita*. Ace is a stubborn man."

"That's an understatement."

"You care for him?"

Lynnie blinked. "You are joking? Why, that mule of a man has been the fly in my buttermilk ever since he took me to the Valentine ball, and before that, when we were kids. I'm glad to be rid of him. Pity the poor girl who gets stuck with him someday."

Pedro didn't say anything. Instead, his attention had wandered and now seemed focused on a plump, middled-aged Spanish lady sitting across the aisle. She returned his smile shyly.

Lynnie looked from one to the other, then leaned over to the lady. *"Señora,"* she whispered confidentially, "this is the trail boss of the great Triple D Ranch; you have heard of it?"

The lady nodded, evidently impressed. "He is hurt?"

"You see," Lynnie whispered, "he was a great hero in stopping a stampede, and now we have to send him home and finish the drive without him."

"Ohh." The *señor*a looked sympathetic and smiled at Pedro again.

Lynnie said, "I am so worried that when I leave the train, no one will look after him on the trip."

The lady squared her shoulders. "Do not worry, *señorita,* I, María Sanchos, will see he gets good care."

Lynnie smiled and nodded. She had already formed a plan as she turned back to Pedro. "That lovely *señor*a

across the aisle is interested in your welfare and has
volunteered to look after you until the Durangos meet
the train."

"Ahh." Pedro blinked and smiled. "You are not
going?"

"Well, thunderation!" She stood up. "I don't see how
Ace Durango can get that herd to Kansas without my
help."

Pedro laughed. "Oh, *señorita,* Ace will be as angry as
the bull that you disobeyed him."

"So let him." She shrugged. "He won't be able to
spare the cowboys and the time to try to put me on the
train a second time. Tell my sister where I am and that
she'll hear from me when I get to Dodge City." She
leaned over and kissed his cheek. "Good luck, Pedro."

"Adios and *vaya con Dios, señorita.* Good-bye and
go with God. You're gonna need it when you go ridin'
into camp. I'd like to be there to see Ace's face."

He'd be mad, all right. The image of just how mad
he'd be made her hesitate. Could she deal with Ace Durango?

A conductor swung up on the car. "All aboard!" he
yelled. "All aboard!"

Lynnie ran down the aisle. "Wait a minute! I'm getting off! Someone unload my gray mare."

In minutes, she sat her horse out by the tracks, smiling and waving to Pedro as the train pulled out
chugging and blowing smoke across the prairie. She
watched it fade into the distance, headed south; then
she reined Boneyard around and nudged her into a
slow walk. The two cowboys' tracks looked easy
enough to follow.

Only one thing really bothered her: Pedro had been
right; Ace would be mad as a rained-on rooster when
she defied him and showed up. No telling what he

would do. She needed to get to Dodge City badly enough to take that chance. Lynnie laughed and nudged her horse into a lope, following the cowboys' trail back to the herd.

Fourteen

Ace let the herd graze a while after Hank and Joe had ridden off to put Pedro and Lynnie on the train. About noon, he and the wranglers finally put the cattle on the trail, knowing they had delayed longer than was wise. It worried him that rain clouds were gathering on the horizon to the north. Should the Red River be flooding when they reached it, they would face life-threatening problems.

Knowing that, again Ace had misgivings. Maybe he'd been wrong not to admit defeat and turn the herd around, since the worst part of the trip still lay ahead. Yet everyone was depending on him to get the cattle through, and Lynnie had been so convincing with her confidence. Lynnie. Damn the stubborn little wench for delaying the drive and causing so much trouble. The Chisholm Trail was no place for a woman, yet he would miss her. Yeah, like he'd miss a boot that hurt his foot, he thought grimly as he rode alongside the herd, urging them along.

By midafternoon, the rain moved in, and men and animals were wet and miserable as dusk came on. Ace finally signaled to bed the herd down for the night.

"Damn it," Ace muttered as he dismounted, "that stubborn girl has cost us a lot of valuable time. By the time we make the Red River, it may be so flooded we can't cross for a week."

Cookie got down from the chuck wagon and hobbled up to stand beside him. "She didn't do it a-purpose."

Ace tried to roll a cigarette, but the makings turned into a sodden mess, and in disgust he tossed it away. "Don't be defending her," he snapped. "I'd like to wring her neck."

The cowboys dismounted all around him, cold and wet.

"It was a purty neck," Comanch said wistfully.

Ace snorted. "Comanch, you been on the trail too long."

Cookie sighed. "Well, the gal was kinda entertainin' to have along—sort of civilizin', like."

"Ha!" Ace turned to unsaddle his black horse. "Entertainin'? You mean annoyin'. I never met a woman who needed turnin' over a man's knee worse than that one."

Cookie guffawed. "Any man tries it, he'd better bring his dinner, 'cause he'll be there a while."

"That's the truth." The cowboys all laughed, then fell silent as they caught a glimpse of Ace's sullen face.

"Cookie, hush up and rustle up some grub," Ace snarled, "and everyone stop defendin' that headstrong little filly."

They were eating a miserable supper, squatting in the mud as Hank and Joe rode in about sundown and dismounted. "We got them on the train, all right."

Ace nodded. "You stay to see the train off?"

Hank shook his head. "Naw, we were in a hurry to catch up with you, so the minute we got them aboard, we left."

Ace sighed in exasperation and put his tin plate on a wet rock. "I told you to see them off. That Lynnie is as tricky as a coyote."

"Aw, boss," Joe said, "she's just a girl; what kind of trick could she pull?"

"Lynnie ain't your average girl," Ace said, and fumbled through his pockets for some dry tobacco. "She's smart, as smart as any man. You never can tell what she might do next."

Joe's eyebrows went up. "You think she's smart as a man?"

Ace thought it over. He had to admit it then, even though it went against his grain. "Hell, yes, she's smarter than most men."

Cookie cleared his throat. "She had a lot of grit to her."

Ace thought about it as he rolled his quirley. *"Sí,* she had grit, all right." Texas had been built by people with grit, the ability to hang in there against all odds. Now that hc thought about it, the camp seemed almost empty without her.

Comanche came over. "I'm gonna miss her. Miss Lynnie was special."

"Yeah," Ace agreed softly, "she was special." Then he realized the crew was watching him, and he lit his smoke and took a deep, angry puff. "Yeah, she was special, all right. The little dickens caused us more trouble than a bunch of wild Injuns."

While the boys went off to get a plate of grub from Cookie, Ace sat down on a wet rock under a dripping cottonwood tree in silence and watched the herd settling in for the long, rainy night. Yes, Lynnie was special, different than most of the women he had known. She was smart and brave and spunky. He'd enjoyed the challenge—until she'd caused the stampede. He was still angry with her, but he'd miss her. He wasn't the only one. The calves, especially the little crosseyed one she'd called Daisy Buttercup, were bawling and searching the camp for her now that they'd been put on the ground for the evening. He glanced at the sky. "Damn, will it ever quit rainin'?"

Cookie paused in dishing up beans for Hank and Joe. "That's Texas for you—either feast or famine when it comes to rain. If the old Red is at flood stage, we'll have a devil of a time gettin' this herd across. That old river has drowned more good cowboys than any ten other streams. 'Course, if we make it to the Cimarron, we have quicksand to contend with."

Once again, Ace wondered if he shouldn't yell "calf-roped," turn the herd around, and go home. His dad wouldn't turn tail and run; he'd take the herd on through. But Ace wasn't his dad. Still, Lynnie had thought he could do it, and somehow he didn't want to face that feisty little rascal and tell her he'd failed. "We'll take it as we find it," Ace said, and snubbed out his cigarette. "I'll take the first guard. You cowboys get some rest."

"Boss, you're as tired as the rest of us," Comanch protested.

"Yeah, but this herd is my responsibility." He got himself a fresh horse and shook the rain off his slicker. The night seemed long and dark to him as he rode the herd, water dripping off the brim of his hat. He hunched his shoulders against the wind and sang to the cattle as he rode. No doubt, Lynnie was almost home by now, safe and dry and comfortable—where he'd like to be. He tried to remember that he was angry with her for the trouble she had caused him, but he missed the give-and-take of her conversation. She was interesting to talk to, not like most girls, whose only subjects were clothes and parties.

Finally, it stopped raining, and the stars came out. Ace leaned on his saddle horn and looked up, remembering that Indian legend said the stars were windows in the sky where the spirits of loved ones could look down on the ones they had left behind. It was comforting somehow.

Hank came out to relieve him, and Ace rode into camp, unsaddled his horse, hobbled him, and turned him out to graze. Then he took his bedroll and went off a short distance from the camp, took off his boots, lay down, and dozed in sheer exhaustion.

A sound. Ace came alert, listening. It was definitely the sound of a horse's hooves. He reached under his blanket, felt for his pistol. Lordy, there was always the possibility of rustlers trying to steal the herd. The sounds ceased. Had he only imagined it, or was it one of the horses from their own remuda stamping around out there? He'd better check. Quietly, he slipped on his boots and stuck his pistol in the waistband of his jeans. Somewhere in the brush, he heard a horse snort. Outlaws? Indian renegades? This herd and this crew were his responsibility—he who had always been so irresponsible. The thought both intimidated and emboldened him.

Ace crept through the brush as silently as his Cheyenne ancestors. Yes, there was definitely someone out there. He heard a horse stamp its hooves and whinny; then he saw the barest silhouette squatting down in the darkness, watching the camp. Ace would hit him before the trespasser knew he'd been discovered. For a heartbeat, Ace brought his pistol up, thinking about picking the man off, then shook his head. A shot would startle the cattle, maybe start another stampede, and he'd been through that once lately. Maybe he could creep up on the intruder, grab him, and snap his neck. Dealing with rustlers, one had to play rough; they were known to be ruthless.

Ace tucked his pistol in his waistband again and crept

up behind the shadowy intruder. This was high ground. Ace could see the whole campsite from here. The son of a bitch was probably waiting until everyone was asleep to attack. Ace wondered how many rustlers were out here. He'd better try to capture this one alive and force him to talk. He crept up behind the form. "Gotcha!"

Even as he dove for the man and grabbed him, his hand clasped over the rustler's mouth. The intruder fought back, and they rolled over and over in the mud. This was an awfully small outlaw, Ace thought in surprise, and then the outlaw sank his teeth into Ace's hand.

"Oww!" Ace let go, but he stayed on top.

"Let go of me, you dirty skunk!"

In confusion, Ace recognized a woman's voice, and then he realized with horror who the woman was. He froze, looking down at the girl under him. Her hat had come off, spilling red hair against the ground. "Lynnie! What the hell are you doin' here?"

She bucked, but she couldn't dislodge him. "Trying to get a no-good *hombre* off me. Get off, damn it!"

"It isn't nice for a lady to swear." He was both annoyed and angry, but to his horror, he realized he was also a little bit glad to see her.

"Get off, I tell you."

She was soft under him, and he was enjoying her discomfort. He grinned down at her. "You little rascal. You're supposed to be on that train."

"Well, obviously, I'm not. Get off, damn it."

Reluctantly he got off, then reached down and offered her a hand, which she didn't take. Instead, she scrambled to her feet unassisted.

Around the fire, Lynnie could see men coming awake, looking about. Frankly, she was relieved to have found the camp, but she wasn't sure of her reception. Ace looked angry enough for a lynching party.

"What the hell are you doin' skulkin' around our camp like a hungry coyote? You know I almost shot you?"

She tried to wipe the mud off. "You wouldn't dare; I'd tell your daddy on you. Anyway, I knew you'd be mad because I came back, so I thought I'd just follow along to Dodge City."

"All the way to Dodge City? You're either stupid or stubborn to think you could pull that off."

She leaned over and picked up her hat. "Necessity is the mother of invention," she said loftily.

"I don't know what the hell that means."

"Doesn't matter," she sniffed, encouraged that he wasn't screaming at her. "Pedro didn't need me, and I figured you'd never get this herd to Dodge without me, so I got off the train before it left the station."

"Couldn't get the herd to Dodge without you? Listen, lady—"

"I'm hungry," she said matter-of-factly, and grabbing up Boneyard's reins, she began walking toward the campfire. "We'd better get some shut-eye if we're to get this herd on the trail by sunup."

"At sunup I'm gonna send you back to the train."

She paused and eyed him. "There isn't another train till next week, and you can't spare the cowboys to wait with me. You'll need every hand you can get to cross the Red with it flooding, even me."

He began to curse under his breath, and she knew that he had realized the logic of her words. "Okay, Miss Priss, you can finish out the trip with us, but I warn you, I'm gonna make it so hard on you, you'll wish you had taken that train."

"If you think you can scare me, Ace Durango, forget it." She was a little annoyed to realize she was glad to see the big, woman-chasing, uncivilized brute. "I accept the challenge. Now, hush up and let's get back to camp."

"I'm goin' to bed, lady," he snapped. "You done wasted enough of my shut-eye time."

She started to correct his grammar but decided by the look in his eye that she had pushed him far enough for one night. Lynnie hobbled Boneyard and turned her out to graze as Ace headed back to his bedroll, crawled in, and put his hat over his eyes.

Some time in the night of steady rain, Ace felt someone shaking him out of a sound sleep.

"Ace?"

He lifted his hat and squinted in the darkness. "What?"

It was Lynnie, and she looked like a shivering, drowned rat. "I—I lost my slicker, and my bedroll is all wet."

"So?" He put his hat back over his face.

"I'm cold. Do you suppose I could have your slicker and a dry blanket?"

He lifted the hat again. "No. *N-O*. You want to be treated like a man? That's what I'd tell a man who lost his slicker: sleep in a wet bed."

She shivered, and her teeth chattered. "Okay, I reckon I deserve that." She started to crawl away.

"Oh, hell," he muttered, "come on in; I'll share my slicker."

She raised one eyebrow, and water dripped off a soaked strand of long red hair. "No, you don't understand. What I want you to do is give me your bed."

"Lordy, if you don't beat all. Because you're a woman, right? I ain't gonna do it, Lynnie."

"Aren't," she corrected.

"Woman, you are pushin' your luck," he warned. "I ain't givin' up my bed—not to you, not to anyone—but I will share. Come on in; your virtue is safe."

She leaned over him. "What will people think?"

He sighed heavily. "Stop drippin' water on me. Since when do you care what people think?"

"You're right. Everyone ought to know I wouldn't let any man pull my bloomers off."

"Perish the thought. Now get in or go away; you're gettin' me wet."

She hesitated, shivered, and crawled in next to him.

He started and pulled away as far as the slicker would allow. "Damn it, you could have pulled off your wet shirt," he complained. "Now you're gettin' me and the blanket all soggy."

She sighed. "You want me to get out? I reckon I might find a dry spot under the chuck wagon."

Now Ace sighed. "Why not in the wagon?"

"Because it's full of calves, silly."

"Of course, how could I be so stupid? Ain't every chuck wagon a rollin' nursery for a bunch of calves?"

"Don't be so sarcastic." She shoved him over so she'd have more room. His big body put off as much heat as a coal stove. As she relaxed, she could feel him tense up. "What's the matter?"

"Nothin'. It's just that when I usually have a woman in my blankets—"

"It isn't fittin' to tell me that," she snapped. Somehow, the thought of him under a blanket with some woman annoyed her no end.

"It ain't fittin' for you to be in my blankets," he pointed out.

"Oh, don't be so logical. Shut up and go to sleep."

"Then stop snugglin' up against me," he complained.

What was the matter with him? "I'm trying to get warm."

"Damn it, you'll think *warm* if you keep curlin' up against me like that."

"Are you threatening me?" She wasn't afraid of him.

"Oh, no, honey, I just love havin' a little drowned, wet rat crawl all over me. Now lay still." He put his hat back over his face and closed his eyes.

"Don't be so arrogant, and don't call me 'honey.' I'm nobody's honey."

"Truer words were never spoken. Go to sleep."

Lynnie took a deep breath, grateful for the warmth that the big man radiated. She snuggled up against his side, and he automatically put out his arm and she laid her head on it. "I'm much obliged, Ace."

"Yeah, sure. Now, quit wigglin'."

She was getting warm now, and she yawned. "I didn't figure you could finish the drive without me."

"Believe me, we could have." His voice trailed off.

She sighed, rolled over on her side, and put her arm across his chest. She was warm now, and it was cozy under the slicker, while the rain dripped at a steady pace. He was breathing evenly, and she was certain he was asleep. "You're not half as mean as you try to make everyone think you are," she whispered. Impulsively she pushed his hat aside and kissed his cheek.

He started and rose on one elbow. "What the hell . . . ?"

"I'm sorry; I didn't think." She looked up at him, feeling very vulnerable and stupid.

His body against her felt as tense as a coiled spring, and he looked angry in the dim light. "Uh, Lynnie, you're too innocent to explain it to; just don't be kissin' a man when you're lyin' this close to him."

"Did I do something wrong?"

He looked down at her, water dripping off his hat onto them both. "I reckon you'd better find another place to sleep."

"You're tossing me out in the rain? Why, you rotten . . ."

She looked absolutely irresistible as he stared down at her. Without meaning to, he leaned over and kissed her. For a long moment, she seemed frozen with shock, and then she reached her arms up around his neck and returned the kiss.

Now he was the one in shock at the heat and passion of that kiss. With a groan, he took her in his arms and kissed her thoroughly. Her lips were warm and full and moist, and he could smell the sweet woman scent of her mixed with the dampness of her hair. Her body was lithe and yielding, and all he could think of was kissing her and kissing her and kissing her. . . .

She came up for air, breathing hard. "I—I think you're right; I'd better find another place to sleep."

Was he loco? His pulse was racing like a stallion's, and all over this prim old maid. "Oh, hell," he grumbled, "I'll find another place." He scooted out of the blankets and got up. "You keep the bed."

"You sure? I hate to—"

"No, you keep it." He turned and strode away, his whole body aching and aroused as he splashed through the puddles over to the chuck wagon. She was too innocent to know what she'd just done to him, and he realized he'd never wanted a woman as badly as his body now wanted Lynnie McBride. *Lynnie McBride? The old maid schoolteacher?* "Ace, my boy," he muttered, "you've been on the trail too long. Remember all the trouble that bit of calico has caused you."

He was as angry with himself as he was with her. Lordy, what in the hell had he been thinking when he'd grabbed her in a hot embrace? He'd wanted to hold her close and go even further than a few kisses. *A hell of a lot further.*

Yes, he decided, he'd been on the trail too long. Once he got to Dodge and into the beds of some of their fancy whores, Lynnie would be as unappealing and as big a nuisance as she'd always been. He crawled under the chuck wagon and lay there sleepless, listening to Cookie and the calves snoring above him. As he lay there, wet and miserable, his anger and frustration grew. He kept remembering the softness of her body and the moist taste of her lips. From here, he could see her curled up, warm, dry, and cozy in his bedroll. Damn the uppity girl, anyhow. Well, he'd make her regret disobeying him and getting off that train.

Morning came, and it was still raining. Ace was wet and aching from sleeping on the wet ground. Cookie's grub was worse than usual. "Lordy, I ain't ever et worse food," Ace grumbled to himself as he ate the heavy biscuits.

"I heerd that. How you expect anyone to turn out one of them fancy meals when the rain keeps puttin' my fire out?"

"It ain't any better when it ain't rainin'," Ace said.

"Well, who got up on the wrong side of the bed this morning?" Lynnie said self-righteously as she yawned and crawled out of his blankets. "I had a great night's sleep."

He thought about killing her but decided the other cowboys wouldn't let him—something to do with a Texan's code about treating women gently. It didn't help any that all the cowboys gathered around Lynnie, happy to see her. He pushed the canned beans around his tin plate and washed them down with thick, muddy coffee.

Cookie hurried to get Lynnie a cup of coffee and looked up at the dripping sky. "Glad you're back, Miss Lynnie."

The whole crew rushed about, tripping over each other to see to Lynnie's comfort. That annoyed Ace.

"You shouldn't treat her so good," he grumbled as he sipped his coffee. "After all, she was supposed to be on that train. We ought to make her sorry she's not."

Comanch looked toward where she'd slept. "You're sayin' that, when you let her have your bed last night?"

Ace felt himself flush. "Hell, she was cold and wet. What kind of a man wouldn't have given her his bedroll?"

"I resent your male, superior remarks," Lynnie said as she tried to comb her wet hair.

"Fine," Ace snapped. "If it rains again, I'll let you find your own warm place."

Joe grinned. "She can share my bedroll."

"Mine, too." The whole crew was smiling at her.

For some reason, that also annoyed the hell out of Ace. "She ain't sharin' nobody's bedroll."

"Well, now, I reckon I'll decide that," she said. "I don't take orders from you."

He ground his teeth. "I can see it's gonna be a long, long trip."

"I don't know why you're so cranky," she sniffed. "Everyone else is acting like a real Texas gentleman."

He started to comment that it might have something to do with sleeping on wet ground without enough blankets, but decided he couldn't win an argument with Lynnie. She was smart, he conceded silently, smarter than most men—maybe as smart as Ace himself. The thought rankled him. "Let's get this herd movin'."

They got off to a slow start, the rain steady as they took the trail.

"Cookie . . ." Ace rode up next to the chuck wagon. "When you think we'll make the Red?"

Cookie ran his hand through his gray beard. "Maybe

late this afternoon. With this steady rain, it's bound to be out of its banks."

"Can't help that." Ace shrugged. "We'll have to play the hand we're dealt."

He rode on up next to Lynnie. "You doin' all right?"

She nodded, rain dripping off the brim of her Stetson.

He looked at her gray nag and remembered suddenly. "Did that old nag outrun my black yesterday during the stampede?"

"Yes." She said it glibly and matter-of-factly.

"Mares don't usually outrun stallions."

"Just because Boneyard is a mare, she's got to be slow and dumb? Haven't I already proved that females—"

"Don't start, Lynnie," he warned her. "Where'd you get that mare, anyway?"

"Borrowed her from Penelope's spread. Her father's planning on winning a bunch of races with Boneyard."

"He may not cotton to your stealin' her."

Lynnie drew herself up primly. "I didn't steal her, I borrowed her."

"Horse-thievin' is a hangin' offense."

Lynnie shrugged. "I reckon I'll have to return Boneyard at the end of the drive. I really hate that; I've gotten quite fond of her."

"Well, you've still got your calves." He nodded up ahead toward the chuck wagon. Daisy Buttercup stuck her head out of the canvas and looked toward them. At least she appeared to be looking toward them. With the calf's crossed eyes, it was hard to tell.

He rode on, leaving Lynnie staring after him in confusion. She was having a change of heart about Ace Durango. He wasn't quite as hard and stubborn as she had always thought him to be. And last night, in his blankets, she had had the most uncontrollable urge to let him kiss her until she was breathless. Or maybe he hadn't wanted to kiss her anymore. Certainly, he had crawled out of that bedroll like red ants were all over him. It was indeed a puzzlement.

Late in the afternoon, they arrived at the river and reined in. Thunderation. It was bad, Lynnie thought, they were asking for disaster if they tried to cross that flooded stream. Question was, could Ace Durango handle this emergency? All their lives might depend on his judgment.

Fifteen

Lynnie looked at the torrents of water and sighed. No wonder they called it the Red. The river that marked the boundary between Texas and the Indian Territory ran the color of blood. Now at flood stage, its scarlet was accented by the white foam and froth racing along its torrent. "What do you think, Ace?"

He rode up, leaned on his saddle horn, and began to curse softly. "It'd be death to half our herd if we tried to swim them across now, to say nothing of our cowboys."

Comanch had joined them. The young half-breed stared at the water glumly. "They say it's killed more cowboys than any river in the West. You think that's true?"

Cookie yelled from the seat of the chuck wagon, "'Course it's true, you young whippersnapper."

She watched Ace's face. The responsibility of this drive was weighing heavily on a man who'd had little responsibility until now. He looked older, more tired. Ace was the trail boss, the one who was ultimately accountable if this drive ended in disaster. Looking at his expression, it was apparent that he knew it and doubted his own ability. "Maybe we'll wait a day or two for the water to go down."

Hank spat on the muddy ground. "Judgin' from the

way the grass is eaten up, Forrester's herd got here a day or two ago and managed to get across before it began to rain."

Nobody said anything, and Lynnie ducked her head. This herd might have gotten to the river before the big rain if it hadn't been for her, the stampede, and Pedro's injury. She determined at that moment to do more than her share as a cowboy on this drive. She owed it to the wranglers.

Everyone waited for the trail boss to speak. "We'll wait," he said finally, "and see if the water goes down now that it's stopped rainin'."

Cookie said, "We can only wait so long with the grass used up like it is."

"You think I don't know that?" Ace snapped. "This drive is my responsibility, and I ain't gonna lose half the herd in that current."

His tone had a ring of mature authority to it that made Lynnie stare at him. It was almost as if he were becoming a man rather than a boy. He needed all the support he could get.

"Well," she said, "we all heard the trail boss. Let's get down and make camp."

"You"—he gestured at her—"you stay out of the way and outta my sight."

She deserved that, she knew, so she didn't argue. He was bound to be angry because of the trouble she had caused, and she didn't blame him. She'd better step softly around the big man on the rest of this trip.

When morning dawned, gray and bleak, the river still ran high and swift, white foam on its crest, and logs and other debris swept along by its swift current.

Ace walked out to the steep bank and looked for a

long moment. What would Dad do in a spot like this? Ace was so unsure of himself, his judgment. If the trail crew knew how uncertain Ace was, they'd lose whatever faith they might have in him.

Lynnie walked up and stood beside him. "What do you think?"

"Hell, do you have to keep creepin' up on me, askin' questions?" He snapped back at her more angrily than he meant to, because he was trying to make a decision, knowing the silent, inexperienced cowboys now drinking coffee around the campfire were depending on him.

"You don't have to bite my head off." She sounded on the verge of tears, and he was ashamed of himself and then angry with her because if it hadn't been for Lynnie McBride, they would have been across the Red before the rain hit. Unexpected things happened on cattle drives despite the best intentions. That's why the Chisholm Trail made men out of boys—if they lived to see the end of it.

Ace returned to the fire and ignored the way the wranglers were glaring at him. They had heard him yell at the girl, and a Texan didn't shout at a lady. *Lady.* He poured himself a tin cup of the steaming black coffee and glanced at her. There was something both pathetic and appealing about the slight girl in her boy's garb. Her spectacles were slightly askew, and her lip trembled when she looked his way.

Cookie glared at him. "Well, Mister Boss Man, if you're through yellin' at the girl, what ya think?"

It was his decision to make, and abruptly Ace wished he had listened and learned more when his father was attempting to teach him about the cattle business. He'd have to do the best he could with little wisdom to draw from. None of these young cowboys had any more experience than he did. "I reckon we'll have to wait a day or two until the river goes down. We try to cross now, we'll lose half the herd swept downstream and drowned."

Cookie grunted. "Can't wait too long. Forrester's herd done et up most of the grass in this area. Our cattle will scatter so bad that we'll never find them again."

Lynnie had returned to the circle. Now she cleared her throat. "I'm sure Ace is aware of that," she said to the cowboys. "He'll make the right decision; he's a Durango, isn't he? And the Durangos are cattlemen for half a dozen generations."

The others nodded and murmured agreement. Ace blinked and looked away. Here he'd shouted at her, and now she was coming to his defense. Well, he didn't need some small bit of calico to look out for him. "Hank, you and me'll ride downstream, see if we can find a better place to cross."

Hank started for his horse as Ace began to saddle Nighthawk.

Cookie looked up from the fire. "Ain't gonna find no better place. I've ridden this trail before, remember?"

"We'll see." He glanced over at Lynnie. She was now hunting down the cows so she could feed her bawling baby calves. It was both a ridiculous and a touching scene, Ace thought: the calves with their ribbons around their necks, and the slight girl with that forest fire of hair pulled back like a pony's tail.

He did find a little better place down the river a few hundred yards, but not that much better. Its only improvement was that the banks weren't quite so steep. He and Hank stared silently at the rushing water.

Hank leaned on his saddle horn. "Looks ten miles wide, don't it?"

"Might as well be," Ace replied as a huge log washed

by, causing small waves of reddish foam. "Cattle get out in that current and panic, they'll try to return to this side. We get a mill churnin' out in the middle, we'll have a lot of dead cattle washed downstream."

"You think our horses will be able to make it to the other side?"

"If not, we'll have some drowned cowboys, too." It was a cool day, but sweat broke out on Ace's face. He had a secret he hadn't told anyone, and he harbored a terrible fear of deep water. "We'll wait until tomorrow and look at her again."

Back in camp, there wasn't much to do except drink coffee, play cards, and help Lynnie with her calves. The little critters were beginning to eat grass now. Watching her, Ace smiled in spite of himself. Just what did the girl think she was going to do with those calves when they got to Dodge City? *If* they got to Dodge City.

"We'll get there, Ace." She came over and sat down on a rock before him as if she had just read his self-doubts. "All the boys have plenty of faith in you."

"I'm not sure I'm up to it," he whispered without thinking.

"Sure, you are." She reached out and put her hand on his arm. "Cattlemen are made, not born, and your dad had to learn all this, too, at one time or another."

"I just wish I'd spent more time out on the range rather than in cantinas and cockfights."

"You'll get us there." She smiled, and once again he thought how gentle and appealing she looked in her oversized boy's clothes. Why, when she smiled, she was almost pretty.

Lynnie McBride pretty? Lordy, he must have eaten some loco weed in his biscuits.

* * *

The next morning, the river was down but still not nearly calm enough to cross. The cattle were lowing and scattering, looking for grass. Ace looked at the water and felt sweat break out on his broad back. The swift-moving red current looked like streaming blood to a man with his secret. "There's no help for it; we've got to cross today."

Even Cookie shook his head doubtfully. "Water's still too high."

Ace snarled at him, "I'm tellin' you, there's no help for it. We'll have to cross today."

Everyone looked at each other.

He was right, Lynnie thought; they had to chance it, but some of them might die trying. Ace seemed far too riled. She sensed something wrong—more wrong than losing cattle in a flooding stream. "If Ace says to try for it, I'm game. Who's with me?"

Cookie shook his head. "Bad current."

The others looked at each other uncertainly.

"Hell," Hank said, "if the little lady ain't afraid, I reckon I'm game."

The others looked at each other, then at Lynnie.

Comanch said, "I ain't gonna be showed up by no gal."

The others nodded in grudging agreement. "I reckon we got to try."

Ace wiped sweat from his face, and she noted that his hand trembled. He looked at the old cook. "You think you can get the chuck wagon across?"

The old man nodded. "And the lady's calves, too."

"Hey, Daisy," Lynnie cooed, and the ugly calf stuck her head out of the back of the wagon and bawled a greeting. Ace frowned at Lynnie. "I'm worried about you gettin' across. You're my responsibility, you know."

"I can swim," she said. "You don't have to worry about me."

"You get caught in a mill of panicked cattle, they'll take you down with them. Anyway, since when can a gal swim? I never met a girl who could swim."

"That's because the silly things never take off those heavy petticoats. I figured if the boys could do it, I could, too, so Crockett, Bowie, and Travis taught me."

He didn't dare tell her or any of the others his secret; she was so smug and superior. "All right, I'll have a couple of the boys escort you across, one on each side in case something goes wrong."

"I'll be damned if you will." Her cheeks flushed in an attractive way when she was angry. "I'll help take the herd across just like the other hands."

"I don't need the aggravation of arguin' with a headstrong female, not when I got so many other problems."

"So fine—stop arguing with me." She mounted Boneyard and went to join the cowboys, who had mounted up and waited near the herd for instructions.

"All right, boys, here's what we do," said Ace. "Cookie will take the chuck wagon across. His mules can swim, and the wagon will float. Then we begin to push the herd into the river. They won't want to go, and they may try to return. We can't let that happen, because it will cause a mill out in the middle that will panic and drown the herd."

The cowboys looked uncertain, and the horses, as if sensing what was coming, stamped their hooves and snorted.

"Everybody ready?" Ace took a deep breath and stared at the rushing water. The red current looked ten miles wide and twice that deep. "Okay, Cookie, take her across!"

The old man slapped his mules with the reins, and

they started forward but hesitated at the water's edge. "Hey, mules, get along, there! Hah, mules!"

With his urging, the mules waded out into the river, hesitating again. Daisy Buttercup stuck her head out the back of the wagon and bawled for her mama. The old cow came to the edge of the water and bawled in answer.

Lynnie watched the wagon, holding her breath as it moved deeper into the fast-moving stream. Her cross-eyed calf looked toward her and bawled for help as the wagon reached deeper water and began to float, the mules' legs pumping like pistons as they started to swim. She glanced over at Ace. His face looked strained and almost pale, and she pitied him this responsibility. Why, he looked almost scared. *A brave man is one who's scared but keeps on coming anyway.* She remembered the credo of the Texas Rangers.

The wagon was out in the middle of the river now, and the current was trying to float it downstream as Cookie lashed his mules and shouted at them. "Ho, mules! Keep a-goin'! Hey, mules!"

For what seemed like an eternity, the wagon fought the current, the mules' legs churning the red water into foam. Then they were coming up on the other side, water dripping from the chuck wagon, all the calves bawling enough to wake up the dead. The mother cows had gathered along the river bank, bawling across the water to the calves.

Ace's face appeared to be drenched with sweat. "Okay, boys!" he shouted. "Take this herd across! Indian Territory, here we come!"

Now there was no more time to think. Lynnie reacted with the others, riding her horse alongside the snorting cattle, shouting and snapping her quirt. The cattle didn't want to go into the river, but the cowboys were insistent, shouting and firing their pistols. The mama cows were in the water now, led by old Twister, and the others came on hesitantly.

"That's it!" Ace yelled. "Get 'em movin', boys!"

Lynnie took a deep breath and galloped Boneyard along the edge of the herd, urging the reluctant longhorns into the water. All along the route, cowboys shouted and whistled as they pushed the cattle toward the river. Old Twister was swimming strongly for the other side. The others, seeing the big, brown lead steer in the water, followed him slowly, and the leaders waded in and paused, but the cowboys drove them on.

"Watch out, boys!" Ace yelled. "Don't get caught in the herd."

Lynnie watched him hesitate, then urge his black stallion into the current, swimming Nighthawk along the edge of the hundreds of lunging cattle. Lynnie rode into the river, cracking her quirt, urging the stragglers forward. Somehow, the cattle had parted, and she had longhorns all around her. She was now in the middle of the swimming mass of flashing horns, and the panicked cattle were pushing Boneyard along.

She gasped as the red water came up around her chaps. She hadn't realized it would be so cold. Around her, all she could see were heads and big horns as the cattle began to swim the river.

"Lynnie, what the hell are you doin'?" Ace had made the other bank and reined in there, he and his horse both dripping water.

She was scared now, very scared because she was caught in the middle of the swimming herd. She couldn't turn back if she wanted to. "What does it look like I'm doing?" she yelled back at him. "I'm bringing the herd across!"

Behind her, cowboys pushed the rest of the herd into the river and rode in themselves.

"Hell!" she heard a cowboy yell. "If that little gal can do this, shorely we can!"

A shout of agreement, and the cowboys who had hesitated pushed the stragglers of the herd into the river. Ahead of her, she could see cattle finding the bottom of the far shore and scrambling to climb the bank. She'd made it halfway now, and all she could see were hundreds of brown heads and flashing horns as cattle mooed and swam.

On the far bank, Ace looked terrified. "Lynnie, get the hell out of there! They begin to mill, you can't make it!"

Leave it to a man to comment on the obvious. She fought to keep her horse moving with the cattle crowding and swimming all around her, the cold current pulling at her horse. "You think I don't know that?" she yelled back, angry and scared.

Then, out in the middle of the river, some of the cattle hesitated and tried to turn back to the safety of the old camp.

"Hey, they're tryin' to mill!" Ace shouted. "Boys, keep them movin'!"

Around her, cowboys fired pistols and slapped quirts in the faces of frightened cattle, trying to make them swim.

"Oh, my God," Lynnie whispered, and it was more of a prayer than a curse. Boneyard's legs churned as she attempted to swim ahead, but around them, cattle were moving into a circle, trying to return to the original bank. All she could see was red water and the whites of terrified cattle's eyes. It was a mill, all right, one of those deadly mills that were legends in Texas. They could lose most of the herd in this river, swept away and drowned, the survivors scattered for miles downstream so that they could never round them up. "Come on,

Boneyard," she urged her horse forward, and the valiant horse was giving her best, but surrounded by panicked cattle, the horse was caught in the crush of a swimming, thrashing brown river of beef.

"Ace, help!" she yelled without even thinking.

He paused just a moment on that safe, far bank, his face white as cotton; then he plunged his great stallion back into the deadly water. "Hang on, Lynnie, I'm comin'!"

He wasn't going to be able to help her, she thought as she struggled to keep her horse from being swept away. She was only going to get him killed, too. "Throw me a rope, Ace!"

He reined in and tossed a loop, but he missed. "I'm comin' to get you. Hang on!" he yelled.

It was a comforting sound, a welcome sound, and yet she feared for him. The water was cold as death, and the world seemed like miles and miles of swimming, bawling cattle. In the water ahead, Ace used his whip to make a path through to her. He looked a million miles away. At that exact moment, Boneyard lurched, and Lynnie lost her seat and went under.

"Lynnie, clear your stirrups!" he shouted.

She came up fighting for air, trying to get her boots out of her stirrups. If she should get a foot caught and not be able to scramble free, she would drown.

She'd lost her hat, and she coughed and choked on the cold water as she thrashed about, her wet clothes pulling her under. She had been swept off her horse, and Boneyard, freed of the extra weight, was now making for shore, leaving Lynnie to try to keep afloat while surrounded by hundreds of thrashing, bawling cattle.

Abruptly, Ace was there, his black horse swimming strongly as he reached for her. She grabbed for his strong, callused hand, but the current was sweeping her downstream. "I—I can't make it!"

"Oh, Lordy!" he gasped, hesitated, and then he was off his horse, in the water with her, reaching for her. "Hang on, honey; you can do it!"

She fought the current, struggling to reach that lifesaving hand, yet being swept farther away as she struggled. Now Ace himself seemed to be in trouble, thrashing, his face panicked.

"Give up, Ace, I—I can't . . ." She went under again and choked on the cold water.

"And miss that women's convention?" he taunted her. "What about women's votes in Texas?"

They were counting on her, she thought, all those women who needed the vote. "Damn you," she gulped, and came up, fighting to reach him. He looked a thousand miles away as she swam, held back by sodden clothes. Finally, she caught his hand and he pulled her to his horse.

"Hang on, girl," he ordered, and his strong arm went around her. Then, grasping on to his saddle horn and swimming, he turned Nighthawk and headed for shore.

She didn't remember much else that day except that Ace had picked her up and carried her out of the river. "You look like a drowned rat," he grumbled as he dumped her under a tree.

She struggled to sit up. Over in the shade of a grove of trees, the chuck wagon was reined in with its load of bawling calves. Ace seemed to be everywhere now that he was once again mounted up on the big black horse. They'd gotten the mill stopped and were driving the wet and bawling herd ashore, roping the stragglers and helping them across. It was almost dusk when the whole herd was safe. The cattle began to graze calmly on the

Indian Territory side of the Red River, and Ace dismounted and walked over to her. "You all right?"

"Thanks," she gulped. "I'm much obliged; I was scared for you."

He grinned. "You'd been more scared if you'd known the truth. I can't swim."

"You can't swim?" She was horrified at the thought. "And yet you came in anyway?"

He shrugged and paused to roll a cigarette, came up with a sodden bag of tobacco and sighed. "I kept thinkin' what Dad and Uncle Maverick would do to me if I let you drown. That was scarier than the river."

She didn't think he was telling the truth, but she didn't push it. "I can't believe you took that chance." She was in awe of him. "That was a very brave thing to do."

He snorted. "Forget it. I would have done it for any of the wranglers."

"Oh. I thought maybe . . ." She wasn't sure what she had thought, and anyway, what did it matter? She was crestfallen as he turned and sauntered back to the cowboys. She would have sworn he had called her "honey." Not that it mattered. She wouldn't have an untamed brute like Ace Durango on a platter with an apple in his mouth. His manners and grammar were crude, and he thought poetry was something cowboys wrote on outhouse walls.

Still, for a man who couldn't swim to fight the Red River to save her life—it had been a very brave thing to do, the kind of thing cowboys would be telling around campfires for a hundred years. It was the kind of thing a real trail boss would have done, and they had gotten the herd across.

While the muddy cattle grazed and Lynnie got her

calves out to dry them off, the cowboys gathered around the campfire, and Cookie got his kettles going.

"We lose any?" Ace asked.

Cookie said, "Only one or two. Must be a new record for crossin' the Red, only losing a couple. I got Joe cuttin' up one of the dead ones. We got beef stew tonight."

After a satisfying supper, the cowboys gathered around the fire to sing as twilight came on. Lynnie had managed to find some dry clothes she'd wrapped in oil-cloth in her saddle bags, and had gone down to the river to wash the mud out of her hair.

Ace came up behind her. "You sure you're okay?"

She nodded and toweled her hair, looking up at him in the darkness. "That was a mighty brave thing, Ace."

He hesitated. "When I heard you screamin,' I came in without thinkin'."

"I reckon you're your father's son after all—a real cowman."

He stubbed his toe in the mud and looked embarrassed. "That means a lot, comin' from you."

"What are you talking about?" she scoffed. "If it hadn't been for me being so stupid and getting myself in that mill, you wouldn't have had to risk your life. I reckon you're mad at me for that."

"Not really. My ma would have done the same thing. You got spunk, Lynnie. Texans admire that in a woman."

"Then you don't care if I finish the trip with you?"

He shrugged. "It don't make me no never-mind. I reckon you've earned the right to go on."

She stood up slowly. He was so big and broad shouldered standing there in the moonlight, and suddenly, she wished she was pretty like her older sister.

"What are you thinkin'?" he asked.

She shook out her wet hair. "Not much. Sometimes I wish I was pretty. In my family, they call me the smart one."

"You ain't exactly coyote bait."

She looked up at him. "Thank you—I think. I'm not beautiful like Cayenne or full of personality like Stevie, or winsome like Angel."

He came closer. "Don't compare yourself to your sisters, Lynnie. You're smart and spirited, and that's a good thing in a woman. Besides, I think you're pretty."

Her heart seemed to skip a beat. "Aw, you're just saying that because you're gallant."

The puzzled look on his dark, handsome face told her he didn't know the meaning of the word.

"Ace, you behaved like a real gent," she assured him.

"Lynnie, I ain't no gentleman. You can ask any of the girls in San Antone or Austin about that."

He was standing close—too close.

"All the girls say you're so charming, you could talk a dog off a meat wagon." Lynnie ducked her head. "I'm sorry you got stuck with taking me to the ball."

"I enjoyed takin' you to the ball," he protested.

"Now you're lying."

"A Texan, lie? If you was a man, I'd wipe up this riverbank with you."

She stepped closer, feeling some emotion she had never felt before. She couldn't identify it. "It's nice of you to say it, anyhow."

"Lordy, girl, let me put it this way; bein' with you is never dull, and most girls—even the pretty ones—are dull." He was looking at her in a way that made her insides turn to jelly.

"Ace, they say even coyote bait begins to look pretty good to a cowboy after he's been on the trail for weeks."

He reached out and put his big hands on her slight shoulders very gently. "Lynnie, believe it or not, there's other things as important as being pretty."

"Not to hear most men tell it." She swallowed hard. "And I know I'll never be as pretty as a lot of those girls you were looking over at the ball."

"But I took you," he reminded her, and then he pulled her close and kissed her.

She forgot then that she hated Ace Durango for being such a smug, superior male animal and that she knew that her sister and Ace's mother had forced him to take her to that dance. She returned the kiss with all the pent-up longing and emotion of a lonely, vulnerable girl, her tongue brushing lightly against his lips until he opened them with a gasp and pulled her hard up against him. She could feel his aroused manhood through both their clothing, and his hands stroked up and down her back as she leaned into him.

"Lordy, girl, Lord!" He seemed amazed at his own reaction to her as he kissed her harder and deeper, turning her so that one of his big hands went into the collar of her shirt, stroking along her collarbone, and then down the swell of her breast.

She knew she ought to stop him, but his hand caressing her flesh aroused feelings in her that she hadn't even known were possible. She pressed closer to him, moaning softly in her throat, urging his hand to stroke and caress her breast while her breath came in deeper gasps. It seemed he was holding her so tightly, she could scarcely breathe.

It was Ace who pulled away, and when he spoke, his voice was shaky. "I—I'm sorry, Lynnie; I shouldn't have handled what weren't mine to touch. I wouldn't blame you if you slapped my face."

Lynnie took a deep breath, too, and tried to straighten her shirt. "Now, why should I? I liked it, too."

"A lady ain't supposed to admit that." He backed away.

"Well, I'm nothing if not honest, am I?"

She saw just the slightest glint of admiration in his dark eyes. "You are shorely different than other girls, and that's a fact. So now I'm gonna do something I don't usually do. Lynnie, I'm a bad *hombre* when it comes to women; any of them will tell you I love 'em and leave 'em."

"I wasn't asking or expecting anything," she said, now on the defense.

"I know that. Most girls spend all their spare time tryin' to catch a husband, but I reckon with all your women's rights stuff, you ain't got time for marriage anyhow."

"You think I'd marry you?" She was indignant. "Just because you had your big paw down my shirt?"

His rugged face turned scarlet with embarrassment. "I said I was outta line, and I'm sorry." He backed away. "But I wanted you to know that marriage ain't in my plans for a long, long time. . . ."

"Mine either." She was so angry, she wanted to hit him; to pound on that big, wide chest and slap that handsome face until his ears rang.

"Well, then, I reckon we're even. Now, you don't tempt me the rest of this trip, and—"

"Tempt you?" Her voice rose. "Of all the conceited . . . Listen, cowboy, you're not what I had in mind at all. When I marry, I want a civilized man; a sophisticate who plans to travel farther than El Paso or Wichita."

"You know I don't know the meanin' of them big words. You think your tame lapdog of a dude would have come out and fought that river for you?"

"I reckon not," she admitted sheepishly.

"Gal, you don't tame a Texan. At least, it ain't likely to happen—especially to me."

"You're a savage brute," she snapped back.

"And most women seem to like me that way." With that, he turned on his heel and made tracks back to the campfire.

Lynnie stared after him. Ace Durango, swaggering Texas cowboy; everything she didn't want in a mate—and yet, it had felt good to be in his arms, protected and loved.

Loved? She snorted. Ace Durango's idea of love cost about two dollars at places with names like the Lace Garter or Miss Fancy's Pleasure Palace. Of course, she was well aware that most of the time, wanton girls would be happy to bed him for free. She wondered if he was good at it. *What am I thinking?* Lynnie's face flamed at the images that came to mind. No, once they hit Dodge, Ace and the boys wouldn't think she was pretty or special anymore, and Lynnie would be right back where she'd always been; in her beautiful sister's shadow and compensating by leading women's rights movements.

So to hell with him. She finished drying her hair and sought her bedroll. They still had many weeks ahead of them, and Cookie had said the worst of the trip was still ahead. Could anything be worse than what they'd endured already?

They hit the road again at first light, the June dawn already hot as they started up the trail through Indian Territory. Days passed with nothing more exciting than an occasional coyote skulking around the herd. Lynnie was beginning to think that Cookie had been exaggerating and that the rest of this trip was going to be as dull as dirt.

And then one June afternoon, quite unexpectedly, they ran across a war party of Comanches.

Sixteen

"Uh-oh." Ace reined in, automatically grabbed for his pistol, and realized he wasn't wearing it. The Colt, along with his Winchester, was rolled up in his bedroll on the back of his horse. He reined in and signaled the cowboys behind him to stop the herd.

Up ahead of him, a small group of warriors rode out of a thicket of wild plum bushes, watching him. They had weapons in their hands and paint on their faces.

Ace could feel the sweat breaking out between his shoulder blades, and it had nothing to do with the hot summer day. "How," he said, and held up his hand, palm outward, to show that it was empty.

The ancient chief, brown and stoic, said nothing. He seemed to be watching the cowboys without expression. Once he might have been majestic, but now his horse was thin and his feathers and beadwork worn and ragged.

If he could dismount and reach his rifle . . . Ace dismissed the thought almost as soon as it crossed his mind, because other Indians were coming out of the brush on both sides of the trail. All the tales he'd ever heard about war parties crossed his mind, and he remembered his father telling of the Great Outbreak of '64.

The chief rode forward, accompanied by a handsome, younger brave. "You got whiskey?"

Ace shook his head. "Got tobacco," he said slowly and distinctly. "We can eat and powwow."

Now the old man shook his head, his face stern. "You no cross our land."

"We'll pay," Ace said. "We want to be fair."

The young Indian brave sneered. "White men never fair."

Comanch rode up just then, accompanied by Lynnie. "Boss, what's the trouble?"

The young warrior was looking Lynnie over in a way that made Ace nervous. "Lynnie, get outta sight," Ace commanded.

"I will not."

Oh, damn her for always wanting to argue the point. This time, it might cost her her hair or worse. Ace's mouth suddenly seemed as dry as gunpowder. "Comanch, you speak the language; palaver with them and see what you can do."

Comanch nodded and spoke a few words of Comanche and border Spanish to the old man. Then the handsome young warrior said something, looking Lynnie over keenly.

Sweat broke out on Comanch's face. He translated. "The young buck wants the girl. He says he'll give ten fine horses for her."

Ace cursed. "The hell, you say. Tell him he can't have her. Tell him she belongs to me and there ain't enough horses in all the Territory to get her."

Lynnie sniffed. "The very idea. You two talking about trading me like I was a piece of furniture or something."

"Lynnie, shut up," Ace said under his breath. "You're about to start a war here."

Lynnie looked at Ace's strained face, then at the handsome young warrior, who was staring at her so intently, it gave her a scary feeling.

The young brave said something else, and Comanch turned back to Ace. "He says he'll up that to twenty ponies. He thinks a girl with hair like fire is pretty and good medicine."

Thunderation. She'd always wanted men to think her pretty, but this wasn't what she had in mind at all. Lynnie glanced around and realized just how many Indians there were, watching from the brush. She had to do something. She rode up next to Ace, reached out, and patted his thigh. "Comanch, tell him I love my man much and expect to have his child. He wouldn't trade me for a hundred ponies."

Ace grinned, his face tight with tension. "Don't tempt me, Lynnie; a few of those warriors have some mighty good horses."

"You wouldn't dare."

Ace turned back to Comanch. "Tell him Firehair is a real hellion and would bring much trouble to his teepee."

Comanch relayed the message.

The young brave looked Lynnie over, smiled, and said something in his language.

Comanch said, "He says he thinks he would enjoy taming her."

Ace shook his head. "Tell him she's a Texan. Everyone knows you can't tame a Texan."

About that time, a very beautiful Indian girl rode out of the brush and reined her pinto pony in next to the young brave. She looked Ace over and smiled archly in a way that annoyed Lynnie. The girl said something to the young brave, and now the young brave nodded and addressed Comanch.

Ace looked the girl over. "Comanch, what is going on?"

Comanch shrugged. "Her brother is offerin' her in trade, and she's very willin'. She says she thinks the big

Texan would be very pleasin'." The young cowboy's face turned beet red.

"The very idea!" Lynnie said. "Tell her he is very pleasing, but only to me."

"Now, Lynnie," Ace said, grinning, "why don't you keep your nose out of this? I might be able to trade some ponies here, and she's real purty—"

"Ace Durango, are you out of your mind? What would you do with her the rest of this trip?"

The cowboys all guffawed, and Lynnie felt the flush rush to her cheeks.

Ace seemed to sigh in regret. "Comanch, tell them the Firehair is too much of a hellion, and I'm too fond of her to trade her off. Tell them we'll cut a beef out of the herd and give a feast."

Comanch translated, and the Indians brightened. Lynnie noted how thin and tired they looked.

The old man now said in broken English and border Spanish, "We share your meat. That is good. We have nothing to offer in return. Once we were great hunters, but the whites have killed all the buffalo, and we live off the little the Indian agent gives us."

"My father is a very powerful man," Ace said solemnly, "as is the brother-in-law of the fire-haired one. We will see if we can get the Indian agent fired."

The Indians passed this word around, and there were many smiles and nods as all the people relaxed.

Ace said, "Boys, let's camp here tonight, and Cookie, bring out the best you got. We're throwin' a party."

"Just so you don't feed them Daisy Buttercup," Lynnie said.

Ace laughed as he dismounted. "Don't worry, they'd be insulted if we offered them your scrawny calf. We've got some steers that are too thin to make it all the way to Dodge."

And so they threw a party, roasting a whole beef over a pit while Cookie made big kettles of coffee full of sugar, and pans full of biscuits. The Comanche didn't seem to notice that the biscuits were heavy. After all, as Ace pointed out softly to Lynnie, they were used to eating army hardtack and inferior flour, so Cookie's bread must taste pretty good to them.

"I heerd that!" Cookie shouted.

The Indians ate as if they were starving, and more and more of them came out of the brush. Lynnie smiled but watched the people out of the corner of her eye, knowing that if the Indians decided to rush them, the roundup crew didn't stand a chance.

Now the Comanche brought out their drums as Ace shared his tobacco around. The people looked happy and full, Lynnie thought, but the way that young brave was watching her made her very nervous indeed. In the firelight, the pretty Comanche girl stepped into the circle and began to dance to the beat of the drum. She paused in front of Ace and held out her hand. He hesitated a minute, but Comanch said, "You mustn't offend them; dance with her."

"I reckon I can force myself to do that." Ace grinned and stood up. The girl pulled him into the center of the fire ring, and they began to dance while the other men nodded and smiled. Lynnie did a slow burn, sneaking even farther back into the shadows. Hell, Ace didn't have to look like he was enjoying it so much. Now the other cowboys were taking turns dancing with the girl.

The handsome young brave looked at Lynnie in a way that made her think he was imagining peeling her clothes off. He said something to Ace again, and Comanch translated. "He says he's ready to up his offer, and he thinks he can handle the spirited Firehair. He says the wilder the filly, the better the mare when the right man breaks her."

"Tell him I've got her broke well enough and I want to keep her." Ace grinned and reached over to put his hand on her knee in a gesture of ownership.

"The very idea!" Lynnie fumed and slapped Ace's hand off her knee.

"Hush up, Lynnie; sit very close and try to appear obedient so he'll know you belong to me," Ace muttered.

"Obedient?" She fumed. "I don't belong to anyone," she argued, "and when women finally get their rights—"

"Would you rather belong to him?" Ace warned. "They outnumber us, or can't you count?"

The stress and warning in his tone caused her to look around and silently count warriors. "Thunderation," she said under her breath, "we're in real trouble, aren't we?"

"So do what I tell you," Ace ordered.

They fed the Indians and smoked and danced, then fed them some more. The hour was late, but the Comanches showed no inclination to leave the camp, and Ace wasn't certain what to do. He knew he didn't have enough men or weapons if the warriors decided to rush them. In the meantime, the pretty Comanche girl was looking at him in a way that made his blood run hot. As he stood in the shadows, she came over to him and put her lips against his ear. "Come out into the night with me," she whispered. "I will make you very happy."

Ace hadn't had a woman in weeks, and the image of this ripe, passionate girl naked in the moonlight roused him. Then, in his mind, he saw Lynnie's freckled face the night he had kissed her on the riverbank. He shook his head. "No can do. My woman would take a skinnin' knife to you."

The girl turned sullen. "You should beat her."

Beat Lynnie? The thought of turning her over his knee was very tempting, but he couldn't even do that without a fight that would take all day. "Beatin' her wouldn't help," he explained. "She's too much woman to be tamed."

"Ah, you care for her, then?"

Ace considered. "Yeah," he admitted finally, "I care for her, damned little ornery wench that she is."

Finally, the Indians were scattering, heading for their blankets. The old chief approached Ace. "A good feast. It has been long since our bellies were full. We will not forget your promise about the Indian agent."

"I will take care of it," Ace said, and he meant it.

"Now I offer a good lodge for the night so you and your woman can make love in comfort," the old man said.

"Oh, no, I . . ." Ace let his voice trail off as he looked into the old man's wrinkled brown face. How could he explain without insulting the old man? If he admitted she wasn't his woman, the young brave would be insistent on trading for her again. "Yes," he answered, "my woman and I will be happy to use the lodge."

He strode over to his men. "Hank, you fellows will have to keep a guard goin' tonight and watch the herd. The old man's offerin' me and Lynnie his lodge, and I can't refuse without offendin' him."

The cowboys looked at him. "You think Lynnie McBride is gonna share a teepee with you? I'll wager she'd rather fight the Indians."

"Thanks a lot," Ace said, tired and surly. "Once she understands the situation, she'll do it. After all, nothin's gonna happen. I'd sooner bed a rattlesnake than try to get Lynnie McBride's drawers off."

Comanch bristled. "You be careful what you say about Miss Lynnie. I'd take her in a heartbeat."

"Comanch," Ace sighed, "I keep tellin' you that you done been on the trail too long."

"Don't I know it? That pretty Injun girl keeps lookin' at me like she's got something in mind."

Cookie guffawed. "That little sweet brown candy worth your hair?"

"Right now, I think so." Comanch grinned.

"You men keep a good watch," Ace warned again, and he went off to find Lynnie.

"What?" She was horrified as Ace tried to explain to her. "I won't do it."

"Well, now, Miss Uppity Lady, you didn't mind crawlin' into my bedroll a while back."

Her face colored. "That was different. Nothing happened."

"Well, nothin's gonna happen now. Matter of fact, I might crawl out under that teepee and meet that Comanche girl."

"You wouldn't dare."

He shrugged, looking puzzled. "Now, just why would you care? Anyway, the only thing holdin' me back is that that young brave would crawl into the lodge the minute I was gone."

She was scared at the thought. "Okay, what do we do now?"

"The boys are keepin' a watch till dawn. Maybe by then we can give the Comanche a few steers and move on. But tonight, I'm gonna pick you up and carry you into that lodge."

"I got two good legs; I can walk."

"Shut up and let me handle this." He caught her arm, picked her up, flipped her over his shoulder, and headed for the lodge.

Lynnie began to make sputtering, outraged threats. "You put me down, you male monster, you!"

"Shut up, woman." He slapped her lightly on the rear, and the braves laughed as he carried her across the circle toward the lodge.

Lynnie, outraged, sank her teeth into his broad back, and he smacked her on the bottom again. Then he stooped, carried her through the door of the lodge, and tossed her on a pile of buffalo robes. He rubbed his shoulder. "You're worse than a bobcat, you know that?"

"And you spanked me. The very idea. How dare you!"

"Stop it, Lynnie; you don't want to tip them off that you're not really my woman, do you?"

About that time, an old Comanche woman came through the door, smiling and offering a fine buffalo robe. Ace nodded his thanks and, as the old crone watched, grabbed Lynnie and kissed her.

The old woman giggled behind her hand and crept out.

"Don't fight me, Lynnie; she might come in again," he said against her lips, and continued to kiss her.

"You can stop now; she's gone." Lynnie pulled away and wiped her mouth.

"Oh, hush, woman. She might come back." He pressed her down against the buffalo robe, his mouth claiming hers, his lips urging hers to open.

Then his tongue licked along her lips in a way that made her breathe hard. "I—I reckon we have to make this look good," she gasped.

"I reckon we do," he said against her mouth, and he was gasping for air, too.

She knew she ought to move away from him, but his hand was stroking the front of her shirt, and somehow, it felt too good to stop him.

He shuddered and pulled back, rose up on one elbow, and looked down at her, breathing hard. "You know, Lynnie, you really are very pretty."

"Have you gone loco?" She wasn't quite sure what to say next; his eyes were intense as he stared down at her.

With a sigh, he lay down next to her. Outside, they could hear the drums beating as the others continued to dance. She was more afraid than she wanted to admit, and she snuggled up against Ace's big, brawny form.

"Lynnie, I wish you wouldn't do that."

"Why not?" She cuddled even closer.

"Young'un, you don't know a damned thing about men. You don't crawl all over a man and then go peacefully to sleep." He seemed tense against her.

"I don't know what you're talking about," she protested. "Besides, I'm not crawling all over you."

"If you weren't so damned innocent. . . . " He rose up on one elbow and kissed her in a hot, hurried manner that made her catch her breath as his hand fumbled with the top button of her shirt.

She knew she ought to stop him, but her heart seemed to be pounding as hard as his. She opened her lips. His warm tongue caressed the inside of her mouth, and Lynnie took a deep breath as Ace expertly unbuttoned her shirt. She knew she should protest, but his hand inside her shirt felt too good to end it. Ace's grammar might not be good, but he knew how to please a woman.

Now his fingers stroked her breast until the pink rosebud of a nipple came up hard and firm. He made a sound low in his throat, and then his mouth found her breast and she gasped at the sensation. She hadn't realized a man's mouth could feel so warm, so wet, so good. Without meaning to, she arched herself against him, taking his dark head in her two hands, guiding him to her other breast.

"Oh, Lynnie," he whispered, "oh, Lynnie, I had no idea you could make me want you like this."

Her breasts were pale in the moonlight as his hands tugged at her pants.

She felt his hand under the waistband, under her drawers and stroking down her belly. Lynnie gasped. "You—you shouldn't be doing that."

"You're right; I shouldn't."

"I ought to make you stop."

"Just say the word." He looked up from kissing her belly. "If you don't like it . . ."

"I—I like it just fine." She caught his head between her hands and brought his face up to kiss her. His mouth was hot, and she could feel his pulse pounding as hard as hers did. She wasn't sure what it was she wanted, but Ace had done this a thousand times; he would know what to do. Then she hated all the girls he had done it with.

He took her hand and put it on his crotch. Through the denim, she could feel the hard, throbbing maleness of him. "Ace, I—I've never done this before; I don't know what to do next."

He sat up suddenly, cursing. "Lordy, I must be loco to be doin' this. I'm sorry, Lynnie; I got carried away."

She sighed with disappointment. "Does that mean you're stopping? I really liked that."

He frowned at her. "A nice, respectable girl shouldn't tell a man that."

"Well, why not?" She was annoyed with him for interrupting those wonderful, exciting sensations. "I was just being honest."

"If I weren't a Texas gentleman, I'd have your drawers off by now." He fumbled in his pocket for a smoke.

"Gentleman? You?" She snorted. Then she felt a deep sadness. "It's because I'm not pretty enough, isn't it?"

He looked at her, seeming to study every line of her face in the dim light. "Lynnie, I never thought I would say this, but I think you're beautiful."

She shrugged. "You're just trying to spare my feelings."

"Don't tempt me, missy," he snapped as he rolled a cigarette with a shaking hand. "I never wanted to take a woman as bad as I want you tonight."

"Really?" She brightened.

"Damn it, really. Now go to sleep." He lit his smoke.

"What are you going to do?"

"Not sleep," he grumbled. "Not after what you've just put me through."

She looked up at him innocently, puzzled. "Me? I didn't do anything."

"Like hell you didn't," he growled. "Now hush up and go to sleep. I'll stand guard."

She started to protest that he had no right to tell her to hush up, but judging from his annoyed face, she decided not to push her luck. She felt safe with Ace Durango on guard, even though they were surrounded by Comanches. She laid her face against his leg. As she dozed, she felt his big hand stroking her hair, and it was comforting.

"Ace," she whispered, shirt half open, hair askew, full lips swollen and wet from his kisses.

"Shut up," he commanded, "and go to sleep, Lynnie, before I throw you down and do something I've been fightin' since way back on the trail."

"I'm not pretty," she said.

"The hell you aren't, but you're prettier with your mouth shut. Now go to sleep."

She started to protest again, saw the anger in his eyes, and backed off. She hadn't realized what a thin veneer of civilization this cowboy had. Deep down, he was not much more than a savage like his Cheyenne ancestors. "All right, Ace," she answered meekly, "whatever you say."

He leaned back against the lodge pole with a sigh, his

groin aching, and smoked. He didn't dare look at her, afraid he might not be able to control himself. He wasn't used to going without a woman for more than a day or two, and it had been weeks. There was something different about this one, though. Lynnie wasn't just any woman.

Ace looked over at her. She lay on the buffalo robes, her hair spread out like a red fan across the fur, her shirt half open so that he could see one of her small, perfect breasts. Right now he would have taken a front seat in hell for her to open her arms to him. What he was feeling wasn't honorable, he knew, and it would only cause more trouble because he wasn't the marrying kind— certainly not to a headstrong women's-rights type like Lynnie. She probably wouldn't have him, anyway, not if he were the last man on earth. Lynnie was too busy saving the world to get hitched up with a man she considered an uncivilized, untamed brute. Well, maybe in Dodge she'd find some pantywaist in a derby hat and flowered vest—the kind of dainty gent who could spout poetry and plant posies.

Ace chuckled at the thought. A man like that could never tame this Texas spitfire; he wasn't sure he could do it himself, and he damned sure didn't want to try. No, better he should stick with the rollicking tarts that danced in cantinas and expected nothing more than a good roll in the hay and a few laughs. He and Lynnie McBride were too much alike in some ways even to think of anything permanent.

Ace sat guard all night and, at the first light, shook Lynnie awake. "We'd better be movin' on, Lynnie."

For a moment, she seemed puzzled as she looked around, and then she seemed to remember. "You rotten . . . ! Taking advantage of me like that."

"Nothin much happened," he reminded her.

"How can you say that when you had my shirt open and almost my pants—"

"You were pretty cooperative," he pointed out.

"A gentleman would not bring that up," she sniffed, nose in the air.

"Okay, I must have been outta my mind." He sighed. "Now let's get a move on. The Comanche may have changed their minds this morning."

Sure enough, when they came out, the old chief was in council with some of his warriors. The cowboys looked tense and alarmed. Ace looked at Comanch. "What is it?"

"The chief says his son still wants the firehaired woman. If he can't trade for her, he's willin' to fight you for her."

The hair rose up on the back of Ace's neck, and he reached out and pulled Lynnie into the protection of his muscular arm. "Tell him I will give the young brave a fine horse and some beef instead," Ace said.

Comanch spoke, and the old man shook his head. The young warrior looked Lynnie up and down in a way that left nothing to the imagination.

Ace could feel Lynnie trembling in the circle of his arm. The young warrior looked lithe and strong. Yet Ace knew what he must do, what any Texan who called himself a man would do. "Tell him I don't want to fight him, but I will to protect my woman."

Lynnie looked up at him, and he saw fear in her green eyes though she tried to hide it. "Thunderation. The very idea of men fighting over me like two stallions over a mare—"

"Hush, Lynnie," Ace commanded. "Get over there by the chuck wagon."

"But . . ."

"You heard me!" he thundered in no uncertain tones.

Meekly, for once, she obeyed. Ace nodded to Comanch. "Find out how this plays out."

"Oh, Boss, you sure you . . . ?"

"I don't have any choice," Ace snapped. "I ain't lettin' him have Lynnie."

Comanch conferred with the chief and returned. "It will be hand-to-hand wrestlin'. If you beat him, the chief will give you the best horse he has. If the brave beats you, you will hand over the woman and ride out."

Lynnie looked scared, and the cowboys set up an angry murmuring. "We'll all fight them, Ace."

Ace shook his head. "They outnumber us, and we don't stand a chance." He studied the young warrior, not at all sure he could take him.

Lynnie caught his arm, and he felt her hand tremble. "I have faith in you, Ace."

The way her green eyes looked up at him made him determined to protect her. "Damn you, girl, I wish you'd stayed on that train."

She smiled despite the fear in her face. "And miss all this fun?"

Ace began to strip off his shirt. "Tell the chief to form everyone into a circle. I will defend my woman."

As Comanch translated, there was a murmur of excitement from the Indians, who began to form a big circle. The young brave stripped down to his loincloth, and Ace took a deep breath as he looked over the muscled brown body. Ace was pretty good in a barroom brawl, but he wasn't sure he could take this lithe young warrior. He glanced over at Lynnie. She looked pale but defiant.

Ace squared his shoulders and stepped into the circle. The young brave grinned and nodded to Lynnie as if to say, *In a few minutes, you will belong to me.*

The thought annoyed Ace as he went into a wrestler's
stance. The warrior circled warily. Ace circled, too, then,
unexpectedly, dove for the other man and caught him
around the legs. They went down in a flurry of dust,
rolling over and over as both sides yelled encouragement. They finally broke free and staggered to their feet,
even as Ace hit the other man in the jaw, causing him to
stumble backward and go down. Ace pounced on him
like a bobcat, pounding him in the face. The Indians
yelled encouragement, and the warrior skillfully twisted
out from under Ace and grabbed him by the throat,
choking him with strong hands.

Ace was gasping for air, struggling to break the
other's grip. Blackness played around his vision as he
fought to escape. His lungs felt as if they were on fire,
and it was tempting to stop fighting, hoping the other
would relax his grip; but then he thought of Lynnie's
fate and brought his arms up, catching the warrior on
the forearms and breaking the hold. Gasping for breath,
Ace staggered toward the brave and slammed him into
a tree. Around him, he was dimly aware of everyone
shouting, urging both men on. He doubled his fist and
caught the other man in the jaw, sending him sprawling.

At this point, Lynnie could stand no more. Before
anyone could stop her, she rushed into the battle and
began pummeling the downed brave. "How dare you
think I'd go with you? How dare you!"

The brave threw up his hands to protect his face as
Lynnie beat on him while Ace stared in horror. Now the
Comanches began to laugh uncertainly and point. There
was no doubt they were ridiculing the young warrior for
having to fight a woman. Ace came striding across the
circle and picked her up, kicking and screaming. "Girl,
you weren't supposed to get mixed up in this."

"Damned if I wasn't!" Now she began to punch Ace,

who held her at arm's length, trying to avoid her small fists. The Indians laughed even louder, and the chief said something to Comanch.

"He says she is too much woman for any man. He would not like his son to have to try to tame her."

"I could have told him that." Ace grinned and held Lynnie at arm's length. "Tell him his son is a brave man, and we give three fat steers in payment for crossin' the Comanches' land."

When Comanch translated, even the beaten brave began to smile. He said something to Comanch, who turned to Ace. "He says if you can handle that filly, you're a better man than he is."

Ace picked up the struggling Lynnie and hung her over his broad shoulder. "Tell him no one can tame a Texan except maybe another Texan. We part friends."

He carried Lynnie over and put her up on her horse. "Now let's get out of here before they change their minds."

She smiled at him, her eyelashes fluttering. "Whatever you say, Ace."

Seventeen

The cowboys cut out some steers for the hungry Indians and resumed their trail drive, with the pretty Comanche girl still smiling at Ace in a bold and inviting manner.

"Lordy, she's temptin'," Ace said, turning in his saddle to look back at her.

Somehow, that annoyed Lynnie no end, and she gritted her teeth and looked straight ahead as they rode, trying not to think about what had happened last night in the teepee.

Things remained calm for the next few days as they drove the herd across the Indian Territory toward the Kansas border. The weather grew hotter as June progressed, and sometimes water was in short supply.

At last they came to the broad South Canadian River, which meandered across the central Indian Territory. It was wide but shallow. Still, it gave the trail hands a chance to water the thousands of cattle and rest their remuda of horses. Then they pushed on north across the parched land to the North Canadian River. This would be their last chance at plenty of water as they pressed on toward Kansas. The cattle seemed to sense this, too, and were loath to move on. Tempers were short and cattle difficult to move as they crossed the plains. Worse than that, Forrester and his herd were eating up the grass ahead of them so that when Ace's herd moved in, the grass was eaten to the ground.

Lynnie sighed and wiped her red face. "My, it's hot."

Ace frowned at her as he rode up. "Lynnie, try to keep your hat on; you look like a boiled lobster."

"You've never seen a lobster," she snapped back. Why was it the sun turned her even redder and more freckled while Ace's tan just deepened, making his rugged face even more handsome?

"Don't bother me with details." He took off his Stetson and wiped sweat from his face. Red dust swirled up as the bawling cattle passed. "If we don't find water soon, we're in real trouble. We need a little luck."

They got it, all right—bad luck. The chuck wagon broke an axle and they lost a day carving up an old cottonwood limb to replace the damaged one. Nothing seemed to matter as the days passed but to keep moving north.

Wolves and coyotes hung around the edges of the herd, spooking the cattle and keeping the cowboys from getting any rest. Here and there, they ran across Indian sign and wondered if they would come under attack. Again the chuck wagon broke an axle and delayed them for a day while it was repaired. That night, all the cowboys were tired and discouraged.

Squatting down by the campfire, Ace sipped his coffee and made a wry face. "Tastes like it was made with water that came out of a cow track."

"I heerd that, you young pup," Cookie yelled. "And for your information, that's just about where it did come from."

Lynnie licked her dry lips and watched her calves nibbling grass. In her mind, she was swimming naked in a cold spring, diving down and drinking all the clear, cold water she wanted.

She looked up to see Ace watching her. "Hey, kid," he said gently, "I got a canteen-full; take a drink."

She shook her head. "I've had plenty."

"Lynnie, don't lie to me. You shared your water with those calves, didn't you?"

"Well, what if I did?" she flared. "It was my water."

Joe walked up and squatted by the campfire. "We ought to kill those calves," he said. "Then we might manage to milk the cows."

Lynnie attacked him with both fists. "No, damn it, not my calves!"

Ace pulled her off the cowboy. "Here, here. Nobody's gonna kill the calves, Lynnie. Besides, we shouldn't be too many days from the Cimarron River. Maybe there'll be plenty of water when we get there."

But what if there isn't? She must not even think that. Instead, she swallowed the lump in her throat. "Sure, when we get there, we'll have all the water we want."

Cookie paused in cleaning his big cast-iron skillet. "The Spaniards didn't name that river 'Wild One,' for nothin'. Cimarron's a devil to deal with—lots of quicksand."

Ace looked at him. "But the safe path across is marked, ain't it?"

Cookie nodded. "Yep, but you can never be sure the quicksand ain't moved some, so's you might be ridin' right into danger."

Lynnie was miserable, thirsty, dusty, and sunburned. The crew looked surly and ready to revolt. If they all decided to abandon the herd and head for Dodge or home, Ace might not be able to stop the mutiny. He was worried, she could tell by the expression on his rugged, dark face. What a mess. She tried to hold back the tears, but they came anyway and she blinked rapidly.

Ace studied her. "You get something in your eye?"

"Y-yes."

"Here, have a sip out of my canteen." His voice was soft, almost gentle.

She started to refuse.

"Look, I'm the trail boss." His tone brooked no argument. "Drink some of my damned water before you pass out and are no good to us the rest of the trip."

"I—I can carry my own weight," she insisted. "I'm fine."

"Uh-huh. Drink it anyhow before I pour it down your throat."

"You wouldn't dare!"

"Lynnie, you keep tryin' my patience and you'll find out."

She decided he was big enough to do it. "Well, just a little." The water was warm, but it tasted delicious. She had to force herself not to empty the canteen. "I didn't realize the trip would be so tough."

"You wanna quit? I could send you on to Dodge with a couple of cowboys. I'm worried about you—all sunburned and sick-lookin'."

So that's how he saw her. He had been lying when he'd told her she was pretty. He'd only been trying to get her drawers off. Her big sister had warned her about men like Ace. She glared at him. "You're not going to do me any special favors. Besides, you don't have enough hands to spare, and how would that look back home if everyone found out you'd sent me on to Dodge because I couldn't take it?"

Ace sighed. "You and your damned equal rights. You know what Uncle Maverick and my dad would do to me if something happened to you?"

So that was his only concern. Well, what had she expected?

"I got myself into this and I'll damned well get myself out."

"Ladies aren't supposed to swear," he reminded her.

"I'm not a lady; I'm a cowboy!" Lynnie shouted, and the cowboys looked at her and cheered.

She studied the green cowhands. They were dusty and sweat-stained and looked almost ready to give up. But there was no way to quit now except to abandon the herd and ride for the Kansas border. "Look, fellas, if I can make it, you can, too. It's only a few miles to the Cimarron."

The boys looked at each doubtfully, and a murmur ran through their ranks. "Reckon if that little gal can make it, I ain't gonna yell 'calf-roped' and be laughed at back home."

Lynnie grinned. "Then it's settled. We'd better all get some sleep so we can get an early start in the morning."

Ace shot her a look of gratitude, but she pretended not to see it.

"I tell you what I'll do; I'll read you some Shakespeare or poetry."

Ace looked doubtful. "Must you?"

"You don't have any culture, Ace Durango. I'll read MacBeth." She got up and went searching through her saddlebags. "You'll like that; it's about an ambitious man, a bad woman, and lots of sword-fighting."

The cowboys were soon enraptured in the story and magically transported to Scotland.

The next few days were tough, and the June sun was hot as they drove the weary cattle at a walk toward the Cimarron. Heat waves rose up from the sun-baked earth, and when a wind came up, dust devils danced out ahead of the weary herd. Just about the time they were ready to drop in their tracks from thirst, old Twister raised his head, sniffed the hot air, and bawled. The other steers raised their heads and sniffed the air, too. They all began to bawl and to move a little faster.

"Hallelujah!" Cookie yelled from the chuck wagon. "They smell water. The Cimarron must be straight ahead."

"Look lively, boys," Ace shouted. "We'll have to keep them between the markers and away from the quicksand. Thirsty cattle won't care where they stop to drink."

The cattle began to pick up the pace, and Cookie slapped his mules with the reins. "Get along, mules; water ahead."

The cowboys cheered and perked up as they rode alongside the dusty cattle. Lynnie licked her dry lips and thought about water, lots of water. "Ace, we're going to make it."

"We ain't there yet, kid; stay to one side. I don't want you trampled."

They could see the river in the distance now, flat and sandy. The cattle were starting to run, and there was no way to stop them—only to slow them and keep them from trampling the leaders when they reached the water. The cattle broke ranks and scattered up and down the shallow river despite everything the cowboys could do.

Lynnie took in the scene. "Oh, dear God, Ace, there aren't any markers."

"What?" He galloped over beside her, took one disbelieving look, and began to curse. "Those dirty skunks, they've pulled them up behind them."

Lynnie shook her head. "Nobody would do something that underhanded."

Ace laughed without mirth. "You don't know the Forresters very well, do you?"

"As well as I want to know them."

"Watch where you try to drink," Ace warned her, and spurred his horse to reach the river ahead of the last of the herd. Ahead of them, cattle were crowding into the shallows, eager to drink, and already some of them were in trouble. She watched Ace make a loop and throw it over a sinking steer's head. "Hey, boys, watch out, we'll lose some here if we aren't careful."

Cautiously Lynnie rode near the river and dismounted. The cowboys were obeying Ace as he barked orders, spinning loops, pulling out cattle that had waded into dangerous areas.

Cookie reined in near the water and studied it. She ignored the temptation to go splashing into the stream and rode over to the chuck wagon. "Cookie, you think you can remember the trail?"

"That's just what I'm studyin' on," he replied. "As I recall, if we take that ford there, right past that bend in the water, the ground's safe. That Forrester is a rotten coyote. Even rustlers wouldn't pull up stakes markin' quicksand." He got down off the wagon.

"Cookie," she said, watching the cattle plodding deeper into the shallow stream, "tell me where it's safe."

The old man pointed, and Lynnie dismounted and led Boneyard across the ground. The sand seemed solid here. Boneyard bent her ugly head and drank deeply while Lynnie fell on her belly upstream from the cattle and plunged her sweating face into the cold water. "Ohhh!"

Then she drank as if she could never get enough. Behind her in the chuck wagon, her calves bawled. "I'm coming, babies." She filled her hat with water and took it back to the chuck wagon. Cross-eyed Daisy stuck her small muzzle into the hat and drank deeply. Then Lynnie returned to the river for more water for the others.

Ahead of her, some of the cowboys were in trouble,

their horses stepping into the mire and beginning to sink. Other cowboys threw them loops and pulled them out.

"It'll be worse out in the middle!" Cookie shouted in warning. "We'll have to be careful when we take them across."

Ace rode up. "Remember the trail, old-timer?"

"I'll have to think on it." The old man took off his hat and scratched his gray head. "If'n I'm wrong, we could lose a lot a beef."

"And cowboys, too." Lynnie had remounted and rode up beside them after watering her calves.

"Lynnie," Ace said, "be careful."

"You stop worrying about me and get your steers across," Lynnie said.

"I'm not worryin' about you," he said. "I just don't want to have Uncle Maverick mad at me; that's all."

They had taken most of an hour getting the cattle watered and pulling the stragglers out of the sand.

Ace rode up to the edge and stared across. It was probably only a few hundred yards across the river, Lynnie thought, but it was going to be the most dangerous part of this trip after surviving the Red.

Cookie limped about, picking up limbs from cottonwoods along the bank. "I'll do the best I can to mark the way across."

"Careful, old-timer," Ace said, and she caught the affection in Ace's voice.

"Listen, you young pup, I kin take care of myself."

"Sure you can," Ace nodded. "But if you get stove up, we'd be without a cook."

"That'd be a blessin'," Comanch muttered.

"I heerd that!" The old man paused in staking out a path through the shallow water. Abruptly, he made a misstep and began to sink. "Oh, my God, quicksand!"

Ace rode to the edge of the water and lassoed him. "Hang on, old man; I'll get you out." He backed his horse away slowly, and the rope tightened. For a long, heart-stopping moment, the old man continued to sink; then the rope tightened and Ace dragged him out.

"Well," Cookie said, "I made a misstep there, didn't I?"

Lynnie looked at Ace and exchanged glances. If the old man made a mistake, they could lose half their herd in the bottomless quicksand of the Cimarron. Cookie tossed off the rope and went back to staking a trail. Out in the middle, the water was not shoulder high on him, but there were dangerous sinkholes in the river bottom that could grab a man and swallow him without a trace before anyone could make a move to save him. It was late afternoon when Cookie finished.

Lynnie looked up at the sky. "You think we should wait till morning?"

Ace shook his head. "We're losin' time, and it won't be any better tomorrow." He took off his hat and waved it as a signal. "Okay, boys, let Cookie take the chuck wagon through; then we'll take the cattle across."

"I'll help." She nudged Boneyard forward.

"You watch out," Ace snapped at her. "I got enough worries without worryin' about you drownin'."

"I'm not the one who can't swim," she reminded him pointedly.

Now the chuck wagon was splashing across, Cookie yelling and slapping the reins at the nervous mules. Then the cowboys herded the remuda of extra horses through. Finally, they began to drive the cattle across.

"Look out!" Lynnie yelled. A couple of panicky steers rushed outside the marked trail, and Hank and Joe turned to lasso them, pulling them back from the quicksand.

Lynnie and Ace watched, holding their breath as the

cattle, mooing and protesting, splashed through the water to the safety of the far shore.

"Keep 'em movin'!" Ace shouted. "We don't want them turnin' and comin' back. Cattle meetin' in midstream will force some of them off the safe path into the quicksand."

The cowboys nodded and kept the cattle moving. Soon everyone was across except Ace and Lynnie, bringing up the rear.

"Okay, Lynnie," Ace said, "now you go."

Lynnie took a deep breath. "Why don't we go together?"

"Sure. That way, I can rescue you if you get in trouble."

"I am not in need of rescue," she replied haughtily, and nudged Boneyard into the water.

Ace hurried to catch up with her. It was almost dusk, and the cattle drive was now several hundred yards ahead, disappearing over the horizon. "This will be a piece of cake," he said, but she noticed that his dark face looked strained, and she remembered that he could not swim.

About that time, a water moccasin, disturbed by the passing cattle, swam slowly through the water and almost under the black stallion's nose.

"Snake! Look out!" Lynnie yelled in warning, but the horse was already rearing in panic.

Ace, caught unaware, lost his seat as the horse floundered sideways and off the marked trail. He fought to stay on his horse, but a stirrup caught him in the head, and he fell, struggling, into the water.

"Ace! Oh, my God! Are you okay?"

He didn't answer even as his horse floundered and regained its footing, splashing toward the shore.

"Ace, for God's sake, answer me!"

He seemed to be struggling to raise his head, and she

could see the blood on his forehead as he tried to swim, thrashing about in the water. "Go back, Lynnie," he muttered, almost unconscious. "Quicksand . . . "

"Damned if I will!" She reached for her lasso and tossed him a loop. "Grab on, cowboy."

She missed him on the first toss, and he sank a little deeper. In the twilight, she could see the apprehension in his brown eyes. "Lynnie, go . . . go for help."

"Damn it, by the time I get back, it'll be too late." She pulled in her rope and made another loop. By now, Ace was up to his waist in the sand. She tossed and he grabbed it, but the rope slipped from his hands. Lynnie built another loop and tossed it to him. "Come on, cowboy, don't quit on me now."

He was almost chest deep, half-dazed and sinking. He caught the rope.

"Ace," she yelled, "put it over your head; can you hear me?"

He nodded, but she wasn't sure he understood. Blood ran down his face. "L—Lynnie, go on," he gasped. "You can't . . ."

"The hell I can't!" She was off her horse, hanging on to her own loop as she struggled through the sand to him. "Back up, Boneyard!" she called to the horse. "Back up, baby!"

"Get away, Lynnie," he muttered. "You can't—"

"Oh, shut up!" She slipped the rope over his broad shoulders. "Now, put your arms through."

He didn't seem to comprehend for a long moment; then he struggled to put his arms through the rope.

She turned to yell at the ugly gray horse. "Okay, Boneyard, tighten that rope! Get us to shore!"

For a moment, the horse paused; then, having been used as a roping horse and trained to keep the loop tight, she began to back toward the shore.

"That's a girl!" Lynnie hung on to the half-conscious man and encouraged the horse. "Keep going, girl."

On the horizon, she saw some of the cowboys coming, now that they had realized two of their crew had been left behind. However, she knew they weren't going to get here in time. It was all up to Boneyard now. Ace was big and almost limp in her arms. "Thunderation, Durango, don't you dare die on me; I can't get this herd to Dodge by myself."

He didn't move, and his skin was bloody scarlet against the pasty color of his face. His eyes were closed, and he didn't seem to be breathing. *It's already too late,* she thought in horror. *Ace Durango is dead.*

Eighteen

"Ace," she whispered, "oh, Ace, please don't die. I need you; we all need you." She couldn't hold back the tears dripping down on his still face.

One of his eyes fluttered and opened. "Is it—is it rainin'?"

"Oh, God, hang on, Ace, there's help coming." She yelled at Boneyard again, "Keep it up, girl. You can do it!"

Ace choked and began to cough up water. "Did—did I hear you say you needed me?"

"Why you son of a bitch! You were playing possum. I ought to leave you to die."

"Now, you can't do that." He grinned up at her. "You need me, remember?"

"Damned if I do! When we get out of this mess, you rascal . . ."

"I liked you better when you were cryin' because you thought I was dead."

"Oh, shut up and hang on to the rope."

The horse kept backing, and the pair pulled free of the quicksand with a great sucking sound. They struggled to make it back on the safe path as the horse dragged them toward shore. Then the cowboys were there, tossing more loops, pulling the half-drowned pair from the river.

"Miss Lynnie, you okay?" Comanch tried to pull her to her feet.

Ace tried to stand but couldn't. "She—she came back to help me. Somebody catch my horse?"

Hank nodded and signaled to some of the others. "Let's get them over to the chuck wagon. I reckon Cookie will stop up ahead and we'll camp for the night."

Later that night, wrapped in blankets, the pair sat by the campfire eating hot beef stew and drinking coffee. Their clothes hung near the fire to dry.

Ace looked at her. "I'm much obliged, Lynnie; I almost didn't make it outta there."

She shrugged. "It was that water moccasin; that's all. It panicked your horse."

"I think I've underestimated you," he admitted.

"Of course. Haven't I been telling you that all along? When we get back home, I'll teach you to swim."

The other cowboys had bedded down, leaving the two sitting on a log, sipping coffee. He reached over and put his arm around her shoulders. "You're as good a cowboy as any on this drive, Lynnie."

His arm around her shoulders felt good, but she would never admit that. "Then you've forgiven me for coming along?"

"I can't imagine how dull it would have been without you." Before she realized it, he reached over with his other arm, put one big hand under her chin, tilted her face up, and kissed her lips gently.

"You don't have to feel that obligated," she protested. "I know I'm not pretty."

"You're pretty," he said, and he kissed her again.

She looked around. All the cowboys had sought their blankets and were asleep, most snoring gently. The crackling fire made a cozy, warm glow. The stars above seemed like diamonds on black velvet. Somehow, she felt differently toward Ace Durango now. They had survived much together: danger, misery, thirst. "You know what, Ace? You're every inch the man your father is, maybe more."

His rugged face softened. "Comin' from you, Lynnie, that's a real compliment."

She leaned her head against his broad chest. "I suppose we'll be in Dodge in a week or two."

He nodded and pulled her closer. "Reckon we will. Never thought I had what it took to bring the herd through."

She looked up at him. "I always knew you did. You're a Durango and a real cowboy."

They both watched the fire as it dwindled down to glowing coals.

"Lynnie . . ."

"What?" She looked up at him, willing him to kiss her.

"Never mind." For the first time, he seemed hesitant and unsure of himself.

Damn it, he wasn't going to kiss her. Lynnie remembered his hot kisses in the teepee and knew she would like him to do it again. She felt the blanket sliding slowly down her shoulder, but she didn't attempt to grab for it. "Soon we'll be in Dodge, and you won't have to put up with me anymore."

"I reckon I'll miss havin' you around," he admitted.

Damn it, kiss me, she thought. Sometimes a woman just had to take the initiative, she decided. Before he could move, she reached up and put her arms around his neck and kissed him. He seemed taken aback, and then he put his arms around her and kissed her deeply, thoroughly.

She didn't know what she wanted, but she wanted more than this. Lynnie leaned into him, and he went down on his back slowly, breathing hard. Both blankets were slipping, but neither of them seemed aware of it. She proceeded to kiss her way down his face and throat.

"Watch out, Lynnie," he cautioned, gasping for air. "You're about to start some real trouble here. . . ."

"Show me," she challenged, and kissed his bare chest very thoroughly.

He made a sound deep in his throat, half groan, half plea, and then he rolled her over, his hands under her blanket as he stroked her skin. She knew she ought to stop him, but somehow, she didn't want to. Her own breath came in gasps as his hot, wet mouth fastened on her breast. In the firelight, she watched his tortured face as his mouth kissed across her nipples.

"Lynnie," he murmured, "oh, Lynnie . . ."

She closed her eyes as his hand went down to touch her thighs. Her lower body seemed to be on fire with need, and her hands were shaking as she let her thighs fall apart.

His hand felt hot and trembling as he caressed her bare belly. "Lynnie, oh, Lynnie, you'd better stop me . . . stop me now."

Was he loco? She wasn't about to stop him. Her own heart was pounding hard as this big man kissed her belly and moved down her thighs. He moved so that he was half on her, his manhood hot and throbbing against her. "Lynnie . . ." His voice was urgent. "Lynnie, I—I can't stop."

"I don't want you to," she said honestly, and pulled him toward her. He seemed to need no more urging before he moved between her thighs. Then he was on her, driving into her, hard and deep. She locked her legs around him, urging him deeper still. She was giving up her virginity out in the dirt by a campfire—not at all the way she had envisioned her first lovemaking, but she didn't care. All she cared about was embracing this big, rough cowboy and getting him inside her—riding her in the most primitive of all acts. The sensation and her emotions were building to a crescendo of feelings.

She had never felt anything as exciting and as wondrous as what she was feeling now, locked in this man's embrace while he rode her hard and fast. He was a big man, and she could feel every inch of him in the hot rhythm they created. Neither could stop now if they were threatened with death; she realized that, and nothing mattered but finishing this wild action they had started. She wanted him deeper still, and she dug her small hands into his lean hips and urged him on as her own excitement mounted.

"Ace," she whispered, "Ace . . ." And then there were no words except to cling to him, holding him tight against her with her legs. She felt him hesitate; then he went rigid, holding his breath and gasping as he poured his seed into her. For a long moment, nothing else mattered except this man and this emotion as they meshed, straining together. Then he relaxed on her, breathing hard. She reached up and gently brushed his hair out of his eyes.

"I can't get enough of you," he admitted, and began to ride her again, their lovemaking more torrid than before. Then she kissed his cheek and held him close as he relaxed against her, his slow breathing telling her he slept. After a long moment, she slept, too.

When Ace woke up next to Lynnie just before dawn, he was horrified. His first thought was: *Lordy, Uncle Maverick will kill me. No*—he shook his head as he scrambled for his clothes—*Maverick won't have to kill me; Dad will do it for him.*

Lynnie stirred languidly and smiled up at him.

"Lynnie, I know what you're gonna say." He hopped about on one foot, struggling to get his pants on. "It was a big mistake; I got carried away and I'm sorry I ruined you."

"Ruined me?" Lynnie sat up and realized she was naked under the blanket. "I'd hardly call making love to me ruining me."

"Shh!" He put his finger to his lips. "The crew might hear you." He grabbed up his shirt.

"You don't want them to know you made love to me?" She pulled the blanket around her, indignation mixed with hurt in her soul, knowing he regretted last night.

"We was both tired and it was the heat of the moment," he said, buttoning his shirt. "Let's just forget all about it, can we?"

"You sidewinder!" She threw her boot at him and hit him.

He hopped away, barefooted, then began to howl as he stepped on a cockleburr. "Damn it! Now, don't get mad, Lynnie. You just took seriously what I was pokin' at you in fun."

"You—you pig, you!" She threw her other boot and hit him between the thighs, causing him to curse louder. "I thought it meant something special, and here you were just behaving like a typical man."

"I said I was sorry." He managed to pull on his boots, which was difficult, considering that Lynnie was throwing everything she could reach at him. "I don't like the idea of bein' fenced in, and I reckon now that I'm obliged—"

"You're not obliged for anything!" she shrieked. "And I wouldn't have you on a silver platter!"

"Shh! You'll wake the others. Let's just pretend this never happened, okay?"

Lynnie glared at him a long moment, fighting back tears. Here she was having feelings for the big brute, and he'd only been doing what men did naturally, trying to top every female they met.

"Fine!" she snapped, and began to rummage around for her own clothes. "You keep your distance for the rest of this trip and we'll pretend it never happened. Besides, I've got too much to do for women's rights to end up cooking and slaving for some Texas cowboy."

He paused. "You're sayin' that if I asked you, you'd say no?" He sounded as if he couldn't believe his ears.

"I *am* saying no," she sniffed, and began to dress as the first light broke over the eastern horizon. "You may think you're God's gift to women, Ace Durango, but you weren't so hot."

He looked first amazed, then disbelieving, and finally crestfallen. "Now, Miss Priss, since you never done it before, how would you know whether I was any good or not?"

It had been good—better than she'd ever dreamed it could be, better than in the romantic novels she had read—but she wasn't about to admit that. Ace Durango had a big enough ego without telling him what a great lover he was. "I just guessed; that's all. I felt nothing."

"Nothin'?" He looked as if he couldn't believe it.

"Yes," she lied, "and it won't be a problem forgetting about last night, because it was quite forgettable. Now, get your boots on; we've got cattle to drive."

"Women!" He put on his boots, grabbed up his hat, and headed toward the camp, where the others were just waking up.

Lynnie watched him go, torn between the soft feelings she'd had felt for him last night, and the cold, hard reality of today. She'd only been an hour's pleasure for the cowboy, and in a few days, when he hit Dodge, he'd be making love to every woman who smiled at him. The thought upset her so, she ignored Ace when she returned to camp. The icy chill remained in the air the rest of that long day as they drove the cattle on toward the northern border of Indian Territory. The sky clouded ominously, but no rain fell.

As the days passed, Lynnie could no longer remember what day it was—not that it mattered. Each day was like the last: hot, frustrating, and dull. It must be nearly the end of June. Lynnie was no longer sure she'd make it to Dodge in time for the big women's convention on July Fourth, but it didn't seem as important as it once had. She and Ace kept a polite, cool distance. If the other cowboys noticed, they said nothing.

One morning, Cookie squinted against the sun. "By my calculations, we ought to be gettin' close to the Western Trail. After that, it's only a few more days to Dodge City."

Thank God for that, Lynnie thought. The sooner she was rid of the big Texan, the better off she'd be. They could both get on with their lives. Somehow, the excitement of the big women's meeting in Kansas had dimmed, and she was annoyed that Ace Durango had been the cause of that. She had never dreamed she could find such ecstasy in a man's arms, especially an untamed brute like the rough cowboy.

Late that afternoon, they reached a big wooden sign pointing the way to the Western Trail. Everyone reined in and looked.

"That's funny," Lynnie said to no one in particular. "The sign points straight up, but somehow, I think we should be turning toward the left."

"Women's intuition," Ace growled, then took off his hat and scratched his head. "What do you think, Cookie?"

The old man reined in his mules and looked up at the sun. With heavy clouds blanketing the sky, it was difficult to tell directions now. "That sign has always been there; I don't know."

Lynnie ignored Ace and leaned on her saddle horn. "You know what I think? I think that polecat Forrester might have moved the sign."

"Think so?" Ace said. "That would be rotten."

The other cowboys murmured agreement.

"Well," Lynnie said, "he moved the warning signs off the quicksand, didn't he?"

Ace scowled at her. "I sure hate to take the advice of a woman."

Lynnie ground her teeth. "Listen, you low-brained bronc buster, I got a woman's intuition about this."

The whole crew suppressed a grin.

"Lordy, girl," Ace sighed, "there's no tracks leadin' off in the direction you're suggestin'."

"If you'll take a good look, there's none straight up, either."

A murmur of agreement from the cowboys, and Hank said, "You know, Ace, she might be right."

Ace's nostrils flared like a wild mustang's. "Okay, I'll admit she's smart; but she ain't that smart."

"Isn't," Lynnie corrected without thinking. "Give me a few minutes to prove my point." And without waiting for agreement, she took off at a canter in the direction she thought the trail should lead.

"Lynnie, damn it, come back here!" Ace yelled after her, but she ignored him. She was still angry and hurt over his horror at having made love to her. Besides, she wasn't going to let a man boss her when he was so clearly wrong.

Behind her, she heard Ace lashing his horse, galloping after her. She ignored him and kept riding. He caught up with her. "Damn it, Missy, what is it you're tryin' to prove?"

"That I'm not stupid just because I'm a woman." She kept her face turned stubbornly toward the trail and didn't look at him.

"You're still mad about our tumble in the dirt?"

"Only you could be so crude as to call it that." She kept riding. "I'm mad that you regret it."

He hesitated. "I didn't perzactly regret it; I just figured I'd made a mess of things."

"Oh, shut up." She blinked back tears.

He cleared his throat as if to say something but seemed to think better of it.

She admitted to herself then that she was angry with herself because she was falling in love with this untamed brute and he wasn't the kind of mate she had always dreamed of. He didn't have good manners, his grammar was atrocious, he wasn't sophisticated, and the only poetry he knew was the kind that cowboys wrote on an outhouse wall.

"Back to the problem at hand," she said coldly. "Didn't it occur to you that there were no tracks or cow pies either direction?"

"What?" Obviously it hadn't.

"Look up ahead." Lynnie pointed. "Plenty of both. I figure Forrester carefully wiped out his tracks and cleaned up behind his cattle for a few hundred yards."

"Why, the low-down snake." Ace reined in and whistled low. "You're right, Lynnie."

She looked at him. She ought to feel triumphant that she had made him yell "calf-roped," but somehow, humiliating him didn't feel all that good. "All right, let's get back to the herd."

"I ain't never been bested by a woman before," Ace said, and his voice was cold.

"The kind of women you choose aren't smart enough to go toe to toe with you—big-breasted girls like Emmalou Purdy, who can't seem to graduate from school no matter how hard I try to help her," Lynnie snapped. She was still smarting from having been used as a plaything like all the other women Ace had bedded. She was nothing more than another notch on his pistol. Well, maybe not his pistol but his . . .

"Emmalou," Ace sighed as if remembering, and grinned.

At that point, she came close to hitting that insolent, grinning face with her quirt, but she decided that if she made that rash move, Ace might pull her off her horse and spank her. He was just the kind of uncivilized brute who'd do it, too. *Oh, Percival, my gallant knight, where are you when I need you so?* Ace would beat him up and shove his book of poetry down his throat if he showed up, she decided.

They rode back to the herd. As they approached the outfit, Ace cleared his throat. "I'd be much obliged if you didn't make me look like a fool before my men."

She smiled maliciously. Here was a perfect opportunity to show how much smarter a woman was, and what a hardheaded idiot he was. Still, she looked into his eyes and softened. As the pair approached the crew, Lynnie yelled, "Ace found the trail. Forrester's herd did go this way after all."

Ace glanced at her, surprise on his features that she was saving face for him. "I didn't do much; Lynnie was right after all."

"Thank you for that," she whispered.

"I figure I owe you for what I did back at the Cimarron," he muttered back.

Damn him for feeling guilty and making her feel like a slut because she'd enjoyed that night. She determined to make the rest of this trip even more miserable for him if possible.

They reined in, and Ace explained to the cowboys about Forrester's trick. "If it hadn't been for Lynnie helpin' me find the trail, I reckon we would end up in Wichita, where they don't want us."

"Miss Lynnie's smart," Comanch said, "smarter than most men. I reckon women like her ought to be allowed to vote."

There was a murmur of agreement among the cowboys, but Ace made a choking noise.

It gave her a momentary thrill of triumph to hear that from the men, but Ace's expression told her he still couldn't stomach the idea of women in government.

"All right, boys!" Ace shouted, "move 'em out!"

They turned their cattle to the left and soon picked up Forrester's trail again. Lynnie tried to be gracious in accepting congratulations from the crew, but Ace spurred his big black horse and rode off to check on the herd.

Lynnie stared after him. Well, what had she expected? She wasn't the kind of girl that Ace was attracted to; she had known that from the start. She'd caught him in a weak moment when there weren't any other women around to make love to, and she'd become the object of his passion. Well, at least she had that memory of a few magical hours to remember.

That night when the sky cleared and the stars came out, Cookie reaffirmed that they were on the Western Trail, no matter what the wooden sign had said. Forrester had behaved like a ornery polecat in doing whatever it took to win. They bedded the herd down, Ace and Lynnie avoiding each other as much as possible because it felt so awkward for both of them. The cowboys were sitting around the fire just at dark, with Lynnie reading to them, when they heard a shout.

"Hallo the camp!"

Lynnie and the others looked up in surprise. Two riders were approaching from the northwest. What the . . . ? She was as shocked and speechless as the wranglers when Willis Forrester and Nelbert Purdy rode into camp.

Nineteen

Willis Forrester leaned on his saddle horn and surveyed the scene: that worthless rascal Ace Durango, a bunch of very young, greenhorn cowboys, one old drunk of a cook who reeked of vanilla, four beribboned calves and some cows that wore matching dainty ribbons on their horns, and that homely girl of Joe McBride's, who seemed to be reading to the crew. The young cowboys' pink faces were clean-shaven and washed up like they were attending a tea party. Over near the chuck wagon, the ugliest gray horse Willis had ever seen was sharing cornbread from an iron skillet along with an elderly steer with twisted horns.

Ace Durango seemed to recover from his shock first and came to his feet, reaching for his pistol. "Forrester, what are you doin' here? Come to gloat?"

Willis threw back his head and laughed. "Why, no, I figured your novice crew might be in trouble, and I came back to see if we could offer some assistance—right, Nelbert?"

Nelbert nodded his fat head. "Sure as shootin'."

Durango frowned at the pair. "You've got more nerve than a loaded skunk to come ridin' in here after movin' those signs."

"Signs?" He raised his eyebrows and pretended to be

puzzled. "Don't know what you're talkin' about, and I'd be much obliged if'n you'd apologize."

"You ain't foolin' us," one of the others said. "We know you moved the signs on the Cimarron and the Western Trail marker."

Willis Forrester didn't want to get into gunplay with Ace Durango. Everyone knew the two Durangos, father and son, were the fastest in Texas. Willis grinned and pushed his Stetson back. "Good thing I'm in such a great mood; otherwise, I might ask you to back that play for insultin' me."

Ace's hand clicked back the hammer on his Colt, but the red-haired gal grabbed his arm. "Let's have no gunplay, Ace."

Willis glanced sideways. Purdy's fat face was dripping sweat. He wasn't any good with a gun. Willis suddenly regretted riding into camp to gloat over the green crew's misfortune. It had been a loco idea. "Now," he said, "let's not get hasty. A man would have to be a low-down snake to move those signs for the hcrd comin' along behind."

Durango looked tougher and older than Willis remembered. "I'd say 'low-down snake' might be a pretty good description."

The boy had matured into a man, a tough Texan, Willis thought. He remembered the Durango heir as a worthless, womanizing, drinking gambler. "I swear to you on my honor"—Forrester held his hand up—"that we didn't move the signs. Maybe the weather blew them down."

"Why are you so edgy, Forrester?" Durango asked. "Why, you're as nervous as a whore in church on Sunday."

Willis Forrester frowned at him. "That ain't fittin' talk in front of a woman."

Durango frowned. "My apologies to Miss Lynnie. She's been with us so long, I think of her as just one of the cowboys. You swear on your honor as a Texan that you didn't mess with those signs?"

"I already said I swore," Willis answered crossly.

The crew looked doubtful and turned toward Ace. He had become a leader, a real trail boss, Forrester thought.

The girl said, "Well, I reckon since you swore on your honor, we ought to give you the benefit of the doubt."

How naive the girl was, and it was evident by the way she looked at the half-breed Durango that she cared about him. Forrester relaxed and nodded. "What's going on here?" he asked. "Looks like a nancy-boy outfit with everyone cleaned up, the lady readin' poetry, and the calves wearin' ribbons, to say nothin' of that crowbait eatin' cornbread."

Durango frowned, and he gestured with his pistol. "Watch your mouth."

"Meant no harm," Forrester said, and started to dismount. "Coffee smells good."

"We didn't ask you to stay," Durango said, his face grim. "As I recall, there's always been bad blood between our two families."

Forrester nodded. "Maybe it's time we ended that feud."

"When I'm satisfied that the Forresters aren't as rotten as I've always felt they were." Ace slid his weapon back into its holster.

Willis Forrester gritted his teeth. Even as he swallowed back his rage, he forced a smile. He didn't want to get into either a fistfight or a gunfight with Ace Durango; he couldn't win either one, and he knew it. Instead, he turned his attention to the sunburned, red-haired girl. "Well, if it ain't Joe McBride's girl. What you doin' here, honey?"

"My name's not 'honey,'" she snapped, "and for your information, I'm helping bring in this herd."

"Yeah," said the old cook, "and we're all right glad to have the lady along."

"Lady?" Purdy snorted. "Now, my sister's a real lady, pure as the driven snow."

"Hmm, she may have drifted a bit," Lynnie murmured under her breath.

"What was that?" The fat man peered closely at her.

Ace shook his head. "Don't pay no never-mind to her."

Purdy sneered as he looked at Lynnie. "Reckon everyone knows about the scandal attached to this gal. What kind of lady would lose her job and end up in Durango's bedroom?"

Ace started for Purdy, but the girl grabbed Ace's arm. "Don't," she said. "I don't want any gunplay on my account."

Forrester smiled. "Right smart girl, even if she has lost what's left of her reputation travelin' with a bunch of men—"

"Forrester," Durango snarled, "you and your fat sidekick there had better hightail it back to your own camp before me and these so-called nancy-boys pull you two off your horses and wipe up a few cow pies with you."

There was an angry murmur of agreement from the others. Obviously, this crew thought the world of the plain, scrawny redhead, and Ace Durango was ready to get violent over her. Willis had made a bad mistake.

"Okay." Forrester backed his horse away. "We just came over to see how our fellow Texans were doin'— afraid with all these green hands and a gal, you might not finish this drive."

The spirited gal stepped up and put her hands on her hips. "We'll make it to Dodge just fine."

Oh, this was so sweet. Forrester leaned on his saddle horn and grinned. "Wouldn't like to make a small wager on that, would you, honey?"

Durango pushed his hat back on his black hair. "Now, that interests me. Maybe a friendly little game of cards . . ."

"No." Forrester shook his head. "My mama taught me not to play cards with a man called 'Ace,' and I've lost too much money to you before." He looked around the silent, hostile circle of faces and chewed his lip, setting up his trap. "Maybe a horse race. The Forresters own the best quarterhorses in the state."

"The *Durangos* own the best horses in the state," Ace rebutted. "Everyone knows old Nightwind's bloodlines. Yep, I'll agree to a race. Now, my black—"

"Uh-uh." Forrester shook his head, amazed at his own cleverness. "I get to pick who I race against. Our two crews could meet out on the plains between the two herds late tomorrow."

Ace seemed to be considering. Forrester knew many of these cowboys were expert horsemen, and most riding fine horses. "Agreed," Ace said. "Our boys are great riders."

The girl had moved over to pet the broken-down-looking gray nag that was eating cornbread from the skillet.

Forrester could hardly contain his pleasure at tricking the Durango heir. "You agreed?"

Ace Durango nodded. "You bet! It'd pleasure me considerable to beat you, Forrester.

The trap was set. Willis could hardly contain his delight. "Good. Now I get to choose, and I say I ride against the girl."

"The girl?" Ace looked like he was choking on a frog. "Naw, that ain't fair."

A murmur of protest went up from the cowboys. They didn't think he was being chivalrous, but Forrester didn't have much use for women except when his sexual appetites heated up.

The McBride girl faced him. She looked headstrong and stubborn. She was almost pretty when she was angry, Willis decided.

"I'll take that bet, Forrester. I can already see how funny it'll be when word gets back home that you were beaten by a girl."

The cowboys laughed, and Forrester felt the blood rush to his face. He had always hated the Durangos and the McBrides, and now he would have his revenge. "I wouldn't count on it, Missy."

"Lynnie . . ." Ace turned toward the plain, stubborn gal. "You don't have to do this. . . ."

"It's my play," she insisted.

"Lynnie," Ace said, "I'll loan you my horse—"

"Naw," Forrester protested, "she's got to ride her own horse. That her old nag eatin' cornbread?"

"Boneyard is a very good horse," she defended her mount, her green eyes blazing. "Okay, Forrester, what do you want to bet?"

He made a mock bow from his saddle. "Ladies first. You pick your prize, honey, and I can tell you, you're gonna lose."

She grinned up at him, as cocksure and stubborn as Ace Durango. They made a good pair, Willis decided.

"All right, Forrester," she said, "if I beat you, we get to move our herd ahead of yours and get to Dodge first."

She was a smart little bitch, he had to hand it to her, but Forrester had another trick up his sleeve. "Done," he snarled. "Now, I get to pick what I want if I win the race."

Lynnie looked up at him. She had never trusted the

rich and powerful Forrester family. They were as proud
as peacocks of the fact that they had arrived in Texas
with Austin's pioneer families, and they were legendary
for doing whatever it took to win. She looked up into his
pale-turquoise eyes. "All right, Forrester, name your
prize."

He laughed. "It ain't you, if that's what you're thinkin'."

Lynnie snorted with contempt. "I wouldn't be seen
out in public with a Forrester. Name your prize, you lily-
livered, sorry excuse for a man."

"Them's fightin' words, but I'll overlook it since
you're only a gal."

"If I were a man, I'd do more than call you names."

Forrester shrugged and smiled. "You agreed that I get
to name my prize?"

She nodded.

Oh, this was going to be so sweet. He grinned and
looked around at the scene. "Anything? I got your
word?"

Alarm bells began to go off in her head, but there was
no way to back down now. "Everyone knows the
McBrides and their reputation for square dealing. You
got my word."

Forrester threw back his head and laughed out loud,
then gestured toward the calves grazing near the wagon.
"Tell you what: I win, we'll have your little pets barbecued and fed to the crew—especially that ugly little
cross-eyed one."

Lynnie felt herself go white. "Eat Daisy Buttercup?
No, anything but that, Forrester. Take a couple of our
best steers."

"You welshin' on the bet?" Forrester sneered. "Wait
until they hear about this back home."

The cowboys set up a murmur of protest, and Ace

stepped to her side. "Don't do it, Lynnie. Forrester, let me put my fine black horse up instead."

"I'll take him as a side bet," Purdy said.

There was a long moment of silence. Lynnie was shaking as she looked around at the horrified cowboys. They all knew what Daisy Buttercup and Nighthawk meant to the pair. Yet she knew that if she won the race and moved the herd ahead of Forrester's, they wouldn't have to breathe Forrester's dust for the last few hundred miles of the trip, and they'd get a better price for their beef by arriving first.

Daisy Buttercup raised her little head and looked at Lynnie. At least, she appeared to be looking at Lynnie. She shook her yellow ribbons and bawled.

Tears came to Lynnie's eyes so that her vision was blurred. "I—I can't. Think of something else."

"Well?" Forrester grinned. "You ready to holler 'calf-roped'?"

"Forrester," Ace snarled, "You low-down polecat. That's no way to treat a lady."

He couldn't resist, even knowing it was dangerous to rile a Durango. "I reckon we ain't decided whether or not she's really a lady."

At that point, Ace reached up, quick as a rattlesnake's strike, grabbed Willis by the shirt, and pulled him from his horse. They went down in a tangle of flying fists under the horse's hooves. The horse snorted and reared as the men rolled and fought.

"Stop it, you two!" Lynnie yelled, but the pair ignored her. She reached into Ace's holster, grabbed his pistol, and fired it in the air. "Stop it, I say!"

The two stumbled to their feet, dusty and torn.

Forrester wiped a thin stream of blood from his lip. "I look forward to the barbecue and takin' your fancy horse, Durango." He picked up his hat, dusted it off against his leg, and swung up into his saddle.

Purdy chuckled, brave now that Forrester seemed to have triumphed. "Ain't this the wench who's always wantin' equal rights? Well, that's what we're offerin'."

Lynnie swallowed hard and took a deep breath. She couldn't back down now. Besides, she had faith in Boneyard. "All right, the bet is on. We'll race tomorrow about dusk."

"Fine, we'll see you then. *Adios*." Willis Forrester touched the brim of his hat with two fingers by way of salute. Then he and Purdy wheeled their horses and trotted off into the darkness.

Ace watched them go, then turned back to stare at her. "Oh, Lynnie, what have you done?"

"It—it's important for us to get to Dodge first," she said stubbornly, and turned away so he wouldn't see her cry. She ran to the gawky calf and threw her arms around its neck. "You aren't going to be barbecued, baby. Tomorrow night, I've got to win that race!"

All too soon, they met up with Forrester's crew on the Kansas plains, between the two herds, just before sundown.

Both crews of cowboys gathered and watched each other uneasily as Ace and Willis Forrester went over the rules again.

Ace looked up and down the flat stretch of prairie. "I think down to that big rock, around it, and back here past this line in the dirt. That suit you, Forrester?"

Lynnie frowned. "Since I'm doing the racing, you might let me have a say in this."

Forrester stood there holding the reins of his fine bay

quarterhorse. "Since when does an *hombre* ask a woman anything?"

Ace frowned. "We've kinda gotten used to treatin' Lynnie like an equal."

His cowboys nodded and murmured agreement.

Cookie took a sip of vanilla. "We reckon Miss Lynnie's earned her rights."

"Yeah," Joe said, "she's as good a hand as any among us."

Lynnie blushed at the praise and patted her gray horse.

Ace looked at her. "Those rules suit you, Lynnie?"

She nodded.

The other crew was looking in astonishment at her horse. "It's a joke, ain't it? That gal really fixin' to race that old gray nag against one of Forrester's best horses?"

Ace's cowboys hurrahed the other side with jeers. "Just you wait and see what Miss Lynnie and Boneyard can do."

"Boneyard?" Purdy snorted and wiped his fat face. "Well, now, that's a good name for that old hay-burner, ain't it?"

About that time, little Daisy Buttercup began to bawl and hunt for Lynnie. She handed her reins to Ace and ran over to comfort the small, cross-eyed calf. "Never you mind, baby, I'm going to win this race."

Forrester threw back his head and laughed. "Hey, boys," he yelled to his crew, "that cross-eyed calf is what we're havin' for supper tonight."

"Naw!" one yelled. "Ain't hardly big enough to feed this bunch, but I'll bet she's tender."

The Forrester cowboys set up a chorus of bawdy laughter while Lynnie blinked her tears back, straightened her gold spectacles, and returned to the starting line. The sun was low on the horizon, but the air was still hot.

"All right," she said, and took a deep breath, squaring her shoulders. "I reckon I'm ready to race."

Both contestants mounted up, with all the cowboys lining up and down the racecourse to watch. Forrester's spirited quarterhorse snorted and reared as his rider held him in check. On the other hand, Boneyard stood quietly, almost as if she were sleeping—or, at least, had her mind on other things.

"Okay," shouted Ace, "I got this red bandanna, and I'll drop it when you're both ready to go. You both got to go up and around that boulder over there and back across this line Forrester's men have drawn in the dirt. You understand that?"

Both nodded. Lynnie squinted through her spectacles and studied the course. The boulder was less than a quarter mile away; an ideal distance for a fine-blooded quarterhorse. That breed had been bred to cover a short distance in the fastest time, which made them ideal for working cattle. Her calves bawled again, and Lynnie winced, hoping that Boneyard could run as fast as Penelope had said.

"Ready?" Ace held the red bandanna up.

Both nodded. Forrester was having trouble keeping his spirited horse behind the starting line. It snorted and danced about. However, Boneyard almost appeared to be asleep. Lynnie leaned over in her saddle and whispered in her horse's ear. "Hey, baby, you've got to win this for Daisy and the other calves. More than that, you've got to show this bunch of male animals that girls can be better than they are. You hear me, sweetie? You've got to win this for all the females in the world."

Boneyard gave no clue that she had heard. Lynnie, on the mare's back, felt no tension or any clue that Boneyard realized she was about to run an important race.

"Ready!" Ace held the bandanna as high as his head, then let it flutter on the evening air as it fell. "Go!"

Lynnie slapped Boneyard with the reins, and the startled mare seemed to awaken and start out at a light canter. Next to her, Forrester dug his spurs into his bay horse and lashed him with a quirt. The horse took off at a dead gallop.

"Giddiup, Boneyard! Yah, baby!" Lynnie urged her gray forward, dust already flying in her face as Forrester's bay galloped ahead.

From the sidelines came the shouts and jeers of the gathered cowboys drifting to her ears. "Hey, that old gray is asleep on her feet!"

"Boneyard will catch up; don't count your win yet!"

Lynnie glanced behind her and saw Ace's grim face. He, too, thought she was going to lose. She had to win, not only to save her calves but to move their herd ahead of the Forrester herd. That would save the day for Ace, make his father proud of him, and bring in a lot of money. "Come on, Boneyard, give it all you've got!"

At this point, her gray horse seemed to realize finally that they were in a race. Her ears went up and she whinnied and quickened her speed. The fine bay quarterhorse was already three lengths ahead of her and running hard for the boulder.

"Come on, Boneyard!" Lynnie was a skillful rider, and her mount snorted and began to run. It was almost as if she wouldn't be outdone by some fancy bay. The quarterhorse was throwing dust in their eyes as it ran ahead of them, and Lynnie could hardly see the boulder ahead. Behind her, she heard the cowboys yelling encouragement and cheering the racers. No one, even her own cowboys, probably thought she could win. "Get moving, Boneyard! They can't eat my calves!"

Boneyard finally seemed to hear Lynnie and

stretched out at a dead run toward the boulder, right on the heels of Forrester's quarterhorse. Rounding the boulder, Lynnie was still behind the other rider. Now they were headed back toward the finish line, the quarterhorse still showing the gray its heels.

"Come on, Boneyard!" She leaned close to the gray's ears, urging her to greater speed. Far up ahead, Lynnie could barely see the yelling cowboys through the dust on each side of the finish line, Ace standing almost frozen to the spot. Dust filled her mouth and eyes so that she could hardly see, and her teeth gritted when she took a breath. The scent of lathered, sweating horses was strong on the hot air. "Now, Boneyard, now!"

Her mare needed no urging. Forrester was still ahead of them, but Boneyard was gaining. The Forrester cowboys had stopped shouting and were staring, big-eyed, almost as if they couldn't quite believe what they were seeing. Her mare was running neck and neck with the bay now, and Forrester glanced over, surprise and anger in his cold turquoise eyes. He lashed out with his quirt, catching Boneyard across the muzzle.

"No fair!" Lynnie yelled as her horse faltered and then regained its stride. "You rotten cheater! Come on, Boneyard!"

The gray, with her rider's urging, ran even faster. The noise along the sidelines was building to a roar as excited men jumped up and down and waved their hats.

"Now, Boneyard, make your move!" She urged the gray on, and the lanky mare stretched her stride even more and began to leave the fine quarterhorse behind. The finish line was only a few yards ahead. Lynnie's head seemed to pound like the thunder of the racing hooves. Up ahead, she saw Ace, his face beginning to show hope. Now he was waving her on and cheering, too.

"Come on, Boneyard!" Lynnie gave the mare every bit of her riding skill, and the distance between the two horses lengthened as the gray's hooves pounded a rhythm and left Forrester in the dust. She was two lengths ahead when she crossed the finish line, and the crowd of cowboys went wild, dancing in circles and hugging each other, shouting with joy.

Lynnie reined in and fell off the horse into Ace's arms.

"Lynnie, you did it! Congratulations!"

She buried her face in his broad shoulder with tears of relief as Forrester rode over the finish line, shouting, "I was robbed! She cheated!"

Ace set her to one side and faced Forrester. "Would you like to back up those words with your fists, Forrester, because I aim to beat your face in for callin' the lady a cheat and hittin' her horse like you did."

The other man reined in and hesitated. "Well, I reckon maybe I was wrong. I just don't understand how that old nag could have beat me."

Lynnie strode over to hug her lathered gray's neck. "Sometimes a mare is better than a stallion," she said. "Now, Mr. Forrester, I'll collect my debt."

Willis Forrester's face was as black as thunder as he nodded in defeat. There was nothing he could do but instruct his cowboys to hold his herd and let the Durango herd move ahead of them. "You ain't seen the last of me yet," he threatened.

Lynnie, riding past him, could not resist turning in her saddle to yell back. "See you in Dodge City, Mr. Forrester."

Even though it was fast growing dark, Ace and his cowboys got their herd on the move and passed the Forrester herd. Ace was jubilant as he looked back and watched the Forrester herd fade into the background.

"You did it, Lynnie. We'll be the first ones to Dodge, and we'll get top price for our beef."

She only nodded coolly, now remembering how fast the big cowboy had been to reject her the morning after he'd made love to her. However, she had another worry; she intended to keep Daisy, but what would she do with her other three calves when she reached Dodge? She hadn't gone to all this trouble so they could end up on a dinner plate.

A few more days passed, and they saw smoke curling up from a chimney in the distance.

Ace sniffed. "Settlers in some dirt soddie, I reckon. It won't be long before they'll be fencin' the whole range and plowin' it up. They'll mean the end of the cattleman."

"Oh, don't be so greedy," Lynnie said. "While we rest and water the herd at that next creek, why don't we ride over and see them?"

"Not interested." Ace shook his head.

"Fine, then I'll go alone."

"Let you ride out alone? I can't do that."

A small flame of hope flickered. "Why not? You worried about me?"

He pushed his hat back. "Of course not. Lordy, you do a better job of lookin' out for yourself than most cowboys. You're as independent as a hog on ice."

"I appreciate the comparison," she snapped.

"What I meant to say," he replied, "was that I'd have to answer to Uncle Maverick and Dad if something happened to you."

"You didn't seem worried about that the night you seduced me."

"Seduced you? Lynnie McBride, you was all over me like bees on a honey tree. Why, I couldn't fight you off."

She felt her face burn. "I don't remember that you tried to. Besides, Ace Durango, you are no gentleman to bring that up. Now, I'm riding over to that settler's cabin. You can stay here if you like."

He sighed in defeat. "I'll go along."

"Fine. I hope you'll ride a few yards behind me; I wouldn't want anyone to think we were together."

"Perish the thought. After all, the farmer might have a pretty daughter."

She looked him over coldly. "I doubt if we have the time for you to get the daughter's drawers off."

He winked at her. "It don't usually take me long. Anyway, if she's purty, I'll hurry it up so we won't delay the drive."

"Fine." She had never been so angry in her life. To think she had wasted her virginity on this galoot. She nudged Boneyard and rode toward the distant soddie with Ace trailing behind her.

"Hello the house!" she yelled, waving her hat.

A handsome young man came out of the soddie and paused in surprise, then waved. "Come on in."

She rode into the yard, where a few chickens scratched in the dust and a yellow hound dog barked lazily. The tall farmer wore threadbare overalls, and his blond hair was tousled and his skin windburned.

"Get down and set a spell." He strode up to her, grinning. "We don't get much company. I'm Sam Reynolds."

My, he was handsome. She let him help her down, favoring him with her warmest smile. "We're just taking a herd through to Dodge and saw your smoke. This your place?"

"My folks." He gestured toward the house, where a

gray-haired couple were coming out onto the porch. "This your man?"

He turned to shake hands with Ace, who was just dismounting.

"Certainly not!" Lynnie said, "I'm Lynnie McBride. He's just the trail boss; that's all."

Ace frowned. "The lady is a little too headstrong to be married."

Sam gave Lynnie a warm smile. "I don't know about that; I like a woman who thinks for herself. I been lookin' for a wife myself, and I think Miss Lynnie's right purty, if you don't mind me sayin' so."

Lynnie blushed in spite of herself. "Why, Mr. Reynolds, a lady never minds hearing she's pretty." She gave Ace a sarcastic look.

The big farmer grinned even bigger. "Why, I'd be pleased as punch to have a spunky red-haired woman. Come on, I'd like you to meet my folks."

"We'd be delighted," Lynnie purred, and took Sam's arm. When she glanced back, Ace glowered at her as he trailed along in the background.

The family was indeed glad to have company and invited the visitors in.

The older woman busied herself about the small sod house, getting food ready. "We aims to do better," she said, "soon's they open the Indian Territory for settlement."

Ace blinked. "You think they'll do that?"

The old man got out his pipe and nodded. "Folks say it's just a matter of time before they open it up. Won't take any time afore farmers will put up fences, start plowing up the ground for crops."

Sam smiled at Lynnie. "That'll mean the end of the cattle trails. Miss Lynnie, I meant what I said a while ago, about lookin' for a wife."

Ace glared at him. "Miss Lynnie isn't interested in marriage. She's devoted her life to women's rights."

Lynnie glared at him and then gave the handsome Sam her warmest smile. "Well, now, the right man might change my mind."

"I don't think so," Ace growled. He was almost sick to his stomach, the way the pair kept smiling at each other. He was surprised himself at just how annoyed he was that Lynnie might even consider marrying this big clodbuster. Why, she was too good to waste on someone like that. She might be too good to waste on nearly anybody, because the average man couldn't appreciate a headstrong, smart woman like her and wouldn't know how to handle her. "We can't stay long. The herd's waitin' for us."

"Wish we had more to offer," the old woman said as she put a pot of fresh vegetables and a pan of cornbread on the table. "We'd like to get a cattle herd started, but we ain't got the money to buy calves."

Lynnie looked at Ace, and it was funny, but he already knew what she was thinking. Lynnie said, "I believe we've got three we could spare."

"That's right," Ace agreed.

Sam colored. "We got no money."

Lynnie looked at Ace again, seeking his help.

"Ma'am," Ace said, "these calves is just slowin' us down, and our crew sure could use some fresh vegetables and homemade bread."

The old woman brightened. "Why, now, that's different, if you think it's a fair trade. I even got some fresh pies I made this morning."

Now Ace smiled and licked his lips. "By any chance, might they be rhubarb?"

"Why, yes, they are."

"Done!" Ace agreed.

So the pair ate, then returned to get the three calves to trade to the farm family.

As they were riding away loaded down with fresh bread, pies, and vegetables, Sam yelled, "Miss Lynnie, should you change your mind about marriage, I'd be glad to have you."

"I'll remember," Lynnie promised as she and Ace rode away from the soddie.

"I'll just bet he'd be glad to have you," Ace sniffed. "You're too much woman to waste on the likes of him."

"Oh?" She glanced over at him, but he was staring straight ahead as they rode.

"Besides that, Uncle Maverick and Dad would have a hissy fit if I came back without you and said I'd left you with some sodbuster out on the prairie."

So that's all it was: he felt responsible for her. She had a terrible urge to knock him off his horse and tie him out on an anthill, Indian-style. For a long moment, she relished the thought of him writhing as the busy little insects chewed away, especially on his . . .

"Lynnie, I have to apologize again about what happened back there at the river when we was just playin' around. . . ."

"Playing around? Is that what you call it?" She was outraged.

"Well, I reckon a girl like you would expect the man to make an honest woman of her—"

"Honest?" she was seething. "So what am I? A whore?"

"Lordy, girl, respectable women don't use that word."

"I suppose respectable women don't wallow around in the dirt with you, either. Let's get one thing straight, Ace Durango. You're under no obligation to me. In fact, I wouldn't have you as a free gift. Now tell that to the boys at the ranch."

He looked at her, disbelief etched on his dark, rugged features. "I'm supposed to be the best lover above the Río Grande," he grumbled. "Women have told me how good I am."

"Maybe other women were big liars," Lynnie snapped, and nudged her horse into a lope.

"I could do better!" he yelled after her.

"You aren't going to get the chance!" she yelled back, and kept her face turned toward the trail so he couldn't see her tears. He was not only untamed, he was uncivilized and unsuitable. Well, in a few more days, they would be in Dodge, and then she wouldn't have to see him anymore. Lynnie was annoyed with herself that in a moment of weakness, she had succumbed to Ace's charms. *Like a dog lured off a meat wagon,* she thought grimly. And now he felt guilty and obligated.

Thunderation. Damned if she wanted him to feel obligated. She didn't know for certain how she wanted him to feel or how she felt. There was no room in her life for this rude, crude cowboy. Once in Dodge, she'd go on with her women's voting crusade, and he could go back to chasing women, gambling, and drinking. Trouble was, she finally admitted to herself as they drove the bawling cattle up the trail, she had feelings for Ace Durango, and she was certain the attraction wasn't mutual. So she must hide her feelings for the next few days. The big cowboy need never know that she'd lost her heart as well as her virginity to him.

Twenty

"There she is, boys; there's Dodge up ahead!" Ace took off his hat and waved it with a whoop. Behind him, the tired crew set up a cheer. He glanced at Lynnie, but she betrayed no feelings other than to say, "Well, I hope I'm here in time for the ladies' meeting."

"Near as I can calculate, " Ace said, "it can't be later than the first week of July. Lots of celebratin' ahead for Independence Day."

"A good time to push for women's rights." Her small chin stuck out stubbornly.

He didn't quite know what to make of Lynnie. Certainly, he had never met another woman like her: independent, stubborn, and headstrong. She wasn't like the silly, giggling girls or lusty, bawdy whores he had known. It was a good thing the trip was ending; she appeared to be barely able to stand the sight of him. He ought to be glad to be rid of her, but somehow, he almost hated to see the trip end. "Get the herd movin', boys," he shouted, "we'll celebrate tonight!"

Ace rode on in ahead of the herd. It was Independence Day, all right. The town was draped with red, white, and blue banners and lots of flags. Most of the stores were closed, but the saloons and dance halls seemed to be doing a big business. Small boys ran up and down the streets setting off firecrackers, and cowboys lounged against the hitching rails, drinking beer and yelling to each other.

Ace rode up to the cattle buyer's office, and dismounted, and banged on the door.

"Go away; I'm closed for the holiday."

Ace banged again. "Well, open up. I've got a prime herd comin' down Front Street, and you'll want to see it."

"Cattle?" The door opened and a small, mustachioed man stuck his head out. "In that case, let's do a little business."

They both stood and watched Ace's cowboys bring the bawling, dusty herd down the road.

Lynnie yelled, "Is there a hotel in town?"

The buyer nodded and turned to Ace. "Is that a girl with those cowboys?"

Ace nodded and grinned, suddenly proud of her. "Yes, and what a girl."

"Ain't too purty," the man said.

"Purty?" Ace said. "Why, are you blind? That's the purtiest, sassiest girl both sides of the Red River." He paused, surprised at his own words. Once he hadn't thought that. Had Lynnie McBride changed, or was it him? He had no time for deep thinking now. Instead, he turned to yell at his crew. "Take them to the stockyards, boys, and I'll see you in the Lace Garter later."

The cowboys set up a cheer, but Lynnie glared at him.

The buyer looked her over. "A petticoat outfit; a gal on a cattle drive. Bet that's a stubborn one."

Ace looked at the redhead moving down the street with the herd. "Lordy, she does know her own mind. There's nothin' wishy-washy or silly about that one, but she's equal to any man in the saddle. Now let's do some business so's I can wet my whistle and celebrate."

The little man nodded. "Fine herd, let's go inside and talk."

"Oh, one thing, there's a cross-eyed calf and old Twister that don't go with the deal."

The other paused in the office door. "A cross-eyed calf? I'll bet there's an interesting story behind that."

Ace remembered back over the past several months as he wiped sweat from his face. "It's been the trip of a lifetime," he murmured, "and I'll never forget it."

Within an hour, Ace had sold the cattle herd for a very big price in some hard bargaining that would have made his dad proud. Whistling and happy, he headed for the Lace Garter Saloon to celebrate. Here and there, firecrackers exploded as small boys ran up and down the dusty streets, celebrating.

Ace blinked as he entered the darkened saloon and went to the bar. "Whiskey."

Most of his cowboys were already there, one foot on the brass rail. "Get a good price, boss?"

"You better believe it. Forrester won't get near that much when he comes in. Drinks for everyone!"

All the cowboys pushed up to the bar as Ace grabbed his whiskey and gulped it. It was the good stuff, and it gave him a warm feeling all the way down. He had brought the herd through and got a good price for it. He could finally look his father square in the eye and not feel inferior. He had no doubt now that he could run the Triple D when he inherited his share. He hadn't done it by himself, though. He had a good, loyal crew and a certain stubborn redhead to thank for his success. In some ways, she was equal to a man; in others, she was still very much a lady.

Old Cookie limped over to stand next to him. "Boy, you left Texas a raw, wet-behind-the-ears kid, but you're a grown man now, a real trail boss. I'd be proud to side you again."

Joe nodded. "You're a man to ride the river with, boss. You need any hands at the ranch, I'd be proud to work for you."

Ace grinned. Among cowboys, there was no higher compliment than to judge a man savvy and smart enough to make a river crossing with a herd without getting anyone killed.

Hank yelled, "Three cheers for the toughest, best trail boss in Texas: Ace Durango!"

Ace felt himself flush as the crew cheered him. "Another round of drinks for my boys, barkeep."

As the men crowded around and glasses clinked, a bald-headed man in sleeve garters began to pound the old piano, not well but loudly. ". . . *Oh, it rained all the night the day I left; the weather it was dry. The sun so hot I froze to death . . .*"

Ace looked around. There was one member of the crew who wasn't here. "Where's Lynnie?"

Hank put his elbows on the bar. "Are you daft? Ladies don't come into bars."

"Don't tell Lynnie that or she'll be bound and determined to do it," Ace murmured, and smiled when he thought about how feisty she was.

Old Cookie rubbed his stubbly chin. "I recollect that after we put the herd in the pens, she headed for the hotel to clean up—said something about a ladies' meetin'."

Ace groaned aloud. "That is the dad-blamedest, stubbornest woman."

He didn't want to think about Lynnie McBride; he wanted to have a good time getting drunk and carousing like he'd always done. Somehow, the gathering didn't seem complete without her; after all, she'd helped bring in the herd. Lynnie. She wasn't as pretty or big-busted or any of the things he'd always wanted in a woman, and yet . . . there was something special about her.

Not that it made any difference, because she sure wasn't interested in him and she was as independent as a hog on ice. Where most women trailed after him, almost begging for marriage, Lynnie had turned up her nose and scoffed at him.

Joe wiped his mouth, drained his mug of beer, and grinned. "Well, now, I reckon it's about time for another kind of fun."

He started for the stairs. Halfway up, the bartender yelled at him, "You're wastin' your time, cowboy; the girls ain't up there."

"What?" Joe paused and looked disappointed.

"What?" All the men echoed. Then they began to look around. "Say, just where are all the gals, anyhow?"

The bartender sighed and paused in wiping the bar. "Well, some little red-haired gal came in a couple of hours ago. She was dressed funny in green gingham with her underpants showin'."

"Lynnie," Ace sighed.

"Anyways," said the bartender, "she gave the whores a big talk about how they could do better than be playthings for men. She urged them to turn over a new leaf, come to some meetin', and help her campaign for women's rights."

The men all turned and glared at Ace.

"Lynnie," he said again, and took another drink. "Yep, that's Lynnie, all right."

Joe came back down the stairs. "Well, without whores and dance-hall girls, what are men supposed to do?"

Ace shrugged. "I reckon you'll all have to get married and make honest women out of them."

"Married?" said the cowboys in shocked horror.

About that time, a skinny man ran through the swinging doors of the saloon. "Hey, come out and see the fun. There's about to be big trouble down in front of City Hall." He had all the men's attention now.

Ace sighed and kept sipping his drink. He had a feeling that he didn't want to know.

"Well . . ." The skinny man wiped the July sweat from his face, elbowed his way to the bar, and grabbed a mug of beer. "There's a bunch of women with protest signs parading up and down the street. A bunch of fellas is hurrahin' them, and some cowboys who're just bringin' in a herd is really givin' the ladies a hard time."

"Forrester," Ace thought aloud as he turned to the man. "Tell me, mister, is there a little redhead involved in this protest?"

The man paused. "Well, yes, wearin' a short green dress with her underpants showin'."

"Them's bloomers," Ace advised him. "They're something the suffragettes wear."

The man scratched his head. Evidently, he didn't know what a suffragette was. "Kind of plain, she is."

"She's not plain," Ace protested, "and she's smart, real smart—a little headstrong, maybe."

"I'll say," the man answered doubtfully, wiping foam from his lip. "I'd hate to be the man tryin' to tame that gal."

"Mister," Cookie said, "the only man in the world who might tame that little spitfire is Ace Durango."

The men all looked at him.

Ace shrugged and sipped his drink. "She ain't my responsibility now that we've made it to town. Dodge City is on its own, and God help them."

Comanch ran into the saloon through the swinging doors. "Hey, Boss, Forrester's herd just got in, and Willis Forrester is mad as a rattlesnake on a hot griddle 'cause I hear he didn't get much for his herd."

"That's his problem." Ace took another sip of beer.

"But he and his cowboys are hurrahin' those ladies Miss Lynnie's got paradin' up and down in front of City Hall. They're throwin' firecrackers and horse manure at them."

He felt a protective instinct for the brave, slight girl. She was no longer his responsibility, and yet . . .

Ace slammed his mug down. "He's peltin' Lynnie with road apples? Come on, boys!"

He was mad now as he led his cowboys out of the saloon and they marched down dusty Front Street.

There was Lynnie, all right, red, white, and blue ribbons on her short green gingham dress with white bloomers peeking out below. She led a mixed parade of painted saloon girls and upright ladies, all carrying protest signs. Daisy Buttercup walked alongside Lynnie, bawling noisily and wearing a sign that read, *Don't Treat Women Like Cows. Give Them The Vote.*

Boneyard stood tied to a hitching post covered with red, white, and blue crepe paper streamers and a sign that urged, *Women's Rights. They Deserve Them.*

Willis Forrester and his cowboys had gathered amid the growing crowd, and they were yelling taunts at the ladies and throwing firecrackers under their feet. Lynnie appeared to be bravely ignoring the unruly, hostile crowd of men.

"Free women!" the ladies shouted as they marched in a big circle with their protest signs. "Free women!"

A drunken rowdy staggered toward them. "Free women? I'll take one. Which one can I have?"

At that point, Lynnie hit the drunken cowboy with her picket sign. Just then, Nelbert Purdy threw a string of firecrackers under Daisy Buttercup's hooves, and the calf threw back her head and bawled in terror.

"Get back in the kitchen!" Willis Forrester shouted. "That's where you gals belong!"

Ace had seen enough. He doubled up his fists. "Lynnie McBride belongs wherever she wants to be!"

He saw Lynnie look up, her lip trembling a little at the onslaught of catcalls and hostile roughnecks crowding in around her and her ladies. "Ace," she called, "oh, Ace, I knew you'd come."

For a split second, he looked at her and wondered why he'd once thought her plain. Plain? She was beautiful—the prettiest girl he had ever seen—and she needed him.

Willis Forrester threw another firecracker, sending the ladies scurrying and shrieking.

"Get 'em boys!" Ace commanded, and then he went after Forrester. He grabbed him and whirled him around. "That's no way to treat a lady."

"She ain't no lady, not with her underpants showin'." Forrester sneered, "I—"

He never finished, because Ace hit him in the mouth and sent him stumbling backward and right into a horse trough. Behind Ace, a commotion broke out as his cowboys waded in, slugging jeering drunks and ne'er-do-wells and clearing a path around the women.

Lynnie, not to be outdone, rallied her ladies, and they charged in to help, swinging their protest signs. Nelbert Purdy had just run out into the street to throw more manure when Lynnie caught him with her wooden sign, knocking him backward so that he crashed into the horse trough right on top of Forrester, who was just trying to get up.

Ace grinned at her. "Atta girl, Lynnie. Now let's mop 'em up!"

He grabbed Purdy by his collar, stood him on his feet, and Lynnie hit him again with her sign, tossing him into a fresh pile of horse manure. Men were now fighting each other, rolling and brawling in the middle of the dusty street while the whores from all the local saloons were right in there beside the more respectable women, shrieking and scratching.

Ace turned to fight off two drunken cowboys as Forrester himself staggered, dripping wet, out of the horse trough. Forrester grabbed Lynnie and took her sign away from her.

"You!" he snarled. "I thought I'd outwit you and Durango when I changed all the signs out on the trail. You've caused me to lose a lot of money!" He picked her up and tossed her in the horse trough.

She went under and came up sputtering and screaming while Ace ran to her rescue, lifted her out of the trough, and stood her on her feet, dripping and undignified, gold spectacles askew. Then he hit Forrester again and threw him under Boneyard's hooves. The gray horse promptly kicked Forrester end over end and into a fresh pile of cow pie that little Daisy had just made.

It was a riot involving a hundred people, drunken cowboys, bystanders, respectable ladies, and whores from the local saloons. Men crashed through store windows, and children ran up and down, shouting with excitement. A terrified team of horses bolted down the street while a pack of local mongrels ran after the runaway team, barking loudly. Shots flew and added to the fireworks as the brawl spread up and down the street. Some didn't even seem to know for sure what the ruckus was about, but it was too much fun to miss.

Lynnie and Ace found themselves side by side, their clothes torn, wet and dirty as they punched Forrester's cowboys. "Lordy, girl," Ace shouted, "what are you doin' out here soakin' wet with your drawers showin'?"

"They're bloomers," she corrected as she tripped a

drunk, and Ace picked the man up and tossed him in the horse trough. "Thanks for joining our protest."

"Protest, hell, I just came to rescue you." He hit Purdy as the fat man stumbled toward him.

"I don't need rescuing," she shouted back as she swung her protest sign. "I can take care of myself."

"The hell you can. It looks like I'll have to spend the rest of my days gettin' you out of trouble."

She paused, not quite sure what she was hearing. "Is this a proposal?"

"Lynnie"—he wiped the dirt from his face and ducked as a drunk swung at him—"I won't take no for an answer; we're gettin' hitched."

"I don't want you to feel obligated . . ."

"Oh, shut up!" he yelled. "You keep gettin' me in all kinds of trouble, and I'd like to have some kind of control over your actions."

"Control?" She bristled. "Control? Why, you uncivilized brute—"

"Uh-oh, here comes some deputies," Ace yelled, "and it's too late to run."

She looked at him, all bloody and with his shirt torn. Abruptly, she felt like a beautiful princess with a handsome knight available for her rescue. "Good, we'll get some publicity for the cause."

Ace groaned aloud. "Honey, I can see life with you ain't gonna be dull."

"Isn't," she corrected, and paused to watch the deputies running along the street. "What happens next?"

"You don't wanna know," Ace groaned.

"This isn't the way I pictured a marriage proposal." She pushed another drunk into the horse trough.

"Me neither. Matter of fact, I never pictured one at all." He shrugged and put his hands on her shoulders.

"Fact is, somebody's got to protect you and help you get out of all the scrapes you get into."

"I'm perfectly capable of looking after myself," she shouted back, and picked up her sign and whacked Purdy with it as he stumbled to his feet.

"I know that, but you could use an ally now and then. I'm big; I can carry a lot of protest signs."

"You don't care that I'm not beautiful?"

He took the protest sign out of her hand, tossed it away, and yanked her to him, kissing her senseless. "Lynnie, to me you're beautiful." And he meant it.

"Hey," someone yelled, "here comes the sheriff!"

At the Triple D Ranch, Cimarron came into the study looking at the paper in her hand. The date was July 5.

Trace had finally recovered from his broken ribs, and he sat on the leather sofa sipping his tequila and patted the Chihuahua in his lap. "What's that?"

"Ace is in jail again."

"What?" He jumped to his feet, dumping the disgusted dog in the floor.

"This wire just came. Lynnie and the whole crew are in the Dodge jail, too. Also, someone named Boneyard and Daisy Buttercup. Now, who do you suppose that is?"

Her husband paced up and down. "Dios! Damn that boy. It's not bad enough that he's always in trouble; he has to get that sweet, innocent girl into it with him. When Pedro told us she was along on that drive, I hoped her good influence would straighten him out, but I reckon he's hopeless."

Cimarron read some more of the wire and smiled. "They got top dollar for the beef. Ace wants you to get the Indian agent to the Comanches fired."

Her husband lit a cigarillo. "I can do that. I've met him, now that I think of it, and he's rotten."

She beamed at him. "Oh, Willis Forrester, Nelbert Purdy, and their whole crew are in jail, too."

Trace paused and smiled. "Well, it's an ill wind that doesn't blow somebody some good. I'd give a hundred gold pesos to see that uppity pair peeking out between the bars."

Cimarron continued to read and smiled, very pleased. "There's more. They want to get married."

"Married?" He was thunderstruck. "Who? Purdy and Forrester? I think that's against the law."

"Double damnation, Trace, haven't you been listening? Our Ace and Lynnie."

Her husband blinked. "Ace and Lynnie McBride? He's gotten her in the family way; that's what it is. Maverick will kill him, and if he doesn't, I will."

"Darlin'," she said, smiling gently, "Lynnie's not as naive as you think she is."

He shook his head in puzzlement. "Do you suppose that sweet little thing knows what she's gettin' into?"

Cimarron smiled. "I think she can handle him. Cayenne and I always thought they would make a good pair."

"You two women must be loco. A more unlikely pair there never was."

"Maybe," Cimarron said. "We'll have to get together with the McBrides and start planning the wedding."

"First you'd better send bail money and get the whole bunch out of jail."

Cimarron grinned, very pleased with herself. "I already did. They should all be on a train heading for home by now."

"In the meantime, I wonder, who in the hell is Daisy

Buttercup? I didn't know there were two girls along on this cattle drive."

"Reckon we'll find out," Cimarron said, and went off to make a list of guests.

It was a lovely wedding and a big one that crisp September day. Most of central and west Texas had been invited, including the cowboys who had helped Ace take the herd up the Chisholm Trail. The little old-fashioned church where Lynnie's blind father preached was full to overflowing. Besides the many friends, some were just incredulous citizens who couldn't quite believe that a plain, bossy old maid like the McBride girl had lassoed the biggest catch in the whole state, and had come to see this event for themselves.

Ace had asked his father to be his best man, so Cimarron sat alone on the front pew and winked across at Cayenne, who was bouncing baby Joey on her knee and trying to keep her many children from running up and down the aisles. The two ladies were most pleased with this love match they had engineered.

Maverick would escort Lynnie down the aisle. Of course, no one was surprised that she had arranged to have the word *obey* taken out of the ceremony. Lynnie had asked Penelope to be her maid of honor. Her bridesmaids were Ace's younger sister, the dark and beautiful Raven, and Lynnie's younger sisters, Gracious, Stevie, and Angel. Maverick and Cayenne's daughter, Annie Laurie, was pressed into service as a flower girl. Ace's cowboys, Hank, Comanch, Joe, Pedro, and old Cookie were acting as ushers.

The old organ wheezed and began to play. First the flower girl, scattering wildflowers, came down the aisle, followed by the bridesmaids on the arms of the ushers.

Penelope was radiant because, as everyone knew, her father had finally relented about Hank, even though he was a poor man with only a few worthless, oil-soaked acres to his name.

When Cookie passed, Cimarron got a distinct whiff of vanilla and sighed. Oh, well, maybe he wouldn't trip and fall down in front of the whole church.

As the radiant bride started down the aisle in a magnificent white dress, a girl sitting behind Cimarron moaned to another, "I don't understand it. She's not even pretty and she lands the most handsome, charming man in all Texas. What's she got?"

Cimarron couldn't resist. She turned around and smiled sweetly—a little too sweetly. "Lynnie's smart and she can go toe to toe with Ace, which is just the kind of wife he needs. By the way, even the plainest girl is beautiful to the man who loves her."

Emmalou Purdy was not present. It seemed that during the summer, that paragon of virtue, the new schoolmaster, Clarence Kleinhoffer, had gotten her in what in Texas is politely called "a family way." Nelbert Purdy had had to take his shotgun to persuade a very reluctant bridegroom to marry Emmalou, and the school board had fired Clarence. The pair had left the state in disgrace.

Ace, with his father as his best man, stood watching as Lynnie came down the aisle on her brother-in-law's arm. Maverick, frankly, looked relieved that someone else was about to take over the duty of keeping Lynnie in bounds. Ace grinned as he looked into her radiant face. She wasn't wearing her spectacles, so he hoped she didn't trip and fall coming down the aisle. He could tame this little Texan, or maybe he couldn't, but it was going to be a great adventure to try.

When she took her place next to him, he leaned over and whispered, "You're the most beautiful girl in the world, honey." And he meant it with every beat of his heart.

Lynnie took his arm, barely hearing the words of the ceremony. She had her man, and it was going to be a great challenge to tame this rough Texan, but she figured she was up to the challenge. Of course, she didn't intend to give up her work for women's rights. Ace had promised to help with her crusade because he wanted his daughters to have the same rights as men.

She looked up at him, loving him like she had never known she could love a man. Half the women in the audience wanted to be Mrs. Ace Durango, but he had chosen Lynnie. He was looking down at her as if there were no one else in the whole world. Almost in a daze, she heard her preacher father say "Diego de Durango the Fourth, will you take this woman to love and cherish now and forevermore?"

Ace seemed to hesitate as if forgetting his real, legal name. His father cleared his throat and nudged him. "Say yes, Ace," he whispered.

The audience tittered.

The minister asked again, "Ace, you gonna marry my daughter?"

"You're damned tootin'!" Ace declared in a loud, honest voice. "Long as I got a biscuit, she gets half."

That was the best promise a Texan could make. Lynnie looked up at him in a daze, loving him so.

"And will you, Lynnie Elizabeth McBride, take this man, Diego de Durango the Fourth, to be your lawful husband, to love and to cherish through sickness and in health, as long as you both shall live?"

"As long as we got that 'obey' thing straight," she said in a determined tone.

The audience laughed, and her father sighed. "I

reckon any man who tries to make you obey had better bring his supper, because he may be there a while."

"I thought," Ace said, "we cleared that all up."

"In that case, the answer is yes," Lynnie said. "And as long as I got a biscuit, he's got half."

The audience fanned itself and nodded in approval, everyone grinning. No Texan could make a more sincere commitment than offering to share his last biscuit.

Father seemed to sigh with relief. "Is there a ring?"

At that point, Ace's dad reached over and handed him the gold band studded with the biggest diamonds Lynnie had ever seen. A murmur of wonder went through the crowd as Ace slipped it on her finger. "Do you see the size of those stones? Why, that ring would buy a whole ranch."

Lynnie let Ace slip the ring on her finger while her father intoned the words. It was a beautiful ring, she thought, and it sparkled like a thousand suns in the dim light of the old church. It glowed like the passion she held for the man who put it on her hand.

Her father smiled and held up his hand in benediction as he pronounced the final words. "Then by the power vested in me by God and the most wonderful and best state in the union—Texas, of course—I now pronounce you husband and wife. You may kiss your bride."

Ace slowly lifted her veil. She looked up into his eyes and saw the love there. "Put on your spectacles, honey. I want you to see who's kissin' you."

Obedient for once, she reached for the glasses that Raven held out to her, put them on, and his handsome features cleared in her vision.

"I love you, Lynnie Durango," he whispered.

"Oh," she whispered back, "I've been meaning to tell you, I don't intend to give up my maiden name."

"The hell you don't!" He took her in his embrace and

held her so close, she could scarcely breathe. Then he kissed her with such passion that Lynnie McBride-Durango forgot about everything else but what lay ahead of them tonight in bed, and the wonderful and exciting life they would lead as each tried to tame the other.

The audience began to titter, and her father cleared his throat. "Ahem. You've got the rest of your life to kiss her, my boy."

"The rest of my life," he repeated.

She saw Ace pull back with reluctance, never taking his gaze from her face. His dark eyes promised that her wedding night was going to be unforgettable.

But right now, they had guests to entertain. They swept down the aisle to organ music while old ladies wiped their eyes and young women sighed regretfully. Outside, a large pavilion had been set up with a Western band and plenty of food, including a whole barbecued steer turning on a spit. Cookie was turning the spit and sipping out of a quart bottle of vanilla while the little Chihuahua, Tequila, lay next to his feet, waiting for his share of the feast. There was plenty of cold beer and lemonade, potato salad and deviled eggs, and cakes and pies and cookies of all kinds.

The whole trail crew was there to help them celebrate. Comanch and Joe got a card game going out on the lawn. Pedro, his leg now healed, took his new bride, the lovely Maria Sanchos, whom he had met on the train, out onto the dance floor to join Penelope and the grinning Hank.

Ace's dad was so pleased with the man his son had become that he'd given him his share of the ranch: thousands of acres of choice land with a hilltop that had a glorious view. A fine new home was already under construction there.

Little Daisy Buttercup, all decked out with ribbons

and flowers, was quietly munching on the floral deco-
rations of the tables as the dancing began, while old
Twister, now permanently retired, grazed peacefully in
a nearby pasture.

Ace took Lynnie in his arms, and they moved out on
the floor. "Lynnie," he reminded her gently, "I'm supposed to lead."

"Now, why is that?" she said stubbornly.

"I think we've already had this discussion."

"But we didn't settle it the first time."

"Oh, Lynnie," he sighed, "I'd forgotten just how stubborn you can be."

"I'm not stubborn; I'm resolute."

He grinned down at her and kissed the side of her
face, sending shivers of pleasure all over her body. "By
the way, I bought you a wedding present."

"Another one? Oh, Ace, you've given me so much already: all the jewelry and building me a big ranch house
on that hill . . ."

"But this is something you really wanted," he murmured. "Penelope's dad didn't really want to sell, but I
convinced him." He whirled her around, and there on
the other side of the pavilion, Boneyard stood tied to a
buggy, all decked out in red harness and flowers.

"Oh, Ace." Tears came to her eyes. "You knew how
much I wanted her."

Ace sighed and held her closer. "An ugly gray horse
and a cross-eyed calf. We're off to a good start, I reckon."

She smiled up at him and kissed the edge of his
mouth. "Daisy is going to be the start of our giant new
herd. Now all we need are a half-dozen children."

He grinned. "I'm available for stud service morning,
noon, and night, Mrs. Durango."

"I can hardly wait."

Of course, they had to stay at the party for several

hours so the crowd could congratulate them and wish them well, but finally, Lynnie went to retrieve her bridal bouquet from the table to throw as she left. Unfortunately, Daisy Buttercup had found the flowers and nibbled them down to a few leaves. Oh, well. Penelope caught it and smiled at Hank Dale, who smiled back and pulled her out on the dance floor.

The bridal couple got in the decorated buggy as the crowd threw rice.

"Hey," Penelope yelled, "that horse isn't used to pulling a buggy."

"Now you tell us," Ace complained as the horse snorted, half reared, and then took off uncertainly. The cans and old shoes tied on behind made noise, which seemed to panic the horse, and she took off at a gallop. Ace sawed on the reins, but the ugly gray mare kept running for almost a mile before she got off the road and crashed the buggy into a haystack.

"Look out, Ace!" Lynnie closed her eyes as the buggy bounced, and when she opened them, she and Ace lay sprawled in the hay, the buggy upended nearby, and the horse grazing contentedly in the field.

He leaned over, picked some hay out of her hair, and kissed her. "I think I'll make love to you right here," he whispered. "Lordy, how I do love you."

"Thunderation. Right here? Where everyone can see?"

"They're a mile down the road and still dancin' and celebratin'. They won't know."

"Sounds good to me," she whispered, and offered her lips to let him kiss her—really kiss her—while molding her body against his. She felt his fingers opening the bodice of her long white dress, and her heart beat a little faster at what was coming next as his mouth moved down her throat. "All right, Texan, tame me."

He grinned and kissed his way down to her breast, his

hand going to pull up her skirt so that he could stroke her thigh, and then he was making passionate love to her. It was as wonderful and exciting as she had ever dreamed possible.

"I'll do my best, Mrs. Durango," he promised as he kissed her again. "I'll do my best!"

Epilogue

The telephone rang and rang and rang.

Cimarron, her hair very gray now, hurried into the library to answer it. "Double damnation, Trace, couldn't you answer that thing?"

"Was it ringing?" The gray-haired rancher stroked the latest Chihuahua in his lap and pretended he hadn't heard the bell. Trace didn't like the newfangled gadget his wife had had installed.

"You old cuss, you knew it was." She picked up the receiver, talked a moment, hung it up, and turned around.

"Ace is in jail again."

"What? I thought when he married that nice girl back in 'eight-five, we'd see the end of that—"

"Lynnie's in jail, too, and so are all our granddaughters."

Trace sighed. "I don't see why they can't stay home and run the ranch instead of galavantin' off to Washington for women's rights."

"Oh, darlin', don't raise your blood pressure." She came over and sat down. "You know how important riding in that suffrage parade during President Wilson's inauguration is to them. There's five thousand other protestors, too."

Trace snorted, hobbled to the sideboard, and poured himself a jigger of tequila. "Ridin' in one of them newfangled automobiles, I reckon. Horses were always good enough for us."

"Time's are changing, and they say there won't be much need for horses in a few years. Good thing Hank Dale hung on to that worthless, oil-soaked land of his. He's about the richest man in Texas."

"We've got a little oil ourselves," her husband reminded her.

"Then that's all the more reason that maybe we should buy an automobile. I saw a Stanley Steamer at a dealer in town."

"Never." He gulped his drink.

She frowned at him. "You know what your doctor said about tequila."

"A little drink never hurt anyone," Trace snapped as he returned to the leather sofa. "I reckon I'll outlive that young whippersnapper of a doctor. You didn't say why the kids are in jail. I reckon our son got that nice, innocent girl in a mess of trouble again."

"Or vice versa." Cimarron smiled. "They're hoping this will be the year Congress will act on women's right to vote. There was some protesters tried to break up the parade, and some brute insulted Lynnie so she hit him with a sign, and then Ace knocked him down and the granddaughters started swinging."

Her husband rolled his eyes as if imploring heaven. "I had hoped the girls might grow up to be ladies, but what can we expect when five of the six are named after suffragettes?"

"They *are* ladies, just feisty like their parents, and

they'll be voting soon if their parents have anything to say about it. A lot of people were arrested."

"Well, I don't want my granddaughters sittin' in jail; wire them some bail money."

Cimarron leaned over, kissed his forehead, and brushed his gray hair from his face. "You old darlin', I already did."

The state capitol, Nashville, Tennessee
August 18, 1920

Lynnie McBride-Durango sat in the gallery with her husband and daughters, waiting for the representatives to enter for the morning's vote.

It was hot, really hot, in the crowded chamber. She patted Ace on the arm and smiled lovingly at him. There was a lot of gray in his hair now, as in hers, but she loved him more than she had ever thought she could love a man. This thirty-five-year marriage had produced six red-haired, wonderful daughters, all married now except for the youngest, Lynnie, who would finish college this year.

Young Lynnie sat next to her and gave her an encouraging nod. "We'll do it this time, Mom."

"Let's hope so. North Carolina voted it down yesterday, the old South has all voted no, and Vermont, Florida, and Connecticut have decided not to take any action at all. If we can't get it through today, it may all be over. I wish Penelope and Hank were here."

"Oh, Mom, you know they're in Europe on a grand tour with their daughters." Young Lynnie pushed her gold-rimmed spectacles back up her freckled nose.

"Who's running the oil company?" her mother asked, looking around at the hot, restless crowd and then below at the empty legislative seats.

Young Lynnie fanned herself. "Junior. Did I tell you he's bought an airplane and a Pierce Arrow automobile just like Grandpa's?"

Lynnie frowned. "I'm not sure a man as old as Trace Durango ought to be racing against your Uncle Maverick's Duesenberg. Men that old ought to stick to a horse and buggy, but I guess your grandma and my sister can't do a thing with that pair."

Her daughter took out her lipstick. "Hank Jr. says he's going to teach me to drive the car and the airplane."

"What?" At that, her father leaned around her mother and glared at her. "Tell Hank Dale Jr. I forbid that."

"Daddy"—Lynnie gave him her most engaging smile—"I'm an engaged woman. You can't forbid me to do anything."

"Lordy, you're just like your mother." He shook his head in defeat. "Young lady, is that face paint you're smearin' on? And your skirt is entirely too short. In my day, respectable girls wore long skirts and bustles."

"Daddy, you're so old-fashioned! Skirts are going to get even shorter. Besides, Mama told me when you romanced her, she was wearing a dress so short her underpants showed."

"Bloomers," her mother corrected, "not underpants. But they didn't show as much leg as you're showing, young lady."

"I'm thinking of having my hair bobbed," young Lynnie said. "All the flappers are doing it."

"What?" Her father glared at her over her mother's head.

"Mama," said her oldest daughter, Amelia—named, of course, for Amelia Bloomer—"can't you make the two of them stop? We're here for serious business."

"Thunderation," Mother said, "Amelia is right; stop it, you two."

"Mom"—Lynnie made a face at her older sister—"when we get out of here, can we go to the movies? There's a wonderful new Douglas Fairbanks film playing. They say it's the cat's pajamas."

"Lordy," Ace said, "that doesn't make any more sense than 'twenty-three skidoo.'"

His daughter rolled her eyes. "Daddy, you've got to learn the latest slang."

Lynnie gestured, her mind preoccupied with the growing crowd in the statehouse. "Be quiet, you two; it looks like the legislators are coming in. As much as I've made the rounds trying to persuade them, we still may lose this by a vote or two."

Ace took her hand. "Then we'll just keep tryin,' honey. Have I told you lately how beautiful you are?"

All six of the girls moaned aloud. "Oh, Dad, really. Not in public."

"Well, she is," Ace snapped. Then to Lynnie: "Have you talked to Mom and Dad?"

Lynnie nodded. "For a couple in their eighties, they sure are spry. I just hope they don't break their necks racing Maverick and Cayenne in those automobiles. Anyway, they called right before we left the hotel to wish us luck. Oh, by the way, Grandpa Trace said for you not to get me sent to jail again, and stay out yourself."

Ace laughed. "The old codger will never believe that a sweet, innocent girl like you might be the one gettin' me in trouble all these years."

Grim-faced men were now entering the big room below and taking their seats.

Young Lynnie was so excited, she strained her neck to see better. "Do you think we'll win?"

Her mother shrugged. "No way of knowing. It's been a hard-fought battle here in Tennessee all summer. If they vote yes, that puts us over the top and makes the Nineteenth Amendment law."

Ace gave her a fond smile. "You know, honey, when I got involved in this fight right after we married, I never thought it would take so long to win."

"We haven't won yet," Lynnie reminded him. "It all hinges on one or two men."

Young Tennessee legislator Harry Burn took a deep breath as he hesitated, then squared his shoulders and entered the chamber, the noise of hundreds of spectators drowning out his footsteps. He was only twenty-four, a first-year legislator. His town and county in the eastern part of the state were very much opposed to giving women the vote. His whole career was surely riding on what decision he made this morning.

Harry paused. The gallery was full of spectators and reporters. Looking up, he saw a sea of paper fans moving rhythmically. It was the most crowded he had ever seen the state capitol. Harry had been up most of the night wrestling with his decision after getting a letter from his mother yesterday pleading with him to give women the vote.

All the legislators were taking their seats as the speaker hammered his gavel for order. Harry could feel the sweat running down his face, and it wasn't just the summer heat. He was about to put his political career on the line. The speaker rapped for order again, and Harry took his seat along with the others.

He smiled as he looked up into the gallery and spotted that red-haired woman, her big Texas cowboy, and all those red-haired daughters of hers. She had been in to see him, asking for his vote as had all the powerful men who were opposed to women's voting. The pressure and bribery had been shocking for an honest young legislator. He nodded to Mrs. McBride-Durango, and she adjusted her spectacles and smiled back.

Harry had made his decision, and he didn't give a damn anymore what it cost him. Now the Speaker of the House had read the motion aloud and was starting down the roll, asking each legislator his vote. It was going to be very close, but the nays were carrying it right now. All too soon, the man was calling his name. "Harry Burn?"

It seemed to echo through the deathly silence. The young legislator hesitated, knowing what he was about to sacrifice.

"Mr. Harry Burn?"

He looked up at that brave red-haired woman and her daughters in the gallery and smiled. He was doing it for women like those so they would have a future.

"Harry Burn, how do you vote?"

He stood up and took a deep breath, looking at the women in the gallery for inspiration. "I vote yes!" He almost shouted it, so that it echoed through the crowded, silent building.

A roar began to build, an excited roar that swept through the statehouse, the Speaker pounding his gavel in vain for order. Reporters were running out of the packed room, running to get the news to their papers. Young Harry Burn's had been the winning vote. To Tennessee belonged the bragging rights now and forevermore. After seventy-two years of struggle, American women now had the vote. The gallery went wild, people hugging each other and cheering.

Harry sat down slowly, taking out a handkerchief and wiping his perspiring face. He watched that family from Texas. The red-haired woman hugged the big Texas cowboy, and the younger red-haired women almost danced in the aisles.

Harry smiled, satisfied. Whatever happened to him,

this would be a day to remember forever. The Nineteenth Amendment had finally passed. From this day forward, American women would have the right to vote. The Speaker still hadn't managed to bring order to the chamber, but no one cared, because it was all over, and the statehouse was the scene of pandemonium.

The legislators were gathered in small groups or waving to people in the gallery. Some of them would not be speaking to him anymore. He didn't care. Young Harry Burn was still smiling with satisfaction and watching that Texas family as he rose, turned, and left the chamber. "Now, ladies," he whispered to himself, "you've finally got the vote. Please, God, make it count!"

To My Readers:

The fight to give women the right to vote began in 1848 in Seneca Falls, New York, and finally ended seventy-two years later on that hot August day in Tennessee, when thirty-six states had ratified the amendment to make it law.

Four Western states—Idaho, Colorado, Utah, and Wyoming—had given their women the vote before the turn of the century. Wyoming, of course, holds the place of honor for being the very first to do so. It is part of their legend that when the U.S. Congress tried to get the Wyoming legislature to repeal that law, Wyoming fired back a telegram, which read, *We may stay out of the Union a hundred years, but we will come in with our women!* Reluctantly, Congress accepted Wyoming as a state with voting women.

I am happy to report that young Harry T. Burn, the first-time legislator from Niota, McMinn County, Tennessee, was not destroyed by his yes vote. He became a successful banker and gentleman farmer.

Despite the hundreds of movies and novels about the twelve-hundred mile Chisholm Trail, its time was brief, about twenty years, from the end of the Civil War to the mid-1880s. Kansas farmers complaining about fever the Texas cattle carried, barbed wire fencing off the Trail, and railroads coming into Texas, which could carry cattle to market more easily and cheaply, ended the necessity to drive cattle hundreds of miles to sell. When the Oklahoma land runs began in 1889, civilization ended those great cattle drives.

Today, the Chisholm Trail roughly follows U.S. Highway 81 through Oklahoma to the west of Oklahoma City. In fact, some of the asphalt was laid directly on the worn ruts. A man from the city of Enid has carefully marked the Trail.

Some Texans argue that the Trail in Texas should not be properly called the Chisholm Trail, since Jesse Chisholm, for whom the Trail is named, never pushed into Texas. Jesse, a part-Cherokee trader, never drove a single cow up the Trail. He died in 1868 and is buried in Oklahoma at Left Hand Spring Camp, a few miles north of the town of Geary.

If you are ever in my home state of Oklahoma, I invite you to visit the big Chisholm Trail Heritage Center, in the town of Duncan, on U.S. Highway 81, about eighty-seven miles southwest of Oklahoma City. Besides having a huge bronze statue depicting the Trail, the museum has a reality movie that will give you the sensation of participating in a real cattle drive.

The old longhorn cattle almost became extinct at the turn of the century, but a dedicated group recognized that these tough old beasts should be remembered, and gathered up a few of the handful that were left and put them at the Wichita Wildlife Preserve in southwestern Oklahoma, where their descendants still live today. Old Twister is modeled after a famous lead steer, Old Blue, owned by Texas rancher, Charlie Goodnight. Blue led many trail drives for some eight years before retiring. He lived to the ripe old age of twenty, and today, his gigantic horns may be seen at the Panhandle-Plains Museum in the town of Canyon, Texas.

I thought you might like to know about what was probably the deadliest stampede in Western history. It happened one stormy night in the year 1876, near the town of Towash, Texas. Some 2,700 of the Wilson brothers' cattle died in that wild race over a cliff into what became known as Stampede Gully.

As always, I'm including a list of some of the many research books I used in writing this novel. You may find some of them at your public library if you want to read more about the women's suffrage crusade, cattle drives, and the Chisholm Trail. I also highly recommend a documentary movie Ken Burns made for Public Television about the fight for women's suffrage called *Not for Ourselves Alone.* Many Public Libraries have videos of this film.

Recommended Reading:

Abbott, E.C. (Teddy Blue). *We Pointed Them North.* U. of Okla. Press, 1954

Adams, Andy. *The Log of a Cowboy.* Bison Books, 1964

Dobie, J. Frank. *The Longhorns.* U. of Texas Press, 1985

Flexner, Eleanor. *Century of Struggle.* Belknap Press of Harvard U. Press, 1959

Gard, Wayne. *The Chisholm Trail.* U. of Okla. Press, 1954

Gattey, Charles Neilson. *The Bloomer Girls.* Coward-McCann, Inc., 1967

Vestal, Stanley. *Queen of Cowtowns Dodge* City. U. of Neb. Press, 1972.

Some of you may recognize some of the characters in this story from earlier books. *To Tame a Texan* is a sequel to both *Comanche Cowboy* and *Cheyenne Princess*. For those of you who have written and asked: all my Zebra books connect in some manner, as I am writing a long, long continuing saga that covers about fifty years of the history of the Old West.

So what story will I tell next? The Civil War hit the Indian Territory hard, pitting friend against friend and brother against brother as the "Five Civilized Tribes" chose up sides. Many of the braves who became soldiers were members of the Lighthorse, the groups that provided law and order in the Indian Territory.

Now, I'm going to tell you two Civil War stories in one book—one about the Creeks, fighting on the side of the Union, and one about the famed Cherokee Mounted Rifles, fighting for the Confederates. Two of the Lighthorse, one from each side and once good friends, will meet each other on the field of battle. These two are both friends of Talako, the Choctaw lighthorseman from my earlier book, *Warrior's Honor.* The Creek loves a white nurse; the Cherokee loves a mixed-blood girl who just might be a spy; all are caught up in the bloodshed and turmoil of the Civil War. This new story will be published by Zebra in March 2004.

For those who would like an autographed bookmark explaining how all my Zebra books fit together in this continuing saga, please send a #10 self-addressed, stamped envelope to: Georgina Gentry, P.O. Box 162, Edmond, OK 73083-0162, or check out my Web site at: www.nettrends.com/georginagentry.

'Long As I Got a Biscuit . . . ,
Georgina Gentry

More By Best-selling Author
Fern Michaels

DO YOU HAVE THE
HOHL COLLECTION?

Experience the Romances of
Rosanne Bittner

__**Shameless** $6.99US/$7.99CAN
   0-8217-4056-3

__**Unforgettable** $5.99US/$7.50CAN
   0-8217-5830-6

__**Texas Passions** $5.99US/$7.50CAN
   0-8217-6166-8

__**Until Tomorrow** $5.99US/$6.99CAN
   0-8217-5064-X

__**Love Me Tomorrow** $5.99US/$7.50CAN
   0-8217-5818-7
